Also by Alan Dennis Burke

Fire Watch

Getting Away with Murder

ALAN DENNIS BURKE

Getting Away with Murder

AN ATLANTIC MONTHLY PRESS BOOK
LITTLE, BROWN AND COMPANY   BOSTON/TORONTO

FIRST EDITION

LIBRARY OF CONGRESS CATALOGING IN PUBLICATION DATA
Burke, Alan Dennis.
    Getting away with murder.

    "An Atlantic Monthly Press book."
    I. Title.
PS3552.U7213G4   813'.54   81-2345
ISBN 0-316-11688-2   AACR2

ATLANTIC—LITTLE, BROWN BOOKS
ARE PUBLISHED BY
LITTLE, BROWN AND COMPANY
IN ASSOCIATION WITH
THE ATLANTIC MONTHLY PRESS

BP
Designed by Susan Windheim
Published simultaneously in Canada
by Little, Brown & Company (Canada) Limited

PRINTED IN THE UNITED STATES OF AMERICA

Special thanks to valued friends and family for their help and support, especially Albert P. Burke, Christine M. Burke, Bobbie Aloyse Jellison, the Jellison Family, Judith Maginnis, Regina Downs, Jean Morelli, Lucy Record, Laurie Burke, Kathy Devine, Margaret Lally, and Gingie Paradise.

Getting Away with Murder

one

WITH ME, she hardly ever wore clothes. Well, it didn't have much to do with me, it was just the way she was. I remember this one day in particular because of the incident at work later. She stood in the center of my room and made a show of it, being naked.

"Come back to bed."

"Tell me how I look," she insisted.

"You look so good, Judy. So good."

Smiling broadly, she drew her initials in dust on my bureau. "Don't you ever clean this place?"

"If I knew you were coming, sure."

She went out to the kitchen and made a sandwich. My apartment was small. I could see her from the bed, over bread, peanut butter, and jelly. "Make one for me."

"Who was your last slave?" she asked.

When I was dressed, she was still undressed. "Aren't you chilly?"

She looked up from the table, covered in crumbs. "Billy, you live like a pig."

"I need to clean up a little."

"You need to move out and start over."

She finished her sandwich, washing it down with a great gulp of milk. Bread crumbs fell on her breasts. "Oh dear." Smiling, she brushed them off. It was part of the show. I never got tired of it.

She began collecting her clothes. "Where do you go now?" I asked.

"Home," she said. "Where else would I go?"

"Sometimes I wonder."

She dropped the clothes at her feet on the rug and paused dramatically. She was short, with a spare, athletic figure. Her hair, hanging to her shoulders, was jet black against white skin.

"How many affairs have you had?" I sat watching.

"What?"

"How many guys? Before me? How many guys before me?"

"Maybe you're the first." She studied herself carefully, admiringly, before sorting her clothes.

"No, really, how many? I'm just curious."

"Fifty." She began to dress.

"No, come on. How many? Really."

"Where's my coat?"

"Does he know?" I asked. "About your affairs?"

"Of course," she said. "I tell him everything."

"Come on. What would he do? If he knew. What would he do?"

"Nothing."

"I can't believe that, Judy. He wouldn't do anything? He'd do something. Wouldn't he?"

"Where's my coat?"

"No, really. What would he do? He wouldn't do anything? Really?"

"I don't know what he'd do." She finally located her coat. "And I don't care."

I had something very serious to say. That's why I was nervous, asking so many questions. But when I finally worked up my courage she was at the door. "I wanted, I thought we could sit down and talk."

ead slightly.

e're goin. You and I. Together."
other time?" she asked.
discuss it now. The thing is, Judy,
having a future. Now, maybe that's
do you think? Ah . . . you don't
ute."
to get married again," she replied.

nough for anyone. Don't you learn
've learned by mine."
y. I said let's talk. About the future.

r right now. If you want to think it
over . . ."

"Sure."

"Take all the time you need. Think on it."

"I will." She paused at the door. "But you gotta remember, you can't count on anything. I am still married. I have that to consider. It means something to me. Maybe I sound ridiculous saying it, but it's true."

Whenever she talked of her marriage, her child, or her husband, I had no answer. After all, what could I offer? A cramped apartment and uncertain prospects. And Judy was a very practical person.

"Billy," she kissed me before leaving, "don't take everything so seriously."

The newsroom was quiet at night. Reporters sat gossiping or reading newspapers. The *Suburban-Citizen* is a small-city daily paper. On the night shift, we saw none of the frantic pressure of deadlines.

"What are you covering tonight?" asked Pam Nealy.

"I don't know," I said.

"The city council isn't staffed yet. It should be a good meeting. On the rapid transit extension. There's going to be a mob up there. Fireworks."

For a few minutes, I thought I might be asked to cover that. Except for me, everyone on the staff had been given an assignment. Then I noticed Paul Burkhalter, hovering around the editor's desk. He wore a smart, black, pin-striped suit. The well-dressed vulture.

"What's he doing?" Pam nudged.

"I don't know." I shrugged. "Promoting the city council for himself, probably."

"Damn sneak. Roy already gave him an assignment. A talk to some church group."

Burkhalter left the editor's desk, smiling. Later, Roy Klijner, the assistant night city editor, came to me. "Bill," he said, "you'll be covering a speech at Saint Mary's. Senator Garnett. That's over at the rectory there. You know it? Saint Mary's?"

"I can find it."

I didn't complain. What was the point? Pam Nealy, however, was even angrier than I. A thin, fair-skinned blonde with a girlish face, she was my best friend in the newsroom. It was a relationship I appreciated only too late.

"Hey, Paul," Pam called to Burkhalter's desk. "That story was supposed to go to somebody else. You know? The city council? It was somebody else's story."

"It's an important story," he called over his shoulder.

I resolved to buy a suit.

"What are you covering tonight, Martell?" Eddie Murphy, one of the veterans of the staff, caught me in the elevator.

"Oh, I'm suppose to cover a speech over at Saint Mary's. Garnett."

"Well. I suppose that's better than covering the goddamn dog officer. Isn't that the story you did last night? The dog officer?"

16

"Yeah."

"And now you have to listen to Garnett?" Murphy shook his head. "From dog shit to bullshit. Why don't they send you up to the city council?"

"I only work here."

I met photographer David Chew in the parking lot. Together, we drove toward Saint Mary's on the east side. "Do you think if I wore a suit," I asked, "you think it would make any difference? I mean, do you think I'd get better assignments?"

"Shhhh!" Chew leaned near the squawking police radio. His car was spiked, front to back, by a long, arched aerial. There were also antennae on the trunk and roof. It all seemed to produce a steady stream of static and nothing more.

David pushed down a narrow street that slithered left and right into the blackness. "So what's Garnett doin tonight?" he asked.

"Nothing. Just making a speech."

"I've been taking a lot of pictures of this guy. You know? I think maybe he has friends in the newspaper business."

"Well, I'm not one of them."

"I took his picture at the Knights of Columbus last month. He went around kissing these old nuns. Kissing them. I didn't know you could do that. Kiss them. Can you do that?"

"Why not?"

"Shhh." He suddenly bent forward.

"What is it?"

"That. Right there. On the radio. Sounds like a bad accident. Bedford Street? Didn't he say Bedford Street?"

"I didn't hear a thing," I admitted.

"Bedford Street. That's just around the block. Why don't we have a look?"

"Well, I don't know, David."

The car jerked forward and around a corner. In a few minutes we were on a wide avenue flooded in yellow light and strangely silent. "Hey," we rolled to a halt, "cops aren't even here yet."

Camera in hand, David scrambled from the car, leaving the door ajar.

A small knot of people had gathered on the sidewalk, some turned away.

Further, twisted in a bizarre manner, as though melting on one side, a compact car leaned on a light pole, tail to a thick granite wall. The car's motor sat in the middle of the street, thirty yards beyond. The severed hood rested on the top of the stone wall.

Alongside the car lay two bodies. Chew hovered near them, taking pictures, strobe flashing.

They were certainly dead. A girl and boy, at an angle to each other, one on the sidewalk, one on the street. Both lay on their backs, legs together, arms at their sides. The boy rested in the gutter and my view of him was obscured, but the girl I could see clearly. She wore a ruffled pink blouse, which was neatly tucked inside her slacks. She was slim and her hair was a wavy cascade collected by a kind of **pin** above her ear. That was the whole thing. I couldn't see a mark on her body. She might have been asleep.

I couldn't see her face. But I didn't want to.

The crowd began to grow, their cars blocking all traffic.

"All of a sudden," a woman said, "I was sitting in my car and I saw them coming. And all of a sudden they speeded up and went, bang, right for the wall."

"They hit the wall?" someone asked.

"They went right into it. I didn't hear any brakes or anything. Just a noise like a bomb. Almost like they did it on purpose or something."

From where I stood, about twenty feet away, I couldn't see any blood. "Are they dead?" I asked.

"Of course, they're dead." Chew consulted his strobe. "This goddamn thing isn't working right . . ."

"How do you know they're dead? You try for a pulse or anything?"

"Don't worry, they're dead. They got their skulls," he touched his head, "their skulls split wide open. Have to be dead. Go look. There's beer cans, empty beer cans all over the car. Stupid-ass kids. Go look."

"No."

"Hey. This's nothing. You should be around when they're still alive. That's when it really gets hairy."

"What a waste." I moved a few feet closer. "She looks what? Eighteen?"

The police arrived, blue lights sweeping into the yellow, then the ambulance, spewing red.

"Should I ask questions?" I waved my notebook.

"Nah," Chew said. "Whoever's on police. Leave it for them. That's all we need. I got the pictures."

Later, at the church rectory, I looked down at my shoe and saw it was covered on the toe by a moist, brownish substance. "What the Christ is that?"

"God." Chew instinctively clutched his camera. "God."

"What? What is it?"

"That stuff from your head. Brain matter." He stood. "Jesus. It's all over my shoes too. I must be tracking it everywhere."

"I think I'm going to be sick." I took a deep, slow breath, scraping my toe on the chair in front of me.

After work, not a single car or pedestrian could be found on the street below the newspaper office. The air was cool, a thin mist touched by the yellow moon and the electric glow of street lamps. I was reminded of the accident, noiseless death. I couldn't get it out of my mind.

"Beautiful night." Roy Klijner came up behind me.

"It is." I was caught off guard.

"Going for a drink?"

"Well, no. Well, I don't know. Why? Who's going?"

"I am," he said. "Hennessy. Lewis. Maybe Burkhalter."

"Burkhalter."

We walked slowly toward Mullins's Bar, shoes clapping audibly on the pavement.

"Did, ah, did David turn in his accident pictures?" I asked.

"We can't run that blood and guts crap."

"Not even one?"

"One," Klijner said. "Maybe. Of the car. If he thinks we're going to run pictures of bodies and shit. Not likely. What if it was your wife or child? Would you want it on the front page of the newspaper?"

"I suppose not."

"Chew is one of those guys, maybe he's seen too much. You know? Oh, I don't doubt it'll pay off for him someday, all this chasing sirens. But it's the shit end of the business and I never liked it."

"No?"

"When I started out, more than once I had to knock on doors. 'Hello, mom. Your kid is dead. Any comment?' "

"Jesus."

"Shit like that," he said quietly. "I suppose somebody's got to do it. Well, not everyone can interview Henry Kissinger. That's why God made editors."

"I knew there had to be a reason."

Murphy, Lewis and Hennessy were already in the bar.

"So, Martell, what'd you cover tonight?" Hennessy asked. "The Animal Rescue League?"

"Very funny." I ordered a Coke.

"Say, Roy," added Lewis. "Give this poor guy a decent assignment."

"I'll give him yours," Klijner replied.

"Shouldn't you check with Burkhalter?" Lewis grinned. "He might not approve."

"Don't worry about Burkhalter," Murphy said. "He's on his way to the *New York Times*. This's only a brief stopover for him."

We traded stories for over an hour. Klijner and I were outsiders in this company. I, because I was relatively new to the staff; and Roy because he was no longer one of the boys, but management. Murphy had no use at all for the assistant editor. "That ass-kisser," he often muttered behind Roy's back. Murphy had expected to be named assistant editor. At his age, he was probably never considered.

Klijner and I left together.

"Don't break up the party," Lewis pleaded.

"What the fuck is this?" Murphy asked. "Where you going, Martell?"

"Out of here," I said. "Before Burkhalter shows up."

"Yeah," Murphy complained, "Bill can't wait to get home to his box of Kleenex."

Klijner and I walked slowly toward the parking lot. The street was empty. I could not forget the accident. I imagined that dead girl, as though sleeping, blouse tucked neatly inside her slacks, dressed so carefully for her last day of life. The car had struck the wall head on, but was pointing to the street when we arrived, back tires flattened, on the sidewalk. How did that happen? I couldn't imagine.

"My wife's supposed to be here." Klijner consulted his watch.

"Well, I should go." In fact, I was quite uncomfortable in his company.

"There she is." A yellow Pinto parked across the street. Judy did not look at us, but stared at the road.

"Night, Bill." Klijner ran to the car and climbed in beside her. They drove away and I felt a curious surge of excitement, a mixture of jealousy and pleasure that came from seeing Judy for the second time in a day.

Two

THE INDIAN BAY MOTOR INN stands on a thick, green lawn overlooking the Atlantic. Everything had begun to go wrong at that place. I had heard about the "Getaway Suites" with bathtubs for two, water beds, and mirrors on the ceiling. "King and Queen for a Night," touted the brochure. "Includes Free Breakfast."

We drove there in Judy's car early Tuesday morning. "This is going to be fantastic," I promised.

"You're crazy." She smiled. "You can't afford this. What about your job?"

"I can't go to work." I winked. "I'm sick. I'm at death's door."

It was a three-hour ride, on country roads, past rocky hilled farms and blotches of cranberry bog. We stopped for breakfast at a small-town diner. Over bacon and eggs, Judy relaxed. The confidence of being a hundred miles from home.

Crossing the street, we even held hands, until Judy impetuously raced ahead without so much as a glance at the traffic.

I gave chase. "Didn't your mother ever teach you to look? That's a good way to get killed, the way you cross streets. Those big trucks, they can't stop on a dime, you know? They'll run you over. They don't care how pretty you are."

She laughed.

"You," I chided in the car. "If you'd take things carefully it'd keep you out of trouble."

"If I was careful I wouldn't be here."

"Well . . . where did you tell Roy you were going today?"

"To my sister's house," she said. "To stay with my sister. That's where I left Mikie. My sister loves having him. She doesn't have any kids of her own."

"Your sister knows about us?"

"She knows about me. In case Roy goes checking up on me, she knows enough."

Later, I said, "I wrote to my mother about you. Just a few lines to say I was going out with a nice girl who was a little crazy in a nice way. I didn't tell her you were married, of course. But I wanted to tell someone about us. I had to tell someone."

"I know what you mean," she said. "I have a friend I talk to, I tell everything. Bobby."

"Bobby? Who is that? I never heard of him before."

"A friend," she replied. "Someone I've known forever. An old, close friend."

"How old and how close?"

She shrugged.

"And you tell this Bob all about us? Everything about us?"

"I have to have someone to talk to. You said it yourself."

"Just what is this guy to you? Is he — do you, you and he —"

"What did I say?" she asked.

"You said he was a friend."

"I said a close friend."

Twice, including once the next morning, Judy took time out to call her son, Mike, though he could say little more than 'Hi, Ma." She never called Roy.

At the Indian Bay Motor Inn, Judy floated naked on a water bed, admiring her image on the mirrored ceiling. "Would you two like to be alone?" I teased.

She turned on her side, studying herself from a different angle, reaching back to slap her own splendid behind. "This bed is great. It feels like you're floating on the ocean. You know? It's July and you're floating on a calm, calm ocean."

"Glad we came?"

"I'm not answering that just so you can say I told you so."

I moved very close, sitting on the mattress, which seemed alive, warm and undulating. "All I want to say is that you look beautiful. And sexy. The most beautiful, the sexiest woman I've ever known."

"Am I sexier than Kathleen?"

My ex-wife's name always stung, like a mild electric shock, but I pretended indifference. "Compared to you," I touched the soft flesh of her hips with the back of my hand, "compared to you Kathleen was barely conscious."

"How am I sexy?" she asked.

"You're just sexy. I don't know. It's the way you look. The way you like it so much."

"And that makes me sexy?"

"Judy." I smiled. "Stop asking so many questions. Let's just enjoy it."

All night, Judy's fascination for the mirror never flagged. "Nice," I noted, "we're both so interested in the same things." But this unconcealable delight in her own body was a part of her vulnerability and appeal. "Sex is great," she decided when we both lay exhausted. "When it's like this, sex is the greatest thing."

We were hurried in the morning. "I've got to be home by noon," she said.

"Well, at least have breakfast. It's free, after all."

She discovered fresh strawberries and cream on the menu.

"Go ahead," I said. "Get whatever you want."

She grinned broadly as the waitress covered them in thick, white cream.

/ 14

"Wicked girl."

"I shouldn't," she said, "but . . ."

When we reached the front desk my problems began. "What's this?" I questioned the desk clerk, pointing to the bill. "This added on here."

"That's — I believe that's for breakfast. Yes. For breakfast."

"But breakfast is free. It's included with the room."

"I see what you mean. Yes, the continental breakfast is included. But you ordered, what is it? Strawberries and cream. Strawberries and cream are not part of the continental breakfast."

"But this charge is nearly three dollars," Judy said. "How can strawberries and cream be three dollars?"

"Strawberries are out of season," he explained. "And then you get the tax."

"But why is there any charge at all?" I waved the tab. "It says on your brochure, 'includes free breakfast.' "

"That's the continental breakfast."

"It doesn't say anything about a continental breakfast. It says breakfast included. Period."

"Well, that doesn't mean you can eat anything, sir."

"Then it should say that."

"Would you like to speak to the hostess?" he asked.

"That's false advertising, what you got up there."

"I'll get the hostess."

As he left, I turned to Judy. "That's unbelievable. First, they tell you free breakfast. Then they try to cheat you into paying for it."

"Two dollars and fifty cents." Judy shook her head. "Most places you could get a whole breakfast for that."

The hostess was no help, repeating everything said by the desk clerk. We argued at length, but I soon demanded to see her superior. She ran to get the assistant manager.

"One thing my father always taught me," I explained. "Go to the top. You don't get anywhere talking to underlings."

"Maybe you should just pay for it." Judy touched my hand. "We really can't afford a scene, Bill."

"That's just what they're counting on. In these kinds of places they figure you'll keep your mouth shut and pay the bill."

"Let me pay for the strawberries." She reached for her purse. "I ate them. And you've already paid enough."

"Hey, I've got the money. It's not the money. It's the principle of the thing."

The assistant manager was a stiff, young man. "I don't see the problem, sir," he said curtly. "Did you order strawberries and cream?"

"Yes."

"And did you eat them?"

"Yes, but —"

"Then why won't you pay the bill?"

"Here we go again," Judy said.

I debated with the assistant manager for ten minutes. He was as stubborn as I was determined. Eventually, I suggested that the manager might settle the dispute. The young man rolled his eyes. "I'll see if he's in."

When the assistant manager was gone, Judy asked, "Are you going to talk to every employee in this hotel?"

"If that's what it takes."

"Pay the bill. Please?"

"No," I said. "We've been talking to the hired help up to now. Wait'll the manager gets here. You'll see some action."

A middle-aged couple had come into the lobby. I only noticed them now, watching our little drama from some distance.

"Let's please get out of here," Judy said. "This isn't worth the bother."

"That's what they want you to think. So they can bully us out of our money. Suppose they clip two bucks from everybody who comes in here, do you know how much money that is? For Christ's sake. They think we're stupid or something?"

"It's only a few dollars, Bill."

"I don't care if it's a few cents. Someone, somewhere has to say no to these crooks."

"I'd rather not go through this," she said.

"I should write an article on this place. I wish it was in our circulation area."

"I'm going to wait in the car."

Judy left abruptly. I felt abandoned, though I understood her need to avoid notice.

When the youthful assistant manager returned he was smiling for the first time. "The problem's been taken care of."

"What does that mean? I don't have to pay?"

"It's been taken care of."

In the car, I was perfectly satisfied. "In this life you stick up for your rights, Mrs. Klijner. You let them, they'll cheat you blind. So you don't let them. Scream loud enough, like I just did, they back right down."

Later, she admitted paying the bill, slipping the money to the hostess on her way out. We argued briefly, but bitterly. The good feeling of our night under the mirror was lost.

"You're not much fun when you get all righteous and stubborn," she said.

"Well, it's not much fun to be cheated either."

"It was only a few dollars. It's no need to act like a child."

"Well," I sneered, "I'm sorry if I spoiled things for you, acting like a child. Like a child. I guess I act the way I am. Maybe that's your complaint. Maybe you're sorry you came out with me. Cause I couldn't be perfect every minute."

"Perfect every minute," she mumbled sarcastically. "Look, Bill, you're not perfect. But you don't pretend to be and that's one of the nice things about you. You took me away and treated me great and I had a wonderful time. So, maybe we'd be better off to remember last night and forget the goddamn strawberries. I'm sorry I ever got them."

"Well . . ." I waited to cool. "Maybe I did get carried away. Sure. I don't know. I guess when it comes to people taking advantage of me, I get a little worked up. So is that some kind of crime?"

Explanations notwithstanding, our relationship never really recovered from the Indian Bay Motor Inn and I mark this incident as the beginning of my troubles.

Three

ROY KLIJNER'S ROUTINE sent him from desk to desk, delivering assignments to each reporter. He chatted easily with them. "No planning board tonight," he tapped my arm.

"What a shame." I avoided his eyes.

"Knew you'd be heartbroken to hear it. Hennessy's sick. How'd you like to take police?"

"Sure. I'll take it. Thanks." I smiled excessively whenever Klijner was near, as if to hide my guilt. How can I go on working here?

At other times I hated Klijner. It was easy to hate him after listening to Judy's horror stories. His mistreatment of her filled me with rage and frustration.

At the police station I was directed to the log book, which recorded every call the police had answered that night. Though they took up a full two pages, most of the incidents were trivial: vandalism, loitering or false alarms, none leading to arrests. Several traffic accidents were reported, but none involved serious injury.

Only one item was worth notice. "Taken into custody, Margaret Shea, 20, of 12 Dinsmore Road; and Robert De Lilio, 31, of 1124 Brace Avenue, charging them with lewd and lascivious conduct, indecent exposure, in a motor vehicle at Shore Drive municipal parking lot." It was the type of story occasionally featured in the "Police Roundup" column. I probably wouldn't use it, but to be on the safe side I began to take it down. After all, the guy might turn out to be a state rep or something.

"What are you copying down?"

"What?" I looked up to see a large, white-haired man in uniform with a name tag, "Captain Adair." He had a friendly red face and blue eyes.

"I said, what are you copying down?"

"The police log."

"I can see that, but what about the police log? Which report?"

"Well, just the usual stuff, Captain." I gave a little laugh.

"Can I see your notebook?"

"Well, no . . . I can't give you my notebook. No."

"I just hope you haven't taken down that Shea thing."

"Shea?"

"That indecent exposure arrest. That's in the book by mistake." The captain took the log in his two meaty hands and closed it, pulling it off the desk.

"Mistake? There was no arrest?"

"It shouldn't've gone in the book."

"No? Well, I don't understand. Are those the right names? Why shouldn't they be in the book?"

"Look," Adair came from behind the counter, "it's like this." He took me by the arm and led me into a corner of the room; which was bright, everything in glossy white paint, lit by rows of neon. "This girl, Peggy Shea."

"Peggy?"

"Yeah. The one right in there. Margaret Shea. Anyway, it turns out she's a nice girl. She got messed up with this bum. They had too much to drink and one thing led to another. Now that can happen to anyone. She's in my office now. Scared to death, poor kid. She's a nice girl, made a mistake." He shook his head. "Well, what I'm trying to say, she's not the usual type we get on a charge like this. And if all this got in the paper it could, it would really hurt this girl. A newspaper story'd do a hundred times more damage than any court action. After all, this isn't really a crime, is it?"

"Captain, what are you trying to tell me?"

"I'm telling you to be a good fellow and forget what you just saw in the log."

"I can't do that." I shook my head. "That puts me in the position of taking orders from the police. I can't do that."

"Be smart. You don't want trouble."

"No." I wasn't about to be bullied. "I've got to do my job."

"Look," Adair softened, "I understand you don't want your story messed with. I understand, but maybe you got a sister. Or a cousin or something. Imagine her in this predicament."

"Captain. I'm sorry about this, but I can't help you. I could lose my job doing what you want."

"If Hennessy was here he'd do it."

"That's his business," I said.

"Let me get this straight. You can't do it? Or you won't?"

"I can't. If it was my own sister —"

"Look, pal, I'm asking as a favor to me. Not to the girl now. But to me. Are you going to tell me no and screw up the police relations for your paper? I'm asking a small, a very small favor here."

"Well, I've got nothing against this girl. And I don't even think these stories should be in the paper. But since they are, why should she be treated any different than anyone else? It wouldn't be ethical."

"Ethical? I suppose it's ethical to ruin a young girl's life for a stupid three-line story in the newspaper. Tomorrow you won't even remember writing it."

"I could lose my job."

"Don't gimme that shit. You could forget the whole thing. Nobody would know."

I was confused. I could, indeed, be fired for withholding a legitimate news story. And imagine Judy's fading interest in that event. Besides, I couldn't think of any reason why this girl should be spared the same treatment given everyone else whose name appeared in the log. Nor could I allow myself to be coerced by the police. But it did sound cruel. I admit that.

"Captain Adair, how about if I take this back to the paper and ask my editor what he thinks?"

"Forget that," he growled. "I want to tell this girl her good name won't be shit in the morning. I want to tell her now so she won't lay awake all night worrying about it."

"Well, let me call. I can telephone the office."

"You make the decision."

"There's nothing I can do," I snapped.

For a moment, Adair's face was disfigured with anger. I thought he might move on me. But he quickly recovered his composure. "Come with me."

"Why?"

"Just come."

I could see her, sitting in an office at the end of the corridor, a tall, skinny girl with long, dark hair. She was crying, face deep red, eyes wet. "What's this?" I asked.

"I want you to meet her."

"No, I don't want to meet her."

"Just say hello," he prodded.

"It won't make any difference. I have to do my job. It won't make any difference if I meet her or not."

Unwittingly, Adair was making it more and more difficult to back down. Several officers were now eavesdropping on our argument. I could imagine that one or more was a friend to Burkhalter, who had sources everywhere. If that reporter heard of my squelching a story he would waste no time telling Jack Olander, the night city editor. Thus, I could lose my job. And Judy.

I moved to the door of Adair's office and stuck my head in. "Hello."

The girl looked up, sniffling. Her face was puffy, shoulders stooped.

"I'm sorry," I said, "but I have to write up your arrest for the paper."

She nodded sadly.

"I'm sorry, but it's only a few lines. It's always way in the back pages, those police stories. Maybe they won't even run it. I could ask about that. I don't know, sometimes if space is short these stories get cut. They don't run at all."

"You want to ask me questions?" she mumbled.

"Oh, no. Like I say, this's just a tiny little story way in the back. But I just wanted to warn you. So you could prepare yourself, sort of. I have to write it, you see. It's my job. I wouldn't. If it was up to me. But it's not. I could be fired if I didn't."

She looked glumly at the floor. How did I get into this? If only Adair had kept his mouth shut, I would have discarded the story on my own. I'd done it before with these sleazy pieces. But the big cop made an issue of it. He pushed. And I pushed. Until there was no backing down.

"Don't worry," I told her, "hardly anybody reads those police stories."

"You're a lousy bastard," Adair whispered in my ear.

We were all a little ashamed of the "Police Roundup." However, after the comics, it was the most popular feature of the *Suburban-Citizen.*

Everyone in the newsroom had an opinion on my encounter with Captain Adair. They stopped work or came to sit near my desk as I related the facts to Roy Klijner and Jack Olander.

"What the hell does this cop care if some honey gets her name in the paper?" asked Murphy.

"I think she might have been a relative," I explained, "the way Adair acted. But, I mean, you had to feel sorry for her."

"It's a good thing you didn't listen to him," Burkhalter said. "They're very strict about that sort of thing around here. You could be fired for sitting on a story."

"Thanks for the tip, Paul."

"It's true," Klijner agreed. "You did exactly the right thing."

"I told him it was a matter of ethics." I shrugged. "Still. We don't really need a story like this. Do we?"

"Adair's got no business censoring that log," Olander said. "We have a legal right to see it and he's giving preferential treatment when he does that."

"That's what I told him," I said. "But. I mean, you don't want me to really write this story. Do you?"

"You bet your life I do," the editor barked. "Lewis. Check out those names in the morgue. I'll lay odds one of these birds is connected to Somebody."

"I didn't know they arrested you for doing it in a car," Lewis said. "I thought they just told you to get dressed."

"Is this going to change your life, Carl?" asked Pam Nealy.

"That Adair is an uncooperative bastard anyway," said Klijner. "He's never done shit for us."

The story, all fifty words or so, was passed on to the copy desk. I never looked to see if it appeared.

Anyway, Adair was wrong about one thing. For very obvious reasons I've never forgotten that incident.

The waitress brought lasagna.

"I love it." Carefully cutting with her fork, Judy balanced a heaping stack, spilling steam and cheese, and guided it home. She chewed slowly, eyes fixed dreamily.

"This is the first time I've ever been jealous of lasagna," I said.

She smiled, eating still. The restaurant was dark and far from town.

"I wish you'd talk."

"I'm eating." She sipped wine.

"Talk between bites."

"Between bites," she buttered bread, "I breathe."

"I'd like to know why you're not fat."

"We're a perfect match," she said. "We both love food. Not like Roy. He eats because he'll die if he doesn't. Can you understand someone like that? I can't. I cook him a delicious meal, spaghetti and meatballs with a salad and an appetizer and fancy dessert. He sits down and eats the whole thing. Not one word. Not one. Not 'thank you.' Or 'that was good.' Or even 'that was bad.' Nothing. If I gave him Franco-American he wouldn't know the difference."

"Don't talk about him."

"I thought you wanted to talk."

"I don't want to talk about him."

"Why not?" she asked. "Why should it bother you?"

"I work with him. I have to see him every day. I try to forget he's your husband."

"What's Roy like to work for?" she asked.

"You like to pick, Judy."

"I'm just curious. I wonder what he's like all day when he's away from me. He's my husband."

"No kidding."

"So I'm curious. Why should it bother you? What's he like?"

"Some people, a few people don't like him. They say he's a sneak, an ass-kisser."

"Who says that?" She smiled with delight.

"But most people figure he's okay."

"Does he talk to people?"

"Of course he talks to people," I said. "How could he do his job if he didn't talk to people?"

"My, my. He sounds like he's nicer to work with than he is to live with. He sounds almost human."

"A lot of people are like that. They act real nice at work and when they get home they let it out on their families. A lot of people are like that."

"And Roy's real friendly to everybody?" she asked. "Is he friendly to you?"

"Ah, cordial. I guess. You know. Well, I guess it's one of the things that bothers me, that he was so helpful when I first came to work there."

She scraped at stray pieces of ricotta on her plate. "Well, I'm glad you're not the loyal type."

/ 25

"What kind of thing is that to say?" I took a deep breath. "You know, Judy, you got a mean streak, a rotten streak in you."

"What did I say?"

"Don't give me that. You know what you said."

"Well," she insisted, "I didn't mean anything by it."

I dropped my fork, appetite gone.

"I'm sorry. . . . Bill? Really. I am sorry. I didn't mean anything."

"You go too far, Judy."

"I really am sorry. It was a stupid thing to say."

"Then why say it?"

After a minute of cool silence she pointed. "Are you going to finish that?"

"You know," I shoved the plate toward her, "if you were honest you'd ask yourself what makes you say cruel things to me. To me. Who cares so much for you."

"And what about the things you say?" she demanded. "Do you think I like to hear how he's so wonderful at work, such a nice guy, mister nice guy? Because he isn't nice. At least not to me."

"Christ, you brought it up, talking about him."

"I know."

"Why should that bother you, anyhow?" I was indignant. "You don't care about him."

"No, I don't care about him. Except I'm married to him. That's all."

"But you don't care about him."

She looked down at the two empty plates. "We had some friends over the other day. And one of the girls told Roy how good he looked. But I don't know. It's strange. But I guess it has to do with the way you feel about a person. Roy, he just isn't, I mean, he doesn't look handsome to me. Of course, he is very handsome. I used to think so. But not anymore. He doesn't look handsome to me." She looked up. "Does that make you feel better to hear that?"

/ 26

"Judy. Why did you ever marry him?"

"I had to." She stared at me. "You hadn't figured that out? Well, I told you before, all my problems come from sex. And that's example number one. Anyway, it sure got us off on the wrong foot. We probably would've got married anyway. But the way it happened, there was always that doubt. Like maybe I trapped him. Like he was some prize and I trapped him. Ha. But it was a bad start and I think it had a lot to do with the way everything went so wrong so fast. You know, the nuns always told us be good girls. Or we'd be sorry. I should've listened to them."

"There's no hell like a bad marriage." I spoke from bitter experience.

"Oh, for sure. I got married. I was so proud because Roy stuck by me. It didn't come out till later how he resented it so. There was that always hanging over us. One time he was mad, he came out and said it. 'I had to marry you.' Maybe I was naive, but I never imagined he'd feel that way. I felt like someone played a pretty mean trick on me."

"Why don't you divorce him, Judy?"

"Oh," she groaned, "why didn't I think of that?"

"Well, why don't you?"

"I've told you before. I can't afford it."

"That's just an excuse," I said.

"I have a baby. I have no skills. No college degree. And no money of my own."

"What about alimony?"

"And suppose he doesn't pay it?" she demanded. "Suppose it isn't enough?"

I knew better than to press the point. We had argued this one before.

When the spumoni came Judy was suddenly agitated. "Shit. Shit. Shit." She buried her face in her hands.

"What? What is it?"

"Don't." She turned to the wall.

"You got a toothache or something?"

"Don't look. My sister-in-law just walked in."

"Has she seen us?"

"I don't know. I've got to get out of here."

I peeked across the restaurant. No one was looking back. Fortunately, we had taken a booth in the back of the large dining room.

"Don't look! Do you want her to see us?"

"What should I do?" I asked.

"Pretend you're not with me."

"How do I do that? We're sitting together."

"Sit somewhere else. Hurry, please."

Confused and embarrassed, I stood.

"Take your spumoni," she gasped. "Please."

"You can have it."

"Jesus Christ, take it!"

I sat at the adjacent table and picked over the dessert.

"Something wrong, sir?" It was the waitress.

"A little problem."

"Will you be sitting here from now on?" she asked.

"I hope not."

Meanwhile, Judy made her way out, a small but lively figure against the daylight from the great picture windows. She stopped at a table occupied by two women, slightly older than she, coolly pretending surprise at the meeting. Roy's sister strongly resembled her brother, round-faced, with brown hair.

For my part, I was humiliated, sitting alone, enduring quizzical, patronizing looks from the waitress.

It was no better in the parking lot. Her car was gone. I walked the street, a block in each direction, to see if she was waiting nearby. No luck. Judy had run. Well, let's face it, it was the sensible thing to do. It would look positively incriminating for us to be seen leaving the restaurant separately and the parking lot together.

I sat on a great boulder painted yellow that marked the

boundary of the parking lot. I waited half an hour, hoping she would return.

"I don't know how all this is done. It's new to me. I've never gone out with a married woman before."

"Well, what do you think?" Judy demanded. "Do you think I do this all the time?"

"I had to spend an hour and a half on buses."

"I'm sorry, but it couldn't be helped." She paced the length of my apartment, stepping over a bowl of stale popcorn. (When you live alone things tend to pile up.) "I was afraid to wait for you. I was scared and I didn't think."

"Well, she didn't see us," I said. "Did she?"

"I don't know. She acted awfully strange. She asked me if I was alone."

"She did? She asked that? What did you say?"

"I told her I was there with a friend. But my friend left early."

"That's a good story," I said.

"It's good unless she saw us sitting together."

"Would she tell, you know, him?"

"She doesn't like me. She never liked me." Judy began chewing her nails.

"I thought your husband already knew you fooled around. Didn't you tell me that once?"

"Don't talk nonsense." Finally, she took a seat on the couch beside me. "I'm wondering if we should see less of each other."

"No."

"Just for a while. Just to be on the safe side."

"No, Judy."

"This started out," she said, "it was just for fun. Didn't I say that? No one gets serious. No one gets hurt. Didn't we agree to that?"

"In the beginning, yeah."

"Well, maybe it got out of hand. For you. And for me. Maybe a thing like this, it's going to get out of hand eventually. But, anyway, at some point, we have to know when to cool it."

"I don't understand."

"I'm thinking of you, Bill. Well, both of us. But you mostly because you haven't really gotten over Kathleen and I'm wondering about how you're handling this. Us. I'm thinking mostly of you. I don't want you to be hurt."

Here it comes.

"I think we should see less of each other, Bill. For your own good. Well, for the good of both of us, really. I know I have a lot to lose. I am a married woman. And a mother. And that means something to me. So, this separation would be a temporary, necessary thing. For my own good. And yours."

I argued fiercely, but to little effect. I should have expected it. If I'd had a decent job, a little money, maybe it would be different. I could offer affection, love. But a woman with a young child must consider how she will eat.

When I went to work Roy Klijner smiled at me. It was a casual, sudden smile, the type you can't fake. Relieved, I knew at once he was ignorant of my relationship with his wife. Of course, he might suspect her infidelity without ever connecting me. His sister could not identify me. Yet, his behavior seemed that of a man whose life was in order. He knows nothing, I decided. He's winning and he doesn't even know he's in a race.

On the other hand, at any time, he might turn on me. A physical attack in the newsroom; it was one of my nightmares.

Judy had decided to see less of me. She wasn't kidding. In three weeks I didn't get a visit or even a phone call. And then came the letter.

Dear Bill,

We always knew this letter would have to be written. But all things must end, even love affairs.

Right now my ambition is to be a good mother for little Michael. Maybe this will also satisfy Roy and things between us will improve. In the

meantime I'm learning to live like a nun — doing without. (Me? Can you believe it?) It's not as difficult as I imagined.
You always wanted me to write something to you — now I have. Sorry it couldn't be a happier letter. I'll always remember our times together. Too bad it couldn't work out better. Oh, well. Maybe in the next life. Try to think kindly of me.

> *Your Special Friend,*
> *Judy*

P.S. You can't change my mind so don't try. It'll only make it more difficult for both of us. A clean break is best.

There could be only one explanation for such a letter — another man. I called Judy, something we had agreed I would never do. The first time no one answered. The second time he answered and I hung up. The third time, wishing to avoid him, I was especially bold. I made the call mere feet away from him, at the office. He watched me dial.

"Hello." It was a woman's voice. A young child cried loudly in the background.

"Hello?" I said.

"Who is this?"

"Judy?"

"She's not here right now. Who is this?"

I hung up. Of course, it was a terrible mistake. I should have worried about the pointed questions Judy would have to answer concerning the mysterious caller. Perhaps that was her nosy sister-in-law answering the phone. I should have worried about this, but I didn't. Instead, I was frantic that she was not home at eight o'clock at night. Where was she?

I reviewed our affair a hundred times, often with regret. To be hurt this way, again. If I had taken up with Pam Nealy, my original intention, how much easier everything would have been.

I had come to the *Suburban-Citizen* six months before from a dreadful job writing a hospital newsletter. Landing newspaper work was a stroke of luck. My disastrous tenure at Carey Hospital had climaxed with a story on candy-striper volunteers headlined "Teenage Candy Strippers Please Patients." My heart wasn't in that job. Fortunately, the *Suburban-Citizen* never checked my references.

From the beginning, Pam Nealy was my ally on the night staff, helping me to adopt the peculiar writing style of the *Suburban-Citizen*, alerting me to the various newsroom taboos. "If you have anything to say about the publisher," she nudged, "say it behind his back."

"What if I have something nice to say?"

"You won't."

Almost a year after my divorce from Kathleen, women were beginning to look good again. Blonde, smiling, and slim, with gold-rimmed glasses, Pam Nealy looked particularly good for some reason. We made a habit of taking supper together. These weren't really dates. Sometimes one or another reporter joined us.

Finally, I asked her to a movie. And afterward, parked by the ocean, we kissed and petted like teenagers. "Whoa," she said, "slow down."

"I can't."

"You're awfully ambitious on the first date."

"It's your fault for being so sexy."

"Leave a little for later." She smiled.

A few days later I met Judy at the *Suburban-Citizen* spring picnic. Within the week we met again, by pure accident, at the beach. Judy was with her son, Mike, a toddler with white-blond hair. He spent the day chasing waves.

"You get a look," I told her. "When you're watching your little boy. It's really something."

"A look?" she asked. "What do you mean? A look?"

"It's hard to describe. It's like, I don't know, like from inside."

"It's because I'm a good mother. That's actually the only thing in my life I'm really proud of. Maybe that's what you see."

Judy and I lay on the warm, white sand. She watched the boy.

I watched her. At first, we talked about Roy Klijner. "A wonderful guy," I said, "a great editor." She was obviously flattered by my attention. I enjoyed having someone to talk to. If there was more on my mind I never acknowledged it, not even to myself.

On another day, she told me her history. She had dropped out of college in her junior year to marry. "I was too young," she said. "Sometimes I think of what I missed, marrying so young."

"What was the big hurry? A woman as pretty as you. I'd have thought you could marry whoever you'd want. Whenever you'd want." Praising Judy was like pumping air into a balloon; she sat back, lips widening to a guilty grin, eyes growing as round as gum balls. "Isn't Roy always telling you how pretty you are?"

"This morning, let's see, what did he say? He said I was getting bags under my eyes for one thing."

"What a thing to say."

"And I look older than a lot of women my age. He's full of encouraging remarks like that."

"He must be blind," I said. "Or stupid. What makes him say things like that?"

"I used to worry about it. What was I doing wrong? But I don't even think about it anymore. It's not my problem. It's his."

We soon went to bed. We did it thoughtlessly, in the best sense of that word. If there was guilt, I reminded myself that no one suffered. Roy Klijner was blissfully ignorant. And Judy, who insisted that her home life was pure hell, enjoyed a little relief. A kind word, I think that was the main thing she was after.

Pam was confused and hurt by my sudden, unexplained indifference; you could see it in her face, that fast-fading hope. But nothing else counted, not Pam, not Roy Klijner. Nothing else could count when Judy was considered.

At times, I scarcely believed it. What did such an attractive, exciting woman see in me? She would come to my apartment and stay for hours, talking, laughing or making love until the room smelled deliciously of sweat and sex.

"All my problems come from one thing." She lay beside me.

"One thing. What's that?"

"I'm too horny. No, really. Listen. I got married because I was horny. I'm here with you because I'm so horny. I just can't help myself. I have no willpower."

"Thank God."

"But don't think I feel guilty about it. I don't. I'm not going to live without it. I don't care what anyone says." She leaned over me. "You must get sick of me, talking all the time."

"I love to listen. Loose women interest me."

"I think most of the people I know, if they saw me here now. With you. I mean, my God. They'd be shocked."

"They'd be jealous," I said.

"I do like it." She grinned, climbing on top, sliding against me. "I do love men. That's my whole problem."

"It's no problem for me."

"You know what my husband does? Whenever we have a fight he stops sleeping with me. Really. He does this to punish me. But it never works. Guys keep coming along."

"Like trolley cars."

She laughed.

"You and him fight a lot?" I asked.

"Oh yeah. Most of the time."

"You don't get along at all, then?"

"There was a time," she said, "when he went off in the morning, I used to daydream he'd get in an accident. That he'd never come back. I wished him dead."

"You didn't think that."

"I did."

"I can't believe it," I said. "I can't believe you ever wished anybody dead. Judy?"

"That's because you don't live with him. Someone who never talks. Who never wants to go out. Who never has a thing to say except everything's my fault. I'm stupid. Did I tell you? I'm a stupid woman. All women are stupid, but me especially. If the car is broken, I broke it. It couldn't have just worn out, it has to be I broke it. If the baby cries, it's because I pamper him. It's always my fault. And this goes on every day, this abuse. This is how I live. Every day of my life."

"Marriage isn't always such a bargain," I said.

"Not for me."

"I could have told you." I held her, feeling a great pity for both of us. "Forget about him. You're with me now. Forget him."

"I do like it," she said softly. "I do like it."

So now she had left me and I was devastated.

At once, my work suffered. One day I was sent to cover a post-midnight auto accident. A car occupied by two married men had struck a car occupied by two married women. None of these people were married to one another. And I promptly turned a very ordinary story into a memorable disaster by mistakenly putting a man and a woman in each car.

The error became apparent next afternoon as suspicious spouses rang the executive telephones off the hook. Lawsuits were threatened and only a prominently placed retraction saved the day.

"Is that the asshole?" Desmond Cooper, the publisher, pointed at me from across the room.

Only Murphy, of all people, recognized the extent of my difficulty. "What's the problem?"

"Me?"

"Yeah, you. You go around here like you know the end is near or something. What've you got? Woman trouble?"

That was all I needed. I told him everything, except her identity.

"Oh, Christ," he said. "Screw 'em and forget 'em. If I was your age I'd be stickin a different one every night."

"Yeah."

"You're young. You'll forget her in a week."

"A week? I couldn't forget you in a week."

four

FALL HAD TURNED BITTER.

My Toyota is small, but has one advantage: the heat comes on quickly. Across a tiny park, I could see the house, gray with white trim, elegantly Victorian. There was a wide lawn, going brown, and a great elm along the sidewalk. The blue Mercury was parked on the street, the yellow Pinto in the driveway.

Never taking my eyes from the front door, I enjoyed a hurried breakfast, a tuna sub and a cherry-filled pie, washed down with two cans of Coke. To keep awake, I listened to the radio, switching from station to station, never satisfied with the music. Nervous. Something to read would have been nice, but I couldn't read and watch the house both, obviously.

A woman, graying, with glasses and a severe expression, walked past, eyeing me. Just sitting there all morning I would attract attention. But it didn't worry me. There's nothing illegal about sitting in a parked car, after all.

I admit a sharp pang when I first saw Judy. After about two hours she came down the front steps, wearing a tan raincoat against the dampness. She walked with great energy, even seemed to skip at one point, as though suffering none of the black depression weighing on me. She looked almost happy.

Or was I reading too much into her walk?

She drove down Hancock Street, toward the business district and the office of the *Suburban-Citizen*. I followed in traffic at a distance of two or three vehicles, confident she would never notice my car with its ordinary pea-green color. As a disguise, I had washed it the day before.

Judy turned on Beale Street, stopping at a small drugstore called The Naborhood Pharmacy. Probably filling a prescription, she was in there nearly half an hour. I was ready to go in after her, at one point. A long line of cars slipped between us when she moved back to the road. But the bright yellow car was not difficult to follow, even at a distance.

I lost sight only once, when delayed at an intersection. But once was enough. I drove nearly a mile, past the shipyard, running yellow and red lights, trying to catch up, but the road was dark-colored cars, trucks, and buses to the horizon.

"Jeez!" I slammed the dashboard. "Where is she?"

I retraced my path, glancing down side streets, hoping for a glimpse of yellow. No luck. My greatest fear was that she had purposely lost me. Which meant she had spotted my car. I had made things worse.

And where would she go now? Who was she off to see?

But there it was. It had to be her car, parked outside of the Super Bowl. Thank God. She was bowling. Of course, I remembered now, she bowled on Wednesday mornings.

I stopped in the parking lot of a small bar across the street, the Alibi Lounge. For a while, I waited. What was she doing inside the bowling alley? Who was she with? Maybe she wasn't in there after all.

The Super Bowl is a split-level recreation center. One steps down from the pool parlor and pinball arcade to lanes of duckpins and candlepins. Judy bowled on the candlepin lanes with a slim, red-haired woman I'd never seen before. They smiled and chatted, seemed to be serious friends. Judy bowled with concentration. Everything about her became quick, the second ball thrown the moment the pins were still. I was impressed with her skill, as ball after ball rolled with speed and accuracy, smashing the pins violently away.

I tried the electronic games in the arcade. Preoccupied, I played poorly, quickly running through a pocketful of quarters. When I looked up Judy was gone. How could I be so stupid? Hurrying outside, I found no sign of her car.

I drove back to the big gray house. In the driveway was the yellow Pinto. Roy Klijner's car still waited on the street. It was one o'clock. I went to eat, despite an upset stomach which was probably due to lack of sleep. For the rest of the day I sat beyond the park, viewing the Klijner house through the trees.

Around three-thirty, Roy left for work. He looked in my direction as he moved onto Hancock Street, but I'm sure he didn't see me. I wasn't going to work myself, having called in sick.

It grew darker, colder. I had to run the heat all the time now. Downstairs, lights began to go out, the bluish television brightness being the last to fade.

I still watched closely, excited when a passing car slowed, expecting it to stop. A tall, well-dressed man would emerge and hurry into Judy's home. I imagined this so clearly. I soon wondered if it hadn't already happened. Was Judy in there now, playing host to a new lover?

. Upstairs, a figure passed the hall window. It had to be Judy. She would be washing. Once, we took a shower together. I knew exactly how she would look now. Rivers of water had traced her figure, the taut skin, smooth and white. "Well," she had giggled, "look at me."

"I am. I am looking at you."

But another time I had made her angry in the shower. She smashed her fist into a mirror. I don't remember the reason for this, something trivial in any case. Judy had an unpredictable, even violent temper. Soon, the upstairs lights went out.

I drove around awhile, bought some fried chicken. It should be explained, I wasn't proud of all this. I had spent the day spying on someone. I knew it was wrong, but I couldn't help myself.

Driving relaxed me. I didn't want to go home. I could see myself, collapsed before the television, hypnotized. By moving, hands on the wheel, alert to the lights and traffic, I could keep my mind off my problems.

In the neighboring big city, I was wary of shadows and the people who seemed to skulk on the fringes of dark streets. Shuffling along the sidewalk were old men who hadn't washed or changed in days, braced for killing winter. More frightening were the people in parked cars in cold, empty alleys.

Soon, I came to corners lit by bright marquees selling movies, plays, nude dancers. I began to consider various bars.

At a traffic light, a girl in a beret came pounding on my window. She was young, still plump in the cheeks, with moist, wide eyes. Her coat was open to her fat hips and a loose-fitting jersey was nudged here and there by her breasts. I rolled down my window.

"Where you goin?" She smiled.

"Ah . . ." It dawned on me what she wanted. "No. Not tonight. Sorry."

"Asshole." She withdrew.

Why pick on me? Of all the drivers stopped at the red light?

Down the street was another girl, short, athletically built, and smiling. I drove on, but grew excited thinking about her. And where would we do it? In the car. On a dark street. Very quickly. With our clothes on. I suppose that's how those girls work. But what if she pulled a knife on me, took my money?

She was gone when I passed that block again. But I wouldn't have picked her up anyway. There were other girls around. I didn't pick them up. It's something I don't do.

I woke early, around eleven, with a careful plan for the day. I made a real effort to keep busy, to clear my mind of Judy. But it was useless. Around two o'clock, during my third straight soap opera, I could sit no longer. I drove to the Klijner house.

The yellow Pinto was gone. I waited, my mind working frantically on the infinite innocent explanations for this. She was shopping. Visiting a friend. At the dentist. In a motel room with another guy. Jesus, you'd think her husband could watch her more closely.

Stopping for a Coke and hamburg, I began retracing the route we had covered the day before. To my relief, I found her car at the Super Bowl parking lot.

Across the street, the Alibi Lounge was practically empty. From my table I could see the yellow car, a bright blur through the green-tinted window. I ordered a Coke without ice.

What was I doing? Wasting my time. Obviously, Judy no longer had any use for me. She now realized what a terrible risk our affair posed to her marriage. Bumping into the sister-in-law that time had done it.

It was over. Face it. I would watch her walk from the bowling alley to the car and never see her again. Ever. Unless she called or something.

I ordered a turkey sandwich from the waitress. I wasn't really hungry, but I like to eat when I'm depressed.

Someday, I would remember her fondly for the wonderful times. Frankly, she was the best in bed. And I would think of that. Not of her cruelty. The way she simply dropped me. Without a word.

I would find another job. Anything to get away from her and her husband. Putting things in perspective, it had been a positive experience. Someday, I would look back without feeling sick to my stomach.

"Another Coke, please."

The lounge began to fill with men from the shipyard offices, accountants, clerks, lower-level executives.

Well, screw her. She could've shown a little consideration for my feelings.

No, I understood. She never promised more than she delivered. It was over. No one needed to say it. I should cherish her memory, appreciate the warm days she gave me. The bitch.

"Could I have another sandwich, please?"

At once, I noticed something strange about the lounge. Even as more customers came there was none of the careless chatter expected after a long work day. Instead, there was nervous whispering and low laughter. And there was Judy, at the bar, her straight, black hair thrown back at them.

I swallowed my drink with a hard gulp. I had not even seen her arrive, yet she was now the center of gravity in that cramped little world. It seemed every man had an eye for her.

Judy was flanked by two empty stools. Everyone knew why. Before long a young man in a plaid suit, red tie, and cranberry shirt sat beside her. He ordered a drink as his friends, a vulgar, leering threesome, gleefully rooted him on from a table close by mine.

Overcoming an initial hesitation, the man spoke to her. He was well dressed, but otherwise ordinary. To me, on the far side of a dark, increasingly smoky room, it seemed Judy barely acknowledged him. She looked unhappy. Yet she fed on the attention and sexual excitement in the room, physically reacting to it, sitting taller, erect, more alert.

"Could I . . . ah . . . could I have another Coke?" I asked the waitress. The room had grown hot, sweaty.

And there were more people suddenly. It was getting dark outside. Judy turned toward the man in the plaid suit. They were talking, leaning near each other. A vague smile came to her lips. My face burned.

It took no more than twenty minutes. He reached out and touched her hand and then her knee. His friends smiled and nudged each other. Whatever he was saying, she seemed to respond, cocking her head, shrugging.

Unhurried, Judy left the bar, every step studied by a dozen men or more. The man in the plaid suit went with her.

It was past ten o'clock when they returned in a silver sports car. He was no gentleman, driving away, leaving her alone in the

Super Bowl parking lot. She stood beside the solitary Pinto, fumbling with her keys in the dark.

"Need any help?"

She turned with a violent start. "Oh, Jesus!" gasping, truly afraid. "You scared me."

"I didn't mean to."

"Jesus Christ!" Her hand went to her throat. "Don't ever do that."

"I said I'm sorry."

"That's a stupid thing to do. Sneaking up like that."

"I said I was sorry. How many times do I hafta say it?"

"What in God's name are you doing here anyway?" She opened the car door.

"I just happen to be here."

"You just happen to be here? At nine o'clock at night?"

"It's more like ten o'clock. And I'm here so I can talk to you."

"You've been following me. Haven't you?" She stood with the door open. In one move she could be inside, driving away, leaving everything worse than before. "You've been poking around my private business."

"That doesn't matter now."

"It matters to me. I don't like my privacy taken off."

"Judy —"

"If you wanted to know something you should have had the decency to come up and ask."

"How would I do that? Judy? How would I do that? I couldn't get in touch with you. You went off. Without a word."

"You're a snoop," she complained. "I thought you had a little more integrity than that, Bill."

"Oh, you givin integrity lessons today?"

"Yeah? Well, what I do, it's none of your damn business."

Unexpectedly, I lowered my voice to a soft, soothing tone. "Judy," I asked, "why haven't you called me? Why did you leave me alone without a word?"

She turned to the car. "I wrote you. Didn't you get my letter?"

"How could you write a letter like that? To me? It was like a business letter."

"I have to go home now. It's better for both of us if I go home now."

"So go home," I said. "I won't stop you, Judy. I won't bother you again. I wanted to talk. I wanted to ask why you didn't care for me anymore. Why you won't see me. I thought you might be in trouble. It didn't occur to me. It should've been obvious, it would've been obvious to anyone, but it didn't occur to me. You never really did care for me. Not really. No more than you care for that jerk in the sports car."

"You do enjoy feeling sorry for yourself."

"Yeah, well, somebody has to do it."

"I have to be home," she said. "I'm cold here."

"Go ahead. Go home. I won't stop you."

But she stood in the parking lot, watching me from the corner of her eye.

"I don't want you to go, Judy. How can you go? How can you just walk away from me? Are there so many guys in love with you?"

She shrugged sadly. "I'm sorry the way it ended. But you don't want to stay mixed up with me. My life is a mess. It's better you stay clear."

"Why not let me make that decision?"

For some time, she leaned against the car, looking wistfully at the sky. "Remember Hubbard Road?"

"Of course."

"If you want to talk . . . I'll be there on Sunday. At noon."

"Why? Why there? Of all places."

"If you don't want to — I've given you the chance to say no. So if you're not there I'll understand."

"Of course. I'll be there."

Once, Hubbard Road had been paved. Now it lay peppered with potholes and powdering chunks of loose asphalt. A dead end, it twisted sharply downhill for two miles, through a forest of conservation land, toward a small river and the concrete blocks of a never completed public works project.

I drove until the trees were small and far apart, with here and there a stray brown leaf clinging to a twig. I pulled to the shoulder.

She came precisely at noon, stopping behind me in the familiar yellow Pinto and coming to sit in my Toyota.

"Hi," I croaked nervously, suddenly mortified because the floor of my car was carpeted with old newspapers, candy wrappers and empty Coke cans. How stupid could I be? And it was plain carelessness. No wonder she no longer liked me. "Sorry for the mess."

"I don't mind the mess, Bill. With you, I'm used to it."

"No, really. Lemme clean it up a little."

"Bill," she caught my hand, "do it later. Please."

I tried to relax. "How are you? You look so good. Did you get in any trouble the other night? Coming home so late."

"Yes."

"Uh-oh. What did he say?"

"Nothing."

"Well, he must've said something."

"He doesn't say anything. He watches television."

She looked out on the marsh that bordered the road. Great blue pools reflected bright sky and silvery dead wood. In summer, when we first made love, in the front seat of her car, it was rich green all over. Now, everything about us was dying of the cold. "You once said you wanted to consider us in the future." Her expression was hard and serious. "Didn't you say that once? Something like that?"

"That's right," I swallowed.

"And what about now? If . . . I mean, do you still —"

"Yes, Judy. I love you."

"Well," she continued, "I can't say, honestly say, I love you. Maybe I do. Or, at least, maybe I will. But I can say I like you,

Bill. Very much, in fact. I care about you. Maybe that's why I was in such a hurry to break it off. Cause it scared me, caring for you. But the thing is, I want to be fair. I don't love you. Yet. And you should decide if that makes a difference."

"Come away with me, Judy. I love you. And that's enough for now."

"If we did that," she said, "if we went away together . . . there are some things you might not think about. You'd go along now. But later you might not find it so easy to accept. Things to do with me —"

"I know. I thought about that. But I'm willing to accept you. I know the way you are. You can't help the way you are. And I can't say I like it. But I'm willing, you know. What I'm, what I'm trying to say. If you have to see other guys it's okay — why are you smiling?"

"Because that's not what I meant. I'm not interested in other guys."

"Well, what?"

"I have a baby," she said. "I couldn't leave him. He comes with me."

"Oh . . . yeah. Okay."

"You don't sound very positive."

"Oh, sure. I am."

"This is important. You have to be positive. My son is the most important thing in my life. He has to know he's loved and wanted. If you resent him he'll know it. He can hardly talk, but he'll know that. Kids feel things."

"I like kids."

"Yeah, but be sure. A young child is a big responsibility."

"Judy, I love you, everything about you. Everything that's yours. I'd be willing to adopt him, even."

"Let's not get ahead of ourselves."

"I'll do anything for you."

She smiled. "You'll like Mikie. I know you will. Everybody does. He's really a wonderful kid."

I kissed her. Later, she talked about Roy, as if to sort out her own feelings. "There's a million reasons to stay with him. He doesn't beat me. He brings home a paycheck every week. I have my house. My beautiful house. And my son has a father. But I can't be happy with him. I don't even like him. I live with the man, but I don't even like him."

"You can forget him, Judy."

"I wish it was that simple. People are going to talk about us, you know. About me. Me especially. It's always a worse sin for the woman. Well, I'm not going to worry about that anymore. What other people think. It doesn't really matter."

"No."

"When I married Roy, everybody was happy. Roy. My family. His family. Everybody but me."

"Judy, I'll make you happy."

"At the time, I thought I was happy. But I was fooling myself. I was really in love with someone else when I got married. That's something I've never told anyone. Remember Bobby? I told you about my friend I talk to."

"You were in love with him?"

"But it wasn't going to work. Sneaking around. Feeling guilty. I'd get headaches all the time, terrible headaches. And we fought, which was the worst. I knew it wasn't going to work. So I broke it up, by going with Roy. And everyone was happy."

"Why couldn't you marry Bobby?"

"Bobby was married already," she said.

"Oh."

"Nothing ever works right."

"This'll work. You and me. You won't be sorry."

"The first month we were married," she continued, "we were having fights already. One day, we had one and he drove off, took my car keys so I was stuck in the house. This wasn't anything special. He'd done it before. He still does it. I stood there watching him drive away and it suddenly occurred to me that I'd be married to him until the day I died. I cried all afternoon. It was the worst day of my life."

I touched her shoulder.

"But I got over it. I don't cry anymore."

"No."

"When I got married I had ideas of being a perfect wife. Doing everything to please. Having fun all the time. But he wrung that right out of me. I wasn't always this way. Being married to Roy you forget how to trust people. It's a scary thing when someone can change you like that. It's like one of those horror movies where they take over your body. It sounds funny but it's creepy." She looked up, inspecting me. "Do you have any money?"

"I have a few dollars."

"I mean in the bank."

"Well, yeah, I have some. Not much."

"Enough to live on? We have to think of that. You'll need to quit your job. It might take time to find another one. And we can't stay in this town."

"Sure, don't worry about money." I began worrying about money. Later, I asked, "That guy the other night?"

"He was a jerk," she said.

"Yeah. He seemed like a jerk." I pulled her close, her head on my chest.

"Maybe tonight," she said, "I'll tell Roy about us. I don't know. I don't look forward to it."

"Don't mention my name."

"He's going to have to know," she said. "Eventually."

"Yeah, but, just, please don't mention my name. Let him find out some other way."

We began working out the practical details of our escape. "I have a lot of things at my place I want to bring," Judy said.

"Things?"

"My furniture. My dishes. Things my mother gave me. Things like that."

"Well, Judy, ah, I don't have space for a lot of things. I've only got two small rooms."

"I'm not going to bring it all. Just the stuff I really want. I'll get the rest after we move to a bigger place. What I want to do now — are you listening?"

"Yeah," I said. "I'm listening."

"Well, is it okay? If I bring my things?"

"Sure. Bring your things. We'll find room. Somewhere."

"Can you be over at my place in the morning?" she asked.

"Your place?"

"Roy's taking Mikie over to his sister's in the morning. But you can drop by my house around eleven and take some of my stuff for me."

"Well . . . I don't know, Judy. I don't want to go over to your house. What if Roy comes home?"

"He won't," she insisted.

"But what if he does? What if he comes back while I'm there? I can just see him pulling up while I'm packing his furniture into my car."

"It's my furniture," she protested.

"Couldn't you bring it along with you? Your stuff?"

"There's too much for one person. I just thought you'd take some of it. That would make things easier for me."

"Well," I said, "I would. I just don't want to be over there. In his house. Loading his things into my car."

"Mmmmm," she thought for a moment, "how about this? I'll put a few things into my car. You come and get it. You'll be there and gone in two seconds. What you do, you take my car. Then, drive it to your apartment. Unload it. Bring it back."

"Where will you be?"

"I'll be busy. For one thing I've got to get to the bank some-time tomorrow, clean out the joint account. I've got to call a lawyer. I've got to do a million things. Do you think it's easy to end a marriage after three years? Maybe all this is simple for you, but for me it's very complicated."

"I never said it was simple, Judy. I've been through it. I know a little bit about it."

"Okay. I'm sorry. It's just, for me, all this is very difficult. In a lot of ways. And it'll make it much easier if I get my things out. Once I go, maybe he won't let me get some of it."

"Okay, okay, I'll do it."

"Really, I appreciate it."

"Yeah."

"You're great." She gave me a warm, long kiss. Soon, Judy would tell Roy Klijner their marriage was over. And tomorrow we would start a new life. I agreed to meet her at two the next afternoon, again on Hubbard Road.

That night, Jack Olander leaned across his desk. "Better give out the assignments, Roy."

"I'll do it," Klijner muttered.

And ten minutes later, "It's getting late. You better take care of those assignments."

"Okay."

But in a short time Olander was moving unhappily from reporter to reporter, assigning stories. It was a rare sight, as the spindly editor generally avoided leaving his large desk at the head of the room. In fact, he generally avoided any movement whatsoever.

"What's with Roy?" asked Pam Nealy.

"Why?" I asked.

"I was just asking him a question. He wouldn't even answer me."

Obviously, Judy had given him the bad news that afternoon. Thank God, she hadn't given him my name.

Or did he drag it out of her? What if he knew? He hadn't looked at me all night. Of course, he hadn't looked at anyone.

From the Sunday papers to the assignment sheet to a pile of obituaries waiting to be edited, he seemed unable to focus on anything longer than a few minutes. At times, he would stare blankly at his ashtray or put his head in his hands and sigh wearily.

"Hey." Burkhalter hurried past, giving him a poke. "What's up?"

Klijner bristled. "Keep your hands to yourself, asshole."

"Well, pardon me."

It wasn't my fault. He'd brought it on himself. It was the payment for years of cruelty. Even so, I didn't like to watch.

Later, driving to a fire (which turned out to be a false alarm), I thought of Judy. I tried to believe it was real. Judy was mine. Forever. No more meeting in parking lots. We would have each other all day, every day. But I kept seeing him, spoiling the daydream.

To my relief, he was gone when I returned to the office. "Where's Roy?"

"Stepped out," Olander said.

"He's been out three times tonight," Pam whispered to me. "Down at Mullins's Bar."

It was dark on the bottom floor, the circulation office closed. As I came downstairs with Pam Nealy a voice called, "What time is it?"

"That you, Roy?" Pam asked.

I leaned against the wall, holding my breath. Why was he down there in the dark?

"What time is it?" he called.

"Time to go home."

"Yeah." He came forward, face in shadows. "Anybody going over Mullins's?"

"I don't know," she answered. "Hennessy and Lewis are upstairs. Why don't you ask them? You should go up and tell Jack where you are, anyway. He thought you might be sick."

"I'm okay. How about you two? Want to come over for a few drinks?"

"Not me," she said. "I'm going home to bed."

"What about you, Bill?"

"Ah . . . awful tired."

"Hey, look," he reached into his pocket, "I know you guys are always broke. My treat."

Neither of us answered.

"Yeah. That's okay. Go home. I can get polluted all by myself."

"You look like you could use some sleep," Pam said.

"I feel like getting shitfaced. What's wrong with that? Christ, it's practically an occupational obligation."

Voices came from above, Hennessy and Lewis descending the stairs.

"Hey," Klijner yelled, "who's thirsty?" He was still shouting as Pam and I reached the street.

"My God," she said, "he's in a bad way."

"Hennessy and Lewis'll take care of him."

"Hennessy and Lewis can barely take care of themselves."

"It's this place," I said. "This place is getting to him."

We came to Pam's car. Klijner's creaking voice haunted me. With luck, I would never hear it again.

"This place gets to me sometimes," I said. "Sometimes I think I don't like newspaper work. Sometimes I think I'd like to get out of it. Sell used cars or something. You sure can't make any money working for these cheap bastards."

"If I were you," Pam said, "I wouldn't quit until I had another job lined up."

"Yeah. Maybe you're right."

"You wouldn't find another newspaper job. Newspaper jobs are rare these days. And they'll never take you back here. They never take people back."

"Small loss." I smiled.

"Well, if you do quit, I'm sure we'll all miss you. I'll miss you."

"I'll miss you too, Pam."

"It's not often," she gazed at my feet, "you work with someone and really hit it off with them."

"Yeah. We hit it off real good, didn't we?"

"You're a nice guy, Bill."

"Yeah," I backed away, "I hope your opinion doesn't change in the next few days."

She had a very puzzled look on her face. And I had no idea what a stupid thing I'd just done.

I should have been happy, but I lay awake. A nor'easter struck in the night and pounded at my window.

So why should I feel guilty? I didn't steal his wife. Judy and me, you couldn't help a thing like that. It just happened. People have to look out for themselves in this world. And they would both be better off apart.

Roy's car was gone. Judy's yellow Pinto was backed against the front porch of their house. At exactly eleven I scurried across the yard, praying no one saw me. Considering Roy's strange behavior the night before, I thought the plan to move Judy's belongings might be canceled. But she hadn't called.

A small bureau was jammed into the back seat of the Pinto. The drawers on the seat beside it, piled one atop the other, were crammed with clothing and jewelry. Two bulging suitcases were on the floor. The keys were in the ignition.

I knocked on the door, at first timidly, then louder. No answer.

What to do? Wait for Judy to come back?

Where could she be? Visiting her lawyer? Gone to the bank?

I couldn't stand around here. The car was packed and ready to go, the keys inside. So I took it.

Mrs. Gartland, the landlady, was on the street as I arrived at my apartment. "A new car, Mr. Martell?"

"Oh, no." I pulled out the suitcases. "This is a friend's car. I'm borrowing it."

"What's the suitcases for?"

"Clothes."

The drawers, the little bureau and the suitcases went to my second-floor apartment in three hurried trips. At one point, I bumped the railing. Odd things fell from one drawer, a few photos, a notebook, a pair of panties wrapped around a small wood carving of a giraffe. I retrieved all of this. I wanted to get that distinctive yellow Pinto back where it belonged as soon as possible. There was a constant, irrational fear that Klijner would drive past and see me. "What the hell are you doing, Bill? Isn't that my wife's car?"

I was about to drive away when I remembered the trunk. Maybe she'd put something in the trunk. I walked to the rear and slipped the key in the lock. It popped up. But the trunk was empty except for the spare tire and jack.

Around noon, I parked Judy's bright yellow Pinto in her driveway. I knocked on the door. Again, there was no answer. I left the keys in the ignition and hurried off.

On Hubbard Road the wind had done a fierce job. Anything fragile was ripped to pieces, all the leaves gone. Along the dike-like road through the marsh every living thing stood naked, rotted growth discharged, clogging the black water. Tree bases, islands of earth, were soggy with the swamp.

I waited here, weighing my future. For the first time, I was worried about money. My job at the *Suburban-Citizen* was over.

So where would the money come from?

I would need a new apartment. Out of town. Big enough for three. Judy was accustomed to a fine house.

But what could I afford? I had five hundred dollars or so in the bank. If I sold my life insurance I might get five hundred more. A decent apartment would cost at least three hundred a month. I might be solvent for two or three months. By then I should find a job. But what kind of job? After the scandal broke I could not expect a good reference from the paper.

Too late, I began to appreciate the extent of my sacrifice for Judy. My whole life was changed. I was not only responsible for her, but for a child as well. Instant family. Was she worth all this?

Where the hell is she? It was already two-thirty.

So, it turns out I'm tied down. Maybe forever. And for what? So she can run around as soon as my back is turned. Okay, I told her I didn't care about other men. But it's one thing to say when you're desperate and confused. It's another thing to live with.

I was growing sympathetic to Roy Klijner.

A car approached. You could see it coming a mile away, which is why Hubbard Road is popular with lovers. But it wasn't yellow, it was blue. Did Judy have his car for the day?

For an awful moment I considered that it was not only Klijner's car, but Klijner as well, come to confront me.

Instead, it was a police cruiser, rolling slowly, bits of rock and loose asphalt popping loudly beneath the tires. One officer stared at me. He was young, square-jawed with a belligerent grimace. I looked away as the cruiser made a U-turn at the bottom of the road, passing again.

Where was that woman? It was three o'clock.

Of course, she was always late. Early in our relationship I'd adjusted to waiting, fifteen minutes, twenty, an hour, wondering where she might be. Time meant nothing to her. One day she didn't come at all, complaining later that her husband had called her to go somewhere. "And what could I tell him?"

What would be the excuse today? Today was too important for dentist appointments or flat tires.

At three-thirty, she was an hour and a half late and the truth began to force itself on me. I saw it in the stinking, stagnant bog all around. She wasn't coming. I could sit here forever. All along, it had been too good to be true.

I reached my apartment at four-fifteen. Roy would be at work. She was home alone. In a few minutes she would telephone. I sat on my favorite chair and waited for Judy's call.

The phone didn't ring. I sat for what seemed an hour, staring at the wall. Nothing. At quarter to five I called her. Busy.

Busy? Who the hell would she be talking to?

I tried again at five. Still busy. Again at five-fifteen. In an hour

I must've called a dozen times. It was busy. Busy. Busy. Busy. I called the operator.

"That number is busy, sir."

"But I've been calling for two hours. You think someone could be talking for two hours?"

"It's happened before."

"Is there any way you could tell if maybe the phone is off the hook?" I asked.

"I can break in on the line, but only in the case of an emergency."

"Yeah, operator. Look, I'm going to have to think this over. Let me get back to you."

What if Roy was on the telephone? Under no circumstances did I want the operator breaking in on his conversation, announcing "An emergency call from William Martell."

Why was I concerned about her? Obviously, she'd changed her mind without even bothering to tell me. That was typical of Judy. Well, the hell with her. I don't force myself on people who don't want me. On the other hand, she might need me.

I decided to visit her house, something I'd never done before. I wouldn't knock on the door until I was sure she was alone.

First, I had to be certain Klijner was at work. Considering his recent odd behavior it was entirely possible he had remained home for the day. That would explain a lot. Perhaps he had begged his wife not to run away. I could imagine the emotional scene. Her relenting.

It wasn't fair. He had so much on his side, money, the house, the child.

"Hello, Bill? Is that you?" Pam Nealy answered at the *Suburban-Citizen*.

"Pam?"

"Where the hell are you? Listen, you better get in here. We're short-staffed and Jack is furious at you."

"Pam? Look, is Roy there?"

"Just a minute."

"Pam? Wait —"

"Hello." It was Klijner. "Hello."

I hung up. A stupid thing to do. Maybe he'd think we were disconnected. But probably not.

I had to get out of the apartment. He might call back. The phone would ring and ring. And like a complete ass I'd pick it up on the slim chance it was Judy. But it'd be him.

Sure enough, racing down the stairwell of my apartment, I heard the phone. But I didn't stop. I kept running.

There was something odd about Judy's house. I found a parking space a block away. It was early evening on a deep, gray day, yet there were no lights. I telephoned again from a booth near the library, in sight of the house. Still busy.

I walked through the park and saw the front door wide open. That was really strange. Klijner's blue Mercury was gone, but the yellow Pinto sat in the driveway where I'd left it.

I ambled uncertainly across the street, so nervous I stumbled on the curb. What if the sister-in-law came to the door? Well, I could say I was selling magazines or something. Stop worrying. Slowly I walked past the house, turned around, and came back to it. I saw no sign of life.

What if Klijner was home after all? A man says "hello" on the phone. One word from a noisy newsroom. I assumed it was Klijner. But I could have been wrong. Maybe it was Olander or Murphy or any one of half a dozen people. Why didn't I think of that before?

The porch creaked loudly. I tried to be calm, quiet. Don't worry. His car is gone. He's at work, of course. I knocked lightly on the door frame. Inside were dead leaves on the hall carpet, the smell of furniture polish.

No one answered so I knocked again, harder. "Hello . . ." I was frightened by the sound of my own voice, an unfamiliar, high-pitched squeal. "Hey? . . . Judy?"

From a back room came a faint, yellow glow, the rear porch light beginning to count as the darkness grew.

"Judy?" I knocked once more and stepped into the hall. Every shade and curtain was closed. "Anybody home?" Unfamiliar with the house, I moved slowly, step by step. From nearby came an unworldly whine. Something was dreadfully wrong here.

The telephone receiver, off the hook, dangled like an outstretched hand from a bookcase in the hall. Carefully, quietly, I placed it on the cradle. There was another odd sound. Pid. Pid. Pid. The faucet dripping.

"Judy?"

I felt my way, hand over hand, toward the yellow light, grasping a chair arm, then a table, then a bookcase. I reached the kitchen, illuminated in dim yellow. My hand was wet. What the Christ? Pid. Pid. Pid. It was sticky, my palm.

I knew. It was blood. Was I bleeding?

I found the light switch. The yellow was gone and everything was red. The faucet wasn't dripping at all. It was blood. In a puddle on the seat of a high chair, a red pond, dripping to the floor. Pid. Pid. Pid.

Pink fingerprints marked the light switch. Blood spotted the walls. It was in tiny pools on the sink, droplets on the stove and in blaring swatches on the floor. Someone had taken time to paint the room in it.

So much blood. Someone was certainly killed in a horrible way. I shuddered. My legs seemed unsteady beneath me and my breathing came in gulps, as if I'd just run a mile. I was next. I was next. He was somewhere in the house. Watching. Waiting to drop the ax on my head. To split my skull wide open.

As I backed out, my heel caught on the rug and I toppled noisily to the hall floor. I fought a powerful spasm and came near to throwing up. Blood sickened me. Now it stained my hand. Judy's blood. Was it her blood?

I became certain her body lay, alive or dead, beside me in the dark. Fearfully, dreadfully, I reached out. Nothing. I waited for eyes accustomed to shadows. I heard breathing. Labored breathing. Gasps of a person near death. But it was only me.

I stumbled to the front door. Cold, fresh air hit my face,

chilled my sweat-soaked body. Traffic flowed past the house. A breeze shook the large elm near the street. In the park, a young couple walked hand in hand as though nothing had happened. Only one of these worlds can be real.

Where was Judy? Was she in the house, counting on me to save her? I should look upstairs. I should go up there. I listened, cocking my head toward the stairs. Nothing. Not a sound. I should go upstairs. But it wasn't really safe.

I stood on the porch, looking everywhere.

The police. Call the police. Use the pay phone. I scrambled down the porch steps.

In one blow, the breath was slammed out of me. I was pushed violently. Then, piled to the ground. I could smell dirt. I can't die. I twisted madly. I can't die like this.

It was a tremendously powerful and excited person. He seemed eager to break my arm. "Don't move. Don't move, you son of a bitch." I felt his knee boring into my spine.

"Aukh . . ."

The voice was unknown to me.

Then, there came a flashlight beam and a second voice. "Jesus, what a horror show. Blood everywhere."

"What'd you do in there?" demanded the first voice. "What'd you do?"

"Noth— No— Ahh —" My arm was jerked roughly behind and up. "Ahhh —" I feared it would break. "Don't . . . I give up. . . ."

"Keep your mouth shut. Keep your fuckin mouth shut or I'll break your fuckin arm."

five

I HEARD other voices.

"Is that the guy?"

"You seen the kitchen in there?"

"A fuckin mess."

Cars drove on the lawn, headlights pointed at me. The man on my back never lessened the pressure, pushing my face down. I tasted grass and soil.

"Let him up."

I was lifted to my feet. My arm ached. I couldn't move it. At once, they handcuffed my hands behind my back.

"What happened in there?" an older man asked. In a dark suit and a cloth overcoat, he was given to a generous middle and a sad face of folds and wrinkles.

"I don't — " I stopped to spit dirt and grass out of my mouth. It drooled across my cheek and I wiped it with difficulty against my shoulder.

"What happened in there?" the detective repeated himself.

"I don— I don't know. I just got here."

"I see."

Police swarmed about the yard. A crowd collected on the sidewalk.

"What's your name?" The detective led me to an unmarked car on the lawn. The back door was open, waiting for me.

"Bill Martell. William. Martell, I mean."

"You live here, Bill?"

"No."

"This isn't your house?"

"No."

"I see. What were you doing here?" He behaved as if the question was merely a topic for casual conversation.

"I came to see a friend."

"A friend?"

"My arm is killing me." I tried to shake the pain away.

"Who's your friend?"

"Judy. Judy and Roy Klijner. I work with Roy at the paper."

"You work at the newspaper?"

"That's right."

"The *Citizen*?"

"Yes."

"And you came to see both of them?"

"Yeah. I guess."

"I see." The detective urged me into the car. There were no latches on the doors and there was a thick, steel screen between the front and back seats.

"I was just goin to call you guys," I said.

"I see."

"From the pay phone over at the library."

"I'm going to give you your rights." He produced a small card.

"Why? What for?"

"Just a routine thing." He held out the card. "Follow along so you can be sure you understand. You can read, can't you?"

"Of course I can read."

"Good. You don't need glasses or anything?"

"No."

He recited perfectly what was on the card, concluding with, "Now, do you understand what I've just told you?"

"I understand, but I don't see —"

"If you want a lawyer, you can call one when we get to the station. If you can't afford a lawyer one will be provided to you."

"Why do I need a lawyer?"

"Exactly."

"I mean, I didn't do anything."

"Then, why do you need a lawyer?" he asked.

Meanwhile, in the gray house all the lights were on, doors open and shades up, as in summer. It was crawling with men, one taking pictures, the blossom of white-blue always telling the room he was in.

A dark young man in a handsome white cqat came to the car. "Hey, Stevie," he said, "can't we get those cops out of there before they screw up this whole thing?"

"Who's in there?" asked the older detective.

"Everybody. And I've got the state police people comin out to go over the place. Jesus," he watched the house, "what the fuck is attracting them all?"

He casually slammed the car door. I was shut in, a prisoner.

For several minutes, I watched a hectic relay of police to and from the house, while the two detectives whispered importantly alongside the car.

At last, the older one leaned in the window. "What do you know about that?" He gestured to the yellow Pinto in the driveway, a few feet away. Two policemen were all over it, having opened the four doors, hood and trunk.

"That's Judy's car."

"What's that dripping from the back?"

"What . . . ?"

"Underneath." He pointed. "Underneath the back of the car."

"Is it oil?"

"What did he say?" asked the detective in the white coat.

"He wants to know if it's oil."

"Yeah. It's oil. Go rub his nose in it."

Was it blood? "Jesus . . ."

Later, the older man decided, "I don't think we're going to find a victim here. Let's get this guy down the station."

"Yeah. Wait a minute." The other approached a pair of police-women leaning against the porch railing. "Get off the porch, you officers. Move those bystanders out of here." He got in the car, muttering, "Fuckin asshole broads."

As we drove, I was struck by how different everything looked. As a reporter, I enjoyed a sort of status in this town. Whatever I saw might become a newspaper story. Thousands would read it. I was proud of that.

Now, I was a prisoner, and the little city seemed an unsympathetic place. "Did you find anything?" I asked, leaning forward to avoid putting weight on my aching arm.

"Like what?" asked the young detective in white.

"I don't know. Where's Judy?"

"Where do you think she is?"

"I don't know."

As we drove past the *Suburban-Citizen,* I kept my head low.

"I didn't hurt her," I said suddenly.

The detectives looked back. "What did you do to her?"

"Nothing. I couldn't find her."

They turned away.

At police headquarters I was fingerprinted and photographed. "We just want you to make a statement, answer a few questions," explained the older detective, Stephen Reardon. I was grateful just to have my arms free. Agreeing to cooperate, I signed a waiver of rights. This was all a misunderstanding. I had only to explain that now and avoid serious problems down the road.

In that spirit, I allowed the state police chemist to take what he needed for evidence. He scraped some dried blood from my hand and took a blood sample from my arm. "May we have your underwear?" he asked.

"My what?"

"Underwear. Do you wear underdrawers?"

"What could you possibly want with my underwear?"

"An examination of your clothing, underclothing, can prove you had sexual relations recently. It cannot, however, prove the converse, that you have not had sexual relations."

"I can tell you right now I haven't had a woman in almost a month."

The chemist raised his eyebrows.

"Well. Is that a crime or something?"

He took my sneakers as well.

They led me into a bare, cubelike room, coated in snowy, fluorescent light with white-glossed concrete walls and white tile floor. Nevertheless, it looked yellow from the dirt, and my blue socks became caked with dust.

I waited half an hour at a small, gray metal table, sitting, flexing my arm, trying to bring back the feeling. Where was Judy? I tried to worry about her. I felt ashamed even thinking about my own danger, which was real enough.

"Hi." Reardon came into the room. "Would you like something to eat? We're sending out for hamburgs."

"I'd just like to get this settled."

"We want to get it settled too. Send you home. But it might take a while."

Soon, Reardon returned with the detective in the white coat, Bob Matteo. Short and energetic, he never smiled, except maliciously. I would develop a sincere and lasting hatred for this man. Several detectives and uniformed officers came and went. I began by telling everything about Judy and Roy and me.

"That's it?" Reardon asked. "That all you can tell us?"

"I told you everything I know."

"I don't doubt it." He sat with me, drummed his fingers on the table, seemed as worried as I. "Don't doubt it a bit. You say you told us everything. I'm sure you did. But there is one thing. The thing is this. What do you suppose happened to her?"

"Happened to her? What?"

"Judy. What happened to Judy? We can't find her. No one can find her anywhere."

"I don't know where, where she is." I fought dizziness. "Upstairs? She wasn't upstairs somewhere?"

"No. No, she wasn't in the house anywhere." He paused and stared a long time, as though expecting me to say something. I had to look away. "What do you think? Where do you think she is, Bill?"

"I don't know."

"What do you think happened to her?"

"I don't know."

"Well, let's suppose something happened to her. There's blood in the kitchen. Well, everywhere really." Again the pause. "Where do you suppose she is? Where?"

"I don't know. Really."

"What would you think?"

"Her husband? He might know where she is."

"No. He hasn't seen his wife since early this morning."

"This look familiar?" Matteo came from behind and placed a large meat knife on the table. It was wrapped in a clear plastic bag. But on the blade and brown wooden handle there was plainly blood, moist, gleaming under the lights, smearing the inside of the bag.

"No." I was choked with shock.

"Do you know what it is?"

"I can . . . what?" I couldn't take my eyes off it.

"Do you know where we found it?"

"In the kitchen?"

Matteo moved around and came close to my face. I could smell his breath, a whiff of decay. "How'd you know it was in the kitchen?"

"The kitchen. It's a kitchen knife. Where else would it be?" I turned from the sight of it.

"Why were you in the house?" Matteo demanded.

/ 64

"I explained all that."

"Tell me again."

"I had an appointment with Judy. She didn't show up. I went looking for her."

"Did you find her?"

"No, obviously."

"Where have you been all day?"

"For a few hours I was waiting over on Hubbard Road there. Most of the time I was in my apartment."

"With who?"

"With no one. With myself."

"So," Matteo accused, "you can't account for a minute of the day. You have no alibi at all."

"Why should I need one?" I turned to Reardon. "Huh? Why should I need an alibi?"

"I think we should be realistic." Reardon put the bloody weapon in a cardboard box. "I think it's likely Mrs. Klijner is a victim."

"A victim?" I shook my head. "A victim of what?"

"Who would want to hurt this woman?"

"I don't know . . ."

"What if she is dead?" Reardon asked.

"No. She's not dead. She can't be. Why don't you people stop wasting time here and go find her?"

"Where should we look?"

"I don't know. How should I know? You're supposed to figure that out. Why ask me? This is ridiculous."

"Don't you want us to find her?" Reardon asked.

"Of course I do."

"Well, help us. That's the only way we get things done. People see things or know things and they tell us. We can't be everywhere, you know. We need people to help us."

"But I already told you, I don't know anything."

"Talk to us. You might think of something."

"I wouldn't. No."

A detective began pounding frantically at the tape recorder. "This goddamn thing never works. Goddamn machine."

"Tell us," Matteo paced the room, "tell us how it happens you took up with somebody else's wife?"

"She took up with me is more like it. She took up with a lot of guys. I told you. It's the way she was."

"Who knew about you two?" Matteo asked.

"No one."

"Maybe someone saw the two of you together," Reardon suggested.

"I don't know. Maybe."

"Maybe Judy told someone," he continued.

"I just don't know."

"You don't know much," Matteo said.

"I guess not."

"If I was in the shit like you're in the shit, wiseass, I'd be comin up with a few goddamn answers."

"I didn't do anything. That's why I don't know anything."

No one responded. I looked at a room of grim, skeptical faces. "Shouldn't I have a lawyer?"

"You want us to call a lawyer?" Reardon asked.

"Yes."

"Okay. We can do that. Who do you want us to call?"

I had no idea.

"Do you have a personal lawyer?"

"I had a lawyer for my divorce. But he was a jerk. Besides, I have no money."

"Well, in that case the court can appoint a lawyer."

"Yeah." I felt suddenly exhausted. It was late into the night. "I don't think I should talk anymore. I think I should wait for the lawyer."

"Okay. That's your privilege."

"I know."

"That's okay. You know your rights. You're a bright fella. You know your rights and we have no intention of infringing on them. We're as interested in protecting your rights as you are."

"Good."

"We want this cleared up."

"Me too."

"I don't wonder. You look awfully tired. I know you're anxious to get home to bed."

"So let me go home."

"The problem is this. If you don't talk with us, we can't get this settled. And if we can't get this settled, you can't go home. We have to hold you."

"What? What for?"

"Illegal entry," Matteo smiled, "for starters."

"Bill." Reardon was at my side. "We don't want to hold you."

"No?"

"No. If you're innocent we want to settle this and send you home." He took a firm, fatherly grip of my shoulder. Home. The word brought a sensation of safety and peace. "Will you help us, Bill?"

"How?"

"Will you answer a few more questions? Just a few?"

"Questions. What?"

"Keeping in mind, it's entirely up to you. You have the right to remain silent. We can't force you to answer questions and we wouldn't want to."

"Well," I said. "What're these questions?"

Reardon poured coffee for both of us. "You're a reporter?"

"Yeah."

"You know, my boy's taking a journalism course at college. You enjoy it? That business?"

"It . . . doesn't pay much."

"That's what I told him. No benefits." Smiling gently, he put a cup of coffee before me. "Here."

It was steaming hot and a single sip seemed to warm me all over. So good.

"How can we clear this up, Bill?"

"What?"

"How can we clear this up? How can we find out what happened to that girl?"

"Why ask me?"

"You must have some ideas. Maybe you've got a theory."

"If I did I'd tell you."

"How do you feel about girls, Bill?"

"How do I feel about girls? What kind of question is that? How do you feel about girls?"

"The usual way." Reardon smiled with his eyes. "I like the girls."

"Me too."

"You liked Mrs. Klijner?"

"Very much."

"She was beautiful?" he asked.

"She is. Very."

"And you went to bed with her?"

"I've already said that."

"It's all right." Reardon raised his hand. "I'm just trying to understand all this."

"Why?"

"Why?" It was Matteo, from somewhere behind me, his voice an exclamation. "Why? We found you in a woman's house covered in blood. Oh, come on now. Why do you think we ask these questions?"

"I wasn't covered in blood."

"Do you know why you're here?" Matteo moved before me.

"To . . . I don't know . . . to help . . ."

"I asked a question." He was inches from my face, jowls red, vibrating. "Do you know why you're here?"

"I —"

"Do you?"

"— what?"

He lowered his voice and moved closer. Speaking directly to my right ear, he said softly, "Your story is bullshit, Martell."

"No."

"It is. I know bullshit when I hear it. I'm an expert."

"I didn't."

"But somebody did," Matteo continued. "Somebody's killed that poor woman."

My mouth seemed locked shut.

"I think it was you." His voice was a mumble.

I shook my head, no.

"I think it was you. What do you say to that, smartass?"

To have it spoken. How could anyone believe such a thing? Dear God, what a mess. Get me out of this.

Matteo took my hand and turned it over. "What's that, Martell? What is it? Is it oil?"

It had mostly flaked away or been scraped off. But you could still see it on my palm, rust-colored, settled in the tiny, criss-crossed cracks of skin. I shuddered involuntarily, repulsed by the policeman's touch.

"You did it." Matteo's whisper was harsh, loud. "You did it."

". . . you're . . . sick."

"Not me, Bill." He straightened. "Not me." Pointing, he said softly, "You."

"Give the guy a chance," Reardon offered. "Let him give his side."

"Let him try." Matteo moved away.

Reardon was constantly at the coffee pot. "We'll give it a rest," he offered whenever I began to flag. "Catch our breath. We want everyone's head clear. I'm not interested in badgering anyone. I want the truth here."

He brought two fresh cups of coffee to the table. "Cream and sugar?"

"I'm not sure," I began. "I'm not sure I should be answering questions without a lawyer."

"I know. It's being arranged. Relax."

"I'm tired. I wish you guys would leave me alone."

"Okay. I understand. But bear with me. I know we're going to have this all cleared up if we take a little time. Suppose you let me ask you one question?"

I sighed.

"Is that okay? One question?"

"What?"

"If, let's hope not, but if some violence has been done to this woman, something unpremeditated, say in the course of an argument, a misunderstanding, what do you suppose would happen to the person who did it? The person responsible?"

"I didn't do it."

"I'm not saying you did. I'm just asking you, what do you think is likely to happen to the person who did do it?"

"I don't know."

"And that's just my point. That's just the thing. So many people are afraid of the unknown. Sometimes the truth isn't as terrible as you imagine."

"I don't know. . . . What's the point?"

"The point is this. For a person with a good job, no previous record, who works a deal with the district attorney, the sentence on this is minimal."

"That doesn't sound right."

"But it's true. You know, we're both men of some experience on these matters. We know about criminal justice these days. You can murder a woman. And if you cooperate, you spend a few years, at most, on a farm. Hard work. Fresh air. Then, you're back on the street. You can start life over."

"That doesn't sound like justice."

"Well, maybe not. Maybe not. But maybe it leaves justice to the individual. Sort of you come to terms with justice yourself. Of course, you can't do that until you're completely open and honest."

"I have been."

"The trouble is, Bill, your story so far, it hasn't settled things. In fact, it looks very bad for you."

"I told you everything. I can't help how it looks."

"Bill." He leaned close. "You know, you seem like a decent enough guy. I thought that the first minute. I said to myself, this guy isn't the usual common criminal."

"Not any kind of criminal."

"No. You're a sensitive guy. You are. I can see you have good and decent instincts. And I like you."

"You do?"

"I do. I don't care what this character says. I'll tell you," he dropped his voice to a barely audible whisper, "we got cops in here. . . . Let's just say, don't let your sister marry a cop. Okay?"

I laughed uneasily.

"Now. The important thing, Bill," he touched my arm, "the real key thing is. For all of us. We have to know if she's alive."

"Alive? Judy?"

"Is she alive?"

"I think, I hope she's . . ." I shuddered. My feet were freezing. I covered one foot with the other. ". . . I'm cold."

"It's tough. Never seeing her again. I know how you must feel. It should hurt. A thing like that."

And it did. I looked at the dried blood on my hand and thought morbidly, pathetically, it had been part of her, made her what she was.

"She can't be dead," I protested. Overcome by exhaustion, tears skimmed swiftly down my cheeks and I watched them splash to tiny puddles on the table top. Judy was likely dead. I confessed the truth to myself. Of all the sad endings to our affair, I could never imagine one as terrible as this. The horror and shock were too great to be real.

"Want to talk about it? Get it off your chest?"

"Poor Judy."

"It's cold out," Reardon leaned close, "near thirty degrees. Let's not leave her out in that. We can get her. Even if she's in the water. We can have her out in a shot."

"No."

"We'll take her where it's warm."

I turned away from him, but he moved to my side, whispering in my ear.

"She must be cold. Don't leave her out there. Poor girl."

"No."

"We'll wrap her in blankets. Just tell us where she is."

"This isn't fair."

"You'll feel better telling us."

I sniffled, drying my eyes.

"Let me help you, Bill. I'll take care of it personally. Look out for you. Listen now, you gotta be practical. Look at the case against you. How's it all going to sound when people hear it? How's it going to sound?"

"Can I wash my hands?" I struggled to seem composed, nearly smiled. "I'm not going to talk to you guys anymore."

Matteo groaned and Reardon moved away.

"I want a lawyer."

"In the morning," Reardon said. "In the morning."

On the way to the lockup, I passed Captain Adair, who stared at me in disbelief. But I was too exhausted to feel the humiliation.

The cell stank of urine and semen. Everything was hard, especially the thin, stained mattress. I collapsed on it, but incredibly, I couldn't sleep.

Some unseen prisoner muttered incessantly. I listened all night, trying to make sense of his ravings. Early in the morning, a man was placed in the adjacent cell. "Hey," he called, "you awake?" He tapped at the brick wall between us. "Hey. I said, you awake?"

"No."

"No? No, I'm not awake? Pretty funny. Hey, that's pretty funny. You know, maybe you don' wanna talk, huh? You don' wanna talk just say so."

I tossed on the squeaking cot.

"What's your name?"

I sighed.

"Ain't got a name, huh? I'm Glenn. What you here for?"

After a long time I answered. "What am I here for? When I find out I'll let you know."

Later, they returned my sneakers and allowed me to wash my face and hands.

Both Glenn and I were driven out of town to the county courthouse. Through heavy traffic I sat in the police car, looking straight ahead, hoping no one saw me. It was dreamlike, only the cold seemed real. The police were silent, unfriendly. None displayed the paternal concern shown by Detective Reardon the night before.

"Think you'll make bail?" asked Glenn, a shaggy young man with a drooping mustache. His clothes were neat, his face frequently smiling.

"I don't even know what they think I've done. Illegal entry, they say. I think."

"You'll make bail."

"I will?"

"Everybody makes bail. They gotta give you bail unless they think you're gonna run away or something."

I tried not to worry, persuading myself that the innocent have little to fear from the law. Given the chance, I could explain everything. And in back of this confidence was another assumption, or hope, that Judy was still alive and would soon make an appearance.

At the courthouse I was astounded to see news people, including photographers and a television film crew. Up to this point, I had imagined the arrest a private matter between the police and myself.

Hustled from the back seat, I was too disoriented even to cover my face, but stared dumbly at the cameras. They came clicking and whirring. "How you gonna plead, Bill?" someone yelled.

David Chew was among them.

"David . . . hey, don't . . ."

Sighting through his prized German lens, he pretended not to recognize me and clicked away.

I was taken inside the courthouse, the press, jostling, locked out behind me.

"Jesus." Glenn was impressed by all this. "What the Christ you do? Illegal entry? Into what? Fort Knox?"

"I didn't do anything."

We were taken to a large holding cell. On the floor was the early edition of the *Suburban-Citizen*. It was bannered with an uncharacteristically lurid headline: "Prime Suspect in Disappearance of Editor's Wife," and in smaller, heavier type: "Kitchen Bloodbath." My name was in the lead. The paper did not exactly embrace me as their own, burying our connection deep in the article. A picture of me, happy grin and all, was prominently displayed.

"Well," I sat staring, "I finally made the front page."

"Shit," Glenn looked over my shoulder, "is that you? Holy Christ! You killed somebody? Christ. What made you do a thing like that?"

There was a picture of Judy, captioned: "Young Mother Feared Victim of Foul Play." I dwelled on it for only a moment. I was determined not to mourn for Judy. It was wasted energy. The only way to help her, if help was still possible, was to convince these people that I was the wrong man.

The story gave a summary of circumstantial evidence. Judy had disappeared sometime yesterday afternoon. Blood in the kitchen matched her type. I was found on the scene. My fingerprints were on the telephone, which was bloodied and might have been used as a weapon. Neighbors had seen me lurking about a few days before. Finally, the district attorney hinted at an even stronger case than so far revealed.

The *Suburban-Citizen* reported all this with the impartiality of a police department cheerleader. I was described as a "former employee," "reclusive personality," "poorly dressed," with "few friends."

I wondered which of my "few friends" had written the story. "I don't know." I rubbed my eyes wearily.

"Looks bad, huh?"

"I think I need a press agent."

"You're really in the shithouse. I mean, especially now they got that capital punishment back. Shit, I wouldn't be in your shoes, Jack."

I was sweating suddenly. I could feel my clothes clinging to my body, my forehead growing damp.

"You know what you oughta do?" he asked.

"What?"

"Cop a plea."

"Yeah?"

"Sure. Ask to see the district attorney's man here. Tell him you'll plead guilty to something else. Instead of murder make it manslaughter. You get a lighter sentence. They're always wantin to plea bargain because otherwise people might hafta work tryin to convince a jury you're guilty. The judge. He might hafta spend six hours a day in court instead of three."

"Plea bargain?"

"Yeah. That's what I'm doin. Of course, I'm down here. It's nothin compared to the shit you're in."

I winced. It was unfair that this thuggish character should take comfort from my problems.

"Sellin things. That's my trouble. TVs and coats and shit like that. I was sellin them outa a truck and some bastard comes in I give him a great deal on a big console television. So when it doesn't work perfect he sends the fuckin state police on my ass. He gets a six-hundred-dollar TV for two and he expects a god-damn guarantee. What an asshole. I try to explain to him, this isn't Sears. You buy a two-hundred-dollar TV, you take a fuckin chance. Fix it yourself."

"And you made a deal with the district attorney?" I asked.

"Not yet. But I'm gonna. That's what I say. When they got you, they got you. Make the best of it. Make a deal. I mean, you make them have a big trial, they get pissed. You're wastin their time, costin a shitload of money. If you're dead, you should know enough to lie down. You make 'em push you over it's gonna be a long time before they let you up. I mean, fuck it, this is serious stuff, killin people."

I laughed uneasily. "There isn't even a body."

"And you can forget that shit. There don't need to be no body."

"Well how can they know if anybody's dead?"

"Anyway," Glenn scratched his face, "where is the body? You musta hid it good."

"I don't know where the body is. If there is a body. It's just. I didn't do anything. I've never been in trouble in my life. I don't even cheat on my income tax."

"Yeah, you stick to that story, sucker, you'll be tellin it when they throw the fuckin switch."

six

AN OLD MAN, though substantial of build, attorney Damien Coughlin was seated, briefcase open, in the tiny consultation room. Frizzy, pure white hair framed the baby-pink crown of his skull. His voice was firm and businesslike. "You'll need counsel."

"I need help."

"First. Let's see if you're eligible to have a court-appointed attorney." He consulted a printed form. "I'm going to ask a few questions. Some of these questions might seem quite personal. Nevertheless, if you want to qualify, your cooperation in answering is vital."

"I'll do whatever you say," I answered.

"Good. The first question. How much money do you have, including your bank account?"

"Well . . . a few hundred dollars."

"Any stocks, bonds, real estate, assets of any kind?"

"My mother sent me a savings bond for my birthday. It'll be worth fifty dollars in five years."

He was in no hurry, filling out his form, leaving me to study the peeling green paint on the wall. "You appear to be eligible," he said finally. "Would you like me to represent you?"

"I need help."

"I ask again, do you want me to represent you?"

"Please."

Having related it to the police several times, I went through my story now as if by rote. Coughlin listened impassively.

After scribbling a few notes, he said, "The assistant district attorney, Mr. Weisberg, tells me his main concern is this woman. Judith Anne Klijner. He wants the body recovered. He doesn't think it serves anybody to leave the issue in doubt another minute. Besides, he'll look good in the newspapers if he can wrap this up fast. So. He's made an offer, a very generous offer, that I think you should consider carefully. If you make a full confession, he agrees to a second-degree murder charge. Murder one carries a penalty of life imprisonment with no parole. Second-degree murder can mean a fifteen-year prison sentence. Now, I don't say these things to frighten you. But I feel an obligation to state the case frankly. This is a very serious predicament you're in and you should know it."

"Fifteen years?"

"For second-degree murder," he said.

"That doesn't seem like much. Not for killing somebody."

"Well, if you'd prefer a longer sentence. That's no problem."

"I don't think you understand, Mr. Coughlin. I don't want any sentence for myself. I didn't do anything."

Coughlin shrugged. "Usually, when they build a case against somebody we must file a discovery motion to find out what they've got. This time, they want everyone to know. An ominous development, I should say."

"What have they got? I read the newspapers, there's nothing except I was stupid enough to walk in that house, which doesn't prove anything."

"They have a little more than that." The old man gazed out the window. At times, he seemed to lose interest in the conversation, which frustrated me. I had been anxious to argue my case. Now, I found that even my own lawyer was not willing to listen.

"Did you tell someone recently you might be quitting your job?" the lawyer asked.

"No."

"A reporter named — let's see, I have it here. Pamela Nealy. Did you tell her you might be quitting your job?"

"Oh yeah," I remembered, "I did. Tell her. I didn't tell her it was definite. Well, you know, I was planning to leave. I was planning to run away with Judy. I was going to leave that job."

"And you called the newspaper yesterday afternoon and asked if Roy Klijner was there? And before he could answer, you hung up?"

"I did something like that, yeah. But it was because I was going over to see Judy. I didn't want to run into her husband."

"That's what you say," Coughlin noted. "But the prosecutor will say different. He'll say you wanted to make sure the husband was out so you could catch the wife alone and attack her."

"Attack her? Why should I do that?"

"Don't ask me. People do that sort of thing. All the time. God knows why."

"I wouldn't hurt Judy. For anything."

"Let's look at your story," Coughlin said. "You say you were running away with Mrs. Klijner. That never happened and we have only your word it was what you even intended. On the other hand, the police say you attacked Mrs. Klijner and made that mess in the kitchen. Now, they can take a jury to the kitchen. They can show some excellent color photos of the blood. I've seen them. The police photographer does fine work, I can tell you. And, finally, they can place you at the scene, in the kitchen."

"Still," I said, "that's all coincidence. I can say it was coincidence. Someone attacked, I guess, they attacked Judy. Then, I walked in."

"Maybe. Do you know a man named Roland Bennett?"

"No."

"You should," the lawyer said. "You just spent the day with him. In the same cell."

"Roland Bennett? No. He said his name was Glenn."

Coughlin reviewed a notepad. "Roland Glenn Bennett. That's the fellow. Did you talk to him about the case?"

"I don't know. Yeah. I guess we talked about it a little. His case. My case."

"Did you tell this man that you didn't know why you killed Judy?"

"I never said that, Mr. Coughlin. I never said anything like that."

"He claims you did. And the assistant district attorney tells me he has the whole conversation on tape."

"No. He couldn't. That guy. I told him the same thing I just told you. The same thing I told everybody. I didn't do anything."

"It's on tape," Coughlin repeated.

"I don't care. I didn't say it. He's lying. They must've fixed the tape. Faked it. I'd like to hear that."

"In the future," he cleared his throat, "do not discuss the case with anyone but me. The newspaper says you have few friends. I can promise you have even fewer today."

"So I've been finding out."

"We're going to plead 'not guilty' today. That's standard procedure at this stage. However, we can change the plea at any time later. We have that option."

"No, we don't. Because I am 'not guilty.' Nothing's going to change that."

He studied me. "I'll make the case for bail. I can't promise anything there. The assistant district attorney is going to ask for a very high bail."

"I get the impression, I don't know, like they're not going to even look for Judy. They're not going to try and find out what really happened to her."

"Unfortunately, if I understand their position, they feel the only way to find out what happened is to get you to tell them."

Guided into the courtroom with two other prisoners, I noticed a front-row bench made up almost entirely of reporters. I recognized faces, joking faces, drinking faces, now solemn. Burkhalter was among them. I should have known it would be him. No one gave the slightest nod of recognition.

I was led to a sort of dock, a semienclosed area, watched over by an armed guard and intended for dangerous people. People sat here because they were in big trouble and running away was worth the risk. As a reporter, I'd seen the inmates before. They wore handcuffs, as I did. They often were dirty, with vacant, even drugged stares. After over twenty-four hours with little sleep or food or change of clothes I must have looked as bad. The two men to my right mostly stared at the floor and worried. Certainly, I did that.

My case was handled after an "assault and battery on a police officer" and a "driving to endanger." When the assistant district attorney spoke, the courtroom was in such disarray even I, a few feet away, had difficulty hearing. One might think murder cases are always held in orderly courtrooms, skilled lawyers debating life and death before hushed throngs. That may go on somewhere, but not in this populous county, where murder is not unique.

The courtroom was a hardwood, high-ceilinged pit. Its loose joints creaked and cracked, echoing every sound a dozen times over. Someone in the gallery sobbed. One of my partners in the dock moaned softly at intervals, holding his stomach.

People awaiting their own day in court came and went by way of the swinging door at the end of the room. The whomp-whomp was constant.

The picture was complemented by Judge Andrews, who occasionally slouched out of sight behind the bench.

Mr. Weisberg, the assistant district attorney, a young, handsome, and impeccably groomed man, sketched the case against me. "The evidence we plan to submit will establish this man's guilt beyond doubt . . ."

But how? I fought to recall everything I'd told Glenn. If only I'd been more careful. In the car it had actually occurred to me that he was a police spy. But I quickly dismissed the idea as silly.

Weisberg spoke as though personally hating me. ". . . should be held over for the grand jury on a charge of first-degree murder . . . and the record shows he presents a clear and present danger to the community . . . he could end the anguish of the Klijner family, but refuses to do so . . . no roots in the community. He has no family here. No friends . . . the record shows it's likely he will flee once bail is posted. . . . In light of the record the Commonwealth asks that bail be set at one hundred thousand dollars."

"Jesus," I whispered softly. I'd never been worth so much. Through this devastating recital, Coughlin sat serenely penciling notes to himself, chatting with a colleague, or staring off into space. Goddammit, pay attention! He had seemed sharp enough. But these old people, they were in and out of it. Was Coughlin capable of saving me? Did he even care? The evidence, finally collected in one place, staggered me.

I remembered being warm, safe and comfortable in my own bed just yesterday morning. If only I'd stayed there.

As Weisberg concluded, Coughlin came to me. "What're my chances?" I asked. "Honestly."

"Of bail? Your chances of making bail?"

"Well, yeah. That too. But, I mean, in general. How's it look so far? What're my chances?"

His eyes lit up. "That deal they offered, given it any thought?"

"I'm not making any deal. I'm asking, what are my chances? How bad is it?"

"Well, it's not good. But we should keep in mind, we don't even have a body yet, do we?"

"No," I agreed.

"That woman could walk through those doors this minute and make the assistant district attorney look like the biggest horse's ass in the Commonwealth."

I looked at the door, half expecting to see Judy.

"And, in the law, anything can happen. Drawing Judge Andrews is a good break. Police call him the felon's friend."

Coughlin moved on the judge, addressing him with near-reverence. "This man isn't a criminal, your honor." The blue-eyed, white-haloed lawyer was dwarfed by the bench. "He has no record. He is a public servant in a real sense as a member of the working press."

A snicker, soft but unmistakable, from the reporters.

The judge appeared uninterested and the noise made Coughlin nearly inaudible. Nonetheless, he proceeded bravely.

". . . my client is also a religious man and once made preparations for entering the seminary before realizing, your honor, that this was not his calling . . ." Coughlin was so inventive, at times, I wondered if he hadn't confused me with someone else. Certainly, he had found much to admire in a man he had known for an hour.

Finished, Coughlin stood expectantly before the judge, awaiting some reaction, I guess. The judge, however, was having none of it. Head down, he seemed deep in thought. It was the only time Coughlin betrayed his actual contempt for the judge, pressing his lips together in disgust and motioning to the court clerk. "Your honor," the clerk said softly, and the judge appeared startled for a moment.

"I was just finishing up, your honor," Coughlin said. "Pointing out that the prosecutor can't say with certainty that any crime has even been committed."

"Your honor," Weisberg popped up, "evidence of a violent crime is, ah, overwhelming. And the evidence against Mr. Martell specifically is equally strong."

"Why does that guy hate me?" I whispered to Coughlin.

"Charlie? Charlie's okay. But he's his own worst enemy."

Eventually, both lawyers wandered uncertainly to their chairs, and all eyes turned to the judge. For a long time we heard only the whomp of the doors, the shuffled feet, coughing, and nervous whispers.

"Yes." The judge brightened, rearranging papers. "Let me say this. In view of the fact that the defendant has no prior record and holds a steady job, bail is set at two hundred and fifty dollars."

Even I heard the prosecutor mumble, "Jesus Christ." Then he stiffened, as if expecting the ceiling to drop on him. The oath had come out louder than intended.

The judge stared angrily for a long moment. "You have something to say, Mr. Weisberg?"

"No, your honor."

"There is a proper form for registering objections in this court. I follow proper form when I set bail according to the Bail Reform Act. I expect all officers of the court to appreciate that. People who can't appreciate that are not welcome in this court."

"Judge was mad at that guy," I remarked to Coughlin later.

"Yes." He giggled. "You'd think *Weisberg* killed somebody."

"I didn't kill anybody."

Coughlin led me to the attorney's consultation room. "You're a lucky fellow. Yes, sir."

"Why was the bail so low?"

"He thinks you're a good risk." The old man glowed. "He wasn't paying attention."

"So, how long can I stay out of jail?"

The public defender made a face, explaining the many motions for continuance available. "This case . . . better we take every delay."

"I'd almost rather get it over with."

"No, you wouldn't. Delay can only improve our position. God knows, it could use improvement. Anyway, there's no reason you should go to jail before you have to."

"I'm with you there."

From the corridor, uninvited, came Weisberg, the assistant district attorney. "Hello," he nodded, leaving me speechless. "Hello there?" he repeated, waving his hand in my face.

"Hello," I croaked.

"Your client okay, Mr. Coughlin?"

"He's okay. A little tired maybe. Your people gave him a rough time last night."

"My people give me a rough time every night." Weisberg sat heavily in a chair beside mine, as though that were the most natural thing in the world, as though twenty minutes before he had not been earnestly attacking my right to exist. He was transformed in other ways. Tie loosened, collar soiled and open, hair slick and hanging in his face, he showed the effects of a wringing workout.

"Well, Damien, guess I screwed myself good this time."

"I guess you did."

"The man is a disgrace, though. Doesn't matter what they're charged with, what kind of case we got, the son of a bitch lets them out anyway."

"He's very trusting," Coughlin agreed.

"I suppose I shouldn't lose my temper. I should be used to it. The other day, we had an assault and battery? The guy was on the street before the poor slob victim was out of the operating room."

"Now, now."

"Incompetent bastard." I was surprised to see the prosecutor didn't hate me, after all. He hated the judge.

"So what is it you wanted, Charlie?"

"Your boy here is going to get some free medical care. Outpatient. This is an order from the court. The Commonwealth wants to be sure he isn't crazy." Weisberg handed the business card of Dr. Sagie Divitre to Coughlin. "He should be there on this date. Hear that, ace?"

"Okay," I said.

"It costs the taxpayers money whether you show or not. So be there. Besides, you're in contempt of court if you're not."

"Nothing to worry about," Coughlin grinned, "Divitre's a good man. Thinks everybody's crazy. And we're fortunate you weren't ordered to the state hospital for observation."

"My lucky day," I said.

"Damien, do you think he's really mad at me?" Weisberg toyed nervously with his tie. Coughlin smiled.

I headed out of the county courthouse with five dollars in my pocket, borrowed from Coughlin. It was late afternoon, the corridors almost cleared. I saw Burkhalter going over his notes on a bench. I even managed to walk past him.

"Hey, Bill." He ran after me. "Where you going?"

"Home."

"Yeah." He was small, but favored jackets with wide shoulders, exaggerating his size. "Need a ride? Lemme drop you somewhere?"

"No thanks, Paul." I walked on.

"Well, we can talk." He kept at my heels. "Did you see my story today? About you?"

"Yeah. I saw it."

"Wasn't it fair? Don't you think it was fair?"

"Sure, it was fair," I replied. "You didn't tie me in with the Manson Family."

"Look, Bill. I try to be fair. I just didn't have much to go on."

"Just keep using your imagination."

"If we could talk, I'd get your side," he pleaded.

"Get off my ass, Burkhalter. Am I plain enough?"

"I'm asking for your own good, Bill. Don't be stupid. Give me an interview, it gets your story before the public."

"My lawyer says not to talk to anyone," I said.

"If you don't talk, all we have to print is what the police tell us. Come on —"

"Who wrote that headline?" I paused for a moment. "That prime suspect bullshit? Who dug up my picture? Who decided I was a recluse and I had no friends?"

"Not me," he insisted. "A lot of my stuff was rewritten. Other things were worked in. You know how it is. Page one, breaking story, everybody's got to get their fingers in it."

"Well, look, Paul. You're a good reporter. As a human being

you're a total asshole. But you're a good reporter, so you must've figured out that the *Suburban-Citizen* doesn't give a flying fuck about me. They're out to put me away forever. And maybe they'll do it. But sure as hell I ain't going to help them."

"Forget the paper." Burkhalter took my arm. "Trust me."

I stared icily at his hand. "You think I killed her?"

"No . . . well . . . I don't know, Bill. Did you?"

"What if I did?"

He let go of me.

"I'm just asking, what if? What if I do things like that? I mean, for all you know, I'm crazy."

He backed away. After all that had happened I must have looked a little crazy.

"I mean, you ought to be careful. Dealing with someone's maybe crazy and kills people. It's not like pestering some city councillor. Is it?"

He retreated slightly, unnerved. Of course, I'm a bit bigger. But this was amazing. Burkhalter was wary of me.

"Get off my ass. I'm up to here with people on my ass. I've had it twenty-four hours straight and I'm not taking it anymore."

I left him in the doorway of the courthouse. There was always the chance he would make more of my words than I meant. No matter. Anything he repeated was hearsay, inadmissible in court. Unless he was bugged like Glenn, getting it all on tape.

That didn't matter either. Somewhere between the courtroom and Coughlin's office I had reviewed my situation and made my decision. Like any reasonable person in my position, I was set to run.

I found my apartment a wreck. The police had gone through it carelessly, smashing cough medicine in the bathroom sink, overturning the bed, emptying drawers on the floor.

Most galling, my new color television was gone.

Outraged, I phoned police headquarters. "Get me Detective

Reardon." I waited, fueling my anger with a quick inspection of the kitchen. Pots and dishes were everywhere, even on the floor, some broken. A cereal box was ripped open, corn flakes covering the shelves.

"Bill, how are you?" Reardon said. "Say, I heard about your good luck today. Congratulations in making bail."

"Cut the crap, Reardon. I want to talk about the storm troopers you sent to wreck my apartment last night."

"We had a legal warrant, Bill."

"A warrant to steal my TV? I'd like to see that."

"Your TV is missing?" He seemed surprised.

"No, it isn't missing. Try stolen."

"Are you sure? Maybe you never had a TV."

"Yeah? Well, I still got the damn box it came in. Unless they stole that too, No . . . they didn't. I'm looking right at it."

"I'm sure our officers wouldn't take your TV. We seized certain property as evidence. But I'm positive no television was included."

"Who's liable for all this damage?" I shouted.

"Come on over, Bill. Come over here, we'll talk about it."

"Come over, bullshit."

"Any time you want to talk."

"You guys think you can shit on me."

"No, Bill. That just isn't true."

"Bullshit." I slammed down the phone, hours of bitter anger, fear and frustration spilling over. I kicked a small hassock across the room. I might have torn the apartment to pieces, but it was already a ruin. I sat, drawing deep breaths, organizing my thoughts.

The television didn't matter. There was no time to sell it and I couldn't take it with me.

Better the apartment stays a mess. The mattress was on the floor, records thrown across it. I couldn't imagine her on that mattress.

The rug was rolled up. I couldn't see her stepping barefoot on it.

The place was unrecognizable. The police had thrown all my important papers in a great pile on my desk. Her picture was there, a color photo from college days. She really hadn't changed a lot. Her hair was in bangs even then, black against pale skin, bringing out the dark brown eyes.

"Wish I knew you then," I'd told her once. "I keep thinking of all the years I didn't know you, wasted years. I wish I saw you first."

She was smiling.

It would have been nice to sit and brood over this. But if she was gone, I was unwilling to go with her. What would that accomplish? I wanted to live. And to live I had to run.

In the morning, I rescued my bankbook and life insurance policy (this was still made out to my ex-wife, Kathleen) from the pile of clutter on the desk. I took them and hurried out.

Coming up the stairs was the tenant from the top floor. We rarely spoke. "Hi," he charged past, calling over his shoulder, "how was jail?" as if passing the time, disappearing without waiting for an answer.

At the police garage, I was led to my car by a chubby sergeant.

"Find anything incriminating?"

"I never seen so much crud in one car in my life." He was genuinely disgusted by this. "I've seen cleaner garbage trucks." The yellowed newspapers, assorted wrappers and cans had been collected in two large shopping bags left on the back seat. The car never looked cleaner.

"At least I don't litter."

In my own car, I felt free. And never was this sensation so acute or so valued. I vowed to remain free. All of my life. No matter what.

Uncertain how widely my notoriety had spread, I drove on lonely back streets. I dreaded facing people. I would not be humiliated by strangers. Always, I felt someone's breath on my neck. But when I turned no one was there. Most of the day I spent driving, going nowhere. Twice I passed the bank, afraid to stop because it was full of customers.

When I finally entered it was five o'clock, dark, closing time. An armed guard indifferently shouldered past with a ring of keys. No one seemed to recognize me. Perhaps I had exaggerated my reputation. My picture in the *Suburban-Citizen* was a year old.

The lone teller, a pink-faced, strawberry-blonde teenager smiled. "Haven't seen you in a few weeks."

I pushed the passbook to her. "Like to make a withdrawal. Ah, all but five dollars." Withdrawing everything involved complications, suspicion.

She consulted the book, then paused a moment, pen poised, my name triggered something. What? She knew it from somewhere. That name. Her smile fell away. Clear blue eyes widened to meet mine and her mouth opened in an expression I had never seen before. It was a look of near-terror and almost sexual fascination.

"Excuse me," she mumbled, moving away, banging into a desk. Eyes still on me, she disappeared into a back room.

What to do next? The guard stood jingling keys at the door or I would have run. Had the police alerted the bank to watch out for me? Could they read my mind, know my intentions? But I've only come to withdraw my own money. I'm not robbing the bank.

Two women suddenly peeked from the back room, staring rudely, as though I was on display. The little blonde returned. Fumbling, she hastily paid the "$486.82," sliding the passbook along with the money.

"You haven't canceled," I said now.

"Huh?" She avoided my eyes.

"The money. You didn't cancel it out of the book."

"Oh, God. I'm sorry. I'm sorry."

"That's okay," I said.

"Please, I'll do it now. I'm sorry."

She placed the book in a large machine, punching at a row of keys. "Oh dear." She made a mistake and had to do it again. The computer stalled before stamping out the totals and the girl looked self-consciously in every direction but mine. "I'm sorry," she muttered. "Really sorry."

"Never mind." I took the book.

People were afraid of me. Some people anyway. At the door, the guard smiled, "Have a nice day," keys ringing as he turned the lock.

First with Burkhalter. Now this. People were afraid of me. And despite myself, I almost enjoyed it.

I remained alert to the possibility the police were following me. I wouldn't return to the apartment. Why should I? For clothes? I could buy new ones. My typewriter? I had no use for it now. I could never earn a living as a reporter again.

I had money and Judy's picture.

Starving, I drove first to McDonald's. Two hamburgs, a cherry pie, and two colas went in a few swallows. I wanted seconds, but passed on it. Already tired, I couldn't afford to eat myself to sleep. I had to move.

Periodically scanning the rearview mirror, I headed north. My plan was to drive as far as possible (at first, keeping to the back routes), sleep by the roadside, then continue in the morning. My destination was Nova Scotia and my relatives in the tiny French community around Yarmouth. Of course, I speak no French and know these people only slightly, but I was certain blood would tell. They would not give me up to a lifetime in prison.

I imagined myself years from now, assimilated. More French than the French. No one guessing my background. A new country. A new person with the past buried. Someday I would doubt the reality of my earlier life.

I outlined a route on the map. Crossing the Maine–New Brunswick border in the morning, when the traffic was probably heaviest, I would be unnoticed. The red pencil took me to Saint John, then around the Bay of Fundy to Yarmouth. When I got there I would be safe.

The car was a problem. I pulled off the highway at a K-Mart

and bought a roll of off-white reflective tape. Behind an empty store, I applied the tape to my license plate. It turned an *L* into a 1 and eliminated an 8 altogether. Now, I would not be easily identified.

In Portsmouth a cracked muffler cost several hours and nearly sixty dollars. By the time I reached Portland, it was well past midnight. Joining the expressway now, I was hungry again and stopped at a Howard Johnson's for a hamburg, two colas, and caramel-coated popcorn. Tolls, repairs, gas, and food were draining my money. It was conceivable my flight to Canada would cost one hundred dollars, over a fifth of my savings.

After the coast disappeared, so did the lights. In darkness, I was often the only car on the road north. It would have been easy to follow me. But the rearview mirror was black, the highway cold and lonely.

Unfamiliar with roads branching from Interstate 95 to New Brunswick, I questioned a toll-taker near Augusta. "Which is the best route, would you say? You know, if you were going to Saint John, say? I just noticed on my map, you can take a ferry from Campobello Island off Route One there."

"Well." He was a young man with bright, black eyes, but like most people in the region, in no great hurry. "There's some say the Route One's faster. Some say Nine."

"Yeah. Which would you say?"

"Well, it's six of one, half dozen of the other, I'd say."

". . . I see. Is there a rest area up ahead?"

"Might be."

In the rest area I was the lone car. A few eighteen-wheelers hummed noisily close by. Setting the adjustable bucket seat to a tilt position, I covered myself in a blanket and fell asleep. An hour later I was awake, my arm tingling as though occupied by a thousand crawling insects. I let it hang to the floor, allowing the blood to flow. My toes were freezing. I turned on the engine and the heater. It was cold in Maine. Winter, an early phenomenon here, was on the approach.

When the car was unbearably warm, I turned it off and fell again to sleep. But the cold soon woke me once more and I had to repeat the whole process. Tossing in the narrow seat, my legs aching for space to stretch, I despaired of ever getting back to sleep.

Tapping. Someone was tapping. Judy at the door. On the car window. A flashlight shone in my eyes. "What?!" I yelled to scare him off. Groggy, I swung my unfeeling arm. He backed away, a great black shadow. "Wha —"

With blue coat and Stetson, he was a Maine state trooper.

"What? What is it?" I rolled down the window. At eye level, his huge black gun sparkled, as if painted, high gloss. He was well over six feet, trim, unsmiling.

"Not a good idea to fall asleep with the motor running, sir."

"Well, yeah . . . I, ah, just running it a few minutes . . . till it warms up in here."

"You okay?" He leaned close.

"Oh, yeah. Sure. Just, I was asleep."

"Yes, sir. I woke you up. I've found people you couldn't wake them up. That car exhaust is a very sneaky thing." He moved away now.

"I'll be careful, officer. Thank you for your concern."

Perhaps I shouldn't sleep in rest areas. Police patrol them regularly. But a motel, what would that cost? Twenty dollars at least. For a few hours' sleep. And the expenses in Canada would be no smaller. I wanted to arrive in Yarmouth with some money in my pocket. Better if I could pay my keep. Maybe I could find work later, on a lobster boat, a farm, in a shop.

I imagined life on a fishing boat. The work is physically hard. I dislike it, at first, but become resigned. Finally, the sea and the outdoors are part of me, filling my lungs with cold, salt air. So much alive. I buy a little cottage on the water and live alone. Judy never appears in this dream, but I remain always aware of her, missing her.

The sun was shining, my car running, the gas needle near "E' and every muscle in my body ached. It was painful to sit upright. Moving one arm was torture, the shoulder creaking. The other arm, asleep again, couldn't be moved at all.

What time? Jesus! It was ten o'clock in the damn morning. My plan to cross the border in the rush hour was impossible now.

I stopped in Bangor for gas and breakfast, doughnuts, an apple, and a Coke gulped down. I had traveled hundreds of miles from my troubles. Why didn't I feel safe?

On Route 9, a roller coaster of narrow roads for one hundred and fifty miles, I passed towns like Crawford, Wesley and Aurora. Sometimes they were no larger than a grocery store and a gas station: "Honk for Service." Then there were great stretches of forest with not a house or a building. In places, snow powdered the grass and touched the great pines at their farthest reaches.

I thought to abandon the car here and hitchhike into Canada. Thus, I could begin to throw off my old life. Living with my mother's cousin, I would become Will Martell from Toronto or New York. Or something like that.

Probably a great deal of speculation would develop around me. Not enough to interest the authorities, but the young girls would be intrigued by the mysterious man from the States. What had he left behind? Why was he so sad?

I could easily hide the car, drive it down a fire trail, leave it among the trees. But a two-thousand-dollar investment would be gone, putting me at the mercy of the occasional driver on his way to Canada. Suppose no one picked me up?

Calais, Maine, which locals pronounce *Cal*-iss, is a small town of solid old homes and shabby storefronts. In the center, the movie theater was playing an X-rated feature, *Young and Willing*. The Canadian customs plaza is across the bridge spanning the St. Croix River. At three o'clock it did a fair business, people going to the grim little town of St. Stephen. St. Stephen the martyr.

I parked beside the bridge, watching cars waved along with a minimum of fuss by Canadian border police. It was easy to cross the bridge. Like crossing the street. Or so I'd heard.

By now, I was missed. "He's jumped bail," Reardon was saying. "Put out a description." Perhaps alerting the Canadians was standard procedure here. Maybe they had my picture tacked to the wall of their little booth.

Running away would convince people of my guilt. And even if I reached safety the real criminal would never be found. And Judy?

I started the engine and got in a line of five cars.

Judy was dead. I still didn't fully believe it. What if she was somewhere, held against her will, waiting for help?

What did happen to Judy?

Had she done it to herself? Gone berserk and run away? But all that blood. For one thing, Judy was intensely proud of her body. She wouldn't scar herself. She might use pills, but not a knife.

Three cars waited in front of me, the exhaust thick and white in the cold.

Someone attacked her and forced her away. It could have been a maniac off the street. It could have been a lover, like the man in the silver sports car. Or that Bob she spoke of. Or it could have been her husband, Roy Klijner.

One car ahead of me, the man in uniform was laughing with a driver, checking something on his clipboard.

I could be past the customs station, driving through Canada in a matter of minutes. And something would nag me. Unfinished business. Judy. It was wrong to run away while there was even a chance to help her. But I excused myself. The chance for Judy was too slim. The risk for me too great.

At the customs booth the official was brisk. "Anything to declare?"

"No."

"How long will you be visiting us in Canada?"

"I don't know. A few weeks, I guess. I'm touring."

"Touring. Eh. All alone?"

"Yeah. I got relatives in Nova Scotia. I'm going to visit them." Shouldn't have told him that. Christ. "Halifax."

"What?"

"My relatives live in Halifax," I lied.

The official crinkled his brow. He hadn't smiled at me. I tried to relax, but it was impossible. My knees were weak.

"Can I see the trunk?"

God, what for? "Sure." I came out of the car. My legs were unsteady, my hands fumbling with the keys. Be cool. Calm down. You're making it obvious.

The officer sorted through the jacking equipment, lifted the tire. Why was I afraid? I wasn't a smuggler.

"What's this?" He squatted by my license plate.

"What?"

He peeled the tape away, uncovering the 8. How stupid could I be? In daylight the tape was obvious to spot. I should've taken it off. Stupid. Stupid!

"I never saw that before," I said.

He grunted.

"Maybe my wife put it there. I can't imagine why."

He slammed shut the trunk, "Wait here," went into his booth and made a telephone call. I sat in the car, waiting. Now I'd done it. I'd be taken back in handcuffs, never be free again. And over something so stupid. What was I thinking of? Sleep. A little more sleep and a decent meal and I could reason clearly. I wouldn't make these dumb mistakes.

The whole idea was moronic, anyway. I could see that now. Those people in Yarmouth, I'd met them once when I was nine. They wouldn't know me if they fell on me. They literally didn't speak my language. I'd be lucky if they didn't turn me in. Christ, how dumb can you be? Why didn't I think these things through?

Now it was too late.

The sensations of jail enclosed me. I remembered the courtroom, sour-faced men with guns all around me. Anyone in the room can get up and walk outside. Not me. I can't leave. Oh, Jesus.

The Toyota was my prison now, a tiny box. And I sat passively waiting for them to close the lid.

I started the little car and backed it up. The Canadian looked from his phone. I made a tight U-turn on the bridge and headed back to Calais. A patrolman at the U.S. Customs and Immigration booth watched my odd maneuver. "Some trouble?" His gate was down.

"They don't want me in Canada," I smiled.

"Not very neighborly."

"No. I, ah, I forgot my license. My driver's license. Back in the motel, see. So I got to go get it."

"Better not let the cops around here catch you without a license."

"No." In the rearview mirror I could see the Canadian hurrying across the bridge.

"They'll lock you up," the American continued. "These cops around here are real hard-asses." He moved slowly, elevating the gate. Unable to wait, I jerked forward, scraping my roof.

"Watch it!" he shouted, but I kept moving.

I drove swiftly away from Calais. All my enthusiasm for Canada was gone. I was headed home.

seven

"BY THE WAY," interrupted Damien Coughlin, my elderly lawyer, "I've been calling the past two days. Where have you been?"

"I took a vacation."

He unwrapped a candy drop. "Peppermint?"

"No thanks."

"They're sugarless."

"If I can finish, Mr. Coughlin."

He moved to a corner of the office, depositing the candy wrapper in a wastebasket wedged between a bookcase and the wall. Coughlin hung his shingle in one of the colonial-style, red-brick professional buildings scattered all over town. The decor was traditional with shelves of law books. The office was larger than most closets, but only just.

"Anyway," I continued, "I got this idea when I was away. You see, there's this friend of Judy's. His name's Bob. She told him all about us, told him everything. I thought, if we could find this Bob, he could prove my story. I really was going out with Judy, running off with her. I didn't hurt her and I had no reason to hurt her."

"No one questions that you and Mrs. Klijner were having an affair."

"They don't?"

"No." He referred to a paper on his desk. "You told the police no one knew about you two."

"No one did."

"Excepting Pamela Nealy. Paul Burkhalter. Your landlady. Let's see. Your neighbor down the hall. Mrs. Klijner's family physician. And so on. Close your mouth, Mr. Martell, this is only a partial list."

"How could all those people know?"

"Love is blind. The neighbors rarely are."

"So," I tried to recover, "now they know I told the truth. Now what? Does this mean I'm in the clear?"

"Hardly." Coughlin sucked ferociously on his candy. "In a courtroom you're innocent until proven guilty. That's not the case when we come to the district attorney. He assumes you're guilty or he wouldn't bring an action. This kind of corroboration, proving your relationship with Mrs. Klijner, might have meant something when questioning began, but at this juncture I'm afraid they're glad to get it."

"Glad?"

"It gives you a real reason for harming her."

"So, it doesn't matter," I shook my head, "they can believe me where it suits them? I can tell the truth and they'll just turn it against me?"

"Well . . ."

"Then what can I do? How can I prove I'm not guilty?"

"We needn't prove that at all," he said. "They must prove you are guilty. A difficult job. Unless, of course, they've got you on tape admitting you did it. That would complicate matters."

"They don't. Unless they faked it. What if they did that?"

"Doesn't sound like my friend Weisberg."

"He may be your friend, Mr. Coughlin, but I don't think he likes me. I'll tell you what I *do* think." I decided to test a theory haunting me all the way back from Maine. "I think Roy Klijner did something to Judy. Yeah. To his own wife. I didn't want to say it at first. I didn't want to even think it. You don't go around accusing someone of something horrible unless you got good reason. But I think who else? There's the obvious motive. She said she was leaving him to come with me. He couldn't stand that. They had a fight. And he did something to her."

"Well," Coughlin shuffled papers on his desk, "we'll have to look into that."

"The police sure won't. They figure I did it. That's all they want to hear."

He coughed. I had come uninvited and now the old man seemed anxious to be rid of me. "Well, look at the time." He finally held out his watch. "I'm due at the pool. You know, once a day, I like to get in and splash around."

"Nice."

"You get any exercise, Martell?"

"Well, just, you know, regular walking around."

"Not enough. You've got to be in decent shape, boy. Your appearance is going to count for a great deal. You'll need good clothes to wear in court." He went to the door, his outstretched hand indicating I should follow. "Remember, when you walk into the courtroom we want the jury to see a neat, responsible, professional man. So dress the part."

"Yeah, but what about what I said? About Roy Klijner?" I stood at the threshold.

"Sure." Coughlin slowly closed the door on me. "We'll sit down together in a few weeks to discuss it. Discuss the whole case."

"But shouldn't we force the police or somebody to look into this now? While it's still fresh in everybody's mind. What happened."

"We'll talk about it," Coughlin shut the door.

I waited at a bar and grill off Shore Drive, a dusty interior, all flaking paint on the outside. In summer, they sold fresh, fried clams from a takeout window. At three o'clock Pam Nealy had no difficulty finding me among the empty tables. She came with a tall, burly man in a thick black beard.

"Hi," she began. "Ah, I hope you don't mind. I brought my brother, Joe."

We shook hands, Joe mumbling, "Hello," his sole contribution to the conversation.

"Well, first of all, thanks for coming, Pam."

"Sure."

"I asked you here. Well, first of all, you know, I'm talking to you as a friend. You won't write about this? About me? Will you?"

"No," she said.

"Good. You know, I say that. Burkhalter, tells me he's going to help me, pulls out his pencil and notebook."

"We're not running any more stories on this. Nothing more till the trial. They're afraid of prejudicing the case."

"You know, Pam, you don't have to be afraid of me."

"I'm not." Unconsciously, she turned her bracelet around and around. Joe was stern and tense.

"Yeah, well, I want you to know this. Maybe it'll make you feel better. I didn't hurt anyone."

She nodded.

"My worst crime, if you can call it that, was getting involved with Roy's wife. Well, I'm not proud of that. But it's not like I killed anyone or did anything like that. I went to that house looking for Judy and I haven't found her yet."

"You should get a good lawyer," she said.

"But you can see I'm not some sort of lunatic, can't you?"

"I never thought that." Pam avoided looking at me, studied her bracelet. If she doubted me, how would I fare before a jury of strangers?

"Anyway," I continued. "There's something I want to ask you about. Remember Roy? Remember my last night at work? Roy was acting real weird. I mean, he was drinking. And he wanted us to go drinking with him?"

"Okay, I remember that."

"Well, I knew then why he was acting that way. It was the thing with Judy, his wife. Did you know her?"

"We met a few times."

"That day Judy told him she was running away. Leaving him. Coming to live with me. Of course, she didn't give my name. Anyway, that time, when I told you I was quitting the paper, that's what I was talking about."

Pam nodded.

"You don't believe me?"

"I didn't say that."

"Pam, I was unlucky. I was in the wrong place at the wrong time. Otherwise, Roy'd be the prime suspect right now."

She nodded uncertainly.

"Don't you think that's true?" I pressed.

"I don't know what to think."

"Look at me. Please." I caught her eyes. I wanted to take her hands, but I was afraid of the brother. "Pam, I'm not the type who hurts people. Knowing me, you can't believe that I hurt Judy."

Her response was curiously off the subject. "I never liked her."

"What?"

"A woman like that. Everybody talked about her."

"Judy?"

"I can believe she ran around with you," Pam said. "She was a flirt. From what I saw. Always hanging all over guys. That invites trouble. I don't mean to speak ill of someone who's . . . probably in trouble, but, I mean, she'd go to a company party and start to drink. And she embarrassed everybody, Roy, everybody."

I couldn't answer her. Maybe it was true. But she shouldn't have said it, under the circumstances. I studied the wall for a moment.

". . . so. How you been doing, Bill?" Pam adjusted her gold-rimmed glasses and brushed away blonde hair. She was not unattractive. On the other hand, she was skinny, soft-spoken, and easy to overlook. One of life's afterthoughts.

"Did you say something, Pam?"

"How have you been living?"

"Oh, well, I got a little money. It'll last a month or two. I hope. My landlady wanted me out. But she's afraid to push the point. People think I'm dangerous." I laughed.

"What've you been doing with yourself? You look pale. You should get busy. Find some work."

"Yeah. Maybe in a few days I'll go over to the paper, see if there's some way I can work there. Maybe in the south office, away from Klijner . . . you don't think so."

"Well, I don't know. It's just the way they act about you over there." She turned her hands over and studied her nails. "I don't know."

"Well, it doesn't matter what they think."

"No."

"I was going to quit that job anyway. Right now I've got plenty to keep me busy. Maybe I'll go find out what really happened to Judy. No one else seems much interested."

Pam managed a smile. She wasn't convinced.

I parked across from the police station, trying to build up the courage to go inside. There was the bare room where they had prodded at me for so many hours. I was on their ground, vulnerable to lies and traps.

A rumpled, flabby man came out of the front door and went to his car. It was Reardon, looking far less imposing than I remembered. I followed him down the street, tooting and blinking my lights. He drove into the wide, empty parking lot of an abandoned A & P, sending his car into a sweeping turn, facing mine.

I approached on foot.

"What do you want?"

"I wanna talk," I shouted.

"Stay where you are."

I stopped, about five feet from his window. It was chilly, overcast and sputtering. Somehow, I'd imagined sitting with him, explaining everything. That awful night in the police station they wouldn't hear my side.

"Talk to me at the station," he said. "Make an appointment."

"Can't go there."

He was afraid of me, watching my eyes, studying my clothes, every fold and wrinkle. I kept my hands free, though my fingers grew numb in the cold.

"I don't trust you guys," I said. "I went in there, to talk to you before and you fucked around with me. You weren't honest. You made me think you were gonna help. But you weren't honest."

"What do you want, Bill?"

"I want my rights." I was yelling. It was windy and you had to yell to be heard. But I was louder than that.

"Bill?"

"Why can't you just listen for once?"

"I'm not going to listen till you calm down."

"You guys. You fuckin guys. Never gave me a chance."

"I said calm down."

"Somebody gets away with murder. You don't care."

"Who's getting away with murder?" Reardon asked.

"He is."

"Who is?"

"Roy Klijner," I shouted.

"You're sure about that? Roy Klijner? How come you didn't mention this the other night?"

"The other night?" I caught my breath, face dripping cold rain. "I was confused the other night. I couldn't think so good. You never gave me a chance."

"Stay over where you are. I can hear you fine."

"It's gotta be him. Who else would it be? You'd have figured it out yourself if you half tried. We were gonna run away. Judy and me. And she told him. Roy. So he killed her. And then, he just waited."

"Waited?"

"Waited for me to show up," I insisted. "He knew I'd come looking."

"Can you prove all this?"

"You could prove it. If you tried. You're all too busy screwing me. After I offered to help and cooperate. Out of the goodness of my heart. I was willing to talk and everything. But you thank me by fuckin me over."

Reardon laughed.

"Something funny? I must've missed it."

"You oughta be more careful, Bill. You're going to get hurt. Myself, I get edgy about people following me."

"You're not even listening."

"You're wrong about Klijner," Reardon said. "He has an alibi. He can account for all of that day. You can't account for any of it."

"What alibi? Tell me."

"All right. Klijner. He went off with the little boy to his sister's house at nine that morning. The mailman saw Mrs. Klijner alive and well at ten o'clock. Roy Klijner stayed at his sister's house until three-thirty, according to his sister. And he arrived at work just before four o'clock. Where he remained until we picked him up."

"I don't believe it."

"Bill?" Reardon shook his head.

"His own sister. She could be lying. Even if it's true about Klijner. Anyone could've hurt Judy. Anyone. It didn't have to be me."

"I thought you were sure," the policeman said. "You told me it was her husband. I thought you were sure of that."

"Well . . ."

"Well, what?"

"Well, maybe I'm not so sure."

"I see." He snickered.

"I'm sure of this. It wasn't me."

"I can prove it was you, Bill."

"No way."

"Oh yes I can. And the thing is for you to face up to it. Come on down the station. I'll turn around right now. We'll go on up there and you can make a statement. Because I'll tell you, things'll go a lot easier on a guy who cooperates."

"Nothing gets through to you cops. I can't tell you anything. I didn't do anything."

"Come off it, Bill. I've heard the tape."

"What tape?"

"I heard you admit it all on tape."

"What?"

"So let's stop bullshittin each other," he said.

"What do I supposedly say on this tape?"

"We want the body. That's why we're willing to deal. We can convict without it. But we want to make this easier on the family. You understand?"

"Tell me what this tape says."

Reardon dropped into drive. The car moved forward imperceptibly, straining against the brake. "When you want to talk, Bill? Give a call. I don't wanna see you taking the full sentence on this. It's so unnecessary."

"You can't bluff me."

He drove away across the flat, empty lot of broken glass and litter.

"You buncha fuckin assholes," I shouted into the rain. "I wouldn't talk to you . . ."

Running away had not been a solution. But where was the alternative? For the next four days I locked myself in my apartment. The phone rang half a dozen times. I never answered it. Mostly, I watched television, a ten-year-old black-and-white portable rescued from the closet, sometimes listening to the radio at the same time.

I fought reality, hoping the world would forget me. If I stayed in my room and never bothered anyone, wouldn't that satisfy them? Couldn't they leave me alone?

My depression touched bottom one morning when I organized all my pills, aspirins, cold capsules, sleeping pills, into formation on the kitchen table. But, by afternoon, I was cleaning my apartment, which still looked the way the police had left it. I swept away the pills. After all, why make it easy for them?

My recovery had begun. A shower and shave changed my outlook considerably. The police didn't want the truth. I looked guilty and that was enough for them. But if they wouldn't ask the questions, I could. A trained reporter, I could do that much.

Once, while vacuuming the living room, I was nearly overcome again with despair. Sure, the apartment might be spotless. What did it matter if I was in prison? What did anything matter? But I fought off these black moods with work, the thorough, mindless drudgery of cleaning my filthy apartment.

It was while organizing the chaos on my desk that I discovered the picture. It was a man I'd never seen before. At least I didn't recognize him. Slim and ordinary, he stood in a parking lot, smiling. Who was he? Where had the snapshot come from?

Several times during the day I studied the photo. There was something naggingly familiar about it now. Had I simply forgotten some important face from my past? Was my memory now a casualty of the tension?

At some point, the truth became obvious. Surely, this photo had been among the valuables I'd transported in Judy's car. Lying loose in one of those drawers, it had probably dropped to the floor and been ignored by the police who reclaimed her belongings. But who was it? And why did it look familiar?

I studied it closely that night, looking beyond the subject. In the background was the stylish nose of a smart, silver sports car. A few days before her disappearance Judy had been in that car.

It was early morning when I sat at my desk and prepared a list of people who might have useful information:

— Klijner's sister — must find name and address.

— Redhead at bowling alley, Judy's friend — must find name.
— Judy's old boyfriend, Bob — Judy claimed she told him everything.
— Man in the silver sports car, photo — picked up Judy at Alibi Lounge.
— Klijner.

Unhappily, the key figures, Klijner and his sister, would never talk to me. But at least I could try the others. I would begin with the man in the sports car. Why did Judy have a snapshot of a man she had picked up in a bar and knew a single night?

From two o'clock to five one day I sat in the Alibi Lounge as it became crowded with people from the shipyard. I watched for the man who had picked up Judy. But the faces suffered an alarming sameness. I couldn't be certain he hadn't gone right past me, unrecognized.

I parked in front of the bowling alley and watched for the silver sports car. I came every day at three and stayed at least until five. In a full week it never appeared.

Finally, following a long shot, I drove to the shipyard offices. The employee lot was surrounded by a ten-foot chain fence topped with barbed wire. There was a guard who barely looked at me as I walked in. I paced the rows of cars until I found that unique color.

He polished it often. Obviously. There wasn't a scratch, though it might have been several years old. You could see his devotion to the machine in the choice of parking spaces. Between the fence and the utility pole, far from the office building, the car was isolated from other, less careful drivers who might open their doors and blemish the pristine silver finish.

Even the interior was spotless, totally without debris. The steering wheel was covered in leather. This was the car. Now to find the owner.

I knew how he would act, swaggering, indifferent to others. He was quite capable of hurting Judy, who didn't respond in any predictable way, unlike a well-tuned car.

At four o'clock came a stampede of people from the offices. I spotted him at once in a well-fitted corduroy jacket and light green tie. His clothes were carefully chosen. Probably he was sensitive about his size, retreating into the car, a second, more powerful body. He had a thin face and sickly yellow complexion.

"You own this car?" I asked.

"I own it, yeah." He lit a cigarette, while hugging his briefcase, which read "Ernest Timmons, Jr." in small gold letters at the top.

"I'd like to ask you a few questions."

"A few questions? About my car?"

I handed him Judy's picture.

"What's this?"

"Do you recognize that woman?"

"Who wants to know?" He moved away.

"Let's just say," I made sure he looked at the picture before snatching it back, "I'm a person who very much needs information."

"Oh, yeah. Well, I'm a person who doesn't have any . . ." He moved to his car, killing the burglar alarm beneath the fender before unlocking the door.

"You never saw her before?" I held out the picture.

"No." He stared at me, calm, cigarette in his mouth, smoke spewing from his nose and lips.

"You're lying and I know you're lying."

"Who the hell are you?" He climbed into his car and started it.

"Why?" I went to the window, knocking. "Why are you lying to me?"

Abruptly, he pushed the car forward and out of the parking space. I watched him drive away.

Ernest Timmons, Jr., was in the Williamsville book. Williamsville is a country town ten miles away. Here, I drove past weathered colonial homes found in odd places along the winding highway; or deep cuts into the earth, trees down, hills sliced away and leveled as housing projects took shape. Later, I drove by housing developments already completed, treeless lawns without boundaries or sidewalks.

Timmons lived on Orchard Street in the Liberty Tree Acres development. It was easy to find his house; with the silver car in the driveway, wood stacked against the garage and a child's scooter near the front door. Somehow, I imagined him living in a cottage by himself. Judy's crazed assailant couldn't have a wife and child.

Or could he? Criminals were bumped to the front page every day, leaving behind legions of disbelieving friends and relatives.

Timmons had met Judy. Yet denied it. He wasn't nervous. Or afraid. He looked at the picture and coolly lied about knowing her. Why?

After dark, I walked to his house. The silver car in the driveway gleamed in the moonlight. Beyond was the wood pile. A great log lay on its end, split at the top by a huge ax. Sap dripped from the ugly rent in the wood.

"Yes?" An attractive woman answered the door.

"I'm looking for Mr. Timmons."

"Ernest," she called. "Somebody to see you." Two or more children were howling within. Mrs. Timmons looked embarrassed. "I better go look after the kids. He'll be right along." And Timmons himself was behind her, his smile fading behind a bank of smoke. When she was gone he said, "What do you want with me? Who the hell are you anyway?"

I simply held up Judy's picture.

Timmons came outside into the moonlight, closing the door.

"You know what happened to Judy," I said.

"What do you want from me?"

"I want you to tell me everything you know about Judy. About what happened to her."

"I don't know any Judy. I told you."

"Come on, now, Ernie. The less you tell me, the more suspicious I get." I held up the picture of Judy smiling. Timmons swallowed, unconsciously jingling the keys in his pocket.

"I don't care if you believe me or not. But I never saw that woman before in my life."

"Maybe your wife would recognize her?"

"My wife?"

"I saw you, Ernie. I saw you pick Judy up in the Alibi Lounge. I can give you the date, even. The exact date. I saw you drive off together in that toy car of yours. Now, it could be I'm mistaken. Could be there's another guy. Looks like you. Drives a car like yours. And he was the guy I saw. The way to settle any doubt, I think. Ask Mrs. Timmons in there. She must know you pretty well. She'll tell us if you're the kind of guy goes in for that sort of thing."

Timmons stood with his back to the door. He lit another cigarette.

"You look cold, Ernie."

"Is this some kind of blackmail?"

"I need answers. You gotta know I mean business."

He opened the door. The cries of children were louder, more urgent. "Marge. Marge, come here."

"In the kitchen," she called.

"I know you're in the kitchen. Get out here."

"Don't do anything hasty," I said.

She came with a facecloth in her hand, a crying child of three or four following. "What is it?"

Timmons took his son by the hand and pushed him into a nearby room, slamming the door, muffling his loud wails. I wanted to run.

"Oh, that's fine," she muttered. "Now, he'll have nightmares."

"Marge, this person has something to tell you."

I shifted uneasily. Evidently Timmons was in no way frightened of his wife.

"Not now," I said. "We can talk about this later."

"Don't come back. Don't bother me again."

"Ernest?" she said as the door slammed shut.

Timmons's reluctance to talk hinted at a man with something to hide. Nor would any good reporter be put off so easily by his hostility. Of course, my first approach would never work. He was not easily cowed.

I phoned him at his shipyard office the following day.

"Just listen," I spoke slowly, deliberately, "listen for your own sake. I couldn't scare you the other night. I was bluffing and you saw it. Okay. Score one for you. Now, I want you to know something and this is no bluff. If you refuse to help me I am prepared to make you pay for that. Hear? Because, you see, I have nothing, literally nothing, to lose. So I mean what I say. First off. I will turn your name over to the police and to my friends on the newspapers. Right now, no one has any idea you even exist. But I can change all that."

After a period of silence he said, "What do you want from me?"

"I just want to talk."

"Talk about what?"

"You and Judy. Just talk. If you've got nothing to hide, and you're honest with me, there's no problem. Just tell me what you know. Then you can walk away. You can forget you ever met me."

"I'm not hiding anything."

"That's good. That's fine," I said.

"So what do you want? You want to ask me something? What is it?"

"No. No. This'll be better face to face." I suggested a meeting in two days at the Alibi Lounge parking lot. Timmons agreed, though he was not enthusiastic, hanging up abruptly.

I walked into the kitchen, my hands shaking slightly. Trying to frighten somebody, pretending toughness — it was a difficult act.

It had all gotten so complicated. I had only a vague idea of what questions to ask. And if the man lied? How would I know?

Coughlin had called that night, inviting me to his office in the morning. He made it sound very important. I wasn't surprised to find the assistant district attorney already there when I arrived.

"Mr. Weisberg," the old lawyer motioned, "has made an offer. I thought you should hear it."

"We're anxious to resolve this matter." The younger man was hopeful, pleasant.

"So am I." I sat down at Coughlin's gesture.

"Then we agree." Weisberg smiled. "And I can get right to the point. We'd like your cooperation. Now, I should say, in exchange for that we're prepared to make a very generous offer. I think you'll be pleased. The fact is, no one thinks you're a menace to society. There's no prior record whatsoever and all the people I've talked to, the people who've dealt with you, they've been favorably impressed with you personally."

"Thank you."

"Well, it's true," Weisberg insisted. "In fact, there seems to be a growing consensus that the crime was possibly an act of passion. Or the work of a temporarily deranged mind. Anyway, it's not unrealistic to hope my office will come around to that point of view. As I say, despite this difficult situation, people like you, Bill."

"Maybe I should run for office."

"Don't make smart remarks," Coughlin snapped. "This is a serious matter."

"What's your reaction?" Weisberg asked.

"My reaction is that you guys don't listen. I can't cooperate. Or I can cooperate. But I can't tell you any more than I already told. I didn't do —"

"Wait." Weisberg put up his hand. "Wait. Before you go on. I want you to hear something. Before you take a position and can't back down." He went to the bookcase behind me and turned on a tape recorder. There was a rustling noise, then a clang that took me back to jail. There were voices on the tape.

"What's this?" I braced myself.

"Just listen," Weisberg said.

"Is that supposed to be me talking? It doesn't sound like me."

"It is you. At the county courthouse."

"It doesn't sound like me."

"Nobody recognizes their own voice on tape," Weisberg insisted.

At one point, a voice, apparently mine, was talking about the newspaper story, saying, "Well, I finally made the front page."

And fellow prisoner, Glenn, replied more distinctly, "Shit. Is that you? Holy Christ! You killed somebody? Christ. What made you do a thing like that?"

A voice answered, "I don't know."

I stiffened with shock. "I never said that."

"You did say that," Weisberg answered smugly.

"I don't remember saying that."

The tape went on. "I think I need a press agent."

"You said it. Recordings don't lie, Bill."

"You're really in the shithouse," Glenn was saying.

"That's not me. On that tape. That's not me."

"Ever hear of voice prints? That is you. I can prove it is."

"No. You faked that somehow. That can't be."

"It is."

"I told that guy. I told him same as I told you. I told him I didn't do anything."

"Not on this tape. Not in this conversation."

On tape, Glenn was doing all the talking, going on about plea bargaining.

"Play it all, why don't you? Play it from the beginning."

"I played it from the beginning. All of it."

"I didn't do it. And I told him that. I know I did."

"It's not here," the prosecutor said. "I've heard this two dozen times. I've got a written transcript and it's not here."

The tape was full of noises, shuffling and banging. Sometimes the voices dropped so low you couldn't hear what was said.

Weisberg put the tape on reverse. Then it began again. The

same question, "What made you do a thing like that?" And the answer, moments later, not disputing the question, a sigh of apparent resignation, "I don't know."

I shook my head. "I can't believe you're doing this to me."

"Come on, Bill. We haven't done anything to you. You've done it to yourself."

"Can they play that in court?"

"This kind of thing?" Coughlin said. "It's been admitted as evidence in the past. Under certain circumstances."

"Now," Weisberg was relaxed, "let's go over this again. Your cooperation is going to mean a lot to us. But it means more to you. You can measure it, literally, in years. Years of freedom in exchange for a few words now. Years, perhaps a lifetime of prison if you don't cooperate."

I began sniffling for no apparent reason, my eyes stinging, nose running.

"It's up to you, Bill."

"I, ah."

"What do you say?"

"I need a Kleenex. Kleenex?"

Coughlin opened a drawer and passed over a box of tissues. I blew my nose.

"Well?" Weisberg asked.

I searched for a place to throw the tissue. There was the wastebasket across the room, but I didn't want to get up. The chair was leather. I seemed stuck to it. It made noises whenever I moved. I stopped moving.

"You don't have to answer me now."

"No," Coughlin agreed. "You don't have to answer him at all. We can discuss this. You and I. I just wanted you to hear the tape."

With a lot of clicking and whirring, Weisberg packed away the recorder.

"It's not right," I said. "It's not right what you're doing to me."

"Just my job." The assistant district attorney moved to the door.

I wouldn't look at him. I stared at the floor. How much longer would I sit and take this injustice? Somebody else's punishment.

"You think about this, Bill. But don't take too long. We won't wait forever."

"You can wait till hell freezes." My voice quivered.

When he'd gone, Coughlin stared at me as though I'd done something wrong. "You told me they didn't have anything on that tape."

"They didn't. They fixed it. That's not me on there."

He nodded.

"You can believe me."

"Of course."

I wanted to weep. Everything and everybody seemed turned against me. As if the facts weren't damning enough, now they concocted lies to persecute an innocent man. "They can't really use that tape bullshit?" I pleaded. "In court? They let them do that?"

"Ah," Coughlin shrugged, "yes and no."

"Yes and no," I mumbled. "Doesn't anybody give a straight answer around here? I might forget you're all lawyers."

Coughlin checked his irritation, allowing me a moment to compose myself. "Let me explain," he said. "The police cannot. Under ordinary circumstances they cannot use this kind of evidence in court. Simply put, your statement was taken without a lawyer present. Therefore, it violates your constitutional right to be represented by counsel."

"I don't wonder."

"Under the exclusionary rule," Coughlin continued, "evidence taken illegally, in violation of constitutional safeguards against self-incrimination, such evidence is automatically excluded from consideration by the jury. Of course, the reason for this rule is obvious, to discourage the government from violating your rights. Do you understand?"

"No, I don't. If the evidence is excluded what are we worrying about?"

"I'm getting to that. Our problem is this. Such evidence *can* be admitted under certain circumstances, as I've already said. Specifically, it can be introduced to rebut any testimony that raises the question of perjury. You see, the court considers perjury such a serious crime, an affront to the very essence of our legal system, that it will allow so-called tainted evidence to be introduced where perjury is suspected."

"Yeah, well what does all this mean in English?"

"It means the tape cannot be included as part of the prosecutor's case. But. If you go to the witness stand you can expect Mr. Weisberg to ask you 'Did you engage a Mr. Glenn Bennett in conversation? And did he say to you this and that? And did you answer this and that?' And if you deny what's on the tape, the cat's out of the bag. Weisberg plays it in open court as proof of perjury."

"But the tape is faked."

"You can see the box this puts us in," Coughlin went on. "In terms of your defense, we have a classic Hobson's Choice. If we don't put you on the stand we lose the heart and soul of our case. But if we do put you on we allow the tape recording in as well to contradict everything you say. Of course, the final decision here is yours. Nonetheless, in my opinion, you must take the stand. Otherwise, we have no case. You must take the stand. And we must reconcile ourselves to the fact that they will try to introduce the tape as evidence."

"If the tape gets in," I asked, "what'll the jury say?"

He shrugged. "Taped evidence can be very damning. And this tape. Well. It's not singing our song, is it? Of course, it depends on how it's presented. They'll have that fella on the stand and he'll swear those are your words. He'll describe the scene. Say you were looking at the story of Mrs. Klijner's disappearance just when you said it. That'll hurt: I just hope the prosecutor doesn't have any other surprises hidden away."

"No. He couldn't."

"That's what you said about the tape." Coughlin seemed a little disgusted with me. "I suppose we've eliminated the idea of dealing with Weisberg definitely."

I glared.

"But you are agreed with me that you must take the stand in your own defense to forcefully deny these charges. So, then, the question now. The question is, how do we deal with this tape? Assuming it's allowed in. I've listened to it three times. Let me see." He consulted notes. " 'What made you do a thing like that?' And you answer, 'I don't know.' Then a pause —"

"I never said it."

"There's a lot of extraneous noise on that tape. Did you notice? It's scratchy. Much of the conversation is indistinct."

"It's faked," I said.

"Then your response, 'I don't know.' Don't know what? You could put several interpretations on that."

"You could if I said it."

"Shhhh. Let me think . . . suppose." He sat at his desk, alternately scribbling over his notes, then gazing out the window. "Suppose . . . now suppose this. Suppose you said, 'I don't know,' and you turned away, mumbled the rest and it wasn't picked up on the recording. Suppose you actually said, 'I don't know what you're talking about.' "

"I don't know what you're talking about?"

"See," the old man glowed, "you remember."

"No, I don't," I insisted.

"You said, 'I don't know what you're talking about.' Understand?"

"You want me to lie about it?"

"Well, if it's going to present some insurmountable moral dilemma you can go to prison instead."

I took a slow breath. It seemed everything was moving beyond my control.

"Claiming the tape is a fake," Coughlin continued, "no one will believe that."

"No?"

"This gives them something to think about. It attacks the credibility of the tape recorder instead of the assistant district attorney. People would rather assume the machine was at fault. No one trusts machines." For twenty minutes, Coughlin coached me on my response to the tape. I remained hesitant. The story seemed so obviously contrived.

"You tell me, Bill," he questioned sharply, " 'I don't know what you're talking about.' Why is it, the last part of that sentence, we don't hear it on the tape? How do you explain that?"

"Tapes are easy to monkey with."

"And . . ."

"And they break," I parroted. "They malfunction. And when I said this I was turning away. And I was probably mumbling like. Cause I was so depressed. I've never been in any trouble before."

"Good point," he mentioned as an aside. "Now. Are there portions of this tape where voices become indistinct? Even inaudible?"

"Sure. All you gotta do is listen."

Coughlin smiled now, his face a mass of happy wrinkles. "Very good." The grin grew. "Very good. You even have me believing."

It all sounded pretty lame from my side.

At the Alibi Lounge, Ernest Timmons was far to the back, away from the other cars in the parking lot. I parked at the bowling alley and finished a can of Coke before walking across the street. It was warm, a bright, Indian summer afternoon. The street was four lanes across. For a time I was trapped in the middle, cars speeding at me from both directions, sometimes so close I could reach out and touch them.

None would stop. I was afraid, imagining some careless driver swerving into me. It happens. This is going to be another bad day, I decided. I was tired and I'd been backsliding toward another depression since hearing Weisberg's tape, going ungroomed, filling myself with junk.

A red light up the road broke the flow of traffic. I ran across the street.

"Let me in."

Timmons's eyes widened.

"Don't worry. I'm not going to shoot you or anything." I opened my coat, showing I was unarmed. "I just want to talk." He sat behind the wheel, an elaborate thing of steel, leather, and plastic. I rubbed my hand across the dash. "Nice car." It was thick with cigarette smoke.

"Let's get this over with. What do you want?"

"I almost didn't show up, you know? I was crossing the street over there and those guys, they'd just as soon kill you as stop. The way people drive." I was fingering the shift.

"Don't play with that," he said.

"It's a funny thing. You run somebody over, kill them, maybe they take your license away. On the other hand, if you kill somebody, more or less on purpose, it's a serious matter. They put you away for a long, long time. I guess the idea's to discourage that sort of thing. I don't know. Ever given it any thought yourself?"

"I don't know anything about that woman."

"Sorry to hear it." I smiled. "Because I figured, on that point, we'd come to some sort of ageement. I know you were with Judy. I saw the two of you together."

"Maybe you did. But that's it. That's the first and last time I ever saw her. I swear. I didn't have anything to do with . . . whatever happened to her."

"Why didn't you tell me this in the first place?"

"I don't care to be involved," he said. "In a murder. A possible murder. That's understandable. Isn't it? After all, I did go out with her that time and . . ."

"And what?"

"I asked you to leave that alone." He pushed my hand away from the ignition.

"All right. Don't have a coronary."

"I'd appreciate it if you'd keep your filthy hands off the up-holstery."

"Sorry. Next time I'll take a bath before I sit in your car."

"There won't be any next time." He patted at the seat where my hands had been, while taking the keys from the ignition, pocketing them.

"Want to get rid of me?" I asked. "Very easy. Talk. Tell me where you and Judy went that night."

"Just around." Bolt upright, he looked nervously at the empty parking lot. "Driving . . . parking."

"Where?"

"Along the Shore Drive there."

"What did you do?" I asked. "When you went parking?"

"The usual things."

"Did you give her anything?" I suppressed an urge to smash his face.

"Give her anything?"

"Like a keepsake. Something to remember you by."

"No," he said. "Well, I brought a bottle of wine, but she forgot it in my car. Good wine, too."

"Nothing else?"

"No."

"You didn't give her anything? You're positive. Because this's an important point."

"I'm positive," he said. "I gave her nothing."

"You never visited her house or mailed her anything or anything like that?"

"I had no contact with her whatsoever except for that night."

"Well, then," I reached into my pocket, "how do you explain that?" I put the picture on his dashboard.

"Where'd you get that?" He almost smiled.

"Judy had it. It's your picture. And I'm wondering where she got it if not from you."

"Well . . . I don't know. She must've took it from my wallet. I guess."

"I'm getting upset." I was sincerely angry. "We're going to start over. And this time you tell me the truth."

"I told you."

"I feel like a fool when you lie to me, Timmons. I don't like that feeling."

"I told you —"

I raised my leg and smashed my heel into the glove compartment. It cracked and the metal bent slightly inward. The snapshot fluttered to the floor. A metal ring flew off the radio. Timmons was stunned. His face turned as red as if he'd been struck.

"You think this is a joke?" I rasped.

"You're crazy."

"That's right. I'm crazy."

He stared at the damage, horrified.

"This is no joke. Do you understand now?"

"You're crazy." He was pressed against the door, as far from me as possible.

"Just tell me." I tried to calm myself. "Where did she get the picture?" Kicking the glove box was pure anger and instinct. It felt wonderful. I would have been happy to kick something else now.

"I gave it to her." His eyes remained fastened on the dented dash.

"When?"

"Two years ago."

"You're lying again."

"I swear I'm not."

"You picked up Judy in that bar," I pointed, "less than two weeks ago."

"So? We always met here." He was searching the floor for the metal ring.

"What do you mean? You always met here?"

"Whenever," he located it, "whenever we went out we met here or a place close by."

"What," I stuttered, "how, how long was all this going on?"

/ *122*

"About two years. Off and on. Look what you've done. This is bent now. It can't be fixed. Christ. There was no need for it."

"Two years. . . . I don't, I don't believe it."

"Well, you can believe it because it's true. Two years ago. That's when I gave her this picture. We had a real thing then. Lately, I hadn't seen much of her. Half a dozen times maybe this past year. So there's no reason to involve me in all this business."

I was disoriented. Whenever I seemed finally to make sense of it all, I got hit with something like this. It wasn't fair. I didn't know her at all. I wondered if she'd ever once been honest with me. "Why?" I turned to Timmons. "Why didn't you go to the police with this information?"

"Information? What information?"

"If you cared about her you'd want to help."

"I can't help Judy," he said. "I don't know what happened to her. And I can't have a scandal in the newspaper. I depend on my security clearance for my employment."

"That's all you're worried about?"

"I mean, if you're trying to say maybe I'm involved in Judy being missing. No. I work in a large department. I was at work the day she disappeared. And I've got forty witnesses."

Later, I was confused and distressed. In one sense, the interview was a success. I was satisfied I'd gotten the truth. But, at the same time, I'd asked all the questions and come away with more questions. It was like driving piles into quicksand.

eight

I RARELY USE my credit card. But why not use it now? Suppose I never paid the bill? Would they send me to jail? I charged an overcoat and jacket, then made reservations at a steakhouse. This time, after some coaxing, Pam Nealy agreed to come without her brother. I was anxious to win her over.

With some regret and longing, I remembered our date and the nights we took supper together. Her shining eyes had given signals and when I touched her she often, unexpectedly, smiled happily. All along, I now decided, Pam had been the friend to rely on, a gentle, trusting person. I'd thrown her over for Judy, but that was largely a physical thing, beyond anyone's control. If I'd used my head in the matter I wouldn't be in all this mess now. Unfortunately, when I went to Judy I was not following my head.

Since my arrest, I'd scarcely talked to anyone. Ordering a sandwich one day I was startled at the sound of my own voice, which seemed to be deteriorating from disuse. I certainly needed a friend.

Pam came to the steakhouse and I was nervous. "I need help," I explained at one point. "I need someone."

"But why me?" she asked over salad.

"We're friends. I think we're friends."

She munched on sliced cucumbers. "What about your lawyer? Isn't he supposed to help?"

"My lawyer? He's an old man. He's not exactly on top of things."

"You should get a new lawyer."

"I'm a charity case, Pam. I take what they give me. Anyway, I'd rather have dinner with you than any lawyer. For one thing, you're a whole lot nicer to look at."

She ordered seafood. I watched for some spark of that interest I'd seen so many months before. She stared dispassionately. What was she thinking?

"You're quiet," I said.

She nipped a juicy, white scallop from the end of her fork.

"You're still upset with me. Deep down, you're upset with me. Aren't you, Pam?"

"Why should I be upset?"

"It's something we never really talked about. About last spring. When we were going to dinner all the time. I guess I led you on. And then I sort of just dropped you. Which, probably you were upset about, had a right to be upset about."

"Well, no." At last, she was flustered. "I was never upset."

"Well, I'm just saying, I wouldn't blame you if you were."

She toyed with her scallops.

"So, I just wanted to say, for the record, to clear the air —"

"Don't." She put her hand up. "Let's please forget it." She put her fork down, exhaling loudly.

"Now I've done it again. I've hurt your feelings again."

"Not at all," she said quietly. "Back then . . . you know, I never exactly expected you to start seeing me regularly or anything like that. I thought you might. It would've been nice. But I didn't expect it."

"I was a jerk not to. I don't blame you if you're still a little bitter."

/ 125

"Please," she shook her head, "I'm not bitter at all. Like I said. At the time I thought you might be interested in . . . but, evidently, you found something you liked better. And that's okay."

"Judy? She wasn't better than you. Don't ever think that."

"Her?" Pam was suddenly forceful. "You and her. I'll never understand that. What was the attraction?"

"I don't know. I guess, she was nice to me."

"What did you see in a person like that?"

"I don't know, really. Just the way she acted." I tried to explain. "How she was so forward about what was on her mind. You know. And, I don't know, I've always had a weakness for that type of woman. And it is a weakness. I know it. I knew it at the time. And still I couldn't help myself. And now look at the mess I'm in. God, Pam, I'm in so much trouble."

It was true. Even if I was acquitted, my life was changed forever. My eyes filled with moisture. It was so unfair.

Pam studied the tablecloth.

I took a hard swallow of Coke. "I want to be honest. I'm asking for your help. But if you say no, I'll understand. I guess. But first I'll answer your original question as to why I'm coming to you as opposed to anyone else. Okay. I'm trying to be honest. Number one, I like you. I never stopped liking you."

She attempted a skeptical smirk, but it was lost in those questioning lips.

"Another reason is that I trust you, Pam. I know you're a decent, honest person. If you can't help me you'll say so. You won't string me along for what you can get out of it. Some people would."

She was listening intently.

"Now. The third reason is this. And I'm sure it's no surprise. I need you, Pam. I'm alone without you."

"But what do you want from me?"

"I don't want you to do anything that's going to bother you, or get you in trouble or anything illegal. That's first off. Okay. Now. Here it is. Do you still have that contact at the shipyard?"

"The shipyard? Well, I know the public relations officer."

"Good. I want you to check on a guy for me." I told her about Timmons and asked her to verify his alibi. I was careful to give accurate details. Pamela's trust was all-important. "And I also need a name. Klijner's sister."

"Oh, I don't know about that."

"Pamela, I have to talk to her. She's the alibi. The whole ball game. If I can't talk to her I might just as well give it up."

"What if they found out I gave you her name?"

"How would they? I'm not going to tell them."

She shook her head.

"It's okay, Pam." I touched her hand, a natural gesture. "Please."

"Jesus. . . . Don't tell anyone you got this from me."

"I won't. I promise."

"Her name is Agnes Gallagher."

"What do you know about her?" I asked.

"I thought you just wanted her name?"

"Well, it won't hurt if you can tell me a little about her."

"She's divorced," Pam said, "divorced a long time. No kids. Works for the state. I think the unemployment office in town. She lives alone, last I heard, down Horse Neck Beach way. On the beach."

"Thanks, Pam. Really."

"I hope I'm doing the right thing."

"You are. You won't regret it." I couldn't help but smile.

Outside the Super Bowl with a box of fried chicken and a Coke, I waited for Judy's red-haired friend. She was likely to be a person Judy saw frequently. Probably they shared confidences.

The manager had recognized Judy's picture, even remembered her friend. "But I didn't know their names. Lots of people come in here. And I haven't seen these two in a few weeks. Why you wanna know?"

In the next days, at odd hours, I came to the parking lot of the Super Bowl and watched people come and go. Judy's red-haired friend was not among them.

I don't read the obituary page. So I saw the story only by chance over the weekend.

A Mass for Judith Anne Klijner will be celebrated Thursday at 8 P.M. at St. Peter's Church.

Mrs. Klijner disappeared under suspicious circumstances over one month ago.

Attending the services will be her husband, Roy Klijner, and son, Michael. Mr. Klijner is an assistant editor at the *Suburban-Citizen.*

I was sickened. It didn't say funeral mass, but it was listed among the obituaries.

Pamela called that afternoon. Timmons's alibi was a good one, she reported, according to his time card. "It wasn't easy to get this," she complained. "They looked at me like I was crazy. My friend the P.R. guy thinks I was checking up on my boyfriend."

But all I could talk about was the mass. "Why are they having it at Saint Pete's? That's not Judy's parish."

"It used to be."

"Are you going, Pam?"

"Everyone from here is going."

"How can they do this? They don't even know if she's dead. I'd never give up hope."

When I arrived at the church the massive front door was wide open. Parked a block away, I watched people come. I was touched to see that Judy had so many friends.

Klijner arrived with his look-alike sister, the little boy in tow. The mass was well begun, the celebrants arrived, when I finally moved toward the side of the towering stucco church. I pulled on the great creaking door, like a dead weight. Then I smelled incense.

"The Lord be with you," boomed the priest, a powerful speaker system filling the place with his deep voice.

"And also with you," mumbled the worshipers.

The vestibule was quite dark here. Feeling along the wall, my fingers blundered into something wet. I had a bad moment, remembering Judy's blood on my hand. But this was holy water and I blessed myself automatically.

The only lights were on the center aisle and at the front where the priest was just now climbing to the looming, swirling white marble pulpit. He prepared to read the gospel. I watched from the darkened archway to the right. In the large church, he was a dot of vestments above the congregation. Though over a hundred people were attending, they clustered in the first dozen rows, on either side of the aisle.

"I am the Resurrection and the life," the words resonated off stone walls, "whoever believes in me, though he should die, will come to live . . ."

I found a bench beside a post with a clear view.

". . . and whoever is alive and believes in me will never die."

Following the gospel, the priest bowed to kiss the book. The coughing and shuffling nearly ceased. The priest discussed Everlasting Life. He also spoke of hope, mentioning Judy, "my own good friend, God keep her." I was thrilled at the warmth and concern in his voice.

"Consider our loved ones," he said. "God's gift. The joy they bring can never be taken from us. This is the most tangible, the most lasting reward life holds. Friendship. Love. If you are tested, near despair, how will God reach you? How else but with a friend."

He went on in this vein. At the conclusion of the mass, the churchgoers, many weeping, passed down the center aisle; Klijner and his relatives, Pamela Nealy at the arm of Jack Olander, Murphy, Lewis, Hennessy, and even publisher Desmond Cooper. None saw me, slumped in the shadows.

For a long time, I waited among the empty pews. Even after the altar boys, laughing raucously, ran out the side door, I could hear the priest padding about behind the altar. When the lights began to go dark, I moved cautiously up the wide center aisle.

It was then I heard the noise, a clattering, like beads dropping on the hard tile floor. A compact bright missile advanced directly on me. In and out of shadow, as frightening as anything I have seen, it was a large, snow-white dog. I leaped backward, horrified, fumbling for safety among the empty benches.

Within feet of me the animal made to halt and would have if the tile floor had offered any traction. Instead, he slid, helpless, slamming loudly into a bench and disappearing underneath, a whining tangle of legs, tail and teeth.

"Angel!" A man pointed a powerful white beam at the reemerging beast. "Angel! Sit!" The light swung to me, standing on the bench. I held up my hand, trying to see past the glare. "All right," he snapped, "he won't bother you now." The white dog panted, returning to its master, who reached down to rub its ears. "Good boy, now. Good boy."

I stepped off the bench with as much dignity as possible.

"Who are you?" The priest's voice was commanding without amplifiers. "What do you want?"

"I was just at the mass. For Judy."

"Judy?"

"I thought you might be able to talk to me. About Judy." The light shone directly in my eyes. I had to squint. "How . . . how well did you know her, Father?"

"I've known Judy quite a long time. Why?"

"I'm asking questions because I'm concerned. I'm trying to find out what happened to her."

"I see." He lowered the flashlight. "I'm Father Ennis."

"Nice to meet you, Father."

"Well, come on, there's a bit more light down the rear there."

I passed down the aisle, the flashlight on my back casting grotesque shadows even to the ceiling thirty feet above. "We need to have more light in here," the priest said. "But, dear Lord, electricity today." I twisted to see massive stone supports like elephant legs, sculptured panels depicting the agony of Christ, the confessional. I was looking out for the dog, his feet tapping behind me.

"Father Ennis?" I turned to him, an indistinct black form. "I . . . I can't see you."

"There's more light down here."

"I just want to help Judy."

"Fine." He motioned for me to slide into one of the pews. There was a little illumination from a single overhead spotlight. On the bench in front, he half-turned to see me. His face was a shadowy terrain of blotches and depressions. "You're not from the police."

"No," I said. "This is just, just my own investigation."

"Who are you?" he asked.

"I was a friend of Judy's. I'm looking into things. I'm trying to find out what happened to her."

The priest's black eyes seemed to see through me. These men always made me nervous. "I thought all this was solved," he said. "I thought the police solved the case."

"That's what they think. I still have some questions. I know, if I disappeared I'd want my friends to be sure. To check every possibility. You can't always count on the police."

"What do you want to know?" he asked.

"Anything you can tell me about Judy's state of mind recently. If she talked about future plans. Anything suggesting she was about to run away."

"I wish I could help you there. But I haven't seen Judy for some months. Years ago I saw more of her. Lately, I'm afraid she drifted away from the church. The way a lot of people have. Besides, the Klijners haven't lived in this parish for some years. Since Roy worked for the paper. They left. A lot of people have gone. Even a few years ago, this area was quite different. I'm sorry, what did you say your name was?"

"Bill."

He leaned closer, studying me. I could smell the wine on his breath, the blood of Christ. "And what was it you wanted to ask about?"

"About Judy's problems. The things she told you about her problems."

"The difficulty there, some of what she told me I can't repeat, unfortunately."

"Not even if it involves, really, a matter of life or death?"

"Not under any circumstances."

"So that's it?" I asked. "You won't help me?"

"I didn't say that. Some things I can't discuss. Some things."

"Okay. Well, let me ask this. Would you say the Klijners had a bad marriage?"

"A bad marriage." He considered this. "Hard to say. At first, Roy and Judy had difficulties adjusting to life together. Not uncommon."

"What kind of difficulties?"

"Disagreements. The usual things."

"Seeing other men?"

"It's never that simple," the priest said. "Seeing other men. Or women. That's a sin in marriage. But, in my experience, it doesn't usually happen in good marriages. When it does it's a symptom of other problems."

"What can you tell me about Roy?"

"Roy Klijner. A good man. Good provider. Good husband."

"In your opinion," I leaned closer, "what would he do if he found his wife was unfaithful?"

"He adjusted to a lot."

"Did he ever hit Judy? That you know of. Was he violent?"

The priest turned away. "I won't answer that."

"Do you think, would you say it's possible Roy had something to do with Judy's disappearing?"

Again, he looked away. On the altar a few candles burned in red glasses, giving a warm glow.

"Would you pick Roy Klijner for a potential murderer? That's what I'm really asking."

He took a long time to answer. "I wouldn't. No, not Roy. I wouldn't expect him to hurt anybody. Not physically. On the other hand, I put my faith in God. People can be a disappointment."

"There's another thing I want to ask you about. Judy talked to me once about a relationship she had before she was married. It may involve a married man. She said his name was Bob."

"Bob." The priest looked sharply at me. "You got that name from her?"

"Yes. And all I need to do is ask this guy a few questions. As far as I know he's not involved. But Judy might have told him something that could be crucial to this whole thing. And in my position I can't afford to overlook it."

The priest stared at me. "What is your position in all of this?"

"I'm concerned for the sake of Judy. Why else would I be here?" I shivered. Of course, by now he'd realized who he was talking to. "I want to help Judy. If she can be helped."

"I wish I could give you the information you want," he said curtly. "But I simply cannot."

"A life," I said, "possibly two lives are at stake here, Father."

"I'm sorry."

"What if this Bob wants to talk to me?"

"I don't understand."

"You could ask him, Father. You could explain the whole situation. Let him decide if he wants to see me. Maybe he'd be glad to help. After all, he was once in love with Judy. Wouldn't he have an interest in finding the truth?"

"Let me think about it." His voice was firm and final. It inspired the dog to a low moan. "Angel!"

"Dog makes me nervous."

The priest smiled.

"Aren't you afraid he'll scare away parishioners?"

"We should all have an angel to watch over us," he said. "Especially at this hour. Especially in this neighborhood."

"You don't think I'm dangerous?" I tried to laugh.

"Angel's with me every night. We've had some problems here. People. They steal things off the altar, they break the stained glass. For no reason. They just break it. My housekeeper was knocked down within sight of the rectory last month. Purse-snatcher. I accomplish things in the world, positive things. Perhaps it's vanity, but I feel a responsibility to preserve myself." With his sad, Celtic face, he was like all those cops.

"I'll bet you have a brother who's a cop," I said.

"Not in this town," he smiled. "Why? Do you know him?"

He led me out, the flashlight and blue-eyed dog at my back. I never got a good look at him.

The local office of the state division of employment security was a huge, busy room, row on row of fluorescent lights and signs suspended from the ceiling: "Line up here for applications." I stood in line and filled out forms. How many checks would I be around to collect? I left my application in a basket and sat.

"Watch." An elderly man nudged me and pointed to an attractive young woman dropping her application in the basket. Two male employment counselors rushed forward. The pretty lady had not sat down when her name was called. "I been here an hour," the old fellow grumbled. "No wonder the government's such a mess."

When my name was called, after more than an hour, I did not respond. I waited until a certain woman counselor was free, then I took a seat beside her desk. Thirtyish, her face cracking into wrinkles. Judy had once described her as a "frustrated old fart." Agnes Gallagher, Klijner's sister.

"If you'll take a seat over there," she never looked at me, "your name will be called."

"I've been waiting two hours. There must be some mistake. Nobody's waited as long as I have."

"Put your application in the basket. Someone will be with you shortly."

I leaned close. "I don't think it's fair I should wait any longer. I think two hours is enough."

Grudgingly, she took the application. "Did you bring your pay stubs?"

"No."

"Were you laid off or fired?"

"I don't know."

"You're not very well prepared for this interview, are you? You haven't even got the name of your employer down here."

"Could you answer a few questions?" I asked.

She looked up at me for the first time.

"It'll only take a minute."

She glared. "I know who you are."

"I'm entitled to my benefits. Like anybody else."

"And someone else can handle them." She was about to rise when I motioned.

"Please. I just want to talk. It'll only take a minute. I came here so you could be comfortable. I didn't want to surprise you on the street or knock on your door."

"I have no reason to talk to you."

"Just a few questions," I stressed.

"I already answered questions. The police."

"Maybe I got different questions. The police got a whole other perspective from me. They start out wanting to prove I did it. I start out knowing someone else did it. The question is who? What do you think?"

"I think you better get out of here."

"Now." I moved closer, but she wouldn't look at me. "You told the police that on the day Judy disappeared Roy was at your house all day, with you."

"It's the truth."

"Are you sure?"

"I don't lie," she spoke quickly. "You say you're innocent. All right. Maybe that's true. If it is, I hope you can prove it. But you won't prove it by making me out to be a liar. I am not a liar. And you won't prove it by blaming Roy, either. He's not to blame. And that's all I have to say."

"What did he do? He was at your house all day. What did he do?"

"I told the police all about it."

"Tell me," I persisted. "I want to be convinced. What did he do all day?"

"I don't know. I don't know what you mean."

"I mean, did he take a nap? Did he play with the kid? Did he watch television?"

"Yes," she said.

"Yes? Yes to what? Which did he do?"

"He did all those things. He was at my house all day. It was a long day."

"He watched television. What did he watch?"

"I don't know. Will you leave me alone? Really, can't you see I'm working?"

"When did he watch television? What hours?"

"I'm not answering any more questions."

"Problems, Agnes?" A man stood by us, watching me suspiciously.

Flushed, Agnes put her hands to her face. "I just don't feel well." She stood uneasily. "I think I better take a break." Never looking back, she hurried off.

I was directed to another desk where my application for benefits was processed. Mrs. Gallagher did not return, though I waited over an hour. No one at the unemployment office thought this disappearing act unusual. No wonder the lines are so long.

I drove around a lot. Occasionally, I went past Klijner's

house. The yellow Pinto was always in the driveway, always in the same place.

One day, while going from the Super Bowl to lunch at the House of Muffins, I found myself on Beale Street. I remembered following Judy down this very street to a drugstore called the Naborhood Pharmacy. On impulse, I decided to visit it.

The store sold everything from toys to toilet paper. A radio played softly. I never got to the pharmacist with my photo of Judy. He was a tall, gray man with mustache and black glasses. The woman at the cash register was younger. She stared at me with real surprise. She was Judy's red-haired friend, her companion from the bowling alley.

"Need to talk to you," I said.

She opened her mouth and shook her head.

"I only want to talk."

The pharmacist came behind her and took her by the shoulders. "What do you want?" He also recognized me.

"I came to talk to this lady here."

"We've got nothing to say," the man barked.

The woman's red hair, a bright, clownish color, was cut short. Her eyes were soft blue, her face freckled. She was unsmiling now, even grim.

"Nothing to say? Is that true?" I asked.

"Don't say anything, Bertie."

"I'm sure Judy told you about me."

"That's a lie," the pharmacist said.

"Let her talk, for Christ's sake."

"Just a minute." The man leaned past to a bemused woman with a baby carriage, waiting behind me. "We'll be with you in a minute." Then he urged his wife to the back of the store. I chased them among the mouthwash and toothpaste.

"Have the police talked to you?" I asked.

"No," she replied.

"I'll handle this," the pharmacist said.

"Look, Jack, I'm not talking to you."

"You should be in jail." He was shaking. "The nerve of you scum. With your trials and appeals, one layer of bullshit on another."

"We're not going to hit it off. I can see that."

"Get out. Get out of my store."

"I just want you to know," I spoke to her, "I'm only trying to find the truth. Judy must've told you about me. I wouldn't've hurt her. You know that."

The pharmacist pushed himself between us. "Take care of the customer," he told her. "This is my store," he told me. "And I'm telling you to leave. If I get mad maybe I'll help you leave." His thick, hairy fists clenched. "Clear?"

Outside, the wind was blowing. Already we were coming into winter. My heavy jacket fit snugly. I stalled in front of the store. I had to find a way to reach her.

Meanwhile, the woman with the baby carriage came from the store. "Excuse me." She waved a note. "The lady in there? Mrs. Spaco. She asked me to give you this." She smirked knowingly. The note read,

Thursday — in front of Mario's Pizza — city mall — one o'clock.

Arriving home, I found a letter from Father Ennis in the mailbox. Judy's mysterious Bob had agreed to talk with me. I was to be at the church in two nights. It was a second, encouraging sign.

I'd been telephoning Pam almost every day now. Sometimes we talked for a few minutes, sometimes longer. At first, she'd been cautious, almost cold. Gradually, involved in my constant efforts to clear myself, she grew increasingly sympathetic.

And Pam's voice became a drug to get me through the day. As might be expected, I began to see her as an ideal figure, gentle, forgiving, even loving. While I grew confident of her trust, I was surprised and delighted when she actually invited me for a date.

Pam drove us toward the nearby big city, refusing to reveal her specific destination. "It'll be a surprise."

"Sure. I like surprises. Nice surprises."

We traveled a maze of one-way streets through Chinatown to the theater district. Friday-night traffic was thick and unpredictable, parking nonexistent. Pam took us down a narrow alley lined with cars. Here we were fortunate to find a single space.

Cold, it seemed quite natural in that dark, narrow alley that I took her arm. "Where are you taking me, Miss Nealy?"

We reached the main street, which was busy with showgoers. Passing one theater, we came to a nondescript tailor shop. Beside it was a door showing a small name plate in the window: "Downtown Tea Room." We went inside.

"What is this?"

"Don't you know?" she teased. Up the narrow, creaking stairway we came into a dimly lit room hosting eight small tables. People sat here, chatting softly.

"An opium den?" I whispered.

"Very funny." We took the only empty table. Pam paid four dollars and two cups of steaming green-brown water appeared. I studied mine from several angles. "It won't bite you," she laughed. "Drink it."

"Yech. It's awful."

"See the lady across the room? With the two old ladies? She's the fortune-teller. She reads tea leaves."

I smiled in amazement.

"Anyway. I thought it might be fun," she said. "Something different. We don't have to stay."

"Pamela. This is a side of you I never figured on."

"I don't really believe in it. Not really. I only come once in a blue moon."

Marie, the fortune-teller, took a deep breath before putting a professional eye to Pamela's cup. Less than five feet tall, she was simply dressed in a sweater and skirt. After spinning the cup in slow circles she emptied the dregs on the saucer. "You're not married, Pamela."

"No."

"But you're considering marriage. I see that."

"I don't know," Pam said.

"But I do. You are considering marriage, which is causing a great deal of turmoil within. There is a conflict between marriage and career."

"My career?"

"I see you with . . . an instrument . . . you're a nurse . . ." Pam frowned.

". . . wait." The fortune teller peered more closely at the leaves. "I can see you with . . . a pencil . . . true?"

"I use a pencil to take notes," Pam agreed. "I never use a pen because they skip sometimes." She turned to me. "I covered a fire once. And it was so cold the ink in my pen froze. I couldn't take a note."

"You're a writer of some kind," Marie said. "Newspapers. You're a newspaper writer."

Pam shrugged. "I think I gave that away."

"Perhaps," Marie suggested, "you will write a story about me someday."

"That's an idea," Pam said.

"This is a crucial time for you, Pamela. A time to make decisions that will affect the rest of your life."

Pam took all this very seriously, staring at the fortune-teller, scarcely breathing. I was cold. Almost everyone in the room wore a coat.

Marie was rubbing her forehead. "You will . . . others will impose their needs on you . . . you've seen this happening, Pamela."

I hoped Pam would look at me, but she was transfixed by the woman.

"But you must attend to your own needs, your own house, dear." Marie looked several times from the tea leaves to Pam. "You're often lonely."

Pam stiffened.

"This sadness is only temporary, young lady. Be patient."

Pam's eyes widened. I wanted to touch her.

"I see. I see that you were not meant to be alone. You try to convince yourself that you're happy alone. But," she reached out, "it can't be true. At this time you will make a crucial decision about people in your life. One decision is the right one for you."

"What's that?" Pam asked.

"I can't say at this time. Perhaps on another visit. Now I tell you only that what you want from life is worth gambling for. And you must gamble to get what you want." Marie's expression suddenly changed as she turned, reaching for my cup, smiling.

"No!" I covered it with my hand. "I'm just a spectator."

"There's no reason to be afraid," Marie said.

"Go ahead, Bill. Let's see what she says."

Marie gave an unfriendly smile. "You don't believe?"

"No, I don't."

"Then why are you afraid?"

"Go ahead," Pam urged.

"How much?" I asked. "How much does it cost?"

"As you like." Marie studied the leaves now washed up on my saucer. I sat back, arm resting on the table, very casual and smug.

"For you as well. This is a very difficult time." Marie looked up. "You're in some sort of trouble."

Pamela shook her head in wonder. I was determined to look unimpressed.

"It's something to do with your work. At work." She looked up again, her eyes seeming to grow. "At your work . . . you're afraid, afraid of losing your job. Right?"

"Something like that."

Marie exuded self-satisfaction. "You said you didn't believe. They always say that. Only believers leave this room."

"What else?" Pam asked.

Marie looked from the saucer to my eyes. "I see a woman in your past."

"Just one?" I asked.

"Of course, there are several. There is Pamela in the present. Now I see clearly the recent past."

"Maybe you would rather stop, Bill?"

"No. Let her go on. What else? Tell me about this woman in the recent past."

"Ah," Marie glanced to Pam, "you should never see her again, this woman."

"Will I see her again?"

"You shouldn't."

"But will I?" I pressed.

"I can't say. The leaves don't tell. They say only that any further involvement with her would be a mistake. You would suffer for it."

"What went wrong?" I asked. "Can you tell me that? What went wrong between her and me?"

"This woman . . ." Brow furrowed, eyes gleaming, Marie was a show of concentration. "This woman was dishonest with you. You trusted her, but she was dishonest."

When Marie went off to another table, I dropped a five-dollar tip and we left.

"I'm sorry." Pam pulled on her gloves as we walked along the street. "I shouldn't have taken you there. It was stupid. I should have realized they'd drag up painful things."

"Forget it. I don't believe that stuff anyway."

"It's all nonsense," Pam said. "I agree." We walked into the alley. "I feel foolish after I go to one of those places." Her voice echoed off the buildings. It was deathly quiet here. "I don't know why I go. Although, God, she was good. That Marie? I went to her once years ago. She's excellent."

We sat in the car as the engine warmed. "Was she right?" I asked. "All those things she said about you? Are you really lonely? I never thought of you as lonely."

"Everybody gets lonely. Don't you think?"

We sat for several moments, the conversation at a dead end. I ached to touch her. "Sometimes," I said dreamily, "sometimes I wish I could start over. Except I'd probably just do all the same stupid things again."

I put my hand on her shoulder. At first, I was going to ask for a kiss, but I got excited and just went ahead and did it. She seemed to like it so I did it again.

"I should have stayed with you last spring."

"Would've saved a lot of trouble," she said.

"You're so beautiful."

"No. I know I'm not beautiful."

"To me," I said. "To me you are beautiful." We kissed again. I thought of suggesting my place, but I was afraid she might think I was presuming too much. "Promise me something, Pam. Promise that if this all works out badly. I mean, if things go wrong for me and I go to, you know, to jail. Well, you'll just forget me and that's all there is to it. Okay?"

She shrugged.

"And, as a matter of fact," I continued, "I'd rather you didn't come to the trial. I don't know if you were thinking of going. But it'll be hard enough for me. You shouldn't have to go through that. Promise me you'll stay away."

"If that's what you want."

I never wanted to pull Pam into this mess. I could not reasonably expect her to show up on visiting day for the next twenty years. Nor did I want her to suffer over my misfortune should I be convicted. On the other hand, her promise to forget me if matters went badly didn't really mean much.

The following day, Father Ennis called to cancel my meeting with Bob. I was greatly distressed. "Yesterday this individual was willing to answer your questions," the priest explained. "But today I got this message canceling out."

"But why? Did he give a reason?"

"Ah, only that it was no longer necessary."

"No longer necessary? Father, that doesn't make any sense."

"Perhaps not."

"Well, look . . ." There was growing desperation in my voice. "Can you try to talk him into it?"

"I'm afraid not."

"Well, can *you* answer some questions —"

"No, no. We've been over that before. I'm sorry I can't be more helpful, but I've done all I can. If the situation should change I'll give you a call. That's all I can do. Sorry."

Another door closed. With my court date fast approaching, few open doors remained. Bertie Spaco was one of the few.

Unsmiling, she sat in front of Mario's Pizza on a bench in the middle of the mall. Shoppers hurried by, kicking dead leaves along the brick walkway. Probably, she felt safer among all these people. Even her Crayola-red hair seemed muted by the black and gray sky. "Hello." I sat beside her, leaving space between us.

"I don't know why I'm here." Judy's friend avoided my eyes. "I must be crazy."

"You're here to talk to me. Help me get at the truth." I was calm, reasoned. The last thing I wanted to do was frighten her.

"Well, it's this way," she said. "I thought maybe you'd have something to tell me about Judy. I thought you'd tell me what happened to her. If you will, I swear, I promise, I won't tell the police. I just want to know what happened to her."

"Mrs. Spaco, I don't know what happened to her."

"I should go. I don't know what I'm doing here, really."

"Please don't go."

"After all," she put her hand to her face, "why should I talk to you? My husband was right. You should be in jail."

"If you thought that," I said softly, "you wouldn't be here. You've got something to tell me, Mrs. Spaco. What is it? What do you think happened to Judy?"

"Judy always took chances." She sniffed in the cold. "I told her. You've got to be careful today. The world's full of crazy people. But she never listened. Nothing's going to happen to me. That was her attitude. She wouldn't listen."

I nodded.

"Most of the time she was fine. Judy was pretty bright. But every so often she'd do something just plain stupid. Get involved with some creep. With men, Judy had no judgment." She looked down, blinking. "I haven't talked about her to anyone since it happened. And now I'm talking about her in the past tense." As she spoke, the red, raw color of winter spread from her nose to the rest of her face. Mrs. Spaco did not take the cold well.

"Would you like to go inside? Get something to eat? Or drink? It's awfully cold out here."

"I should go home. I really shouldn't stay."

"You and Judy were close?"

She nodded vigorously.

"How long did you know her?"

"Since high school. Really, I can't stay here."

"She told you about us?" I asked.

"No . . . well, she maybe mentioned somebody, some new boyfriend. Maybe it was you. I don't remember. All she said, she said she was seeing this guy and he wasn't crazy, which was a big plus, she figured."

"Did you know Roy?"

"We didn't get along," she said. "One of those things. I didn't like him. And he didn't like me."

"Why was that?"

"I didn't like him because of the way he treated Judy. He didn't like me . . . I don't know, because I didn't like him, I guess."

"Do you think he could have hurt Judy?"

She looked up, as if grateful for the question. "I'll tell you the honest-to-God truth. When I read in the paper what happened I kept waiting for them to arrest him. When they said you did it, I had to wonder." She looked carefully at me.

"What made you think it was Roy? Was he violent? Did he hit her?"

"Wouldn't surprise me," she said.

"Maybe you'd know about this. Judy talked to me once about a guy she went out with before she was married. A guy, he was married himself, as I understand it. According to her, she talked to this guy all the time. And I think he might have some very important information."

"Can't help you," she shook her head.

"His name was Bob. Did Judy ever speak of him?"

"Not to me."

"You're sure?"

"I said so."

"Where were you, Mrs. Spaco, on the day Judy disappeared?"

"Working. In the store."

"And when was the last time you heard from her?"

"Weeks before that," she said. "I don't remember exactly."

"Do you think Judy could have run away?"

"No. Not Judy. Not voluntarily. She wouldn't leave her little boy behind. If she ran away she would have taken him with her."

"Yeah," I said. "But nowadays women do that. More and more. They take off, leave the kids. It happens."

"Not to Judy. She loved her child. She certainly wouldn't leave the baby behind with him. He's no good with kids."

"Can I call you later?" I asked. "I don't want to keep you. But I'd like to call you again, maybe. In case I think of any more questions."

"You can call me, I suppose. But don't let my husband know. He doesn't want me involved in this. He never even knew I was still friendly with Judy. You see, like a lot of people, he never approved of her."

Money was becoming a real problem. As my supply dwindled, the world darkened considerably. Unpleasant notices arrived from the telephone company, Edison, and the credit-card people. It seemed like a conspiracy.

Where could I get some money? My mother, in Florida on social security, had nothing to spare. The *Suburban-Citizen*, however, owed me a few dollars in expense money. Most reporters received severance pay. I hadn't. And it couldn't hurt to ask.

As I approached the building, my own rising anger surprised me. "The *Suburban-Citizen*" gleamed before me in gold-on-black letters six feet high. The newspaper and the people working for it had treated me unjustly. They had attacked me in print. Fired me. Deserted me.

Just past four o'clock, the newsroom was cluttered with people coming or going from the day and night shifts. Their reaction to my appearance was striking. Some glared at me. Fingers froze over typewriters. The noise level dropped dramatically.

I didn't look at anyone as I crossed to Jack Olander's desk. Carl Lewis was in Roy Klijner's seat. Both Olander and Lewis saw me coming and seemed astonished. "Hi," I began. They just looked. "Nice to see you. I've come for some expense money I'm owed."

"I — I don't know anything about that," Lewis muttered weakly.

"I'm owed expense money. About eight dollars, I figure. I thought they'd mail it to me. But they didn't. And right now I need the money."

"Expense money? I don't, I don't know anything about expense money."

"Well, you can look in the desk. See if there's an envelope with my name on it."

"Desk?" Lewis fumbled, flustered.

"Desk." I tapped it. "This desk. Roy's desk. Look in the drawer for an envelope with my name on it. My money. I want it."

Slowly, he opened the middle drawer, eyes carefully sweeping right to left. I marveled that in a crowded room I could hear my heart pumping. Silent, the reporters sat in chairs or on desk tops; thinking the same thing, *I wonder if I can get a story out of this?*

Lewis finally found the envelope and turned to Olander. "Should I give it to him?"

"It's his?"

"Yeah."

"Then give it to him." Olander was loud.

Lewis extended the little package. "You figured wrong. Only six dollars and eighty-five cents." In pencil, the envelope was labeled clearly, $6.85. Full of noisy change, it slid heavily into my pocket.

I wasn't ready to leave. There had to be something else to say. I looked foolish, coming in for six dollars and eighty-five cents. "Ah . . . ah, I was wondering . . . about, about coming back to work."

"You don't work here anymore," Olander said.

"Oh, I don't? Really? Well, nobody told me."

"I'm telling you."

"Oh? Well, maybe you can tell me why? How come I don't work here anymore?"

"Go home, Martell. You're embarrassing yourself."

"Yeah. Well, I have another thing to say. It's this. I don't think it's right. The stories you guys did on me. I mean, I used to work here." I leaned close to Olander, lowering my voice. "I thought I had friends here."

"We do our jobs. You'd do exactly the same."

"But, these stories. They weren't even fair."

"You got a complaint?" the editor growled. "Take it upstairs to public relations."

"Yeah . . ." My hands were clenched. "If I don't work here anymore. What about my severance pay? Huh? What about that?"

Olander sighed loudly, slapping his pencil to the table. "Look, I've got nothing to do with severance pay or any other kind of pay. Upstairs. Take it upstairs."

Upstairs was one long corridor of doors labeled "Personnel," "Executive Editor," "Public Relations," and at the end, "Desmond C. Cooper." The young publisher sat beneath a Winslow

Homer seascape. The room was done in redwood with a little fireplace and a huge mahogany desk. A girl sat on a couch near the window. "Who are you?" Cooper squinted.

"I work here. Or, at least, I used to."

"Have you made an appointment? I don't have anyone on my calendar. What's your name? How did you get in here?"

"My name's Martell. I used to work general assignment —"

"I . . . I know who you are."

"Desmond, can we go?" the girl said. "You said this would only take a minute."

"What do you want, Martell?" I heard a measure of respect in his tone.

"I came to see you about the stories you been running. About me."

"What's wrong with our stories? They're fair. We only put down the facts."

"The facts? No." I moved toward his desk and he warily rolled his chair away toward the wall.

"If you've got some complaint, my suggestion is that you put it in writing. Put it all down on paper and pass it along. I promise to consider it carefully. But be very specific on what's bothering you."

"What's bothering me? I can tell you right now. I want to know why. Why are you people out to screw me?"

"We only report the news. We don't take a stand on something like this, we just give the facts. You should know that. You're a newsman."

"Desmooond?" the girl complained. "Can we goooo?"

"Yes." He looked past me. "Let's do get along. We'll be late."

"I'm sick of the runaround." I was frustrated. "Everywhere I go. That's all I get. The runaround."

"In a way, it's understandable you're upset." Cooper was on his feet, reaching for his fur-lined coat. "You've been through a difficult, emotional period. You see the news stories and it's quite natural you resent us, even though we've only recorded the facts. I can understand perfectly how you feel."

/ 149

"You've taken everything. Everything to make me look bad, make me look guilty, and you've put that in the paper. And anything for my side, you've kept it out."

Cooper gestured to the girl, who came bouncing to his side. "You know what?" he said. "I've got to go now. But, really, if you'll make an appointment —"

"Just tell me why. How come no one's on my side? Are there payoffs or something? Is Klijner behind it?"

"I have to lock up." Cooper swung the keys. The girl was behind him, impatient to leave, having no interest in all this. Her skin was flawless, uniformly pink and smooth, lips a soft, natural red, slightly open. She chewed bubble gum. "You better go," the publisher said.

"Well, wait a minute. There's something else I want to know."

"If you'll make an appointment."

"Am I fired or suspended or what?"

"Now," he said. "You certainly don't want to work here anymore. It wouldn't make good sense. For any of us."

"Well, what do I do? I have to work."

"That is a problem. If I were you I'd get right down to the employment office and file. Have you got a good resumé?" The girl on his arm, Cooper moved out the door.

"What about severance pay?" I called. He pretended not to hear, so I skipped past, coins jingling, and faced him in the corridor. "I'm entitled to severance pay."

"Severance pay?" He locked his door. "I don't know where you get that idea."

"Everybody gets severance pay."

"You've been misinformed. We allow severance pay in certain cases. But that is totally within our discretion. Check the contract. You'll find no mention of severance pay." Cooper angled past with the girl. It was no use arguing further. I'd tired of lost causes.

The publisher stood in the elevator, staring back at me, the girl on his arm. Then the doors closed.

nine

I MET COUGHLIN for lunch at Howard Johnson's restaurant. "You look like hell," he said, squirting ketchup all over french fries and fried clams. "You can't let yourself go like this. Get a haircut. Shave. Keep a regular schedule. You can go to bed late, but get up early. Too many people die in bed."

"You're not listening to anything I say." I clutched my cola.

"I'd offer you some lunch, but, my God, you look like you've gained twenty pounds since I last saw you. That doesn't make a good impression."

"Is that all you can say? I mean, for God's sake, I could use some help."

"You know," he smiled tolerantly, "if I went around like you I couldn't function. I need to be calm to be effective. Now, while you've been working yourself up to a nervous breakdown, I've been preparing this case. And I'm quite satisfied that we'll mount a formidable defense."

"Defense? You have a defense already planned?"

"I'll make a brief explanation," he said. "First, we'll present character witnesses on your behalf. You gave me some names earlier. I've contacted some of these people and they've agreed to testify for you. David Ansel."

"My old college coach."

"Vincent Smith. And Pamela Nealy. These people will counter a lot of that bad publicity, you know, the idea you have no friends."

"That's good," I said. "I like that."

"I had thought, also, of bringing your mother up from Florida. She'll say what a good fellow you are. Now, no one expects her to say otherwise. But sometimes it has a good effect if the jury sees your mother."

"My mother doesn't know anything about this and I'd like to keep it that way."

"She'll have to be told," he said. "Eventually."

"Not if I win. If I win she never has to know."

Coughlin ordered pecan pie and coffee for dessert. "If you won't allow your mother to testify there is someone who might be just as helpful. Now, unless I'm wrong, you were married at one time."

"What about it?"

"The prosecutor wants the jury to think of you as a certain type of citizen, a ne'er-do-well, unstable, as I've indicated. They'll paint that picture. And a failed marriage will be part of it."

"Lots of people get divorced."

"Lots of people," he smiled, "don't get indicted for murder."

"I'll explain. I mean, we tried it for two years. And it just didn't take. So big deal."

"Whose idea was it?" Coughlin asked. "Getting divorced?"

"Whose idea? You mean who first suggested it?"

"Yes."

"It was mutual."

"Mutual?"

"Yeah," I said. "Well, she hired a lawyer and did all that first. If that's what you mean."

"I see."

"She's very independent."

He nodded.

"But the way it was, it was like this. She wanted a certain type of life." I shifted uneasily. "I have a certain idea of what a wife should be. Like, Kathleen thought nothing of it, if they wanted her to work some night, she went right off to them. It didn't matter what I wanted. What I wanted, screw it. That was her attitude. Anyway. Eventually, we couldn't agree on anything. We just had such different ideas. So, we just, you know, went off in separate, different ways. You know?"

"Was it an amicable separation?"

"How do you mean amicable?"

"Still friends?" he asked.

"Not exactly."

"Still speaking, at least?"

"Well. Not exactly."

Coughlin shook his head, grumbling.

"Why, Mr. Coughlin? If we're friends or we speak or what, I mean, what difference does it make?"

"As I said, the prosecutor may refer to the broken marriage. But we can actually turn that strategy on its head," he leaned forward, "if we can put your wife on the stand as one of your character witnesses."

"Would she do that?"

"I don't know," he chuckled. "She's your wife."

"Well, I haven't seen her in over a year. I don't know if she'd cooperate."

"Then you'll have to ask."

My cola was gone now. The lawyer commenced an earnest assault on his pecan pie.

"So," I asked, "is that it? Is that our case?"

"Our case?" He chewed. "No. As far as our case goes, in a very real sense, you're it. You tell your story to the jury. They find you a trustworthy individual. And they believe you instead of Weisberg's tape. But we've been over that before."

"Suppose we prove that that tape's a fake. Prove it absolutely."

"How would we do that?" he asked.

"Oh, there's ways. They got experts, they can tell when the tape's tampered with. Remember Watergate? They figured out how they erased some of that tape. They can tell all sorts of things."

"I'm afraid that kind of evidence would be very costly." The lawyer frowned. "And I'm certain the court would never assume such an expense."

"I think it's worth the cost. To me it's worth the cost."

"But do you have the money? If it costs, let's say, as little as one thousand dollars, and these things can often cost much more than that, expert testimony, but could you come up with so much money? One thousand dollars?"

"I have this." I produced my savings bank life insurance policy.

Coughlin examined it with a professional eye. "This is made out with your wife as beneficiary. You might need her signature to cash it. And I doubt you'd get as much as a thousand for it."

"Look, if I can't get enough money off the insurance policy, maybe I could borrow the rest."

"You're under indictment for murder. Who would lend you money?"

"VISA?"

Coughlin laughed.

"I don't know. I could get it somewhere. Maybe . . . would you lend me the money? I'm good for it."

"I'm sure you are. But I don't have it. Besides, we couldn't be certain what these tests would prove. They might not prove anything."

I scanned the restaurant. People were eating, smiling, talking. No one had my problems. "I keep thinking, why don't we try to find out what really happened? To Judy, I mean."

"But you tried that," Coughlin said, "didn't you?"

"I still think it's her husband. I'd love to talk to him. I think he did it."

"Can you prove that?"

/ 154

"I thought, I mean, for Christ's sake, I thought there was something you could do."

"I couldn't do anything you haven't done already," he said.

"You mean that's it? That's my case? A couple of lousy character witnesses and hope the jury believes me? That's it?"

Caught with his mouth full of pie, Coughlin could only shrug.

"I don't believe this, Mr. Coughlin. There's got to be something I can do. I haven't hurt anybody. I haven't done anything and it's just not fair all this comes down on me."

"You were just unlucky," he suggested. "That was your mistake."

"I was unlucky? Well, how do I get lucky? What do I do?"

"I gather you don't go to church," he said.

"What's that got to do with anything?"

"When I'm in trouble," he said quietly, "I find it helps to go to church. Of course, I understand, a lot of people, young people, they seem to think it's a better world without religion. Perhaps. Myself, I like the world less and less. Sometimes, I'm glad my life is largely behind me. I have this feeling that things are going to get worse. Although the situation is quite bad already. I remember a time when people hurt each other for reasons. Maybe not good reasons, but reasons. For money. Or because they were angry. Or jealous. Today. Today, you see a lot of people, they hurt for no reason. They hurt for the sake of hurting. Maybe they like to see others suffer. I don't pretend to understand it."

"That . . . uh . . . I don't know why you tell me all this. I never hurt anyone."

"Yesterday," he pointed to his newspaper, folded to one quarter and lying beside the pecan pie, "yesterday a man went into a liquor store. He ordered the clerk to the floor, tied and gagged him. The clerk was a man with three children, working a second job. Isn't that always the way? So, the holdup man cleaned out the cash register, helped himself to some of the product, and on the way out he shot the clerk in the head. My God. An act like that. It's incomprehensible."

"That's nothing to do with me," I insisted.

"If they catch the killer. Do you know what will happen to him? Well, there was a time, when I first began practicing law, when there'd be no question. That individual's fate would be a foregone conclusion. Well, maybe I've become a little slow in my old age. These younger men have all the answers today. And this new system seems to make sense to a lot of them." He chuckled, a bitter laugh.

"I want whoever hurt Judy, I want them to suffer," I said, "but if you don't get me off they won't suffer. They won't even get caught."

He nodded.

"I didn't do it. I thought you believed me. You do believe me. Don't you?"

The coffee cup at his lip, he smiled warmly. "Would I defend you if I thought you were guilty?"

I called my ex-wife, Kathleen, that night. It wasn't easy. She still lived in a tiny apartment on Chestnut Street. She was pleasant during our conversation. "Don't believe what the newspapers say," I pleaded. "I didn't hurt anyone."

"I know better than to believe newspapers," she replied. "I know too much about them."

"Yeah."

We arranged to meet at Lincoln's Department Store, where she worked. That she even agreed to this was encouraging. And I was beginning to see Coughlin's point. A divorced wife would be a much more telling witness than the still-married woman whose self-interest is at issue.

"I don't like this." Pam Nealy stopped her car at the edge of Horse Neck Beach. Yellow weeds and bramble surrounded the road. "Shouldn't you call first, tell her you're coming?"

"She wouldn't agree to see me. But she's a real mouse. Once I pop up she'll talk to me. I know it. I can break her down."

"I'm worried," Pam said.

"I don't like this either. But I go to trial in a few days. If I don't get some answers I'm going to lose. I'll go to jail. Forever. So I don't have any choice. Understand? I have to do this."

She sat behind the wheel, watching the lonely oceanfront home across the meadow. I followed a sand path through the high grass, past the roadside mailbox of Mrs. Agnes Gallagher. The cold, rocky beach looked as forbidding as the freezing surf thrown against it. "What do you want?" She was at the door, eyes wild at seeing me.

"Just to talk." The room beyond was paneled, polished, neat. She tried to close the door, but I jammed my foot inside. "I told you, I have more questions. If you — *owww!*" She had slammed the door against my foot with all her strength. A sharp pain numbed the entire limb. I pushed forward, bursting into Mrs. Gallagher's living room. "My foot!"

"Get out of here. Get out of my house."

"My foot!" I hopped and stumbled to a chair. "Jesus Christ. You broke my foot."

"Get out," she demanded, shouting. "Get out of here!"

I wriggled off my sneaker. I thought I might see blood or a terrible malformation. But there was only a slight redness and swelling.

"I'm going to call the police."

"Yeah," I moaned. "Call a doctor for me."

"Get out," she rasped. "Get out of here." She went to the telephone table, opening a drawer.

"You don't have to call the police. Come on, all I want to do is talk, for Christ's sake. Just answer a few — what . . . ?"

She was holding a gun. No one had ever pointed a gun at me before. It looked real, the dull black metal finish, the bright wooden handle. It was small, fitting neatly in her hand.

Probably she was afraid, with something terrible in her expression. But I didn't look at her face. There was the gun. And only the gun. I could imagine the bullets inside, lined up, waiting to be released.

I was tempted, for a moment, to be unafraid. After all, it was a tiny woman with a tiny gun. But don't let it fool you. It can kill you. The bullets can rip you apart. They can tear into your face and smash your bones and destroy your brain. All she has to do is pull the trigger. She might do it too. Crazy enough to pull the gun, she might be crazy enough to pull the trigger.

"You don't need that." My voice grew high-pitched, pleading.

"Get out!" Her tone was hard and clear, as though she was not afraid at all.

"Okay."

"Move."

"Lemme get my sneaker on."

"Out. Now."

"Okay. Okay." I began shuffling sideways, limping for the door, sneaker in hand. I couldn't take my eyes from it. The little hole. The black spout. "Don't . . . don't . . ." I put my hand out.

"I could kill you. No one would doubt my right to kill you." She seemed to be debating the idea. "I could get away with it."

"No. You'd be sorry."

"Maybe."

I was at the door.

"Get out."

"On my way."

"Don't come back."

"I wouldn't."

It went off, a sharp crack that was hardly as loud as the wind howling outside. She was surprised, staring at the smoking weapon.

I looked down, searching for holes or blood. "Am I shot?" I moved my arms, my legs, felt my torso. "Where am I hit?" I had to be certain I wasn't shot. I've heard people are shot and don't realize it. "You shot at me."

/ 158

"No, I didn't."

"Jesus, you shot at me."

"It was an accident."

"You tried to kill me."

"I didn't."

"You did."

"It was an accident," she said. "Don't make me have another."

I looked around for bullet holes in the wall, the windows or the door.

"Get out, I said." She shook the gun. It might discharge again. She didn't know what she was doing. She was crazy.

Limping to the car, I was turned around backward most of the way, expecting that lunatic woman to be following. At any moment, she might leap from the tall grass, firing. Pam's car was a welcome sight. "What happened to you?" She eyed my sneaker.

"You won't believe this." I tried to catch my breath. "She nearly broke my foot. Let's get outa here."

"Did you talk to her?"

"She took a shot at me. With a gun. She's crazy. She's a god-damn nut." I pulled on my sneaker, wincing.

"She took a shot at you?" Pam backed the car away. "Are you sure?"

"It's something you don't make mistakes about. She was as close as you to me almost. And the gun went off."

"God."

"Yeah. Tell me she doesn't have something to hide. I was right. I know it. I know it. But, goddammit, how am I gonna prove it?"

I bounced in my seat all the way home. It was like surviving a bloody auto accident. Only afterward did the horror sink in. "I could've been killed."

"Better stay away from her," Pam said.

My hands shook. I wanted to hide in my room and never come out. The world was a dangerous place. Pam reached over and held my hand. "I'm glad you're with me, Pam. I couldn't even drive now. Look, I'm shaking."

"I'm driving," she said, "so don't worry."

"Yeah. You're great, Pam. I appreciate you."

In my apartment, I settled on a large, padded chair, drinking Cokes and eating compulsively from a box of Oreos. Pam took the box away. "Have some tea." I could remember the gun. The tiny slot at the end and smoke crawling over the barrel. I replayed the scene a dozen times. The idea of being chased away by a woman, quaking before her, was humiliating. It made me angry. "She could've killed me. Those people. They think they can kill anybody. That's what happens when you get away with it once. The second time, the second time is easy."

"Don't get yourself all worked up," Pam said.

"You wouldn't believe me before about him. About Klijner. Do you believe me now?"

"Hey," she said soothingly. "Don't get mad at me. I'm on your side, remember?"

"He killed Judy and he made it look like I did it. It's the perfect revenge. He gets rid of his wife and he gets rid of me at the same time."

"Drink the tea."

"And now he thinks he got away with it. Smug bastard. Somebody oughta kill him." I slammed my fist on the arm of the chair.

"Don't." Pam covered my hand with hers. "Don't upset yourself. That's what they want."

"Yeah. Yeah." But I couldn't relax. "Somebody oughta kill him," I muttered.

Later, the television was on, no one watching. Pam stood at the door with her coat on. "Are you sure you'll be all right?"

"Oh yeah. I'm okay now."

"I hate to leave you like this."

"You can stay," I said. "If you want to. I'll take the couch."

She hesitated.

"It's late to be driving home now, Pam. That's why I mention it. But if you can't stay — Does someone expect you?"

"No. No one."

"I'll make the bed for you," I said.

"I'll take the couch. You don't have to give up your bed for me." She took off her coat. I studied her black slacks and turtle-neck sweater.

She made soup next, saying, "You don't need a heavy meal."

I didn't want to misinterpret anything. I sat on the couch after supper. If I went to prison I wouldn't see a woman for a long, long time. She sat beside me, watching with some sympathy. "I used to see you in the newsroom, Pam. At first, I was afraid to ask you out. It took me a long time to do it because I figured a girl as nice, as pretty as you must have a boyfriend."

She smiled, leaning her head on my arm. "I've never had much luck with boyfriends."

"Don't think about it." I put my hand on her shoulder. "That's all in the past now." She was nervous, studying me. I pulled her close.

"Wait." She took off her circular, gold-rimmed glasses. Without glasses she looked less girlish, her eyes seemed tired. We kissed finally. She slid closer. I came away expecting to see Judy. But you couldn't make any mistake in the light. Pam was tall and blonde. Judy was small and dark.

"Is this a good idea, Pam?"

"I'm not asking questions tonight."

I kissed her while reaching to turn off the light. We took off her sweater and I began unbuttoning her shirt.

"Don't expect much in there," she said.

"It's fine."

"Really? You think so?"

"I never lie to half-naked women." I pulled at her clothes. I wanted to have them all off and slide my hands over every bit of her. She was thin, angular. Not like Judy. I concentrated on pleasing, touching the tips of my fingers along her thighs. And as she sighed and rocked, slowly, it could have been any woman, it could have been Judy. "This isn't fair to you," I said.

"I'm not complaining."

"You're cute in your glasses."

"Those things."

"Pam." I was touching her, everywhere. "I want you to feel good. Tell me what you like. We'll do everything you like."

"Let's go. Let's try the bed." She bounced onto it, pulling me by the hand.

"You look nice. Running around without your clothes on. You know? You look nice."

"Except I'm freezing." The winter, penetrating my apartment, brought goosebumps out all over her.

"Do you like that?" I asked. "Showing off like that?"

"What?"

"Without your clothes on?"

"I don't know." She sat on the bed. "Why?"

"You look nice. That's all."

"How are you today?" In shirt-sleeves, Dr. Sagie Divitre, the court-appointed psychiatrist, ran his hand through his blue-black hair. He was dark, an Indian, with a faintly British accent.

"I feel great." I sat across from his desk.

"Really." He was in his thirties, full of nervous, jerky movements. "Suppose you tell me about that."

"I feel great. What is there to tell? I just feel good. Things are looking a little better in my life. You know?"

"Fine. Nothing wrong with that. Fine."

"How do you feel?" I asked.

Divitre seemed surprised. "Me? I, I'm fine. I'm fine. But this must be a difficult time for you."

"Well, yeah. But I've been trying to stay busy. I've had lots to do. Preparing my defense. It's kept my mind occupied."

"It doesn't bother you to talk about Judy Klijner's disappearance?"

"No, why should it?"

He nodded.

"I mean, I didn't have anything to do with her disappearance. Except I happened along at the wrong time."

He made a note. There was a long silence as he stared at me.

". . . ah, I tell people this. About how I was just in the wrong place at the wrong time. And I'm telling people this all the time. Sometimes I think, I think I should have cards printed or something."

He nodded again.

". . . I, ah, I don't know if anybody believes me when I tell them that."

He was briefly motionless, hands clasping the arms of his chair, still staring at me.

"It's true though," I said.

"Aha."

"Look, if you've got any questions . . ."

"Tell me. Why do you think the police arrested you?" he asked.

"I don't know. Evidence. Circumstantial evidence mostly. But I guess they figured I was a likely suspect when they picked me up in the house. It's just, afterward, they got lazy, didn't bother to check any other possibilities."

"How do you feel, personally, toward the officers who arrested you?"

"Well . . . I don't know." I shrugged. "They're off my Christmas list."

"How do you feel about the way they treated you? Aside from the fact they're off your Christmas list."

"I don't think they were fair. Well, I agreed to cooperate. You know? And they took advantage of that. They tried to badger me into confessing."

"Did they?"

"And they got that tape there?" I went on. "Do you know about the tape?"

"The tape?"

"It's all phony. I'm not sure it was even my voice on there. You know? But if it was, I figure they spliced the tape. They took an answer to one question and put it after another, altogether different question. So I sounded like I was agreeing to something when I wasn't. Do you know what I mean?"

He made a note.

"It surprises you. You can be as cynical as hell about the law and the police and the way things work, but you don't really appreciate what injustice means until it's done to you. When they lie and break the law, the police. Jesus. You want to cry. It's so unfair. You can't believe the police, of all people, you can't believe they can be so dishonest. I mean, God, they want to send me to jail for a long, long time."

"That makes you angry?"

"Well, yeah, sure, it makes you angry."

"How does that anger feel?" he asked.

"How does it feel? I don't know. How does anger feel? Haven't you ever been angry?"

"Of course."

"Well," I asked, "how'd it feel?"

"It felt different at different times."

"Oh. Well, that's the same with me. I feel different at different times."

He smiled.

"I don't know. Sometimes I get mad. I want to hit somebody. Sometimes I want to scream. It's so unfair. You feel it all over. You feel it in your fingers, in your gut . . . I don't know . . ." Why had I said that? I must have sounded like a complete fruitcake. And Divitre was taking it all down.

"I mean, sure I get mad. But I get over it. It's just normal anger, you know? People are going around accusing me of killing somebody. Let's face it, that's what they all think. And it's bad enough you're close to somebody like Judy and you lose her. But on top of that you don't get any sympathy, all you get is people saying . . . saying you're some sort of killer. . . . I don't know . . . it's . . . it's hard. . . . I don't know. I don't know."

Divitre was poking his nose as if it itched.

"Tell me about your family?" he asked.

"My family. Yeah. Well, my mother and father are in Florida. Trying to keep warm. My mother doesn't like the cold up here. I don't think they've heard about this. At least, I haven't told them."

"And what kind of relationship did you and your father have?"

"A regular father-son relationship. I don't know. Sometimes we didn't get along. Like anybody else. You know? Well, we fought sometimes, but doesn't every kid? My father was a good guy, worked hard. I looked up to him. But, the thing was, you couldn't tell him anything. He was right. If he said black was white? It was white and nobody could say different."

"I sense a little resentment." The doctor was no longer poking at his nose. His forefinger had actually disappeared within. I looked politely away. "What about that, William?"

"Huh?"

"Anger? Between you and your father? Would you like to tell me about that?"

"I don't know . . ."

"Do you find that difficult to discuss?"

"Well, no, except there isn't much to tell. We'd argue about things. What? What do you want me to say?"

"And your mother?" Incredibly, he continued working at his nose. I began to wonder if this wasn't some sort of psychological trick to test my reaction.

"My mother?"

"How did you feel about your mother? Did you get along with her?"

"Well, she was . . . my mother. I liked her. She was my mother, after all."

"And what kind of relationship did your mother have with your father?"

"My mother and father? I don't know. They got along okay. I don't know. Could you please stop that, Doctor?"

"Excuse me?"

"That. What you're doing there. It's kind of a bad habit, isn't it?"

His finger was poised not far from his face. He looked at it, somewhat surprised and embarrassed. I felt sorry for him. He'd done it unconsciously. But it was disgusting. "Is something upsetting you?" he asked.

"Yes. Well, it's a bit upsetting. Don't you think?"

"What do you think?"

"I just told you. I think it's a little upsetting."

Now, the doctor removed his glasses and gestured with them. "Are you often so openly hostile with people, William?"

"I'm not hostile."

"If I may say so, you are."

"All I did, I asked you very nicely to stop picking your nose in front of me because, to tell you the truth, I find it offensive. Is that so unreasonable?"

The doctor took a deep, noisy breath, composing himself.

"It's just good manners," I said.

"I might have — this is silly even discussing this. But I might have brushed my nose at one point because it itched. No more."

"I can't believe this."

"What? What's wrong, William?"

"You were picking your nose. And now you deny it."

"Yes, I could have let your remark pass," he was becoming more brazen, "but I think it's important, if we're going to accomplish anything together, that ours is a relationship based on reality and honesty."

"Jesus Christ."

"Are you angry, William?"

"How much longer do I have to be here?" I leaned back, allowing my eyes to go unfocused. I'd been anxious to cooperate. I had an insane dream. Dr. Divitre and I become fast friends. I impress him with my even temper and humor. He stands up in court and shocks Weisberg by saying, "In my opinion, the defendant is not guilty. He couldn't hurt a fly." But this was a dream.

Divitre's purpose was no different than the assistant district attorney's. I was being tailored to fit a prison cell. In a matter of days they expected to have me in it.

I arrived early in the afternoon at Lincoln's Department Store, settling in the coffee shop, watching for Kathleen. How would she look after more than a year? I used to drive past the apartment, occasionally catching sight of her through the front window. But I hadn't done that in a long while, since before Judy.

She was extremely well dressed. That went with the job. She came through Appliances and Hardware swinging her arms, gold on one wrist, an elegant pendant watch around her neck.

How was I to greet her? I was suddenly excited and afraid. Standing, I took her hand, "Hello, Kathleen," and kissed her as she turned a cheek to me. "You look good." But she was noticeably older. My appearance seemed to shock her. She stared.

"You think I look good?" she sat down. "Thank you."

"You've lost weight. Well, since I last saw you."

"I jog." She looked critically at my stomach. "You should try it."

"Are you still in ladies' underwear?"

"Er, there is no such department here. And never was. I used to be in Sleepwear and Intimate Apparel if that's what you mean. But I'm no longer in that department. In fact, I'm now supervisor over it and several others."

"Supervisor?"

"But I might be quitting soon," she said. "I might take a year off. Travel. Go to Europe maybe. Anyway, it's one possibility. Arthur's been talking about relocating in Texas. According to him that's the place to go. Texas. Everything is Texas, Texas."

"Arthur?"

"Of course, you never met Arthur."

"No," I said.

"Well, come on, Bill. You didn't think I'd joined a convent, did you?"

"I didn't say anything."

"He wants to marry me. But, just now, I don't want to get involved in that again, marriage."

"I know how you feel."

"Not that I regret our marriage. I don't. I look on it as a learning experience. It was valuable in that sense."

"It was. It was. And we had some good times. Didn't we?"

"So. What can I do for you, Bill?"

"Well," I cleared my throat, "I have to talk to you about something. I don't know how to put this. You know, we talked on the phone about this trouble I'm in."

"When I first read it I was sick. I couldn't believe it was you."

"Neither could I. Because it isn't me. This thing is all a terrible, awful mistake."

She nodded slowly, hair in stiff, auburn bangs bumping her forehead.

"The thing is, I couldn't hurt anyone, Kath. You know me. I have my faults, sure. But I never hurt you, did I?"

"You were never violent."

"So. The thing is, I need your help, Kathleen."

"What can I do?" she asked.

"Testify."

"Testify? Me? How can I testify?"

"As a character witness." I handed her Coughlin's card. "This is my lawyer. He can explain what you do. Well, basically all you do is tell them about my character. You know, I'm a peaceful guy. Tell them, I don't know, tell them how I gave blood every year. Like that. It'll have a real positive effect."

"A positive effect on who?" she asked.

"On the jury."

"You mean, I say all this in court?"

"Well, yeah."

"In court? With reporters and everything there?"

"Kath, I'm on trial for murder here."

"I'm not saying I won't do it. But you're asking a lot. I have to think."

"Think?" I asked. "What's there to think about?"

"Well, for one thing, my name should not be messed up in this. It's bad enough my mother calls whenever you're in the paper, but a lot of my friends don't even know I was married before. That's behind me. You're behind me."

"Kathleen. Do you think it was easy for me to come here?"

"My life is finally, finally getting itself straightened out. Getting involved in this, well, I just have to think about it."

"You believe me, Kath? I mean, when I tell you I'm innocent?"

"Just don't pressure me. I don't like to be pressured. Maybe you learned at least that much in two years."

"I had nothing to do with this. I need help to clear myself."

"I just want time to think."

"Do you want me to beg? Is that it, Kathleen? Do you hate me so much? Still?"

"Don't flatter yourself."

"You blame me for the divorce. Don't you?"

"I don't care to discuss it."

"It wasn't my fault, Kath."

"I suppose it was mine?"

"I was willing to try. Right to the end I was willing."

"I don't believe I'm having this argument. Again," she told the wall. "I don't believe it."

This was all very familiar. *Prove that you care* had been the battle cry of our marriage. An extra night at the department store was good for a screaming match; an overflowing pail of garbage became a test of wills. With Kathleen, nothing could be taken at face value, not even a murder trial.

"I never should have come here." I felt suddenly limp. "I knew you'd say no. I knew it."

"I haven't said no."

"I'm not surprised. If you'd stayed by me in the first place, if you'd cared, I wouldn't be in this mess now. I wouldn't be in all this trouble."

"Maybe they should arrest me," she said.

"Go ahead and make jokes, but pardon me if I don't laugh. Going to jail has really screwed up my sense of humor."

"God," she snorted. "Poor Billy."

For a while we avoided looking at each other. We never had learned the art of fighting, each with a knack for using the wrong weapons at the wrong time. Well, what a fiasco. "I'm going to leave." I stood. "I'm sorry I came here. I'm even sorry for what I said. It's like you say, I'm no longer any concern of yours."

"Just go away." She patted her pockets, searching for tissues. "Go away and leave me alone."

"Forget I even came here. I seem to be bad luck for a lot of people lately."

"Bastard." She blew her nose and waved me off.

I'd handled it wrong, all wrong, losing my temper in spite of myself. Fighting with Kathleen was like riding a bicycle, it all came back so easily. Coughlin would not be happy.

"In a few days," Damien Coughlin stood in his tiny office, "we'll go to court. How do you feel about that? Nervous?"

"Yeah. I guess. Yeah. I'm nervous."

"Well, don't be. Preparation is the most important element of any defense. And we will be prepared. Today I want you to review your relationship with Mrs. Klijner and your actions on the day she disappeared. Understand?"

"Again?"

"Don't make speeches. Don't give opinions. Just tell what happened. Everything that happened. Whether it seems important or not."

I outlined the course of my affair with Judy, including in great detail that last day.

"And on this day of her disappearance," Coughlin asked, "you went to the Klijner house twice?"

"That's right. The first time I went over to pick up that stuff of Judy's, a couple of suitcases and a bureau. A little bureau. I didn't want to go over there. She insisted. And, well, I guess I had to bring the car back. But that took a minute. Dropping it off. So, now that I think of it, I guess I was over there three times."

"What happened to those things? The suitcases and bureau?"

"I assume the police got them. I left them in my apartment and the police probably took them when they searched my house. They stole my television, you know?" I had told this story, it seemed, a hundred times. But I answered my lawyer's questions as carefully as possible.

"The way I figure it," I concluded, "the first time, when I went to get the stuff, taking her car, she was probably there. In the house. Maybe she was already dead. I figure Roy was in there too. He heard me coming. And he was in there with her body. I was knocking on the door and he was inside, praying I'd go away."

"You think Klijner killed his wife? You still think that?" Coughlin asked.

"I do."

"Well, I have certain problems, certain questions with that. For example, why did he kill her? I'm asking why. The assistant district attorney and the jury will ask the same thing if we introduce this question. What was the direct and compelling provocation for this serious crime?"

"That's easy. She was running out on him. With me. He took a nutty and killed her. I mean, that's obvious."

"It might be obvious to you," the lawyer arranged his notes, "but to me it's only maybe. I'd rather not go to court with maybes. If we could prove she had, in fact, agreed to run away with you, that bit of evidence might make Klijner's motive easier to sell. Unfortunately, even that can't be proved."

"Well, why not?" I asked. "What about all her stuff she gave me? Suitcases and stuff. Doesn't that prove she was running away with me?"

"The prosecution is going to say you stole those to make a murder look like a robbery."

"But Klijner did it, for Christ's sake. I'm sure he did it."

"You may be right," Coughlin conceded. "But I'd rather not openly accuse a man without some proof. That could backfire on us. Especially where we run head-on into a solid alibi. My feeling is this. We can suggest that Klijner is guilty only by carefully, subtly planting that idea in the jurors' minds. But an attack on Klijner, I think, would be counterproductive. The prosecutor would quickly counterattack and ruin us. You can see that, surely."

"Oh, sure." I was angry and frustrated. "Except I'm not so impressed with Klijner's alibi." I now related the incident with Mrs. Gallagher. Coughlin listened in mounting fascination.

"You did that?" he said finally, ears bright red. "You went to her house?"

"Sure. How else was I going to talk to her?"

He stared at me, his old, balding head bobbing.

"What? Why?" I asked.

"You're harassing the district attorney's witness. That's going to land you right back in jail."

"Well," I asked, "how else am I going to talk to her?"

"You don't talk to her. If anyone talks to her I do."

"Well, I think she's lying, Mr. Coughlin. She tried to shoot me. How about that?"

"In her place I'd shoot you myself."

"But I'm not kidding. She shot at me. Something like that. It should get her in trouble. Not me."

"Were there witnesses?"

"Well, no," I admitted.

"You take my advice, you stay away from those people. We're in enough difficulty as it is. We've got no better than a one in twenty chance of winning this case. Don't make it worse."

One in twenty? Did he really mean it? I was afraid to ask.

"Is this how you plan to dress in court?" he asked.

"What? . . . No." I was dressed for the cold in a sweater, jeans and sneakers. "I got a suit at home."

"A new suit?"

"No," I said. "Well, a good suit. It's a good suit."

"You want to look smart. You want to wear something stylish, but conservative. Avoid the loud and flamboyant. Dress like the governor."

"It's a good suit I got. I — I just don't have money for anything new. I don't have much money. You know? I haven't been working."

"Well, if you need money for clothes I can lend you a few dollars."

"That's very good of you."

"Now," Coughlin said, "before we wrap this up is there anything you want to ask me?"

"Well, yeah, I want to know if I'm going to the stand definitely. You know, to testify?"

"What do you think we've been preparing for the last two hours?"

"I just wanted to be sure."

"You can't be forced to testify." He moved for the door. "You have your fifth amendment right to remain silent and no one can make any inference from that, legally speaking. However, practically, the jury will probably be influenced by any reluctance to defend yourself."

"I want to defend myself," I said. "Tape or no tape."

"Good."

"The thing is, as I see it, they've got a lot of evidence, circumstantial evidence, against me. All I've got, so far, is my own word. I have to testify. Or I've got no defense. I'm no lawyer. But that's how it looks to me. Maybe I'm wrong."

Coughlin said nothing.

In the *Suburban-Citizen* my story was front-page news again, including a photo. "Klijner Murder Trial Opens Tomorrow." I was given the lead: "Alleged killer Bill Martell goes on trial in superior court tomorrow in the disappearance of Judith Anne Klijner." The story nowhere mentioned my previous affiliation with that newspaper.

What stung was the expression, "Alleged killer Bill Martell. . . ." How musical. "Killer Bill." It had a ring to it, like Hammering Hank, Bullet Bob. People would remember it.

The scab-infested *Suburban-Citizen* was trying to bury me. Nothing new in that.

Ten

THE COURTHOUSE WAS CLUTTERED with old men in dull blue uniforms and sheriff's badges. I spotted at least five in various places in the courtroom, watching, contributing nothing I could see. "Where is everybody?" I asked. The gallery was practically empty. With its grand, cross-beamed ceiling two stories above, the room echoed every noise.

"We're only picking the jury today," Coughlin glared at me, "pretty boring stuff."

"Something wrong, Mr. Coughlin?"

"That suit."

"My suit? What about it?"

"It's a summer suit. And this isn't summer."

I looked at myself. Admittedly, I was out of place in pastel blue. "No one'll notice."

"I wouldn't mind," the lawyer grumbled, "but I said I'd lend you money for a new suit."

"Well, I'm sorry, but I went to get a new suit and they wouldn't take my credit card. I was over limit. And it was too late to call you."

Coughlin turned away, muttering.

Judge Harvey was a small, fat man, my idea of a used car salesman. He tended to ignore me, as if minimizing my importance. Nonetheless, I was the star of this show.

As it turned out, my trial was always sparsely attended. Most of the spectators were directly involved in the case. Sometimes reporters attended, sometimes not. Roy Klijner usually came, accompanied by his sister, Agnes Gallagher. While he was a picture of grief, she seemed mean and tough. If anyone was a potential murderer she was. I was nervous even turning my back on her.

"That's that Mrs. Gallagher," I told Coughlin.

"You stay away from her."

"Don't worry. She gives me the creeps."

Court opened with an elaborate, singsong introduction by one of the officers. "Hear ye, hear ye," he deadpanned, "all those having anything to do with the honorable justice of the superior court of the county of Norfolk, draw near and you shall be heard. God save the Commonwealth." Archaic language remains popular in the superior court.

The potential jurors were brought for examination, one by one.

"How's this work?" I asked several times.

"We have a number of challenges," Coughlin finally answered. "In fact, I can reject a certain number of these people for no reason, because I don't like the way they comb their hair, because they walk funny."

I was surprised at the seating arrangement. Weisberg, the prosecutor, was closest to the judge, his table abutting the clerk's rostrum. This seemed unfair, giving the jurors the impression of a connection between the judge and prosecutor. (Who takes complaints on a thing like that?) My attorney was seated farther away. I was still farther, in a docklike front-row seat. Coughlin was forced literally to lean over backward just to speak to me.

As my lawyer and I conferred at his table, Weisberg came over, smiling. "Where in hell you get that suit?"

"I stole it."

Coughlin put up his hand, silencing me.

"We're still willing to bargain. Your client knows that, Damien?"

"I tell him whenever I see him, Charlie." The old man smiled sourly. "Every day."

"Well . . ." The assistant district attorney moved away, ready to deal with the first potential juror.

"What you said the other day," I whispered, "about, you know, about having a one in twenty chance. Is that true?"

"I said that? Well, I've been tired lately."

"Then it isn't true?"

"Of course not," he said. "Why? Thinking about Weisberg's deal?"

"No. For the millionth time. No."

A blue-haired woman with a huge handbag took the stand. The clerk, a natty dresser with sideburns and thick, red mustache, asked a list of questions devised earlier by both the prosecutor and defense counsel to test for possible prejudice. One of Weisberg's questions measured attitudes toward adultery. "Can you reach a decision in this case without regard to the sexual proclivities of those involved, judging only as to the facts of the case?"

"Yes," the woman replied simply, wearing the most benign expression, lips in a perpetual grin. Perhaps she was pleased by all the attention. I studied her, thinking of my mother.

"How do you decide?" I asked Coughlin. "I mean, how do you decide which people you want on the jury?"

"It's largely a matter of experience," he said proudly. "You get a feel for this after you've been at it as many years as I have. Oh, today they have professionals who do nothing but pick jurors. They're specialists and that's their job, picking juries. They get all the statistics and put them into a computer. It's very involved, what they do. I guess they've had good luck with that. But the expense. Besides, I don't think they have much to offer over a good, experienced attorney. For my part, I try to eliminate people predisposed to believe the prosecutor's case. People with an excess of respect for authority. Maybe they work for the government. Or they wear those little American flag pins. Call everybody sir."

When the clerk finished with the blue-haired lady, Coughlin stood to announce, "Challenged."

The woman reacted with a pout, taking the rejection personally. In seconds she was whisked away. "But, what was wrong with her?" I muttered. "I thought she was nice."

"Shhh." Coughlin put a finger to his lips.

Other jurors were rejected for more obvious reasons. They admitted reading of the case in the *Suburban-Citizen* or hearing of it on television. One man was excused after showing the judge his ticket to Bermuda. "I wonder if that would work for me?" I asked Coughlin.

"Shhh."

It was not going to be easy, picking sixteen jurors. Compounding the problem, the court proceeded at a pace more suited to the Bermuda vacation. Sitting between ten and four, the judge recessed a minimum of three times, for a total of over two hours. Often, my case was interrupted for arraignments. On some days, court let out as early as one o'clock. From the beginning, I found these delays annoying. I was anxious to have it over and settled.

"Sit up." Coughlin approached me during one recess.

"Huh?"

"Sit up straight. Look alive. Sit here with that hangdog expression and people are going to see a guilty man. Listen," he squeezed my shoulder, "you've got your whole life to be tired. Be awake in here."

The selection of jurors made no sense to me. One day, Coughlin accepted a second blue-haired lady. When I asked for an explanation he merely waved. "Later." This would be his attitude throughout. The idea of consulting me for my opinion never entered his head.

After three days, the jury was selected, ten men and six

women, including four alternates. They were retired people, professionals, a bus driver, a beautician, and so on.

"The best we could hope for," Coughlin said. "They'll give us a fair shake."

"They look mean to me."

It was growing dark as I moved to the back door. I thought I had eluded any reporters, but two shadows lurked in the corridor. "Hey, hot shot." It was Matteo, the cop. "Where'd you get the Day-Glo suit?" I knew his voice at once.

"I don't talk to you. I don't talk to cops."

"No problem." He moved from the shadows. "No one wants you to talk. It's better this time if you listen."

"Listen? To what?"

"What do you think?" He was grinning in my face. "We're selling tickets to the policemen's ball."

"Really? I didn't think you cops had balls."

"Funny. Still a real funny guy. Halfway to prison and he still finds time to make jokes, keep us amused."

Someone was behind me. I could feel him at my back, the second man. And suddenly, I was being urged down a dark hallway. "Got a problem with you, Bill." It was Reardon, calm, fatherly as ever.

"A problem with me?" My voice cracked. We were alone.

"You've been out bothering people, Bill. You been making a goddamn pest of yourself. That's the problem, you know?"

"Bothering who?" If I could push past them and run . . .

Matteo brushed lint from my lapel. "You've put on weight, hotshot."

"Hands off."

"Better start watching what you eat."

"Look, I don't have to listen to you guys. You know?"

"You don't want to listen to us?" Matteo feigned injury.

"Really, Bill," Reardon said, "if you didn't want to listen to us you shouldn't have gone off bothering Mrs. Gallagher."

"I didn't bother her."

"We must have heard wrong," Reardon said. "We heard you broke into her house. You didn't do that?"

"I didn't break in. I walked in. She opened the door."

"Then you were there? You were at Mrs. Gallagher's house?"

"So?" I asked. "I was there. So what of it?"

"Not good, Bill. Really, that's not good. You shouldn't be bothering that poor woman."

"Poor woman? Hey, you guys should go talk to her. That crazy lady took a shot at me. And she slammed a door on my foot besides. Now, that's assault, isn't it?"

"She slammed the door on your foot?" Matteo asked.

"Yeah."

"Which foot?"

"I don't know. This one." I pointed.

Matteo stepped closer. Both of them pushed against me. Matteo placed his heel over the arch of my foot and leaned forward. The pain was instant and intense.

"Hey . . . hey, cut it out. Hey —"

"Excuse me," Matteo said.

"Get . . . off my . . ." I couldn't pull my foot away. Trying, I managed only to lose my balance. I fell against the wall.

"Don't yell," he gasped in my ear. "I hate loud noises."

"Leave Mrs. Gallagher alone," Reardon said. "Leave Roy Klijner alone. You've hurt these people enough. Understand, Bill?"

It was a spike cutting into me. My heel wiggled. My arms were pinned by their bodies. My eyes teared. I lost my breath, could feel my face burning. This wasn't right. "Ahhh . . . get off . . ."

"We want to be sure you understand," Reardon said.

Matteo began grinding his heel into my big toe. Something inside seemed to be crunching.

"Tell me you won't bother these people ever again. I want you to tell me that."

"Okay . . . okay."

Matteo stepped off. I slumped against the wall, but the two policemen held me up.

"This may seem harsh," Reardon said. "But we're only trying to avoid a lot of trouble in the future."

"Yeah." Matteo was gleeful.

"You've got to be careful from now on, Bill. We're keeping an eye on you."

They backed away. I staggered. My throbbing leg could barely support me.

"I think he understands," Reardon said.

"Get up." Matteo propped me against the wall. "Come on, you're not hurt."

"Get . . . get your fucking hands off me, greaseball."

"Hey!" Matteo's fist came up.

"No." Reardon pulled him away. "He got the message. He knows he made a serious mistake. And next time he'll have no excuse."

I hobbled home, an ugly gray mark on my black shoe. Working the gas pedal and brake with my heel. I didn't want to see the damage. But, as I climbed the stairwell, the pain was unbearable. I knew I'd been hurt badly. At my toilet, I pulled the shoe off. The bottom of my sock was dark red with blood. I emptied the shoe, thick red streams pouring down the drain. "Oh . . . jeez . . . jeez . . ." I pulled the sock off, not wanting to look.

The nail was hideously mangled, at a virtual right angle to the big toe.

The emergency room was empty when I arrived. Two nurses put me on a cot, pulling off my sock. "It looks bad," the doctor said. "But it's not as bad as it looks."

"It hurts." I watched the huge light above. What was to become of me? When they can rough you up. Anytime they feel like it.

"You're going to lose most of the nail. But it'll grow back. It'll bother you a few days. You'll be okay if you keep it clean, don't let it get infected. How'd it happen, by the way?"

"Guy stepped on it."

"Must have been a big guy."

"A cop. He was a cop."

The doctor smiled at this, as if I were joking.

Later, I heard a commotion and the emergency room filled with people, including police. A stretcher was wheeled in. A teenaged girl, with long, straight dark hair followed it, like a mourner at a funeral. She was cut above the eye, dribbling blood down the side of her face, crying, "I'm sorry. I'm sorry."

A nurse took her aside and forced her to answer questions about Blue Cross, names and addresses. Lying, watching the ceiling, I listened. "Is Barbara going to be okay?"

"The doctor is seeing to her."

"It's all my fault."

"It was an accident."

"Is Barbara going to be okay?"

"I already answered that."

Covered with blankets, Barbara didn't move at all. She was wheeled into the elevator. The doctor scarcely looked at the new arrivals. He was intent, bandaging my toe. "You know, doctor, if you want to go take care of them? I can wait."

"That's okay." He continued winding the bandages.

When I left, the nearly hysterical girl was in the waiting room, still bleeding. "Let's fix that cut, dear," the nurse coaxed.

"Take Barbara first."

"Barbara's already gone to the O.R."

"It's my fault," she whined. "Oh, God. It's all my fault."

I drove around awhile. For some reason that girl stuck in my mind, reminding me of an accident I'd seen months ago.

My lawyer wasn't surprised on Monday when I explained the reason for my limp. "Let me check this out." He went off to the assistant district attorney. As I waited, the wall clock ticked loudly in the empty courtroom, giving the wrong time.

"Well." Coughlin returned. "He says there's nothing to it."

"Nothing to what?" I spun to see Weisberg arriving at the back of the room. "Don't tell me he says they didn't do it?"

"Well . . ."

"How can he say that? How can he lie like that? They pushed me into the corner and stomped on my foot. They deny it?"

"Evidently."

"You asked them? The two cops? You asked them yourself?"

"Not them," he explained. "Weisberg."

"They're a couple of damn liars and him too, probably." I kept turning to look at Weisberg. He stared placidly ahead. "They're all liars. They are. You don't think I stepped on my own foot. Do you?"

"No." Coughlin patted my shoulder.

"Well, what can we do about it? We just let them get away with it?"

"I know how you feel," he spoke softly. "But you're in a difficult position. We can file a complaint. Just, I doubt it'd get far. They'd simply come back with this business over at Mrs. Gallagher's, which puts us at a stalemate. Wouldn't you say? I think the most effective step is to let me talk to Charlie again this afternoon and I'll give him hell on this."

"And that's it?"

"Again," Coughlin shrugged, "you have no witnesses."

Weisberg got off to a slow, stuttering start. Approaching the jury, he fumbled, then dropped his folder. Papers flew across the room. Weisberg and others went down to collect them.

"We, ah, will prove that William P. Martell did murder Judith . . . ah, Anne Klijner, dispose of the body, and was literally, was caught literally red-handed. With blood on his hands. Witnesses will testify to finding him fleeing the scene upon the arrival of the police."

Radiators in the old courtroom hissed noisily. The room grew very hot. One older juror appeared to doze with her eyes open. I watched her breathe, chest heaving rhythmically, hypnotically.

Coughlin, in contrast to his younger adversary, was not the least hesitant, but vigorous and sharp. "Today you have an opportunity to save a man from a great injustice. Do we all know the meaning of circumstantial evidence? Because of circumstantial evidence the wrong man stands accused today. . . . Remember, this isn't television. I'm not Perry Mason. I'm much better-looking, for one thing." There was soft laughter. "Unlike Perry Mason, I can't produce the real criminal. In real life, criminals don't confess on the witness stand. And my job is not to solve the mystery of Judy Klijner's disappearance. But I will show that Bill Martell had nothing to do with it."

Good. I wanted to cheer. Finally, someone was speaking out for me.

Daniel O'Connor did not wear his police uniform on the witness stand. His deep, authoritarian voice was the loudest, clearest noise in the room. He recalled the night a prowler was reported at the Klijner house. "After circling the building, I sent my partner around the back. I approached the house from the front."

"What did you then observe?" Weisberg asked.

"Well, I heard a noise and saw a person at the front door."

"Was the door open at this time?"

"Yes," the policeman said.

"The front door?" Weisberg asked.

"Yes."

"And where were you, officer, at this time?"

"I was down on the ground. Off the porch. Standing on the ground."

"Did the person in the doorway make any obvious motion or gesture or say anything to make you aware that he had seen you?"

"Well. He looked right at me. He looked right at me and he sort of started."

"He started?"

"Like this." The witness made a sudden, abrupt movement. "Exactly like that."

What a liar.

"Now," Weisberg continued, "the man on the porch. In the doorway. Could you identify him?"

"I could."

"Do you see him in the courtroom?"

"He's right there." O'Connor pointed. "In the light blue suit."

"Let the record show the witness points to the defendant, William Martell."

I shrugged, almost smiled. It's disconcerting to have people pointing at you, talking about you as though you have no feelings.

"You saw Mr. Martell in the doorway?" Weisberg resumed.

"Yes, I did."

"And he saw you? Apparently."

"Yes, he did."

"What did he then do next?" Weisberg asked.

"He started running."

"In which direction was he running?"

"Away. For the street," the officer said.

"How fast was he running?"

"He was running. Really moving. As fast as he could for a few steps. He only got a few steps because I jumped him. Stopped him, making my arrest."

"After you arrested him, did you engage in conversation?"

"Yes," O'Connor said.

"What did he say to you and what did you say to him?"

"He said, 'I give up.' And I told him he was under arrest."

"He said, 'I give up'?"

"Yes."

"As though he expected to be arrested."

"Objection," Coughlin bellowed.

"After the arrest," Weisberg said, "did you go into the house?"

"Yes. My partner was already in there. So, when some other

officers arrived and took custody of the suspect I did go inside."

"What did you observe inside?"

"Ah, blood. Everywhere. In the kitchen, I mean. It was everywhere in the kitchen."

Weisberg displayed large, bright color pictures of the bloodied kitchen. I caught only a glimpse, and even from a distance it left me dizzy, back in time, fumbling in the dark of her house. "Officer O'Connor, is this a fair and accurate representation of the kitchen as you found it?" the prosecutor asked.

"Yes."

The photos were allowed as evidence and passed among the jurors.

Damien Coughlin asked a few questions for the defense. "Officer, you say the defendant was running from the house? Do you know why he was running?"

"I assume he was running because he saw me."

"Assume?" My attorney turned importantly to the jury. "Assume?"

"Yes."

"And one more question," Coughlin said. "When you went inside and discovered all this blood, did you discover whose blood it was?"

"No."

"Did you discover a body?"

"No."

As soon as the policeman left the stand, the judge glanced eagerly to the clock. A recess was called. O'Connor's testimony had taken less than an hour. "How do you feel?" Coughlin asked.

I shrugged. "I'd just like to get this over with. Why do they drag it on and on?"

After the recess, Weisberg called Linda Jellison, Judy's teenaged neighbor. "You called the police?" the prosecutor asked.

"Yes."

"Why did you call the police?"

"I saw this man who —"

"Speak up, dear," Weisberg said.

"I saw this man around Judy's house."

"You saw a man?"

"That's right," she said. "I saw a man."

"Did you get a good look at this man?"

"I did. Yes."

"Were you outside when you saw him?" Weisberg asked.

"Was he outside?"

"No, you. Were you outside?"

"No, sir," she said. "I was at the window. In our front room."

"How far away was the man you saw?"

"Not so far. About, I guess, about thirty feet."

"Could you identify this man?" the prosecutor asked.

"Yes."

"Is he here in this room?"

"Right there," she motioned at me, "that's him. He walked right near our house and I saw him good. He's put on weight, but that's him."

"I didn't get that," Coughlin said. "After, 'I saw him good.' "

"She says he put on weight," Weisberg called over his shoulder, "but that's him."

I sucked in my stomach.

"Now," the prosecutor continued, "Miss Jellison, tell us what you observed while watching Martell."

"I looked out my window. And he was like looking all over. I don't know. He just, just sort of acted real nervous. He walked past the Klijner house once. And then he turned around and came back. And, then, he went up to the porch. And he walked right in there. In the door. I didn't see anyone let him in."

Roy Klijner was sworn in. I could study him now. He looked awful, his face thin, pale, and lined. The way a killer looks.

"Mr. Klijner." Weisberg treated him with exaggerated care.

"Can you tell me, on the day your wife disappeared, did you have a conversation with her in the morning?"

"Yes." Klijner avoided looking at me.

"To the best of your memory, what did she say to you and what did you say to her?"

"Well, Judy'd been talking about going back to school. She wanted to look into that . . ."

"Jeez," I muttered to Coughlin, "a lie."

"Quiet." He turned around, waving.

"She wanted to drive in town and talk to someone about taking some courses," Klijner continued. "Anyway, I agreed to take Mike, our little one, to take Mike to my sister's for the day. My sister's very close to the boy, you see, and she had the week off."

"And did you drive your son to your sister's house?"

"Yes."

"What time did you depart from your own house?" Weisberg asked.

"We left around quarter to nine. Mike and me. And we got there, at my sister's, around nine. Maybe a little later, after nine."

"Mr. Klijner, can you tell us, briefly, where you were for the rest of the day?"

"Well, at my sister's house. There was no reason for me to go back home. To an empty house. We were there till around twenty to four and then I had to go to work. And I got to work just before four. And stayed there, until, well, until the police called."

"After you said goodbye to your wife, around quarter to nine, did you see her again, at any time, for the rest of the day?"

"No. I never saw her again. Ever."

Weisberg left that remark hanging while he shuffled through his notes. The jurors were glued sympathetically to Klijner. One woman, middle-aged with thick glasses, had clasped her hands as though praying. Meanwhile, one of the court officers was glaring at me, lips pursed in utter contempt.

"Mr. Klijner, did you and your wife ever quarrel?"

"Occasionally."

"Would you describe yours as a happy marriage?" the prosecutor asked.

"Yes. We were happy. Don't get me wrong, we had disagreements like anybody else. But we enjoyed each other. We were close. I never realized how close . . ." His voice dropped, became barely audible. ". . . since she's not there . . ." He shook his head. Eyes unfocused, speaking quietly, he was an effective witness.

I made a coughlike groan of disbelief. Everyone glared at me. Except Klijner, staring straight ahead. The judge looked down, disapproving. Coughlin leaned from his seat. "You're not doing yourself any favors. You only antagonize people with that stuff."

"Tell me, Mr. Klijner," Weisberg resumed, "did you observe signs of unhappiness from your wife? During this period. Just prior to her disappearance?"

"No."

"Do you have any reason to believe she has run away?"

"None whatsoever."

"Had she ever run away before?" Weisberg asked. "Gone off without telling you where?"

"No. Never. Not for a day even."

"Was she, just prior to her disappearance, was she behaving in an eccentric manner? Did she behave as though unbalanced in some way?"

"No."

Weisberg nodded with satisfaction. "Now, I want to bring your attention, Mr. Klijner, to the objects we have on my desk over there." He pointed to Judy's two suitcases and small bureau. "Do you recognize them?"

"My wife's things. Her suitcases. Her bureau."

"What kind of bureau is that? It's kind of an odd size."

"Judy used it for her socks and underthings and stuff," Klijner said.

"Earlier in the day, did you get a chance in my office to

examine the contents of the suitcases and the little bureau?"

"Yes, I did."

"What is the contents of the suitcases and bureau?" Weisberg asked.

"Things taken from my house on the day Judy disappeared. There's a silver tea service, you know, the pitcher and creamer and some old china that my wife prized . . . ah, Water —"

"Anything else?"

"Waterford crystal. Jewelry. Silverware. Brass candlesticks. Things like that."

Weisberg opened the drawers of the bureau and one of the suitcases. Coughlin was at his side, examining the contents. "Your honor," asked the assistant district attorney, "perhaps we could have the jurors come over and examine these items, which we would like introduced as evidence, if no one has objections."

"We can delay that until tomorrow," Judge Harvey decided. "I think we'll recess at this point. . . ."

"Can't we ever get this over with?" I complained as the courtroom emptied. It wasn't even three o'clock. "I'm sick of this delay, delay, delay. I feel like a part-time job around here."

"That's the way it's done," Coughlin said soothingly. "Relax. Get used to it."

Of course, I couldn't sleep that night. Klijner's lies kept me tense and frustrated, pacing and eating. I imagined myself on the witness stand, rebutting him. Given the chance to tell my story, I could win them all over. At long last, someone would hear me.

But would my day ever come? These delays seemed specifically designed to drive me insane. Coughlin said nothing the following morning, but I knew I looked worse than the day before, harried and lined. My concentration was deteriorating steadily as well. And my anger made me unpredictable, likely to speak out at times when silence would serve me better.

"Mr. Klijner," the prosecutor resumed questioning where he had ended it the previous day, "do you find any clothes in these drawers? Or in the suitcases?"

"Sweaters. The crystal is wrapped in a couple of sweaters. So is the silver."

"No other clothes can be found in the suitcases or in the bureau?" Weisberg asked.

"Not really."

"Did your wife often pack these articles, dishes and jewelry, when taking a trip, going away for a long time?"

"No," Klijner replied.

"Would she be likely to leave home with nothing to wear but sweaters and silverware?"

"Your honor," Coughlin called, "if I may, I have problems with that. My brother seems to be asking a question, but he is actually stating a conclusion. An erroneous conclusion. May I point out, it is not uncommon, though it is perhaps unfortunate, that separating spouses grab the silver on their way out the door."

Some laughed at this remark. "Strike the last question," Judge Harvey instructed.

"Mr. Klijner," Weisberg portrayed some outrage at the laughter, "putting the witty remarks aside, what became of the things your wife usually kept in that little bureau?"

"Her socks and underthings. I found them in a pile beside our bed."

For a moment, Weisberg let us dwell on that pathetic picture.

"And could you estimate the value of the articles now in the suitcases and the bureau?"

"Oh, well, I couldn't be sure. I'd have to guess. Certainly they're worth a few thousand dollars with a diamond ring and some other jewelry. Maybe eight or ten thousand."

Coughlin began ordering his notes for cross-examination. Klijner looked uncomfortable for the first time, shifting in his seat. He was self-conscious in avoiding even a glance at me.

"You gotta really nail this guy," I told Coughlin.

"Aha."

"Jeez. He lied a dozen times up there. Everything he said. He gave a whole phony idea of what was going on."

The defense attorney moved off. "Mr. Klijner, were you aware of the love affair between your wife and Mr. Martell?"

"I wouldn't call it a love affair. An affair."

"But you knew about it?"

"I knew about it."

"Then your married life wasn't exactly the untroubled idyll you've been describing."

"I never said that," Klijner turned to address the jury. "We had our troubles. But we —"

"Mr. Klijner," Coughlin cut him off, "when did you find out about the affair with Bill Martell?"

"Ah, after it was over. She confessed the whole thing."

"How did you feel about it?"

"I was sorry it happened," Klijner said. "I was sorry."

"How did you feel toward your co-worker, Bill Martell?"

"No different. My wife never told me it was him. I couldn't have guessed it was him. I thought we were friends. I always —"

"Just answer the questions," Coughlin said, "please."

I rolled my eyes and looked away. What a performance Klijner was giving.

"Did your wife have any other affairs?"

"Not that I knew of." Klijner shrugged.

"Could she have had other affairs without your knowledge?"

"I suppose. It's possible."

"No more questions." Coughlin sat down.

It was beyond belief. "Hey," I muttered until he turned to look at me, "why don't you challenge him?" The old man came to my side. "Why don't you challenge him?"

"I did challenge him. I introduced considerable doubt on the matter of his story. I raised the possibility of other lovers, other men with motives."

"But he lied up there. That shit yesterday about going, Judy going back to school, for one. She wasn't going to school. That was a lie. A goddamn lie. Why don't you challenge him on it? Ask him for names. Who were the appointments with? At what schools? What were the courses in? Ask him enough questions you can trip him up."

"No, I've put doubt in the minds of the jury," Coughlin explained. "That's enough for now."

"It's not enough."

"Look, you're upset because the prosecutor is presenting his case and it's a good case. But we knew that. Don't forget, we'll have our turn. That's when we can make points of our own."

"But he's lying," I insisted.

"How do you know he's lying? How do you know she didn't tell him just what he says she told him? Maybe she was the liar."

Coughlin treated me to lunch at a nearby coffee shop. I continued to plead for further questioning of Roy Klijner. "You're all upset," my attorney said. "Try to forget the trial for a little while. Clear your mind of it."

Good advice. And it worked for about two minutes, until I happened to turn and see Weisberg and his assistant at a nearby table. The prosecutor was at ease, attacking a rare roast-beef sandwich with animal enthusiasm. Soon, I would face that man on the stand. His intention was to put me in jail forever. It was hard not to take this personally.

Judy's white-haired mailman, suspiciously named Hatchet, told of seeing her at ten o'clock on the morning of her disappearance. "What did you observe on meeting Mrs. Klijner?" Weisberg asked.

"Well, she was friendly. I gave her the mail and we talked about the weather. We'd had a storm that night, I remember."

"From your own observations, did Mrs. Klijner give any indication that she was under some emotional stress?"

/ 193

"No."

"How well did you know Mrs. Klijner?"

"I saw her most every day. Over a period of two years. Mrs. Klijner was one of the nicer ladies on my route. Always left a big tip at Christmas. Sometimes she'd offer a cup of coffee in the winter. A cool drink in summer."

My landlady, Mrs. Gartland, took the stand. She glared at me with obvious distaste. The jurors saw this. Mrs. Gartland explained how I had arrived at the apartment just before noon in an unfamiliar yellow car. "I knew it wasn't his car. It was a nice car. Clean."

Weisberg showed a picture of Judy's Pinto. "Is this a fair and accurate representation of the car you saw?"

"Yes."

"I show you exhibits six, seven, and eight." The prosecutor gestured to the suitcases and bureau. "Are these the items Martell took from the car?"

"Yes." She seemed quite satisfied. This was one way to evict me.

Meanwhile, Coughlin was suddenly at my side, his hand digging into my shoulder. "You took her car?" he asked urgently.

"I told you that."

His yellowed eyes bulged.

"I must have told you that. I did, Mr. Coughlin."

"Jesus," he muttered softly, "Jesus, Mary and Joseph."

Finally came a short, burly man with great dark hands, Detective Mayes from the state police.

"Detective Mayes," Weisberg was increasingly easy and confident in the courtroom, "you examined Mrs. Klijner's car?"

"Yes."

"What did you find?"

"We found nothing out of the ordinary in the passenger section."

"What about the trunk?" Weisberg asked. "Did you —"

"Yeah. Well, I was getting to that. We looked in the trunk and it was, well, you had blood in there."

At the end of the day, Coughlin and I went to the attorney's consulting room. "I wish you'd told me about taking that car," he said.

"I told you. I know I told you about it."

"You can see how that looks. You took the car. You were seen in the car. Then, it turns up full of blood. You can see how that looks."

For long stretches neither of us spoke. Well, it was bad. Worse than I expected. Finally, my chance had come to save myself. And I was losing.

Coughlin tried to raise my spirits. "We'll have our day."

"The jurors," I said, "sometimes those people would look at me. You know? But by the end of the day, they wouldn't. Some of them."

"He's presenting a good case. No doubt about it. Well, Charlie does a professional job. My God, I get tired." He stretched out, looking every year of his age, no longer vigorous but exhausted. And I had been ruined in there.

The next day's session was cut short by the judge, who had to attend a funeral. Four witnesses were called. Detective Mayes finished his testimony, telling how he'd discovered fingerprints on the phone and a bloody palm print on the kitchen wall of Judy's house. Photos were shown.

A fingerprint expert made a brief appearance, establishing that the bloody prints were mine, as were prints on the car door and trunk. The jurors glanced frequently at my hands. I finally put them at my side.

Weisberg next presented a burly state police chemist named Devlin, who looked vaguely familiar, talking expertly and endlessly about blood. Based on his examination of blood in the kitchen, he placed the time of the attack at "ten to twelve that morning, according to spectroscopic analysis." The blood type was determined to be AB negative.

"Did you run tests on the blood found in the trunk of Mrs. Klijner's car?" the prosecutor asked.

"Yes, sir."

"What blood type was it?"

"AB negative," Devlin said.

"Is that an unusual blood typing?"

"Well, relatively rare. Yes."

"Now, Mr. Devlin, you had access to Mrs. Klijner's medical records?"

"Yes, sir."

"What was her blood type?"

"AB negative."

Weisberg let the jury digest that exchange before asking, "Mr. Devlin, were you present when a scraping of dried blood was taken from the defendant's own hand?"

"Yes, sir. I took it."

"Did you discover the typing of this blood?"

"Type AB negative."

"Was it the defendant's own blood?"

"No, sir. From him, he let us take a blood sample. His blood is O positive."

Finally, a police officer named Grant was produced who had seen me on Hubbard Road the afternoon of Judy's disappearance.

"Could you describe the area?" Weisberg asked.

"It's a state reservation."

"A state reservation. What sort of place is that, officer?"

"In this case, it's a place with trees. Lots of trees, miles of trails. Trails for hiking, but wide enough for cars. Cabins. Swamps."

/ 196

"People?" Weisberg asked.

"Not many. Not on the weekdays, anyway."

"So this would be an ideal place to conceal evidence of a crime?"

"Objection!" Coughlin cried.

"Or even a body."

"Object! Object, your honor!" My lawyer put some vehemence here, but Weisberg had made his point.

Given his chance, Coughlin asked Officer Grant if the Hubbard Road area had been given an extensive search.

"Well, it's a huge area."

"Was it given an extensive search, officer? Please answer yes or no."

"Yes."

"Was a body found?"

"No, sir."

"Then you didn't find Mrs. Klijner?" Coughlin continued.

"No."

"Or any trace of Mrs. Klijner?"

"No."

While all this testimony was not as bad for me as on the previous day, it was bad enough. Resting the Commonwealth's case, Weisberg looked satisfied, even smug. Coughlin's motion for a directed verdict of acquittal was summarily denied by the judge.

"That judge doesn't like me," I told my lawyer.

And the delays and mounting dread over my inevitable trip to the witness box continued to take their toll. I couldn't sleep. I was always tired. Dark pouches and severe lines appeared around my eyes. I could run my fingers through my hair and come away with handfuls of it.

That night, running the shower, I was horrified by screams, a woman, faintly heard. I turned the water off and it stopped.

eleven

IN THE MORNING, Weisberg entered the court smiling. He patted a policeman's protruding gut. "Oh, you should talk," the officer said. Both laughed. The prosecutor was celebrating. Right in front of me.

Coughlin appeared behind him, also smiling, They chatted amiably, the prosecutor and defense attorney. I didn't like it one bit.

Of course there was a delay, this time for a meeting of the grand jury. My trial was postponed until afternoon. Coughlin, Weisberg and I were hustled off to the lobby, where Pam Nealy sat quietly on a bench.

My front row seat was taken by a tall, extremely thin man named José Ruiz. He wore handcuffs and chains around his waist, a surly half-grin on his dark, acne-swept face. Flanked by two officers, he passed us in the hall. Was he in my future?

"I'd just like," I muttered to Coughlin, "I'd just like to have this over with. To have my say and get it decided. Why do they drag it out so?"

I walked Pam down the corridor. "I hate this place," I muttered. "It stinks of lawyers." And they were everywhere, like undertakers in their dark, pressed suits, leaning against the walls, sitting on benches, gossiping, at intervals along the worn, stone corridor. "There's a back way." I pulled her down a small stairway. "You shouldn't be here, Pam. People are going to notice. They'll see us together. That isn't going to be good for you."

"I had to come."

I was happy she had. "How do you think it's going? My case? Well, it'll go a lot better today, I can tell you. Maybe . . . I don't know, after lunch you'll see. It'll get better because we start to give our side, our defense. I'll have to testify. That scares the hell out of me."

From the bottom of the stairwell came a police officer with wide, boxy hips. He looked up, eyes widening with recognition. It was Captain Adair. "Hey, Martell." He smiled malevolently. "It's you. The police reporter."

"Come on," I gasped to Pam, "let's get away from this jerk."

Of course, Adair hadn't forgotten our first meeting and the young girl booked for lewd and lascivious conduct. Just a thing that happened a thousand years ago. I'd written that story and sent it in, thinking I'd done the ethical, professional thing. I'd since changed my ideas on press ethics, but the gloating Adair would not be interested.

"I been following your troubles," he said as we hurried past. "I wanted to tell you something."

Pam looked at him, but I skipped for the exit, head down.

"I'm not going to forget what you did," he called. "I don't care how this trial comes out. I'm not going to forget."

At McDonald's, we ate in the car. "They've had my picture in the paper again," I complained.

"On page ten."

"Yeah. Until the verdict comes down. Then I'll be back on the front page. The verdict. How do you think they'll decide? Well, you haven't been in court. It'll go better, start to go better today. Or did I already tell you that? Jesus. My head's all screwed up lately. I'd have a nervous breakdown, but I can't. Gotta keep my head. Find a way out of this. If there is a way out of this. And I gotta testify. I have to go on that witness stand and make them believe me."

"There's still a good chance," she said.

"What makes you say that?"

". . . Ah, well, you. You said. You start giving your defense today, don't you?"

"Yeah. That's true. Jesus. Jesus, Pam. I wish I had a future. I'd find a way to thank you. Everything you've done. But I don't think I have much of a future, you know?"

"Don't."

"Well, it's true. If I go to jail there isn't much I can do for you. My car. You can have my car, if you like. It looks like hell, but it runs okay."

"I don't want your car, Bill."

"What made you come to court today? I asked you not to come."

"Mr. Coughlin told me to come. I'm supposed to be a character witness."

"Oh."

"I would've come anyway, like yesterday. I would've come, Bill, except you asked me not to."

"You're a wonderful person, Pam. A wonderful, beautiful woman. At night, cause I can't sleep at night. I think about you. Your hair. Your hair's the color of honey almost."

"It's bleached."

"Still. It's beautiful. You've heard that before. Guys must've told you that before." I felt her hair.

Pam couldn't help but smile.

"Jesus, Pam, there's got to be a way out of this. There's got to be something I can do. I don't want to go to jail." I felt close to Pam. Though, for now, we were like Judy and Roy had been, a forced marriage, never knowing what my free choice would be. "I keep thinking about the priest," I said suddenly.

"The priest?"

"Yeah. The one was going to get me to see Judy's old boy-friend, that Bob character. It was funny. First the guy, the boy-friend I mean, he was going to see me. Then he wouldn't. If he was going to see me he had to have a reason. I know the priest figured who I am. And he told this guy. And the guy agreed to see me. And then he changed his mind. Does that all sound funny or what?"

"It sounds funny," she agreed.

"If you were working on a story and some guy gave you a runaround like that, you'd be suspicious, wouldn't you?"

"I'd keep digging, Bill."

"You bet you would. I keep coming back to that priest. Father Ennis. Exactly what he said. I keep trying to remember that. 'Bob won't see you because he's not, he's not . . .' What? No. He said this. He said he won't talk because 'it's no longer neces-sary.' Yeah. That was it. Stuck in my mind because it seemed an odd excuse. But what the Christ does it mean?"

"Have you asked the priest?"

"He won't, he won't talk to me. Either he's scared of me or pissed off or something. I don't know which. It just gets me more curious. I keep thinking somebody's got to know some-thing. You know? Or else why did the priest even bother with me?"

Back in court, Dave Ansel, my old college coach, caught me from behind, clasping my shoulder. He was almost jovial, atten-tive as Mr. Coughlin explained what was required on the witness stand. Anse was so persistently positive I was reminded of peo-ple who try to lighten the atmosphere at wakes and funerals. He'd gotten older, heavier. Certainly, he no longer challenged students to one on one. Did he really believe in my innocence?

"We have a problem with your other friend," Coughlin said.

"Vinnie?"

"Do you see him in the courtroom?"

I scanned the faces, among them Roy Klijner, Agnes Gallagher, Paul Burkhalter and Pam. But no Vinnie. "I guess he's not here."

"Well, that's okay," Coughlin said. "Three character witnesses are probably enough. These seem like they'll be very good on the stand."

Coach Ansel couldn't have been more helpful, praising my wonderful attitude. "Never a bit of trouble. An easy guy to coach." Of course, that was several years ago, as Weisberg happily stressed in cross-examination. "Have a nice day." Anse winked at me on his way out.

When Pam skittishly approached the witness stand I called for Coughlin's attention. "I just realized, Mr. Coughlin. Did you say we had *three* character witnesses?"

"That's right."

"There's Pam and Anse and you said Vinnie wasn't coming. So, who's the third?"

"Your wife." He pointed to my right. Kathleen was in the second row, airily ignoring me, a small, thin, bearded man at her side. "She came to my office over a week ago. Didn't you send her?"

As Coughlin's interrogation began, Pam still could not relax, arms stiffly to her side, actually shaking at one point. Yet she was a forthright witness. I was no monster, just a pleasant, reasonable person. Good and decent. I liked that.

Even the prosecutor was patient, almost friendly toward Pam. "Miss Nealy, how well did you know Mr. Martell?"

"Pretty well."

"Did you see him outside of work at the *Citizen*?"

"Not . . . sometimes," she said.

"He had a reputation as a loner, didn't he?"

"I wouldn't say that."

"Were you aware of his relationship with Mrs. Klijner?" Weisberg asked.

"Well, only from rumors."

"But you knew him well?"

"I did. Sort of."

"Miss Nealy, on the night before Mrs. Klijner's disappearance, did Mr. Martell say these words to you, quote, 'I hope nothing happens in the next few days to change your opinion of me'? Unquote."

"I don't remember the exact words."

"Is that the sense of what he said? Yes or no."

". . . Yes," she conceded.

Probably that didn't help. My lunch had gone down, lying on my stomach, a stagnant glob of discomfort. Very shortly, I would go on the stand. I had to be assured, remembering to look the jurors in the eye. I took a deep breath to relax. After Kath. I was next.

What was my case. I was my own case. I had to make them believe me. That wasn't impossible. I'd convinced Pam, Coughlin, even Kathleen, evidently.

But how do you make yourself assured when you're so afraid?

In a smart tan suit, she was sworn in as Kathleen Lally. Coughlin prefaced nearly every question, "Like any young, married couple . . ."

"I married Bill because he was gentle, honest, and he was very nice to me. He made me feel good. In the beginning, anyway. He has a knack, I think, for making a woman feel special. He's good with words. And, there were other reasons, romantic reasons I can't easily explain. I was just attracted to him."

True confessions in open court. The jurors were rapt at this soap opera come to life. Much more exciting than spectrographs and fingerprint experts. I wanted to go home. Who expects to have their life dissected in public?

"You divorced after two years, Kathleen," Coughlin said. "What went wrong?"

"Sometimes, in marriage, it isn't enough to be honest or attracted. For one reason or another the man or the marriage doesn't live up to expectations."

Coughlin nodded, as a father to a daughter. "Did you and Bill fight?"

"Of course."

"Was he violent?"

"No."

"Did he strike you?"

"Never."

"Now, Kathleen," he leaned close to her, "you had two years of a sometimes unhappy marriage. Are you saying he never lost his temper and hit you? Even once? Think carefully before you answer."

"He never hit me. Ever."

"Well, did he ever threaten you?"

"No," she said.

"Did he ever lose control so you were physically in fear of him?"

"No."

"Was he moody?" Coughlin asked.

"Not especially."

"Any dark depression?"

"No," she said.

"What was your reaction on hearing of Bill's arrest in this case?"

"Shock. Disbelief."

"Has anything happened to mitigate those feelings?"

"No." She was firm.

"Do you believe the man you married, the man you lived with for two years and have known for four, do you believe this man" — he pointed — "Bill Martell, is capable of murder?"

"No. If I did I wouldn't be here."

Taking his turn, Weisberg sought to unnerve Kathleen by sharply raising his voice. "Miss Lally, when was the last time you saw your estranged husband?"

"About three weeks ago."

"And before that?"

"Oh. Over . . . about a year and a half ago."

"Miss Lally, how did your estranged husband, Martell, how did he react to the divorce?"

"He seemed to accept it. I guess."

"As a matter of fact, he might have been deeply affected in any number of ways by the divorce, but you wouldn't know because you didn't see him for more than a year afterward."

She blinked.

"Isn't that true?"

"It's true I didn't see him."

Weisberg paced before the jury. I had to overcome my fear of him. I must remember to answer questions truthfully and precisely. He was tricky.

"Now, Miss Lally, did your estranged husband have any unusual sexual preferences?"

"I beg your pardon?"

"You know, did he have, for example, did he have sadomasochistic tendencies? Did he have weird fetishes?"

Kath looked around, her expression half of anger, half of amusement.

"Come on, Miss Lally."

"If you must know, my husband's primary sexual preference was for taking care of himself. As near as I can tell there's nothing unusual about that. For a man."

Some were laughing. Burkhalter would be taking notes like a madman. I knew without looking.

Weisberg wouldn't give up. "How would you describe your sex life with Martell?"

"I wouldn't. My mother brought me up better than that."

"I don't see where all this is going," Coughlin complained.

The prosecutor switched gears. "Miss Lally, you claim your divorce resulted because Martell didn't live up to expectations. Could you be more specific?"

"It was a number of things. He wasn't very neat, for one, never picked up after himself. Which doesn't seem like much. But I got pretty sick of it. I felt it was inconsiderate. If he really cared . . . well, it was a number of things."

"Are you telling us you divorced the defendant because he was untidy?"

"He was very untidy," she said. "But there were lots of reasons. That's just typical. For another thing, he slept all day. Like twelve hours sometimes. And was out of work a lot."

"He slept twelve hours a day," Weisberg prodded. "And chronically unemployed. Is this normal behavior?"

"Bill was lazy. Is that considered normal?"

There seemed no point to all this, unless it was to humiliate me.

Kathleen was just leaving the witness box when Judge Harvey announced an adjournment. Thank God. My testimony could wait until tomorrow.

As my wife walked toward us, Coughlin turned. "Go to her. The jurors might see it."

I took her arm. "Thanks, Kath." I kissed her on the cheek, though the jurors, filing out, had their backs to the action.

"After all that," she seemed exhausted, "I sure hope you're innocent." And she slipped away, leaving the room just behind Klijner, escorted by her gnomelike boyfriend.

"Hey," I turned to Coughlin, "I should ask her to sign my life insurance policy. I'll be right back." I hurried out, passing Pam. "Be right back," I told her. I chased down the corridor, intercepting my wife near the stairs. "Kathleen."

The two of them turned.

"Kathleen. I forgot. I got to ask you one more favor. A small favor. Really."

She was irritated. "This is Arthur," she grumbled. Gesturing to me, "My ex-husband needs no introduction."

A queer thing happened now. I could not shake hands or even say hello to this Arthur. I stared at him, tried to speak, but could not.

"I'll be right with you," she finally told him, "please."

He squeezed her hand. "Don't be long, Kay."

Kay? I watched him moving down the stairs, almost graceful, not really gnomelike. Physically, he was my opposite. Why did she like him? Was he up every morning at six?

"Well, what is it?" Kathleen smirked.

I smiled, hoping to soften her. She still cared, if just a little. "I didn't think you were coming. What made you change your mind?"

"I didn't do it for you," she said.

"You just like courtrooms."

"I didn't want it on my conscience. I didn't want someone, anyone sent to jail without a fair chance and have that on my conscience."

"Well," I said, "whatever the reason, you were great. You even made me sound like a nice guy."

"I perjured myself."

"I'm still grateful."

"I don't mean to be rude, Bill, but I'm in a bit of a rush. What do you want?"

"Well, the thing is, Kath, I'm running out of money."

". . . Oh?"

"I don't want your money. The thing is, I've got that savings bank life insurance policy. I'd like to cash it in. But you're the beneficiary and I need your signature."

She reached into her purse and produced a pen.

"Ah, I don't have the policy with me right now. Could I bring it around later?"

"Don't come to my apartment," she said. "Call me at work."

It was awkward for a moment. She looked away as I studied her face. Always, I'd wanted to do right by her. Something went wrong. I had failed. "That's all," I said. "Unless. I'd like to say thanks again. You were great today. It made me proud and sad both. It made me think how much I lost when I lost you."

"Here it comes."

"No, I really mean it, Kath."

"I'll tell you something," she gazed down the stairs, "I never wished you well. You made me miserable enough, so why should you be happy? But this." She looked to the courtroom. "I never wished this on you. Anyway, in a week or so I'm going to take a vacation till it's over. And if you lose I'm going to try not to think about you again. Ever."

"I suppose that's best."

Pam was still at the courtroom door. Inside, Coughlin arranged papers in his briefcase. Most everyone else had gone. Without the fancy-dressed lawyers and their phony-formal speeches this was no more than a shabby, ill-kept building. The scum of the earth passed through here. And it showed.

"Pam. I've got to see Mr. Coughlin a minute," I managed a smile. "Then I'll be right with you."

"Don't do me any favors." She backed away.

"What?"

"If you'd rather go off with her, I won't stop you."

"Off with her? With who?"

She glared, a look she'd never shown before.

"Pam . . . that's silly."

"Is it? All I know is the whole time I was a witness for you and I was scared I kept looking to you. For help. And all you did was keep turning around. To her."

"Pam . . . I didn't."

"No wonder you told me not to come to court. Has she been here every day?"

"No."

"I saw you," she whined. "Everybody saw you kiss her."

"I was told to do that."

"I'm not stupid," she gasped. "And I don't like being used." Her eyes were red, but she wasn't so much hurt as angry. This real rage was a side of Pamela I'd never seen or even guessed at. There was no reason for such jealousy. And I was a little frightened by it.

"Where are you going?" I called as she hurried down the corridor. But she didn't answer.

"Here." Coughlin handed me a folder. We stood alone in the huge courtroom. "This is a copy of your statement to the police. Memorize it. Every word. When Charlie gets you on the stand, which'll probably be Monday, he'll try to fool you. He may do this. He'll look down at a copy of your statement. He'll say, 'Didn't you tell the police you saw Judy on the day in question?' He'll say something like that. A question like that. And unless you have memorized everything, maybe you'll begin to wonder if, just maybe, you did say that in some context. And you'll be afraid to deny it and be proved a liar."

"But that's just a trick."

"And if you even hesitate answering certain crucial questions some jurors will think you're lying anyway."

"They can do that? Play tricks like that? In court?"

"Watch out for Weisberg. Your wife made him look a bit of an ass today, but don't underestimate the man. He enjoys playing tricks on people. For example, you'll notice how he'll jump from subject to subject to keep you off balance. That sort of thing."

We left the courthouse together. Bracing myself against the chill of dusk, I watched for Pam. "You were never married, Mr. Coughlin? I think you did the right thing there. I don't know about these women. . . ."

"Trouble with that little girl?" He twinkled. Sometimes the old man seemed to enjoy my problems.

"Yeah. Well, she's starting in on how I'm using her. Which isn't true." Or was it? I no longer knew for certain. At least I tried to behave honorably toward Pam. I sincerely liked her. How deep that affection went I did not know myself. God, I would be happy to see all these legal problems behind me. I could sort out my life.

"I wouldn't worry." Coughlin took the granite front steps cautiously, one by one. "She'll come around."

"You think so?"

"Women aren't easily discouraged. Some women."

"No?"

"I defended a fellow two years ago," he said. "And I'll never understand this. He was up for rape. A very ugly rape where he beat the poor woman half to death."

"He was guilty?"

"No question."

"How do you defend someone like that when you know he's guilty?"

"Well," he paused on the sidewalk, "that's an old question. As many times as I've been asked I've never been able to offer an adequate answer. What I do, I try not to bother about a man's guilt or innocence. After all, I'm not the judge or the jury and it's not my responsibility. At the same time, I know my job and I do it to the best of my ability. You might say I do it with blinders on."

"And that works?"

"I hope so. After all these years."

Was he wearing blinders now?

"But what was I saying?" the old man continued. "Yes, about this rapist. Well, he committed this horrible, horrible crime and do you know what? He had a woman, a sweetheart, coming to the trial every day. Very pretty too. I even pointed her out to the judge when we were pleading for a reduced sentence."

"What was his sentence?"

"He got twenty years, that fellow. But he won't serve all of it. What I couldn't understand, and I'd like one of these woman's libbers to explain this one, why did a pretty girl, who could have had her pick of the fellows, I'm sure, why did she stay with a man who'd committed at least one, but probably several brutal sex crimes against other women?"

"Mr. Coughlin? What's all this to do with me?"

"Well . . . nothing."

"You're always bringing up these stories to me. About murderers. And rapists. Why is that, Mr. Coughlin?"

"Just an old lawyer's war stories." He chuckled, reaching up to my shoulder. "Don't be so sensitive now. Go home and get some rest. And don't worry about women. In fact, don't worry about anything. Go home, study your statement and sleep."

I called Pam when I got home. She hung up. Frankly, I was annoyed. This was hardly the moment for a jealous outburst. Under the circumstances, Pam's anger was almost irrational.

I spent the night reviewing my first encounter with Reardon and Matteo, growing enraged once again at the way they blithely assumed my guilt and alternately tried to badger and trap a confession.

My mood was grim when Pam suddenly arrived. Sitting on the couch in a wet raincoat, for a long time she watched me. "Aren't you going to say something?"

"Like what?" I studied my statement, every question and response. If only they'd grilled Klijner like this.

"I didn't come to check up on you. I don't care if she's here. Or was here."

I snickered.

"Don't laugh at me." She was hurt.

"Pamela," I put down the transcript, "I'm laughing because you're ridiculous. This, what you're jealous about, is something that was buried six months into our marriage. I'm not interested in Kathleen and I can promise she's not interested in me. In fact, she wouldn't be caught dead in my company." An unfortunate expression; it caused Pam nearly to flinch.

"Well, like I said, Bill, I didn't really think she'd be here. And I know you're under lots of pressure. So I know you're not responsible for everything you do."

"I am under a lot of pressure." In the tiny apartment I was a few feet from her.

"I'm not going to make it worse," she said.

"Thank you."

"I've helped you a lot."

"You have, Pam. And I'm grateful."

"I'm willing to go on helping. But I don't want to be used. If you don't really care, tell me so I'll know. I might still help. As a friend. But I want to know."

"Pam," I bent near, "I do care." I needed her badly, a soft, sympathetic, human face; it was easy to believe I loved her.

"And there is really nothing between you and your ex-wife?"

"Nothing."

"I couldn't stand it if you lied," she said.

"I wouldn't."

"If I found out you did I don't know what I'd do. I don't know what."

Sitting in court, I was oblivious to all but the coming ordeal. My hands. I'd bitten my fingernail so badly blood oozed from the corner.

Coughlin was marvelous. His first questions were conversational, friendly. A little background was provided. I began to relax. Still, I was full of nervous tics, sucking air noisily through my teeth, scratching my nose.

I gave a brief life history. We came to my employment with the *Suburban-Citizen*. Now I remembered to look at the jurors. This was hard. I expected them to hate me and I was sure to see this in their eyes. But they were merely curious. I grew confident, explaining how I had fallen in love with Judy. By afternoon, I was actually incisive, taking them step by step through the day of her disappearance.

"Did you see Mrs. Klijner that day?" Coughlin asked with sympathy.

"No."

"Not even for a few minutes?"

"No."

"When was the last time you saw Mrs. Klijner?"

"The day before," I explained. "The day before she disappeared."

"On the day in question, what were you doing on Hubbard Road?"

"Waiting for Judy. We were supposed to meet that day on Hubbard Road."

"And why did you go to her house late on the day in question?"

"I was worried." I looked eagerly to the jury. "I was worried because she was supposed to meet me. I waited on Hubbard Road. I waited at my apartment. And finally, I went to her house to find out what was keeping her."

"Did you make any observations on reaching her house?"

"Well, it looked strange, with the door open. I saw the door was open."

"All right," Coughlin said. "You arrived at the house. What did you do next?"

"I had to go inside, see? For all I knew she was in there, needed help. Anything could've happened with the door wide open and everything." I had the jurors' attention, if not their sympathy, as I described the bloody scene inside the house, including how I had stumbled in the dark.

"Why did you run away from the house?" Coughlin asked. "Where were you going?"

"I was going to the pay phone across the park there."

"But wasn't there a phone in the house?"

"Yeah," I said. "But I wanted to get out of the house. I was afraid."

"Afraid? Why were you afraid?"

"There was blood in there. Everywhere. I'd never seen so much blood. I thought, whoever did this is still around and they'll kill me next. So I ran. I'm not proud of it. But I was afraid. You know?"

"How did you get blood on your hand?" Coughlin asked.

"Ah, it was everywhere. And it was dark. And I must've put my hand in it, you know, not realizing it."

Not realizing it, I was pumping my knee up and down, swiftly up and down.

"When you were arrested, Bill, did you tell the police, 'I give up'?"

"Yes, I did."

"Why did you say that?"

"Because he was twisting my arm," I explained. "The officer who arrested me. He jumped me from behind and started twisting my arm. I thought he was going to break it. So I said, 'I give up,' hoping he'd stop."

"One more matter. The two suitcases and the bureau that the prosecutor showed us. What were you doing with those things?"

"Oh, yeah. Well, that was earlier in the day. I, ah, was taking that stuff to my place as a favor to Judy."

"Why did you take her car?" Coughlin asked.

"Well, we thought it would be simplest that way. She, ah, she left the keys in the car and loaded the stuff in it and I came along and took it."

"Did you go inside the house at that time?"

"No," I said.

"Did you see Judy Klijner?"

"No."

"Did you steal the suitcase?"

"No."

"Or the bureau?"

"No."

"And lastly, did you, in fact, murder Judith Anne Klijner?"

"No. How could I? I cared for her. So much." I bowed sadly, my eyes suddenly stinging. But was I weeping for myself in this awful predicament, or for Judy?

Twelve

OVER THE WEEKEND, Pam and I went to dinner. "My last meal," I joked.

"Don't talk like that," she complained. "Let's try to forget all that for one night."

It was impossible at the restaurant. I dreaded going inside, confronting the hostess, the waitresses. Dozens might recognize me and say something. "Let's not go in," I said. "I'm sick of restaurants. Let's drive around instead."

At nine o'clock the town was clogged with cars, particularly around the shopping centers. "Take a right," I said.

"Where are we going?" Pam asked.

We passed the park and beyond was his house, surrounded by cars. All the lights were on inside, like a party. The yellow Pinto still waited in the driveway. "That's Roy's place over there."

She drove away at once.

"They're going to start asking him questions," I said. "If I win, if I win he's going to be the suspect. Prime suspect. I wanted Coughlin to ask him some tough questions, but he didn't think it was a good idea. Well . . . I think I've got a chance. After the other day. It went good the other day. What do you think?"

"I wish I could've been more help. I was so nervous."

"You were fine, Pam. I mean, just you going up there. You know? It showed the jury that a nice, decent, attractive person like you is on my side." I stroked her back. "You did fine for me."

"I tried."

"You mean a lot to me. You show me nice things can still happen."

Her eyes brightened.

"You're the most important person in my life, Pam. The most." I flattered her shamelessly. In fact, since our jealous confrontation I no longer trusted Pam completely. "This weekend," I continued, "I get ready for Monday. Weisberg goes after me on Monday. But I'm ready and I'm not really worried because all I've got to do is keep to the truth."

She nodded.

"I mean, don't get me wrong. Monday. It's the most important day of my life, probably. You think you were nervous? I get sick just thinking about it. But I'm going to go on that stand and I'll be all right. And the jury's going to see that."

We went to my apartment. "I've got some pretty good steaks in the refrigerator," I said. "But it can wait a little." I lit candles and poured wine.

"You don't have to do all this," she said.

"I like to do it. How do you expect me to act, all alone with a pretty girl? Don't you like it?"

"I like it." She kissed me, but I kept talking. I felt strangely energetic.

Later, I asked her to walk around the room, "Just so I can watch you."

"Why?" She smiled.

"Because you're so pretty. You have a beautiful body, Pam. With beautiful hair."

"I'd rather climb in bed with you."

In bed, I held her, running my hand again and again over her smooth, bare skin. "You sure know the right things to say," she whispered. "I wish I could believe it. I wish I was as beautiful as you say. I wish I was beautiful for you."

"I never say anything that isn't true, Pam. To me you are beautiful."

She drew closer. "I thought we could be together before. But we lost each other. But if there's one good thing, it's now we're back together. Billy. This's how it's supposed to be."

And we began to make love, vigorously. I wanted to leave something she might remember, long for. Though I was gone, she'd never forget me. And I tried to observe and retain everything, wanting to have in mind always that look on her face. In a year I might call on an image, her body, naked, seeming to shiver, her knees drawn up. It would all be mine to enjoy again, anywhere.

After, she lay beside me, long blonde hair across my chest. "That was fun." She sighed.

"Jesus, Pam, I couldn't live without you." I held her in a bear hug. "I know what I'll do. I just won't let go of you. No matter what happens. I just won't let go."

She smiled as if it were all that simple.

Sometime after, I said, "If I do go to jail. You'll have to forget me. Like you promised. Okay?"

"Let's not worry about what's going to happen. If you go to jail . . . I'll have time to worry when it happens. If. I don't care what you did. I don't care what they say about you. I'll still be with you."

"What did you say?"

"I said I'd still be with you." She kissed my cheek.

"No. Before that you said something. You said you didn't care what I did. Didn't you just say that?"

"No, I didn't say that."

"Pam? What do you think I did?"

"Nothing."

"You don't believe me." I rolled away. My voice became louder than intended. "I've told you I didn't do anything. And you don't believe me. You. Of all people."

"No. That's not true."

"You come up here. You eat with me. Make love. And all the time thinking I'm guilty."

"No," she said.

"Christ. You're no different than the cops."

"You're not being fair." She pulled the spread over herself, as if the room had suddenly grown cold. "I do believe you." In candlelight, her face was no longer happy, her eyes were quick and watchful. "I do."

It snowed lightly on Monday morning. I heard church bells as I awoke. Time to be in court. "How do you feel?" Coughlin asked as I arrived.

"Fine."

Tapping my shoulder, smiling, he was actually solicitous. "The important thing is composure. Take your time. If you're uncertain of a question ask him to repeat it. Think through your answers. In some cases, the judge will allow you to consult with me if you think it necessary. Look at the jurors. And I'm talking about eye contact. Be yourself. And stick to the truth as you know it."

Weisberg came at me with his disarming near-smile. A court officer adjusted my microphone as the prosecutor leaned close by, telling the clerk, "This courtroom, never liked this courtroom. Too many stairs."

I was trying to relax. But relaxing is a difficult thing to do on purpose. Were the jurors growing sympathetic? Their eyes searched me. Looking for the truth? Or merely fascinated by the "murderer"?

"I've been going over your testimony and previous statements." Weisberg waved a pad of notes. He was civil, lulling. I tensed for the surprise attack. "You've described your feelings for Judith Klijner as very strong. Would you use the word love?"

". . . Yeah. Love. I would." My voice remained steady, but sweat trickled down the side of my face. In January I was sweating.

"And what were her feelings toward you? As you perceive them. Would you say that she returned your love?"

". . . Ah, I, I don't know . . . I guess, maybe she did. It's hard to say honestly. She liked me. I can say that for sure. She was willing to run away with me. That must've proved something."

"Yet you told the police that she cheated on you. You told them she picked up strangers in bars."

"Well, yeah, she did," I admitted. "That one time. Only one. As far as I know. But we were having some disagreements then."

"Did it make you angry when you discovered Mrs. Klijner had been seeing other men?"

"It didn't make me happy."

"Did you suddenly realize that perhaps her affection for you was not as great as yours for her?"

"No. I don't remember thinking that."

"But it did make you angry," Weisberg insisted. "The question I'm wondering is how angry. For example, did you feel like giving Mrs. Klijner, giving Judy a good, hard shake and telling her not to do it again?"

"No. I didn't feel like doing that at all. If anything I felt sad."

"Are you ever violent?"

"No," I replied. "Never, really."

"Never. That's very unusual. Most of us get mad sometimes. We bang the desk. We yell. Shake our fists. You don't do those things?"

"Well, yeah. I do that stuff. Sometimes."

"Then you do become violent," Weisberg insisted.

"If you call that violent."

"Well, isn't it? Hitting a desk. Isn't that violent?"

"I think violent, that's more like hitting someone who feels it, a person."

"Which you've never done? Hitting a person?"

"No."

"Ever been in a fight?" Weisberg asked.

"Not since high school."

"Not since high school? My. That is a good record. Maybe you can explain how you manage to be so peaceful. We'll send the recipe along to the U.N."

"I don't like to fight. And since I'm bigger than most people I don't have to."

"Could you be goaded into a fight?" Weisberg asked. "Provoked?"

"It wouldn't be easy."

"How about killing? Could you be goaded into killing someone?"

"No," I said.

"Not under any circumstances?"

"None that I can imagine."

"As you describe yourself," Weisberg rubbed his chin, "you seem to have an actual aversion to violence. And it leads me to wonder. If you did get very, very angry — and you admit you do get angry sometimes — but if you did get very, very angry and you committed a violent act, the ultimate violent act. Is it inconceivable that you would block it from your mind and your memory?"

"Wait a minute. Is it inconceivable? Yes, it is inconceivable."

"You say that. But how can you be sure? If you don't remember it."

"Object to that question," Coughlin snapped angrily. "That's very unfair, your honor. The witness has already stated that he had no blackout of memory."

"Strike that question," the judge ordered.

"Are you feeling all right?" Weisberg asked suddenly.

". . . Huh? Yeah, I'm okay," I said.

"You look a little pale to me."

"He looks fine to me," Coughlin called irritably.

"Let the witness be, Mr. Weisberg," the judge said.

"Then let me ask a question about his memory. Mr. Martell, how well do you remember the day in question?"

"I can remember everything important."

"And what do you mean by the word 'everything'?"

"Everything," I began. "I mean everything important. There's no gaps of time in the day. I have a good memory. If something's important I don't forget. As a reporter, you know, that's part of my job. I pretty much make a note of everything important. Up here," I touched my head. "And I don't forget."

Coughlin looked worried.

"Now," Weisberg nearly smiled, "you testified that on the day Judy Klijner disappeared you spent a lot of time on Hubbard Road. What were you doing there?"

"Waiting for Judy. Like I said before. Judy was going to meet me there."

"I see." Weisberg came closer. "She was going to meet you there and, if I've got it right, the two of you were going back to your apartment with the object of setting up housekeeping together. Is that correct?"

"Yeah. That's right."

"Well, okay then, Mr. Martell. My question is this. Why were you meeting her on Hubbard Road? If the two of you planned to live together, openly, why meet like criminals in an isolated part of the state reservation? There was nothing to hide any longer, according to you. So why not meet at your apartment where you both, supposedly, planned to live?"

"Because —" Why, indeed? Jesus, that was a good question. It had never occurred to me before. ". . . Ah . . ."

"Now we know you were on Hubbard Road. You admit it. We have the statement of a patrolman who saw you there. Alone, apparently. So that part of your story isn't in doubt. In fact, there's no way you could lie about not being there. You were seen."

"Object." Coughlin looked aggravated.

"Strike that," the judge ordered, "the remark about lying."

"I still have this question." The prosecutor turned importantly to the jury. "Why were you on Hubbard Road?"

". . . Ah, it's —" The jurors looked at me, expectantly. Think of something to say. Anything. But nothing came. Weisberg's trap was ingenious. I was making it all the more effective by my fumblings.

"Put that crackerjack memory to work, Mr. Reporter." Weisberg tapped his head.

"Give the man a chance to answer," Damien Coughlin called. "The floor is his."

". . . Ah, yeah, what was the question again?"

"I don't blame you for wanting to forget it."

"Your honor!" Coughlin cried. "This isn't cross-examination. It's the third degree."

"Ask your questions, Mr. Weisberg," Judge Harvey chided. "Keep your comments to yourself."

"Mr. Martell, why were you on Hubbard Road waiting for Mrs. Klijner when you could have met much more conveniently at your own apartment?"

". . . Well, it's like this. I never even thought of that. We went together a long time and we always, we always got together in the reservation. So that day, I don't know. One of us picked Hubbard Road. And I, we, we didn't question it. Because we always went there."

"Then it was force of habit?"

"Yeah. I guess, something like that."

"Are you telling us that force of habit brought you nearly ten miles out of your way? That's half an hour or more depending on the traffic. A half hour wasted." Again, Weisberg was speaking to the jury. This guy, his eyes confided, this guy is lying. My stomach churned. Be calm. I was in peril, losing it all. But it was better to stay calm.

"I guess," I said, "I guess, maybe, we were thinking, maybe we'd meet there if anything went wrong. If one of us changed our minds. We'd meet there first. Just in case."

"But, Mr. Martell, you'd already taken some of her things. You'd gone over to the Klijner house and snooped around —"

"One moment," Coughlin stood, "we don't like that word, 'snooped.'" His interruptions allowed precious time to recover. But I could only reflect on how badly it was going this morning.

"Let me make a suggestion." Weisberg was directly before me, both hands clutching the railing of the witness box. I could smell his mouthwash. "Let me suggest to you that you weren't on Hubbard Road to meet Mrs. Klijner at all."

"I was."

"Suppose you were there for another reason?"

"No."

"To your knowledge, Martell, is the reservation virtually honeycombed with hiking trails? Trails through the woods, trails through the swamp?"

"I, I guess."

"Have you ever been on those trails?"

"Hiking, maybe. I guess."

"Did you bury Mrs. Klijner's body off one of those trails?"

"No."

"In the swamp?"

"No."

"In the swamp where even the police couldn't find it?"

"I said no."

"Are you sure?"

"No. I mean yes. Yes, I'm sure."

"You're sure," Weisberg shook his head, "and of course you're the man who never forgets anything important."

"Ask me a question," I said.

Weisberg nodded agreeably. He seemed to be enjoying himself. "Mr. Martell, you admit taking Mrs. Klijner's yellow Pinto on the morning in question."

"I took it. I explained why I took it."

"What time in the morning did you arrive at the Klijner house to take the car?"

"About, I'd say, eleven o'clock."

Weisberg glowed with satisfaction. Ten to twelve o'clock had been given as the estimated time of the attack. I was digging my own grave here. "Do you know a Roland Glenn Bennett?" he asked.

"I met him."

"When was that?"

"In jail. Here. The day I was arraigned."

"You had a conversation with Mr. Bennett at this time?" Weisberg asked.

"It wasn't exactly a conversation. Mostly, he talked and I listened."

"Did Mr. Bennett ask why you killed Mrs. Klijner?"

"I never killed her," I insisted.

"But did he ask you this question?"

"I don't know. Maybe. I guess he did, probably."

"What was your answer?"

For a long time, I just sat there, feeling ill, sweating, my face burning.

"Was your answer," Weisberg prodded, "your answer to the question 'Why did you kill Mrs. Klijner?' or words to that effect. Was your answer 'I don't know'?"

"It was —"

"A yes or no response will do, please! Yes or no?"

". . . No."

Smirking, the prosecutor was already back to his notes. "Mr. Martell, did you tell the police you thought you knew where Judy Klijner could be located?"

"I . . ." In fact, I couldn't remember saying anything like that. But why should he ask the question? ". . . No."

To my relief, he accepted the answer, went on to something else. "Isn't it true that Mrs. Klijner was trying, tactfully, to put an end to your romance with her at the time of her disappearance?"

"No. I don't know where you get that."

"Did she tell you, in effect, not to try and see her? Did she tell you that?"

"No," I replied evenly.

"Did she say her ambition was to be a good mother, devoting all her energies to her son and trying to satisfy her husband?"

"No."

"Are you sure? Are you sure she never communicated these things to you?" He still held his notes in his hand and seemed to be referring to them. But Coughlin had prepared me for these tricks.

"Yeah. I'm sure. We were running away together. She wanted to be a good mother, sure. But she was coming with me. She wasn't going to improve things with him. She was coming with me."

"Quote. 'All things must end, even love affairs. You can't change my mind, so don't try.' Unquote. If Judy were alive today couldn't she testify that these were her words to you? And these. Quote. 'A clean break is best.' Unquote."

"No," I insisted.

"Judy is not alive. As you know. So she can't testify. Except," he waved the paper in his hand, "except here." Weisberg let the gray photocopy fall into my hand.

"What?"

"Is this a fair and accurate representation of a letter written to you by Mrs. Klijner?"

"Oh . . . this."

"Oh, this?" he smiled faintly. "The man with the great memory. You did receive that letter, then?"

It looked bad. My knees were actually shaking. It was quite visible to anyone. "This, this was written before. It was written before we were going to run away together. A month before. When we had a fight."

"Now that I've dropped it in your lap you no longer deny its existence. You agree that Mrs. Klijner did write it?"

"Well, yes. But before, before we were going to run away. She wrote it before . . ."

"Unfortunately," Weisberg sniffed, "I find no date on it."

"Can I see that?" Coughlin was at Weisberg's elbow, his face a squint of annoyance. "We weren't told anything about this, your honor. Why weren't we told about this?"

"It's just come to our attention, Damien," Weisberg answered mildly.

But Coughlin was sincerely angry now, muttering, "I can't believe I'm hearing you, Charlie. This is a cheap trick."

"I didn't get that," said the stenographer.

"I didn't say it," Coughlin snapped.

"Approach the bench." Judge Harvey gestured wearily. The stenographer moved her portable operation to the side of the bench opposite the witness stand in order to record the argument.

"Just where does this come from?" Coughlin rasped audibly, waving his copy of Judy's letter.

"The defendant's own room. Which we searched with a warrant."

"Your honor, they searched that place the night of the arrest. Now how, explain to me how this doesn't come to me until today? If they have evidence, I have, in the interim, filed a discovery motion to see that evidence. He's been sitting on this letter three months."

The judge, with his back to me, was inaudible.

"Your honor," Weisberg said, "I understand why Mr. Coughlin's upset. But, honestly, we took a vast quantity of material, written material from the defendant's room. He is a journalist. And we had to go through all this stuff, newspaper stories, old school assignments. Even a three-thousand-page novel. An intern on my staff had to read everything. Page by page. Looking for any correspondence or diary-type notations relating to the case. Now, we don't have the largest staff, so the boy did this in his spare time. And he only came up with this letter this morning. There simply wasn't time or opportunity to tell Mr. Coughlin. Sorry, Damien."

"Don't tell me you're sorry. I'm not being tried for murder."

"Now wait a minute," the prosecutor slapped the letter with

the back of his hand, "this guy must've known we had it. We took it from his room. It's addressed to him. If you don't know about this, Mr. Coughlin, don't complain to me. Your own client is withholding information from you."

"My relationship with my client is not your concern."

The judge silenced them. Both lawyers retreated. The letter was introduced as evidence. Copies were passed to the jury. They pored over Judy's words, studied the firm, feminine lines of her handwriting. A woman looked from the letter to me. Her eyes were not friendly. I had lost them.

The letter was clutched in my hand. "I'll always remember our times together. . . . Try to think kindly of me." I'd forgotten the letter. And now, it was as if Judy spoke to me, recalling the value of being free and alive just as freedom slipped away. The feelings I'd blocked came rushing to me. Judy. I wanted to weep. This time for her. But the courtroom was not the place.

"Is there anything you want to tell us about this letter?" Weisberg asked.

She was often selfish and inconsiderate. But Judy had an instinct and enthusiasm for life. I agonized. She knew what she wanted and took it. She crossed streets without looking. "Hey," I'd told her, "that's a good way to get killed." And she'd laugh like someone who expected to live forever. No one was more likely to get run over than Judy, or more certain to be surprised when it happened.

"Mr. Martell, anything to say?"

"No."

"Nothing to add concerning this letter?"

"No. Nothing, except I've told the truth. I know how it sounded sometimes. It's just a terrible mix-up of things all come down on me. Some people, some people have lied up here. But I haven't. No. I haven't."

It was silent. I'd won their attention. Nothing else.

In the attorney's consultation room, Coughlin stared glumly

out the window. "That letter." He shook his head. "I wish you'd told me about that letter."

"I forgot."

"That letter. Really wounded us. I tell you it really wounded us."

Us?

Well, I didn't care about that anymore. For the first time I saw things clearly. Reading the letter brought so much back. I understood Judy and I knew something I didn't know before.

Coughlin stared into space. "Now they'll come back with that tape on rebuttal," he was mumbling, "which should just about finish matters..." It was useless talking to him. As I went out the door, he was still mumbling.

At The Naborhood Pharmacy, Bertie Spaco was not happy to see me. She said nothing, stocking shelves as I approached. "I have to talk to you."

"My husband's coming right back," she replied.

"Then I'll have to talk fast, won't I? I wanted to ask you about Bob. This married friend of Judy's. I mentioned him last time."

"I don't remember any Bob," she said.

"You said that before. Anyway, I went to see this priest. Father Ennis? I suppose you don't remember him, either. Well, anyway, he was going to set up a meeting. With Bob. It was all agreed. And then it was canceled. Last minute. Because Bob figured it was unnecessary. This happened just before I talked to you at the city mall. Do you know where I'm going on all this?"

"No." She returned to the register. At noon, we were alone in the store.

"I thought I was supposed to meet Bob. But it wasn't Bob. It was never Bob. I just shortened the name without thinking. It was Bobby. And the meeting turned out to be unnecessary because it was already scheduled. Between you and me. Roberta."

"You must be crazy." She snorted.

"Tell me about it."

"It's not true." She put her elbows on the top of the cash register and rubbed her temples, as if gripped by a headache.

"The thing of it is, Mrs. Spaco, I wouldn't bother you, but I think you can help explain what happened to Judy."

"No."

"Oh yes, you can. Because I think Roy killed Judy. In fact, I'm sure of it now. At first, I thought he killed her because of me. But I always wondered. Even if he knew about me, which now I don't think he did, but even if he did why should he care? I mean, I'm no movie star or anything. Besides, she saw men from time to time and he knew. A dozen times she threatened to leave him. He didn't kill her for that. But. What if she was leaving him not for another man, but for a woman? What do you think? Here's a guy with a real important, visible position in the town. On a very conservative newspaper. How's it going to look if his wife shacks up with another woman? He'd be humiliated, wouldn't he? Any guy would."

"We weren't going to do that."

"But you were lovers. You and Judy. At one time, anyway, you were lovers. I'm right about that."

She fixed her gaze on the cash register.

"And Judy called you Bobby."

Her lips were thin, drained of color.

"Yeah," I said, "it's just about the last thing I would've thought of. With Judy. I guess I don't know much about the way people can be. When you get down to it I'm just ignorant. In fact, I didn't figure it out completely until today. Started doing some arithmetic. You know, adding things up, things that've been bothering me for some time. Like you. Why did you, with your husband having fits about it, why did you still agree to see me? Maybe you knew I was innocent. For sure you knew something. And it made you feel better to talk to me. You could do that much. And then you could sleep nights. Huh, Bobby?"

She was unmoved.

/ 229

"Now, today, in court, this's how it all came together. This's interesting. I took a lesson from Judy. What she taught me. She was a great one for appearances. But she never let the rules get in her way. So I had to remember. Judy was capable of anything. After that it was obvious."

"What do you want from me?" asked Roberta Spaco.

"Just getting to that. You see, I figure Roy, maybe he found out about you two seeing each other again. So, when Judy told him she was actually going to do it, run out on him, he just assumed she was running with you."

A customer came in, announced by a little bell above the door. An older woman, she looked nervously about. Tension was evident. "We can't talk here," Mrs. Spaco said.

"Well, we have to talk somewhere. You're looking at a very desperate person. No lie. And I'm not going to take no for an answer."

Thirteen

I PICKED UP Mrs. Spaco a block from the drugstore. Sitting in my car, she was burrowed into a maroon parka that touched the red in her hair.

"Well, what should I know?" I tried to sound friendly, soft-spoken, calm, hoping to put her at ease. "It's about you and Judy. I just think this thing between you two is at the bottom of it. Judy being missing. What do you think?"

"I don't know," she said. "Honestly, I don't."

"But you're wondering about it. Aren't you?"

"Maybe I am."

"Roy Klijner knew about you two. Didn't he?"

"Judy told Roy," she said. "Years ago. Just like I told my husband. When you're married things have a way of coming out. We never should have told them. My husband is very protective. Well, he has this idea I was seduced into this whole thing by Judy. And I guess he decided pretty soon I shouldn't see Judy anymore. He says he understands. This sort of thing happens when you're young, he says. I never should have told him. But, when you're married, I don't know, I guess you feel guilty keeping secrets."

"What was Roy's reaction to all this?"

"His attitude was strange as far as I could tell. At times, he was really against it. He never actually said anything to me. But, sometimes I got the feeling he hated me. He's got a real hang-up on something like that. I'll bet he's a little that way himself."

"How do you mean?" I asked.

"Judy told me once, he was always asking about it, wanted all the details. And once, when he found out we went for lunch together, he asked her what we did. What did we do? Nothing. We went out for lunch. And, she said, he was actually disappointed to hear that. Sometimes he made fun of her about it, which she didn't like. And he made jokes about all three of us going to bed together. So, he was a little weird himself if you ask me."

"You think that's weird?"

"I don't know," she said. "I don't know what's weird. But I know I wouldn't go near him."

"No."

"He never understood us. People don't understand."

"Judy said you started, you know, going together at an early age."

"Going together . . . yeah. High school."

"Who broke it off?" I asked.

"She did. She thought it was wrong. Well, maybe we both broke it off. It bothered us. We thought it was a sin in those days. Well, maybe it still is. But I don't know how we were so awful compared to some people and the things they do. We didn't hurt anybody or anything. But, it's true, we felt bad about it. And that's when we went to see Father Ennis. And she met Roy after that and got engaged. And I got married. We thought that was the right thing to do. Maybe, if we were young today, maybe our lives would be different. But not in those days. If you were that way you didn't talk about it. People looked down on you. They hated you, even. Well, it would be nice if you could just live the way you want and not be bothered by people."

"But since you've broken up you've seen each other," I said.

"We stayed friends."

"Just friends?"

"I don't know how you think these things are. We started out, we were friends. And we were always more friends than anything else. I like to think. We went to concerts together, studied together. And you're interested in boys at that age. But, I think the reason a lot of girls get involved in this type of situation is because boys, at that age, they're very immature. Compared to girls. We complemented each other, Judy and I. We were so close. And it just happened. It could have happened to anyone. One day we were in her room, or my room. I don't remember. And I told her how much I cared. And I remember I said, 'I wish there was a way for two girls to show how much they care for each other, the way a boy and a girl can. . . .' I don't know why I'm telling you this."

"What happened after you two got married? I'm asking if you ever got back together. You know, romantically, I guess you'd say. Because, if you did, and her husband knew about it, don't you see the motive that gives him?"

"For a while we just forgot each other. I had my marriage, my kids. She had her own family. We didn't bother each other. We told ourselves we made the right decision. We were normal. Like everybody else. And if we were unhappy . . . well, I don't know, probably we would've made each other unhappy too. . . . Sometimes I think people aren't meant to be happy. I don't know anyone who's happy, really happy."

"You did see her again?" I pressed.

"About a year ago she called me. She was upset. Wanted to talk. So she picked me up and we drove to a place of ours, a place in the reservation."

"Hubbard Road."

"She took you there too?" She smiled. "I think she took everyone there. Anyway, that time, we got there and we had a big, long scene. Crying and everything. She was so unhappy with him, Roy. He's a bastard. So that started us up again. And pretty soon she told Roy she was miserable. She wanted to go off on her own."

"What did he say?"

"He said she could go without Michael. He threatened all sorts of court action, legal action. Which, that put an end to that. She was afraid of losing her baby."

"He knew about you?" I asked. "I mean, he knew she was seeing you again?"

"He knew. No one had to tell him. Although, maybe she did tell him. I told her not to, but she never listened to me. I guess he was always jealous of me. And the funny thing is, it wasn't the same when we got back together. Judy and I. It didn't last long. We still cared for each other. But we were different people. I couldn't have left my husband. The fact is, I don't think I was ever really that way. You know? It was just how things happened."

"Mrs. Spaco, would you tell this story in court?"

"No!" She was shocked.

"It doesn't have to be in open court. Probably you can have the judge close the courtroom and only the jury hears what you say."

"For me, that's twelve people too many. Besides, those newspaper reporters will find out. Somebody will find out. Now, if it was just me, fine. I'd do it. But I have to consider my family, my children. Mr. Martell, my mother and father still live in this town."

"I know it's difficult," I said.

"It's more than difficult. Please don't ask me to do this. I'm not going through life with that, everybody knowing. It'd be one thing if I thought it would help Judy. But no one can help Judy now."

"You can help me."

"It won't help you. But it'll ruin me."

"Mrs. Spaco, times have changed. You said that yourself. People will understand —"

"Times haven't changed that much. Some people just wait for something like this. They never say anything to your face. But when your back is turned they talk. And they never forget. For twenty years they remember and remember. When you're dead in your grave they still talk about you."

"You know why you can help me? Because you're the only person who knew that Judy and me were in love."

"How did I know that?" she asked.

"Because she told you. You're the only person she told."

"She never did."

"That's not true." I hadn't expected this. "You know she told you about us. She told you everything."

"No. If she talked it was all generalities. Never any names."

"You can be subpoenaed. I can call you to testify whether you like it or not."

"Call me up there I'll have no choice. I'll just have to deny everything. I'll tell them I was never in love with Judy. I can make people believe. We had to make up stories all the time."

"What you're talking about," I said. "That's perjury."

"I don't care. If you force me, I'll go to jail. But I won't tell that story in court. So please, please stop asking me to do something I can't do. I just can't."

"It's interesting." Coughlin sipped coffee in the attorney's consultation room, waiting out yet another delay.

"Don't you think the jury should hear it?" I asked.

"Well, I thought you said the woman won't talk."

"Right now she says that. But put her on the stand, confront her with it. She'll have to tell the truth."

"Awfully heavy-handed," he said. "Could easily backfire. Besides, she's right, you know. This doesn't prove anything."

"It raises a lot of questions, doesn't it? It shows someone had plenty more motive than me. Mainly, Judy's own husband, who had plenty of opportunity besides."

"You see," the old man was struggling, uncharacteristically, to be tactful, "this introduces a rather, how should I say, unsavory element into the courtroom."

"Unsavory element? Mr. Coughlin, this is a murder trial."

"No, you don't understand what I'm saying. It's a little like a political campaign. When one politician finds himself behind late in the game he begins mud-throwing, making charges, sordid things, very often, unsubstantiated for the most part. Which is what we'd be doing because we can barely suggest a motive in Mrs. Klijner's homosexual affair. In fact, it's pretty far afield for me. Now, in a political campaign, when this tactic is tried, it almost never works. The voters see it as a desperate move by a desperate man. And they resent it. Especially if it's sexual. By the same token, juries don't appreciate being dragged pointlessly into scandal."

"Mr. Coughlin, with all respect, I don't care if they think I'm desperate. I *am* desperate. I look at these people. Jesus. They're about to put me away."

"Now. You can never predict how a jury is going to decide."

"Never predict? For God's sake. I don't feel safe in the same room with those people."

"We've had some bad surprises," Coughlin said. "Most of those were your fault. The letter. And the car. But, don't forget, our day isn't over yet. We have final arguments. Then we can appeal."

"Mr. Coughlin, I have nothing to lose. Let's get her up here. Get the jury thinking. Then, call Roy back to the stand and . . . I don't know, maybe you can get something out of him."

"I don't know what putting those people on the stand would accomplish, except it will annoy the court because we will be wasting their time."

"I'm being tried for murder. I couldn't care less if they're annoyed."

"This is only going to make a bad situation worse."

"Well, for Christ's sake, if you have that attitude how the hell can you expect to accomplish anything?"

"I have this attitude because I don't see the advantage of taking two young mothers, one of whom is no longer here to defend herself, and ruining their reputations in open court. In any case, I doubt she'd testify. And, under the circumstances, you can hardly blame her."

"You're pretty cool about all this," I said.

"I'm honestly concerned for your best interests. This tactic is not in your best interests."

"You can afford to be cool. You're not looking ahead to what I'm looking at."

"I've given my best."

"All along" — I was standing to say this — "all along you thought I was guilty. Didn't you?"

"I don't concern myself —"

"You don't concern yourself. That's a lot of shit. If you thought I was guilty you shouldn't have taken my case. You shouldn't've taken me to this, where they're all set to destroy me and I haven't had a chance to defend myself."

"I've done a good job for you. You're the one who's destroyed this case. All by yourself. If you'd told me about the car, about the letter. I asked you, point-blank, do those people have any more surprises? And you told me no."

"Well, I forgot. And when was I supposed to tell all this anyway? You wouldn't talk to me. I wanted to sit down and prepare myself. I see you when you can fit me in. Between the fish fry and the pecan fuckin pie."

"Don't use that language to me. I don't take that. Not from you."

"You know what your problem is?" I leaned over his desk. "You're too damn old for this job."

The blue eyes were unblinking.

"You're a goddamn old, old man and you ought to be in a home playing checkers where you can't hurt anybody."

He gave no sign of anger, save a faint blush.

"Right from the start. Right from the start I knew I should get another lawyer. I wanted to ask if you thought I was guilty. But I was afraid. That should have been the tip-off right there. And you put on this big fuckin front. Like you know so much. When you're really too old to be doing anything for anybody. Too old. Too fuckin old."

"Are you finished now?"

"Just about. Thanks to you I'm just about finished."

The old man drew himself up. "I shouldn't say this, but you brought it on yourself. The fact is, if you eliminated all the lawyers who think you are guilty you would soon eliminate all the lawyers."

"What's that suppose to mean?"

"Simply, you are guilty. And that's obvious to anyone involved in this case."

I sat back, strangely relieved. At least, I knew where I stood.

"Now, I have defended guilty men. Men I thought were guilty. And won acquittals."

"Ha. There's a goddamn recommendation."

"In your case, I tried to prod, to suggest that you make a deal with the district attorney's office. You refused. Several times. Well, you can lead a horse to water, but you can't make him drink. Can you? Still, I kept that option open as long as possible. Right up to the day this trial began. You wouldn't take it. And now it isn't there anymore. Oh, don't look so surprised. The assistant district attorney is not deaf and blind. He can see how the trial is going as well as you can. He needn't make deals."

"Well," I said calmly, "that settles it. There's no way you can be my lawyer anymore."

"That's up to you. And the court to decide."

"You did this on purpose," I said finally. "You deliberately sabotaged this case."

He looked annoyed.

The judge squinted as sixteen jurors were led from the room. "What is it?" he demanded. Coughlin prodded me.

"I'd like a new lawyer," I said.

He rolled his eyes. "Everybody up here." Coughlin, Weisberg and I moved to the bench. "What's this all about?"

"I have no faith in Mr. Coughlin as my lawyer."

"And what brought this on?"

"Well, he thinks I'm guilty."

"Mr. Coughlin?"

Coughlin was clearly tired, disgusted by the whole affair. "Your honor, I haven't really considered that question. I've involved myself in preparing the finest defense possible. I've done my best. Let my work speak for itself."

"He's lying."

"You." The judge pointed. "You speak when you're spoken to. Understand? And I don't appreciate people coming into my court and attacking the integrity of one of the most respected members of the bar."

How's that for impartial? Obviously, this man was no friend of mine.

"Most of our problems," Coughlin went on, "come from bombshells Mr. Martell never prepared me for. I've done my best."

I was seething, listening to his lies.

The judge glanced at Weisberg.

"This is an obvious ploy," the prosecutor piped in. "The defendant sees how the case is going. He's clearly laying the groundwork for an appeal on the basis of inadequate defense."

"Can I say something?"

The judge peered at me.

"He told me he thinks I'm guilty, your honor. He just told me. Just now. I don't care what he tells you. But that's what he told me."

"And did you have anyone in mind to replace Mr. Coughlin?"

"I don't care. I'll defend myself if I have to."

"Do you know anything about the law? Courtroom procedure?"

/ 239

"I know this, I'm innocent. I know that and Mr. Coughlin doesn't."

The judge shuffled papers until we were seated. "The request for a change of counsel is denied. Mr. Coughlin will continue to represent the defendant. The ruling is made in his, the defendant's, interest."

It didn't seem right. At least, I should have the satisfaction of going down with an honest effort. Coughlin collapsed wearily in his chair. Surprisingly, he was not gloating, but had a distasteful, detached expression on his old face. Our argument had taken a lot out of him. There would be little fight left for Roland Glenn Bennett and the tape. Perfect. Just goddamn fucking perfect.

Weisberg's assistant brought in the recorder. The prosecutor himself briskly passed the defense table, giving Coughlin a keep-up-your-spirits nod.

"Tired," the old man sighed as the jury returned. I barely recognized the rebuttal witness, ex-cellmate Glenn Bennett. Cleanshaven, in a conservative suit, he testified on our morning together. "Why were you placed with Mr. Martell?" Weisberg asked.

"Well, yeah," Bennett said. "That guy, Novio, that guy asked me to go, to go in there."

"You refer to Mr. Novio from my office?"

"That's right."

"Did he give a reason when he asked you to do this?" Weisberg questioned.

"Because. He set me up with this microphone. So he could get it all on tape. Whatever I said."

"Everything you said?"

"And Martell there too," Bennett added. "Everything he said. I was talkin to him. Novio, he says, 'Talk to this guy. Let him talk about this thing, what they arrested him for.' So I did that. I didn't make it obvious. You know? I just let him talk."

Weisberg pushed the buttons and the tape began. My voice.

Was it my voice? Really? It was confused, tired, scared. I could feel sorry for myself, remembering my first night in jail. The same incriminating words came out, Bennett's profanity clearly offending some jurors. "Shit. Is that you? Holy Christ! You killed somebody? Christ. What made you do a thing like that?"

On the stand, Bennett broke into an appropriate, nervous grin just as I answered, "I don't know."

I don't know. It had the ring of a complete sentence. I was beginning to panic, knowing suddenly that Coughlin's jerry-built explanation would never work. No one would believe I'd said, "I don't know what you're talking about," least of all me.

The tape went on, Bennett babbling about plea bargaining. I felt a little relieved. Few seemed to appreciate the significance of the little exchange. Perhaps, many missed it on the scratchy, noisy tape.

Weisberg turned the machine off. "Now, during the course of this conversation, Martell makes reference to the front page."

"Yeah. That's the newspaper," Bennett responded. "Mr. Novio left the newspaper in the cell to get us talkin about the arrest. So he says somethin about bein on the front page, Martell there, he said that. And he was lookin at the newspaper and I was bendin over lookin at it too. You know. I hadda stay close to get the thing recorded. So they could pick up what he was sayin. You know?"

"Mr. Bennett, at some time in the conversation you ask a question. I quote here from a transcript. You say, quote, 'Is that you? Holy Christ. You killed somebody? Christ. What made you do a thing like that?' Unquote. And that is a question, by the way, isn't it?"

"Yeah. For sure."

"So you asked the question," Weisberg resumed. " 'What made you do a thing like that?' And Martell replies, 'I don't know.' "

Had I said it after all? Suddenly, I had the answer. "Psst," I called to Coughlin.

Of course, I'd said it. But not in answer to Bennett's question. Exhausted, dazed, I'd been talking to myself. *I don't know.* It was a sigh of despair.

"Mr. Coughlin," I called again, frantic to share the good news. But he was motionless, slumped lazily over his desk. Not even following the testimony. My God, I thought, don't do this to me, old man.

"Mr. Bennett," Weisberg continued, "when you asked Martell, 'What made you do a thing like that?' "

"Yeah. I was pointin to the story. The newspaper. It said this girl was missin. Gone. Blood everywhere. So I said, 'You killed her? Why'd you do it?' Or I said somethin like that. Whatever it says I said there, that's what I said."

"Mr. Coughlin," I muttered. "Jeez." Why didn't he at least look at me? Had he given up out of spite? He was actually asleep. My God. Hunched over the table, his head lay on his arm. Reaching over, I nudged him. His shoulder dipped and his head tilted toward me. The look on his face.

"Ahhhh!" I stood straight up. Weisberg stopped in midsentence. Bennett began to relax. The judge looked down severely. A few court officers moved forward.

Coughlin's eyes were closed. His lips were crooked and bluish.

"I think — I think he's sick or something. Mr. Coughlin?" I moved close and touched him again. The body moved slightly, a dead weight. Weisberg had his hand, searching for a pulse. "I didn't do anything to him," I said. Court officers surrounded the stricken man.

"Give him air."

Even the judge was off the bench. And most of the spectators pushed forward, whispering, creating a low, moanlike sound in the room.

"Call a doctor."

"Give him air."

For now, I was forgotten. This was some relief.

Two younger court officers took his chair from opposite sides and lifted. He sagged forward, but a third officer caught him. And this odd party waddled into the adjacent jury room, carrying the seated lawyer as if he were the Pope. I followed, feeling some obligation to stand by my attorney, though it was more than he'd done for me.

They gently laid the stricken man on the floor. His legs and arms flopped, had to be arranged. Shoes were removed. Someone unbuckled his belt and pants, another took off his tie and loosened his collar. Now, the judge, his clerk, Weisberg, and his assistant stood among the uniformed officers, wondering what to do next.

"Is he breathing?"

"Heart attack. Must be."

"Did he say anything? Do anything?" Weisberg asked me.

"No. No, nothing. But, I mean, I was listening to you. And I turned and he was, he looked like he was sleeping there."

"We should do that mouth-to-mouth," Judge Harvey directed. No one moved.

"Anyone had that CPR?"

"Try the courtroom. See if anyone out there is familiar with CPR."

An adventurous court officer went on hands and knees and began breathing into Damien Coughlin's old, wrinkled mouth. At intervals, he stopped. "I don't know. I don't know if I'm doing this right."

"Pinch his nose shut."

"Hold his tongue. You're supposed to hold his tongue or something."

"This is dreadful," the judge muttered.

"Shhh, judge," whispered the clerk, "maybe he can hear you."

"Oh, of course."

"Would you like to wait outside, judge?" Weisberg suggested. "There's no reason to wait here."

/ 243

"Must be something we can do," he answered. "You." He came at me with quick, fearful eyes. "What happened? How long was he lying there? With his head on the table?"

"Like I told Mr. Weisberg, your honor, I wasn't looking."

"How was he this morning? He seemed fine to me."

"Oh, he was okay, sir, you know." I was desperate to make a good impression. But the judge was so distracted I surely made no impression whatever.

"Then, there wasn't any warning?"

"No." I tried to forget our bitter argument. But I couldn't escape it. Coughlin was dying. I might be partly responsible.

"Did Damien have heart trouble?" The judge regarded the old man's body with horror.

"I don't know," Weisberg said.

"If my wife was here," the judge continued, "she'd know what to do. She's taken all those courses. Have a little heart trouble myself, you see. I don't like this. A thing like this. I don't like to see it."

"Come outside, your honor," the clerk urged.

As Judge Harvey left the room, two paramedics arrived. They carried bags of equipment. Clearing away the impotent men in suits, they worked on Coughlin, applying an array of gadgets to his body. Shortly, they were consulting monitors and none of these made them happy. "Shit," one complained.

"Will he be okay?" Weisberg asked.

"Get these people out of here."

An oxygen mask was put on Coughlin's face, his coat and shirt were pulled open, his undershirt was cut away.

"I'm still getting zip." One attendant consulted his instruments.

They poised a large black object over Coughlin's heart, working with great hurry. A charge of electricity jerked the old man off the floor. He twitched with life. I'd seen something like it on television. But I wasn't prepared for what happened next. He made an awful gurgling sound, vomit spewed all over the transparent oxygen mask. The paramedics worked to clear it out. The floor was suddenly wet beneath him. The odor grew unbearable. I couldn't stay any longer, staggering into the courtroom, sick at heart, sick to my stomach.

After they took Damien Coughlin away, the room was set on by men with mops and cans of spray disinfectant. Despite the cold, all the windows were opened. But the odor was not easily gone.

"As a result of today's tragedy" — Judge Harvey's black hair and mustache stood out on his white face — "as . . . as a result of the sudden, the untimely death of Damien Coughlin . . . a fine man and a fine lawyer . . . as a result of Mr. Coughlin's sudden death the court sees no alternative but to declare a mistrial."

Weisberg was on his feet, hands on his hips. "Your honor."

"Mr. Weisberg." The judge motioned him down.

The jury was thanked and dismissed.

"Boy," a court officer came near, "you sure lucked out of this."

The assistant district attorney passed me, his face reflecting bitter disgust.

I didn't want to think it. But I couldn't help myself. Down the courthouse steps, in the cold, I repeated it to myself again and again. In the whole thing, it was my first decent break.

fourteen

"DON'T SHUT ME OUT," Pam telephoned that night, pleading, "I can't stand to leave things this way. I gave you a totally wrong impression the other night."

"Oh, that. Forget it."

"Bill, I never thought you were guilty. Not now. Not ever."

"Forget it, Pam. Really. I have."

After a pause, she asked, "Should I come over? You must need company."

"No. I mean, I'm pretty much exhausted."

"It must've been awful for you. That poor old man."

She threatened to visit for breakfast. But I managed to get away early next morning, enjoying pancakes and Cokes at one of those restaurants where you never leave your car. Just now I couldn't face her.

Perhaps I was unfair to Pam, lumping her with Coughlin. Both secretly believed in my guilt. Of course, only the old attorney had actually done something about it. Coughlin had plotted to lose the case. This was the only explanation for his courtroom tactics. The public defender became the public avenger.

Of course, I was sorry about the old man. But, right now, my own life was on the line. I needed money. I could live on unemployment, but suppose I decided to run. It was an option I'd been rethinking very carefully. It might be done. With a little care. A little luck. A little cash.

Consider the alternative. I saw no hope of winning the retrial. I would certainly be sent to a maximum security prison. Weisberg would dangle the bait. "Tell us where the body is. We'll transfer you." Maximum security. José Ruiz and his friends. "Tell us where the body is." How long before they killed me?

That afternoon, I turned the apartment upside down looking for the savings bank life insurance policy, my only quick source of money. I searched every pocket, drawer and wastebasket, but saw no sign of it.

I sat on the couch. Think. Where did I have it last? Or had the police broken in and stolen that too? I remembered showing it to Coughlin at Howard Johnson's. "Your wife might have to sign this," he'd told me. Then . . . Jesus! Coughlin had never returned it. Of course. He must've absently put it with his own papers.

I imagined them closing the lid on him, my money in his pocket, a very smug look on his face.

Lawrence Fabiano's law office was a converted garage attached to his ranch-style house. Of course, it had carpets and shelves of law books, but it was unmistakably a converted garage, the driveway leading directly to the front door.

Fabiano himself was a man in a hurry. At times, he talked faster than I could listen. "I look forward to developing a solid, spirited defense. That is, if you decide I should represent you."

I nodded in agreement.

"I have one strategy in particular I want you to think about."

"Yes?"

"Publicity."

"Well . . ."

"Good publicity. Starting with a press release I've already prepared." He began searching his desk top. "Announcing our agreement that I will represent you. This is, assuming we do, in fact, work together."

"I'm not keen on publicity, Mr. Fabiano."

His eyebrows bounced in surprise.

"You know," I said, "being on trial for murder, it isn't exactly my fault, but it's not something I'm really proud of, either."

"I see your point. On the other hand, it's not quite a secret."

"No."

"You've already gotten a great deal of publicity. All of it bad."

"I know."

"My intention — oh, here's the release," he said. Attached to it was a studio photo of the lawyer himself. "Anyway, my intention is to counterattack. To push out the bad publicity with good."

"I understand. But I don't see how that helps me. Any kind of publicity."

"Well," he folded his hands, "it's a point we can discuss."

"Before I decide on any of that, Mr. Fabiano, I have a problem. And I wondered if you could help me."

"Shoot."

". . . Yeah. Mr. Coughlin was holding something for me. I'd like to get it back. It was a life insurance policy. A savings bank life insurance policy."

"No problem. All of the papers and notes having to do with your case will be turned over to me. Or whoever represents you."

"How long will that take?"

"Oh, I'd say a few days." He lit a cigarette.

"Suppose I can't wait a few days. Suppose I'm really low on cash and I need money now. Like yesterday, in fact. So how can I get it?"

Fabiano's grin faded. He shrugged. "If you can't wait, get in touch with the family. Tell them your problem."

"How would I do that? Get in touch with the family?"

"Try the phone book. But you ought to wait till after the funeral. By the way, are you going to the wake?"

"Me? I doubt it. I mean, I'm sure they don't want me at the wake."

Cigarette smoke advanced on me, a rolling blue cloud.

"There's good sense, going to this wake," the lawyer explained. "Namely, people involved in this case will be there. Clerks, judges from every court. Lots of people. No one really liked the old bastard, but he hung on so goddamn long he knew everybody. When these big shots see you, paying your respects, it's going to have a good effect. One day you're before the parole board and someone remembers, 'Oh, yeah. This guy. Had the decency to go to old Coughlin's wake.'"

"Parole board?"

"Okay, maybe it does nothing for you. But there's always the chance. It's politics. Like wearing a good, clean suit to court. Now that has less than nothing to do with anything, logically. If you could determine guilt by wardrobe, life would be a hell of a lot simpler and I'd be out of work, God forbid. But you won't find atheists in foxholes or raggy bums on trial for murder, I can promise you. So, I'm saying, go to the wake. For your own good."

I agreed to Fabiano's representation. It didn't matter. I would be long gone by the time my new trial date arrived.

"You won't regret this." The lawyer smiled. "You see, I'm willing to walk that extra mile so you'll get the best possible defense. That's the way I am. Couldn't do it any other way."

Coughlin had insisted my guilt or innocence was of no interest to him. With Fabiano this was actually true. We agreed to attend the wake together, leaving from his office at seven. Perhaps someone there would know where my life insurance policy had gone.

A big man in a wool coat, Larry Fabiano set a vigorous pace on our walk to the funeral home. "Maybe I shouldn't go," I said.

"I'm not dressed for this." I ran my hand across my nylon parka with its tattered right sleeve.

"The important thing is to be there."

It was early evening. I'd imagined an empty room and the solitary closed coffin. Evidently, every lawyer, politician and policeman in town was here. The room rumbled with conversation. "What's with all the cops?" I asked.

"Don't you know?" Fabiano smiled. "Coughlin used to be counsel for the patrolmen's union. Of course, that was years ago. Didn't you know?"

It figured.

"That's his sister." My lawyer pointed to a thin, handsome woman, a young priest to her right, the coffin to her left. Her hair was thick, as snow-white as her brother's. She reached out to anyone who approached. "I can't remember her name. What was her name? I met her once. . . . Wait here."

Fabiano abandoned me, plunging abruptly into the mass of dark suits. The white and gold coffin was like marble. The deceased's old hands were folded, entwined with a rosary, his face rouged.

It wasn't my fault. He was an old man and his time had come. At least, he went quickly.

"The notorious Mr. Martell." Weisberg, the assistant district attorney, loomed before me. I would have happily seen him in Coughlin's place. Yet he could be civil, almost casual. "What are you doing here?"

"I came to pay my respects."

"Touching."

"Mr. Coughlin did a lot for me," I said.

"He was good enough to die. Or you'd be in jail tonight."

"I don't see it that way."

"Enjoy your freedom, Martell. While it lasts." He said this with chilling composure, then he was gone, off to mingle with state senators and city councillors.

"Her name is Margaret." Fabiano was beside me. "The sister? I thought that might be her name. Come on, let's say hello."

"Maybe later." I was developing an instinct for this sort of thing. I knew here was no place for me.

"Suit yourself." The lawyer approached the casket, knelt and prayed. "Miss Coughlin." He next clasped her hand. "Margaret. I'm sure you don't remember me. Larry Fabiano, a colleague of Damien's. Just to say what a dreadful loss."

Her smile was forced through grief and confusion. I remembered her brother, alive, preparing for court.

I had made a mistake even coming here. I shoved my hands in and out of pockets, wondering what to do next, how to act. Weisberg watched me from a corner where he conferred with his boss, the district attorney.

Weaving uneasily through the crowd, I headed for the exit. At one point, the mayor shook my hand, offering condolences. Certainly, he had no idea who I was. "I'm sure," I heard a man say, "that's the way old Damien would have wanted to go. In harness." Obviously, the speaker hadn't been there.

In the hall, someone tapped my shoulder. I turned to an ill-fitting brown suit and the great red face of police Captain Adair. "We should have a word," he said.

I edged for the door, but he stepped in front of me.

"Over here." Adair gestured to the water cooler. "It's a little bit private." Sometimes, people came through the front door, the cold blowing in behind them. The hallway was filling with the overflow from two ongoing wakes. "What I'm going to say. The reason I'm going to say this. It's to do with that business when you were a police reporter. You remember that business?"

"You know, I'm really in a hurry."

"Do you remember that business, Martell?"

"Vaguely."

"I suppose it wasn't much to you. Just a day's work to you."

"I'm sorry, but —"

"Don't." He came menacingly close. "Don't say that. We had a disagreement at the station. I tried to tell you your job. You put me in my place. Which you had every right to do. I respect that. But, in the end, you did the decent thing. You didn't run the story."

"Oh . . ."

"I've seen a rare thing in you, Martell. Compassion. And I don't forget. Of course, I'm not in any way involved in this prosecution and I can't do much to help you." He bent for a drink. "In fact, it doesn't do me any good to be seen talking to you."

"I appreciate —"

"Just listen. You went out on a limb for me and now I'm going to do the same for you. I happen to know, Martell, the assistant district attorney is seeking a warrant to arrest you."

"Arrest me? What for?"

"Something about harassing someone. Some woman named Gallagher. It's mainly an excuse from what I hear. They figure they had that trial won. And they figure you know it. And now they're scared you'll bolt on 'em."

"Arrest me . . ." Once they got me back in jail I'd never get out. Enjoy your freedom. While it lasts.

The hall was growing noisy with people. "Now," Adair continued, "it could be they've got hold of a warrant to pick you up tonight. I don't know this. But it could be. And I tell you all this, in case you got things to put in order. I owe you a favor, Martell. And this's it."

Locked away in prison, I would be dependent on Fabiano to fight for me. Imagine putting your life in his sweaty hands.

"Anyway," Adair said, "if anyone should ask, I never said any of this."

I was too shocked even to thank him for the information. As soon as he was gone I hurried for the door. "Excuse me, excuse me." I pushed aside an astonished woman.

The large, brass handle felt cold as I touched it, opening the front door. Detectives Reardon and Matteo were coming up the walk. Christ. I was too late. They had come to arrest me already. "Hey, Martell!" Reardon called.

I pushed back into the crowd, slamming the door. Shoving bodies aside, I was panicked now. "Out, out of the way."

"Hey."

"Watch who you're pushing."

There was a back door. But Matteo was probably racing to cover it. And there were doors left and right. I imagined blundering into a storeroom of dead bodies. I opened the door on my right and stepped inside, shutting it behind me.

"Can I help you?" The man's face was caught in the soft glow of a desk lamp. The bright, buzzing closeness of the corridor was gone. It was cool, dark and quiet. "Can I help you?" His voice was soothing.

A figure, probably Matteo's, ran past the window, feet clattering on the pavement.

"Huh?"

"Are you all right?" the undertaker asked.

"I need to sit down. All those people." I staggered a little. Reardon was out there, searching for me among the mourners.

"Here." The man sprang to unfold a chair. "Sit down."

"Thank you."

"Can I get you something? Water?"

"Yeah. I could use a little water." I held my head as though dizzy. "I don't feel well."

"Tell me, do you need medical attention? Should I call a doctor?"

"No. No, it's nothing like that, nothing serious."

"Just wait here, then. I'll get you some water." He went out, leaving the door ajar.

I couldn't sit here. Reardon was probably passing my picture around. I was hardly inconspicuous in a ragged parka, knocking people over. Surely someone had seen me come in here.

I couldn't let myself be arrested. If I let them put me in jail I would never get out.

The window opened easily. I put my leg outside and felt for the ground. Farther. Farther. Where was the ground?

The undertaker was at the door, holding a paper cup. But he didn't see me.

Where was the ground?

The undertaker was turned, talking to someone. Reardon?

I ducked my head under the window. The cold outside felt good on my face. I breathed deeply.

"Hey."

I dropped on one foot into the U-shaped gutter alongside the house, hitting harder than I expected, feeling the abrasive cement on my palms.

"Hey!"

On my feet, I was off, running down the street. They shouted after me. But I didn't even turn. About ten blocks away I fell on someone's lawn, behind a thick hedge, exhausted. Great white clouds of breath floated toward the moon.

But what now? My car was parked near Fabiano's office. Suppose the police had it watched. As soon as I got near I would be arrested.

So now I had no car.

Nor did it seem practical to return home.

Another problem was money. I had less than ten dollars.

In short, I needed help. And I could get it at only one place.

Pam was not surprised to see me at the door.

I'd been walking all night in the freezing cold, mostly on back streets. Once, I saw a police car and crouched behind somebody's garage until it passed. My hands stung with cold. My nose was running as well. "You look frozen," she said.

"I am frozen. Yeah." Inside, I held out my car keys. "Remember, Pam? Remember I told you I want you to have my car?"

"I don't want your car, Bill."

"I know. I know you said that. But I was wondering, wondering if I could, you know, sell it to you."

"Sell it?"

"I need a couple of hundred dollars, Pam. Look, I feel like a real ass trying to get you to buy it after I said you could have it for free, but, you know, I need the money. It's worth a lot."

"You don't understand, Bill. I don't want your car. I don't

care what it's worth. I have my own car. I don't need yours."

"Well, you could sell it. I'm sure you could get a thousand, over a thousand."

"If you need money," she said, "why don't you just ask for it?"

"Well, okay, how much have you got on you? I mean, right now."

"Just a . . . just a few dollars on me."

"That's not enough."

"Tomorrow I can go to the bank," she said.

"What time?"

"When I get up. Listen, Bill, what's the rush? All of a sudden?"

"The rush is they're going to arrest me."

She was surprised.

"They would have picked me up tonight but I ran."

"But why?"

"But why? Like they need a reason?" I moved into the living room, trying to get warm. How long would it be before the police came here, looking for me?

"What are you going to do?" she asked.

"I'm not going to jail. Obviously. I'd never get out." I collapsed on her couch. "I just want to go. Someplace where I can start over. I want to have a normal life again. I want to be like everybody else. Blend in. And then I can," I closed my hands over my face, shutting out the world, "I can relax."

She sat stiffly across from me. How quickly our relationship had chilled. "Do you have any Coke?" I asked.

She brought me a Diet Pepsi. Dehydrated by the cold, I drained it anyway, in a few swallows. Leaning back, eyes closed, I might have dozed.

"I suppose it's best," she was saying, "that you go."

"I have no choice."

"But it's too bad. Now. Even if they never catch you, they'll always say you did it."

"I can't help that."

"I thought you were making progress?" she asked.

"I've asked all the questions, yeah. Sometimes I got answers even. And every so often I thought it would fall together and make sense. But it never did. Never. Not really. Sure. Some people know things and they won't talk. So how do I force them to talk? There's no way."

"I've had an idea," she said. "All along, I've had this idea. I never wanted to tell you because I know you won't like it and maybe you won't like me for saying it. But maybe I should say it anyway."

The couch was so soft. Pam's apartment was done in bright but gentle colors.

"Sometimes," she continued, "when you can't find the truth like this, it could be because you don't really want to know what it is."

"What are you talking about?"

"You keep waiting for things to make sense. Which they never will, because you won't face the obvious."

"The obvious?"

"The problem is," she said. "As I see it. You won't get anywhere trying to figure a way out of this mess because you refuse to accept all the possibilities."

"I still don't understand what you're talking about."

"For one thing, you insist on trusting that bitch, Judy Klijner."

"Judy? What has Judy got to do with anything?"

"Well, I don't know about you, Bill, but I get really suspicious when someone's supposedly dead but there's no body."

"Are you saying Judy —? That's ridiculous."

"Why?"

"For one thing it's ridiculous," I insisted. "Judy could never be involved in a thing like that."

"Your problem is, you see a woman like that, she's what you think she is. What you want her to be. You decided Judy Klijner was such a poor sweet thing. She wasn't that at all. Not ever. Even before all this she was always one kind of person. A user.

She used you, as one prime example. Whether you realize it or not." Pam paused. "I shouldn't have started this. I know you're mad at me. And I wouldn't say any of it except that I care about you. I want to help and now you're mad at me."

"No," I said evenly. "Go on. Keep talking."

"She cheated on you with that guy, what was his name? The one at the shipyard. Telling lies was nothing unique for her. I never liked her."

"So you've said."

"You know, there were others before you. At least one at the paper I can name."

"If Judy is alive," I began. "This is ridiculous. Why would she do such a thing?"

"Pick a hundred reasons. For one thing, I hear a lot of talk at the paper about a huge insurance settlement. Klijner's quitting, you know. They say he's going to retire on it. Move to Florida or something. Suppose him and Judy cooked up this whole thing together?"

I shook my head. "Insurance settlement? Why didn't you tell me about that before?"

"I only just heard about it."

"But . . . what about all the blood?"

"Of course there was blood," she said. "And lots of it. If you wanted to convince someone you were dead, of course there'd be plenty of blood. They couldn't very well provide a body."

"I don't know."

"They found the car all bloody," she pressed. "And you were in that car. Now, whose idea was it for you to take the car?"

I'd always thought I'd been set up. But by him.

"I'm sorry," Pam added with some emotion, "but it hurt me to read, to read how you told them all in court you loved her. She had you fooled. She's still got you fooled. And it's so frustrating to watch. She didn't deserve you, Bill."

Judy alive? I couldn't accept the idea. But I was fascinated.

Pam agreed to lend me her car and a few hundred dollars. We

would meet next morning at the bank. "What are you going to do?" she asked.

"Take your car and find a place for a nap. I can't stay here. The police are bound to come looking sooner or later."

"That's not what I mean. I mean, what are you going to do after?"

"I'm not planning any further than that." I left the keys to my car, explaining where she could find it. "Just remember this, Pam. If I told them I loved Judy that was in the past. You are the only person I think about now. I love you. I want to be with you. Only you."

I slept in a rest area off the expressway. Once, a state police cruiser rolled slowly past. But no one bothered me. It got very cold, Maine all over again. From time to time I ran the heater, sleeping for one-hour intervals. My legs were cramped. Though the light blue Ford was larger than my Toyota, it had less interior room.

Judy alive? It was nonsense.

I was awake most of the night, thinking of Klijner. I'd talked to everyone else. Why not him? A parting shot on my way out of town. There was nothing to lose. Or was I afraid of what he might tell me?

Unshaven, I breakfasted at a diner far from town.

Insurance policy. That anyone should make money off this. It was obscene. Imagining him counting the money, spending it, having it in his hand. I wanted to smash something, I was so angry.

When I finally arrived at the bank, Pam was at the drive-in window in my Toyota. In the parking lot she handed me two hundred and fifty dollars. I remained groggy, but grateful. "Any trouble getting the car?" I stood beside it.

"No. No, it was right where you said."

"Did you notice? Was anyone around it? Like police or anyone?"

"I didn't see anyone."

"Anyone follow you?" I scanned the street and parking lot.

"I didn't see anyone. Like I said."

"I'll have your car back, Pam. When, I'm not sure."

"Just do me one favor," she said. "Call me so I'll know you're all right."

"Don't use my car for a few days if you can help it. If they find out you're driving my car they'll know I'm driving yours."

"Okay."

"And, ah, the money. I don't know when I can pay back the money. But I wrote this out. It's a bill of sale. I don't know if it's legal. It gives you my car."

"You don't have to do that." She reached out to me. "Just get away safely. That's all I ask."

"So the car belongs to you. In case anything happens to me. It's nothing. The car. I wish I could give you, well, whatever you'd want." Her young face was bright red with the cold and sad in a way I'll never forget.

"I'm thinking I'll never see you again," she said.

"Well. I don't know what to say." Only one person in the world cared and I was leaving her behind. I climbed back into the little Ford. My eyes ached. Not enough sleep. The world seemed faintly unreal. And I must've looked like hell.

"It's not fair." She leaned against the door. "This whole thing. It's not fair at all."

"This isn't the way I want it to be. You can see, I don't have much choice."

"Some people do all the suffering," she decided. "And some people get away with murder."

Did she mean Klijner? Or Judy?

I drove slowly through town, wary of attracting attention. A big insurance payoff. I'd pictured him killing Judy in an angry rage. That was bad enough. But suppose it was all premeditated. Done for money. Suppose he was laughing now at how easily I'd been suckered in.

Suppose Judy was laughing with him.

I drove far from the city. After a chicken sandwich and a few Cokes, I visited the Lakeview Sport Shop, a vast supermarket with everything for the sportsman, tents, fishing reels, guns. If I planned to talk to Klijner I should take precautions. Agnes Gallagher had taught me that.

In a glass case, like watches or jewelry, they were lined up, muted black barrels chained and locked to the display board. Polished handles. Of varying shapes and sizes. "I'd like to buy a gun," I told the clerk. "Handgun. Something big."

"A target pistol?"

"I need something . . . I'll tell you what I need. I'm a salesman. See? I go into a lot of really bad areas. In town. I want something big. I figure it'll scare people. You know? Sometimes I carry a lot of cash. This way, anyone gets ideas, this'll scare them away."

"You have a permit?" he asked.

"A permit?"

"You need a permit, man."

"There's no way to get around it?" I asked.

"Not here. There's plenty of places to buy guns without permits. But this isn't one of them. It's not legal, you know."

"Maybe you know someone," I asked, "someone who sells guns that way?"

"No. No way. I don't. No. And you could get in big trouble carrying one that isn't registered."

"Well, how do you get a permit?"

"You get it from the police chief in your town," he said. "But you better have a damn good reason to ask for it. They won't want to give it to you."

He didn't know the half of it.

"How about a knife? Do I need a permit to buy a knife?"

"Ah . . . no. I could show you some hunting knives."

Like the guns they were arranged in a glass case. Some came with attractive tanned leather holsters. I bought the biggest, a mean-looking thing with a wide, stainless-steel blade. I could see my face in it. On the tan sheath was stitched a pine tree. "Will that do you?" asked the clerk.

"I think so."

"Still. You better watch out. You keep this in your pocket or something, you're carrying a concealed weapon. That's big trouble if you get caught."

fifteen

IN THE LATE AFTERNOON I drove past Roy Klijner's house. His car was parked on the street. Judy's Pinto, however, was gone. A lamp glowed in a front window, the remainder of the house was dark.

I wondered if he'd finally sold the Pinto.

Some minutes later I drove past again. Nothing had changed. His big, blue sedan was still there. The house was dark, except for the single light. And a police car was coming up behind me.

"Jeez!" I swerved a little.

Don't panic. He's not chasing you. I braked abruptly at a red light.

Stop looking in the rearview mirror. Pretend he's not there.

I turned left.

So did he.

"Jesus." I went a little faster. I could feel the muscles in my back tightening. Don't do anything stupid. He's not following you. Relax. Stay calm. Don't screw up.

Every time I looked in the mirror I saw him.

But he had no reason to follow me. I was driving Pam's car. He couldn't see my face in the dark.

I pulled into the parking lot of a Chinese restaurant. The police car hurried past. He hadn't been chasing me at all. A coincidence. I sat, collecting myself. I couldn't allow them to catch me.

On the restaurant pay phone I called Klijner's number. Maybe he'd changed the number. Maybe he wasn't answering the phone.

More likely, he was not home.

At eight o'clock I drove past the house again. It was unchanged. And then at nine and ten, it was exactly the same. At eleven the single light in the front window went out.

So, someone was home.

I called again. Still, no answer. Most probably, the lamp was on a timer. No one was home. Then where could he be? I knew of only one place.

I rolled slowly down Seaside Lane toward Horse Neck Beach. To my left I remembered the thorns of a blackberry patch and a single, sandy path. This was the back entrance to Agnes Gallagher's beachhouse. I peered over the bramble. There, glowing like a half-moon, was the top of Judy's yellow car. Klijner was here.

Seaside Lane is a dead end, not connected to the Gallagher house. Beyond a broken fence and a few flattened bushes was the ocean. By walking down a narrow path I could approach the house from the beach.

My sneakers were swallowed by sand as I walked through sparse, long dry grass and over a large dune. Off the water, the wind was steady, fierce and damp. I reached in my coat pocket among sticks of gum, tissues and loose change for the steel blade sheathed in leather. At some point, I should have strapped it on my belt or something. My freezing fingers curled around it.

Agnes Gallagher's house had a deck on the beach side. Along the deck was a picture window. Inside, a television set produced a bluish glow. A man, certainly Roy, was watching it, slumped in a reclining chair. He looked warm, comfortable, while I was outside, freezing.

Keeping low over the sand dune, I dropped to my knee. So cold. The wind burrowed under my coat, chilling my skin. My fingers were quickly numbed.

At least, the howling weather would cover any noise. Keeping to the scrubby bush that surrounded Mrs. Gallagher's neat lawn, I made my way to the front of the house. I saw only one car in the driveway, the yellow Pinto. Mrs. Gallagher's car was gone.

On the porch, I pulled the knife. A single street lamp helped me find the door. Houses and cottages were all around. Happily, none had a good view of me.

So now what? I was at Roy Klijner's door with a knife. Do I knock? At midnight he would certainly be on guard. Suppose he answered with that gun in his hand.

Suddenly, my blade seemed quite small. Against a gun, useless. I could imagine Klijner snickering. Hearing voices, I pressed near the windowpane. It was the television. Crazy. On the porch with my knife I listened to people laughing on television.

I could see little of the room. I remembered it as small. The hallway, leading, evidently, to the game room, glowed with television light. The window seemed to be locked as I gave it a good tug. Probably they were all locked. Agnes Gallagher seemed the sort who left little to chance.

So, how do you break into a house?

Just the idea was frightening. Maybe I should have thought this over more carefully. Breaking and entering. What did I know about breaking and entering?

The storm door was unlocked. It opened noiselessly. She kept it oiled. Encouraging. And easy. Almost too easy.

The second door was thick panels of wood. I grasped the icy metal knob and took a deep, slow breath. Now, very slowly, very firmly, I turned it clockwise. It rattled and stuck. Okay. Okay.

Wait a second. Try it the other way. I swallowed with difficulty. The storm door, on a spring, was pressed against my back. A cold, rickety thing of glass and metal, it rattled with every movement.

Now. I turned the doorknob slowly counterclockwise. It clicked and stopped. Damn. It was locked. What now?

Thieves often broke into houses with credit cards. Didn't they? As I understood it, you slipped the credit card between the door and doorjamb. The hard edge of the card lifts the tongue from the catch. But I no longer had a credit card. Besides, I'd probably just screw it up.

And even if I got in, what? Klijner would have the perfect excuse to shoot me. Jesus, why think of that?

Maybe he saw me crawling over the dune. Maybe he was inside right now, pointing the gun at the door, waiting for me to open it. God.

Instead of a credit card why not the knife? I could slide it between the door and the jamb and sort of pry the door open.

And then he'd shoot me. The second I walked in the door. I'd lie on the floor, a hole blasted in my stomach. Him standing over me. He'd wait for me to die before he called the police.

But, of course, Klijner wasn't expecting me. Long ago, he'd decided I was too scared or too stupid to be any threat to him. He's smug and arrogant and thinks he's getting away with murder. He won't know better until he sees me.

The knife slipped easily into the crack between the door and the jamb. Lots of play. I pushed on the weapon. The door squealed like a living thing. I stopped moving, breathing. Jesus. Jesus, he must have heard that. I listened for him, my ear on the door.

I heard the wind, a ceaseless scream.

My heart thumped at my ears.

And the laughter still came from the television.

Nothing else.

Maybe Roy was asleep.

I pushed on the knife. The door squeaked again, a noise to wake the dead. But it seemed to separate from the jamb as though it might pop open. I pushed it harder. It made more noise. Still, it gave the promise of swinging inward, open.

If I could just give it one hard push. For one moment it would make a loud noise, but then it would be open and the noise would stop.

I pushed against it heavily, grunting. The door cried and cracked, the hinges rattled. And it didn't open.

Lights came on inside.

Oh, Jesus.

Someone. On the other side of the door. Someone was walking around.

Jesus.

I pressed against the door.

"Who's there?" It didn't sound like Klijner. The voice was high-pitched, tense. He was afraid. But it didn't make me feel any better. "Who's . . . who's there?"

Jesus. Now I'd done it. Jesus. I clutched the knife. If he opened the door I would use it. On him. Before he could shoot me. I would slash him. I could imagine the sensation. I was ready. Ready.

The door rattled. I could feel his warm hand at the knob. I raised the knife, forced myself to breathe. I would need strength. This is his own fault. My hand shook. He's forcing me to fight.

But the door didn't open. He was merely testing it, making certain it was locked.

I could hear him at the window. I tried to flatten myself on the door, making sure not to touch it, allowing the storm door to swing nearly shut behind me. My legs soon ached, holding this awkward pose.

Now he was at the phone. I could hear the dial. His spoken words were indistinct. The television drowned him out. Someone said quite clearly, "We'll be right back."

While Klijner was on the phone, I carefully, slowly allowed the storm door to close. Then, I took two long steps off the porch. Like a soldier under fire, I scurried into the blackberry patch.

Of course, he was calling the police. I withdrew along the sand path, toward the beach and the dune guarding it. In less than ten minutes they arrived. Flashing lights bounced off the house, sand and trees like some blue Fourth of July. But because of shrubs all around me, I could lie flat and remain undetected.

One police officer met Klijner near the front porch. They chatted as his partner walked around the house. A flashlight beam searched among the trees, behind the trash barrels, under the deck.

God, it was cold. And lying still made it worse. I dropped my knife and slammed my hands together for warmth. But I could barely manipulate my fingers and no longer could feel my toes. I moaned aloud. Yet the wind blew the sound away. And beyond was the ocean, tide coming in, spraying the beach, adding to the din.

The two policemen and Klijner, who was coatless, bouncing up and down, now approached the police car with its electric colored flashers still ricocheting wildly off the house and my freezing fingers. The light, revolving, coming my way at intervals, gave the three figures the illusion of jerky, unnatural movement, like a silent movie.

And now the freezing sky filled with tiny ice crystals, glittering to life whenever the frigid blue brightness swung around to sting them. It gave the air a fantastic, unforgettable appearance, as if aswarm with tiny blue diamonds.

But I had no time to admire the sky. Behind the sand dune, I crawled along the beach toward the house. When I reached the deck, my legs felt as though they were encased in concrete. I rose painfully to an upright position and paused at the steps, allowing blood to circulate, bring awareness again to my extremities. I was unable to feel the knife in my hand. I flexed my fingers.

I had to work fast, while Klijner was out of the house. The sky was still whirling with the blue police lights. I could be reasonably certain he was still speaking to the two cops, probably describing me, telling lies.

At the back entrance was another metal and glass storm door, and a windowed wooden door. I yanked at the storm door. It was locked.

With the butt end of the knife I smashed a hole in the glass. Reaching in, I opened the door. Just then, the blue light died. What did that mean? Were the police leaving? Was Klijner back in the house? Were all three men surrounding me at this moment? Without a pause, I smashed the window on the wooden door. It was rather high and a long, uncomfortable reach to the doorknob and the chain lock inside. Because of my long arms I was able to do it.

The door swung open. I entered the house. No one challenged me. Glass crunched beneath my feet. The room was empty, the television unbearably loud. It was just noise.

Knife poised, I closed the door behind me. Warm in here. Thank God for that. Somewhere, someone was crying. A child.

I moved cautiously. The child screeched louder. I began to worry that his cries would bring the police inside.

My fingers were thawing, the dull pain like an electric current, coming, going.

Down the hallway to the front room, I studied the door where Mrs. Gallagher had shot at me. Outside, the police sat in their car, Klijner standing alongside. Now the cruiser pulled back, bouncing over ruts frozen in the sand, then roaring forward, up the street. Klijner was returning to the house.

I would greet him with the knife.

Suppose he picked up a chair, tried to fight?

No, I've a better idea. I went to the telephone table and pulled at the drawer. It stuck, locked. Hurry the hell up. He was on the porch. Using the knife, I pried at the top of the drawer. The table lamp threatened to topple. Steadying that with one hand, I gave a hard pull up. The drawer sprang open.

In the same place where Agnes Gallagher had found it was the gun. Flat black. And polished wood grip. Small. A woman's weapon. Just lying in the drawer. And with a child in the house. People can be so stupid.

When Klijner walked in I pointed the gun directly at him. His mouth opened, but he said nothing.

"Shut the door." I held the gun out where I could see it. Was it even loaded? How about the safety? Didn't guns have safeties to prevent accidental firings? Well, it was too late for that now.

Klijner didn't move.

"Shut the door. You're not going anywhere. Don't think you're going anywhere."

"No," he shut it, "I'm not going anywhere."

"Lock it."

He pulled a chain lock across. "How . . . how did you get in?"

"Don't do anything stupid while I have this gun. Your sister, this is your sister's gun. And she pointed it at me once. It went off practically by itself. You know? So don't do anything sudden. And don't do anything stupid."

He was stiff with fright. Did he think he was about to die? His eyes were so alive, looking everywhere at once. I enjoyed seeing someone else squirm for a change. "What do you want?" he asked.

"First off, I want you to quiet down the little boy in there."

"Okay." But he didn't move. "I'll have to go in the room and talk to him."

"I don't care how you do it. Just get him back to sleep." The shrill howling was doing a job on my nerves.

"His room is right behind you there. How should we do this?" He didn't take his eyes from the gun. I knew exactly how he felt. I'd been in his position.

"We should do it," I beckoned, "we should do it very slowly." I took one small step backward. He took one timid step forward. But we couldn't continue in this manner. There might be a toy or who knows what on the floor behind me. That's all I'd need, falling on my ass. "Wait a minute." The gun pointed at him, I took quick looks to my rear.

Watching Klijner, I noticed for the first time that we were the same height. Also, I spotted an occasional strand of gray in his hair. He was older than I remembered, the face lined and pink after being outside. Yet, already, small drops of sweat appeared on his forehead. He wanted to live. He wasn't ready to face God, not with so much to answer for.

In the narrow hall, I was past the child's room. The house was of recent construction, the walls of cheap panel, the door thin. It was really a cottage. The little boy screamed almost hysterically, with nothing to muffle the sound.

"What's the matter?" I asked.

"The lights," Klijner said. "The police. It scared him."

I followed him into the room. The light was a large plastic globe, a replica of a basketball. The child stood in his crib, sobbing now. His eyes were wide and distressed, blond hair matted with sweat. There was a salty smell peculiar to small children.

"What's the matter, Mike?" His father tried to sound calm, reassuring. He held the child. "What's the matter? What's the matter?"

The boy stopped crying, but remained disturbed, looking to me, regarding his father's odd, nervous behavior. The light swung from the ceiling creating shadows, looming, then shrinking away. "Shhh. Daddy's got company. You go to sleep." But the boy was not appeased. Lying down, his body was rigid, fearful.

"You got the poor kid scared worse than when we came in here," I said.

"I know what I'm doing."

"You got the heat so high." I was sweating in my winter parka. "It's not healthy."

"If you get out of here," Klijner said, "maybe I can get him back to sleep."

I backed into the hall. "I can see you from here. So don't try anything." I was alive to every noise. Suppose the police came back. Suppose they were peering in the windows. I had assumed Klijner and the child were alone in the house. What if someone else was here? Maybe he had a girlfriend hiding in the closet or sneaking out the back door. His sister's car was gone. But his sister might be here.

Or Judy.

He was bent over the child. "Daddy will be right outside. Okay? You go to sleep."

On television, the loud laughter was frequent and cynical. It offended me. There was nothing funny, nothing to laugh at.

"Hurry up," I said, and the child immediately began to whine again. It took another five minutes to calm him. I was terribly uncomfortable in my padded parka. But I dared not take it off, or drop my guard a moment.

"I'm coming out," Klijner said.

"Stand here in the hallway and then I'll tell you what to do." I stepped back, pointing the gun. The weapon seemed surprisingly light when I first picked it up. But it was growing heavier with every minute. I kept changing hands. Once, I slipped my finger over the trigger. Mostly, I kept away from the trigger.

Klijner left the light on and door ajar. He allowed himself a long look, as if he might never see the boy again.

"Okay," I whispered. "Is anyone else in the house?"

"No."

"Where's your sister?"

"On vacation," he said. "Gone all week."

"I hope so. I hope you wouldn't lie about this."

"No."

"Cause I wouldn't want people barging in on us."

"They won't."

"Good," I said. "Let's go shut that noise off, that television." We moved to the back room. I switched on a small lamp beside the recliner. Klijner shut off the television. The colors, smiles and laughter faded to a single white dot in the center of the screen. Then, that died too.

Except for the wind it was quiet.

"Now what?" He remained still, avoiding sudden moves. Every minute the gun pointed at him.

"You sit down here, Roy. I want you to be comfortable."

Moving slowly, carefully, he sat in the recliner.

"Sit back in it."

He rocked back, feet leaving the floor, body almost horizontal. Now, he would be easier to deal with. He could hardly spring on me from that position.

The child began to cry again. Damn. Would he ever go to sleep? "He'll quiet down," Klijner insisted. "He'll cry himself to sleep."

I sat in a straight-backed chair. Allowing too much comfort would be a mistake. I hadn't slept very much the night before. And tonight I needed to remain wide awake. "Tell me where Judy is," I said.

"I don't know." He stared at the gun, which was propped on my knee. Perhaps he was familiar with it. Maybe he was noticing the safety.

I resolved to assume the safety was off. When I got a chance I would examine it more carefully.

"Do you believe God punishes people for their sins?" I asked now.

"What?"

"Myself, I'm not sure about it. And, I think, in case it's not true. In case there is no God and nobody punishes people after they die. In case of that. I think it's important to punish them while they're still alive. Ever think of that?"

"What do you want from me?" he asked.

"But the trouble is, when it comes to punishment, the trouble is the courts just screw it up. I've seen that firsthand. Twenty years, they told me. If I took them to Judy's body? I could get off with twenty years. Or less. Does that sound fair?"

"I . . . I don't know what you want me to say."

"What is your life worth, Klijner? If I shot you? Is twenty years enough?"

The child's crying stopped at some point. It was silent again except for wind blowing through the broken windows, like whispering.

"I know about the insurance," I said.

"What?"

"And I know about you quitting the paper, moving away."

"It's no secret," he said.

"Don't pretend it isn't important. You're retiring on the insurance money. Isn't that true?"

"No."

"How much money is it, Klijner?"

"Well. It could be a million dollars and you couldn't retire on it. Not in this day and age. With all this inflation."

"When I want an economics lesson I'll let you know."

Klijner gave a hopeless shrug. Slowly, he was pushing the recliner upright.

"Someone planned this whole thing," I said. "By that I mean it was premeditated. In the legal sense. I figure this because your car wasn't there that day. What you must've done, you drove the car here. And you got back to your house somehow. Maybe your sister drove you back. Or someone. And you made sure no one saw you."

Klijner was relatively impassive, though I had his concentration totally. He seemed particularly attentive to the pistol.

"When you got home you made that bloody mess in the kitchen. And later you made another mess in the car. You did all this deliberately because you knew I'd be coming along. I took the car. I walked in the kitchen looking for Judy. Oh, yeah, I was a very cooperative guy. Made to order. Fingerprints everywhere. Witnesses. You must've been delighted."

For a moment he looked less sure of himself.

"How am I doing so far?"

"You're guessing," he protested. "And all your guesses are wrong."

He was still pushing forward in the recliner. Slowly, imperceptibly, his feet had come almost to the floor.

"Don't."

"Don't what?" he froze.

I checked the aim of the pistol on my knee. It was pointed somewhere to the center of his body, head, chest, stomach, depending on how far back he was leaning.

"In court," he spoke softly, "in court you said you couldn't kill anyone. Under any circumstances."

"Well, don't bet your life on it."

He talked of killing. Nothing like it had crossed my mind. Until he said it. He was afraid of the gun. The gun. It was all I had going for me. "You're wondering how you're going to get out of this," I said. "The way I feel about it is this way. Either you tell me what I want to know . . . or don't think about getting out of this."

"I have to go to the bathroom," he said. "I don't feel well."

The zipper on my parka was down all the way. But I wore a sweater under that. And I was soaking in this overheated house. The heat numbed as quickly as the cold. I wasn't sleepy yet, but I resolved to beware of grogginess. Stay alert. "Where's the kitchen?" I asked. "We're going to the kitchen."

Slowly, down the narrow hallway, Klijner went first. He was restless with the gun at his back, continually turning to look at it. "Now, where's the kitchen?"

"Over there." He pointed left, to a dark doorway.

"Okay. You go in. Very slowly. Don't do anything sudden. Understand?"

"I understand." The barrel of the gun floated hypnotically at his back a few feet away.

"When you get to the kitchen," I said. "First thing. Put on the light."

He took a step past the archway, reached up and turned on the light. The kitchen was cramped, with a small, square table exactly in the middle. "What now?" he asked.

"Do you have any Coke?"

"No."

"Christ. Then make me some coffee." I grabbed a banana from a bowl on the counter, peeled it with one hand, biting away the skin. Meanwhile, I never took my eyes off Klijner. He went to the sink and filled the kettle. He reached for instant coffee on the shelf and cups on a hook nearby. "No," I said. "Put it in a glass. Biggest glass you got. With sugar." I stood at the doorway, the gun damp and uncomfortable in my hand. The kitchen was too small for two under the circumstances.

He poured a teaspoon of sugar into a large glass beer mug.

"More sugar," I said.

I watched closely, taking care he didn't poison or drug me. The kettle whistled. He lifted it from the gas, pouring it, steaming into the glass. When he picked up the glass by its handle, I imagined him wheeling, hurling the scalding liquid in my face.

"No, no," I snapped. "Put it down and pick it up from the top."

"The top?" he asked.

"That's right. Keep your hands off the handle. Pick it up from the top. With your fingertips."

"But . . . I'll burn my —"

"I don't give a good goddamn. Okay? Just do what I say. What the Christ do you think this is? I'm not kidding around here. Pick it up and put it right here."

I took a cautious step backward as he hurried to deposit it on the counter. Then, he shuffled away, blowing on his fingers. "Maybe you better make some for yourself." I took a sip. It was steaming hot and sweet. "It's going to be a long night. Make some for yourself."

I drank the coffee very quickly. I had grown thirsty in this hot-house. "We're going to see Judy," I said. "You're going to take me to her."

"I can't."

"It's not like you have a choice, Roy. You're going to take me."

"Or what?"

"Or don't ask."

sixteen

"IF YOU HURT ME," Roy Klijner was saying, "you'll be hurting an innocent man."

"I don't think so. I think if we get into that car you'll drive me right to her."

"I don't know where she is." His voice was high-pitched. "Honest to God I don't."

"Maybe we'll take a walk on the beach instead."

He stared at the gun, a tiny black hole at the end of the barrel.

"And if you think I'm kidding, Roy, it's probably because you don't know what I've been through the past months."

He began compulsively scratching his wrist, tearing at it, without a conscious thought of doing this.

"Do you believe me, Roy?"

"What?"

"You believe me?"

"Yeah."

"Good, we're getting somewhere. Now. Where is Judy?"

"Anything could have happened to her."

"Don't whine, Roy."

"Maybe she just went crazy, berserk, and ran away. I often think that."

"Where is she, Roy?"

"What do you want me to say?"

"I want the truth. Tell me where she is, you goddamn son of a bitch. Tell me!" I gestured with the gun. His eyes followed it everywhere. "Let me tell you, when your sister had this gun it went off practically by itself. Now, that is something to think about."

The child began to cry again.

Klijner bowed his head. "Tell me what to say. I'll say it."

"Answer the fucking question." I pushed halfway across the room, knocking the table into him. It frightened both of us. But this hysteria accomplished nothing. I took a deep breath. Stay calm, calculating.

"Last night, Roy, last night they tried to arrest me again. They already wrecked my apartment. I lost my job. People who used to be friends won't talk to me. My whole life is maybe ruined forever. And you know something? Shooting you won't make it all better. But it'll help."

He sagged.

"Where is she?"

"I can tell you," he admitted.

"Do that."

"I, ah," he struggled for composure, "I got in a fight with her."

"Yeah?"

"She hit her head. That's, that's what killed her."

Was this the truth? At last? I watched him closely. He avoided eye contact. "Where is the body?" I asked.

The child was howling again, calling "Maaaa . . ."

"In the woods," he replied.

"What woods?"

"I don't know what all this proves."

"What woods? I'm asking you this for the last time." I lifted the pistol slightly. My hand was shaking.

"Okay. Okay. Don't get excited. I'll tell you."

"Where is she?"

"In the reservation."

"Hubbard Road? You mean Hubbard Road?"

"Yeah. That's it."

"Good. That's good. Doesn't it feel better to tell the truth?"

He collapsed in a chair, elbows on the table, running fingers through his damp hair. I wished I could sit down. My eyes ached worst of all and I was frequently rubbing at one or the other. I wanted so to believe his confession. But Pam's suspicions infected everything. If Judy was alive.

"We're going to go there," I said.

"Go where?"

"To the reservation. To Judy."

"I don't . . . I doubt I can remember where she is."

"You'll remember, Roy. When you get there. It'll all come back to you."

"We can't go tonight," he said. "My son. We can't leave him here alone."

"Don't use the kid for an excuse. He'll be all right."

"Don't you know anything about children? At that age he has to be watched at all times. You can't leave him on his own."

"We'll take him with us," I said. "I'll look out for him. Don't worry."

"We can't take him with us," he scoffed. "It's freezing out."

"Would you rather leave him here?" I asked. "Because that's the choice. We take him with us. Or we go without him. But we're going."

The child stopped crying as Klijner dressed him in a winter suit that covered him from neck to ankles. Barely awake, the boy only glanced at me, uncomprehending. "I'm going to give him a bottle," Klijner said. "Some warm milk and a sleeping pill."

"You give a sleeping pill to a kid?"

"Would you rather listen to him scream?"

"That doesn't seem right, drugging a little kid."

"His mother gave him pills," Klijner insisted. "Whenever we went on a long trip."

He prepared the bottle in the kitchen, sitting the groggy child on the table where he swayed and at one pointed threatened to topple. Taking a sleeping pill from his pocket, Klijner cut it in half with a butter knife. I felt drowsy myself.

Klijner carried the child, little legs protruding on either side of his father's back, arms wrapped around his neck. The wind blew. I was cold again, pointing the gun at the back of the man's skull, trying to zip my parka with one hand. I couldn't do it and settled for holding it together. "We'll take your car," I said.

"The Pinto?"

"Do you see any other car around here?"

"I don't have the keys," he said.

"You better have the keys."

"I don't. They're in the house."

"You better have the keys," I raised my voice. At times I must have seemed out of control. I did this purposely to frighten him. But, often, I had to check myself from going too far, losing control, in fact.

"Oh, wait a minute." With difficulty, he balanced the child while digging into his pocket. "Yeah, I guess I have another set here. Yeah. I forgot. I just completely forgot I had these. I don't usually wear this coat."

I snatched them away. "Okay. Let's go." We filed down the sand-ridden lawn toward the driveway. He kept turning to me. "Keep your eyes front. Watch where you're going."

At the car, he stopped, "What should I do now?"

"Open the door and put the little boy in. Then we'll go around to the driver's side."

He sat the boy on the front seat, where he started to cry. "Shhh. Daddy's here. Shhhh. Be quiet." He pushed the warm bottle into his mouth. Closing the door, he went slowly around the back of the car to the driver's side. I was always a step or two behind.

"Okay. Open the door and get in the front seat." As he did this

I got in the back. It was even colder in the car. The windows fogged. "Here." I held out his keys. "Start the car. And don't turn around."

The car suffered several false starts. "What's wrong?"

"It's cold. Sometimes it doesn't start in the cold."

"It better. You hear me, Roy? It fuckin better start. For your sake." I held the gun. I was actually enjoying the enormous power in the gun.

The child whined. "Drink your milk," Klijner said softly. The car shook and started. Little Michael cried louder, competing with the noise of the engine. "It'll take a minute," Roy said. "It has to warm up for a minute."

Without warning, the boy was standing, silent, looking right at me. "Sit down," Klijner told him softly. I shrank into the corner, not knowing where to point the gun.

"What's the matter? I thought he was going to sleep."

"Drink your milk." The father stroked his head. "There's a blanket beside you. On the seat there. Can I have it?" I passed a small wool blanket to the front. Klijner spread it over his son. "I'm going to slip the seat belt on him and lock his door. Okay?"

"Go ahead," I said.

He did this. "The milk . . . he's all right. He'll go out soon. A few seconds." Klijner was gentle with the boy. What did that prove?

As we rolled slowly up the street, a police car came sweeping around the corner. I ducked to the floor. "Don't stop. Don't slow down. Don't even look at them."

I waited for blue lights, sirens. But we rolled quietly along. There was little traffic on these roads. Klijner said nothing. The steady hum of the engine and the growing warmth soon put the child back to sleep. I allowed my parka to fall open. "Gimme a little of that heat back here. Put on the blower."

On the expressway, the traffic was amazingly thick. "Two o'clock in the morning," I mentioned idly. "Where the hell are all these people going?" I realized the gun was pointed to the floor, probably at my own foot. Watch that. Don't get careless.

"I want to ask about the little boy," I said.

"He's asleep now. Finally."

"I heard him tonight. He called for his mother."

"He misses her," Klijner said. "He misses his mother."

"No. After three months. Kids forget. I know that much. At his age they forget."

"Maybe they do. He hasn't forgotten."

We turned off the expressway, directly onto the reservation road, a fine, wide blacktop with a thick yellow line down the middle. It twisted and turned about stands of pine, ledges of sharpened granite, and naked birches, luminous white by moonlight. I saw only an occasional car, though I kept alert for the police.

I was excited as we rounded a familiar turn. Hubbard Road was only a few minutes away. And a great mystery would be solved. After three months of horror I could sleep again.

"Slow down, Klijner."

"What?"

"Slow down, I said. You're going to drive right past it."

"Oh."

"What are you doing? That's the turn. Right there. Stop."

We stopped with a lurch in the middle of the road.

"Jesus Christ. What kind of game are you playing? There it is, right there. What's wrong with you?"

"I forgot," he said.

"You forgot. Bullshit."

We rolled down Hubbard Road, the car bouncing over great potholes, stones and loose macadam. For a while, as we went steadily downhill, gaining speed, the overgrown tangle of trees cut the moonlight from the narrow road. We seemed to be descending into a black pit. I became afraid of something in the night, hanging over us. I searched for the moon, but could see only dark outlines of leafless branches. "Where?" I asked. "Where is she?"

/ 282

"I don't remember."

"Come on. Don't pull that shit now. You know where."

"I can't, I can't remember. Honest to God." He stopped the car. The trees were nearly gone. The swamp was before us and the end of the road in sight.

"It was Hubbard Road?" I grunted in his ear. "It was on this road?"

"It was on this road. Yeah. Somewhere. Near this road."

"Was it one of the trails? One of the hiking trails from this road?"

"Yes. One of the trails. Yes, that's it."

"Good. Good, we're getting somewhere. Which trail?"

"I don't know."

"Well, think."

He pointed.

"You better be sure. I'm not fucking around out here forever. If you say you're sure you better be sure."

He drove up the worn, dirt path. An evergreen forest soon closed in and we were jostled riding over thick tree roots and deep, rain-washed ruts. At times, I doubted the car would survive this trip. But Klijner pushed on, as though he'd been this way before. The headlights pointed out the route, long white fingers picking among the trees.

"You're sure this is it?"

"I said so," he retorted.

In the reservation cabins are available for lease. But not around here. Nothing lived in the freezing black beyond this car. And I was relieved, in spite of myself. Alive, she had betrayed me. I no longer expected to find Judy alive.

"You buried her down this trail?"

"I said yes."

Once, the car seemed stuck, but he pumped the gas, jerking us forward. The sleeping child moaned dreamily. In the distance, I could see a strange, white glow. "How far do we go?" I asked.

"I don't know."

"You better know." And later I asked, "Tell me how far we go."

"We go a ways."

Presently, the trail narrowed, the car hesitated, grinding over a rock-ridden rise of land. Klijner gave it gas, but the engine strained, roared, and died. All was silent except for him, breathing as though he had pushed the car rather than driven it. The oil gauge light made all our faces red and the headlights still beamed into the woods. "Is this the place?"

He gave a tremulous sigh.

"Is this it? Is she here?"

"I don't remember."

"You don't remember. You don't know. I'm getting sick of hearing that. Is she here or not?"

"You know, in the dark," he said. "It's hard to tell in the dark."

"Did you drive all the way before? Or did you have to get out and walk some of the way?"

"I drove."

"You mean down that way? Toward the lights?" I asked.

"Yes." He nodded.

"Okay. Okay, let's go down that way."

He made to start the car.

"No. Let's walk. You can't get the car past those goddamn boulders in the dark. You'll rip out the transmission. Let's walk."

"What about Mike?" he asked.

"He'll be okay. We're going to come right back."

"You want to leave him here alone?"

"We can't take him with us," I said. "Christ. What are we going out there for?"

Klijner stared at the sleeping boy.

"Hand me the keys."

He did.

"Turn out the lights."

Without lights it was darker than I expected, positively black. What was out there? I might be better off not knowing. "Get out of the car."

As Klijner moved from the front seat, I moved from the back. Cold. I could feel dead leaves and twigs cracking as I moved. In the dark it seemed so much worse to be cold. And Klijner was an indistinct shadow. "The boy," he muttered.

"I told you, we'll be right back."

"He'll wake up while we're gone. He'll be scared. Anybody would be. Alone in the dark."

"He's out. He's not going to wake up for nothing and you know it." I slammed the door shut. The boy never stirred. "We won't be long."

What were we going to see? Nothing. I was convinced.

We moved carefully toward the curious horizon of light. I kept my eye on Klijner's back, his dark brown coat that sometimes threatened to disappear in the blackness. My greatest concern was my footing. Even when I could look down, it was difficult to see the ground. Once, Klijner stumbled and actually fell to his knees.

"Get up."

"I'm all right." He came unsteadily to his feet. "Watch out. There's a log or something here."

My fingers ached from the icelike gun. It seemed I'd been carrying that pistol for days. I was constantly switching, holding it in one hand, allowing the other the warmth of my pocket.

"I got to go the bathroom," he said.

"What?"

"Really. I got to. I'm sick." Klijner staggered toward a small bush. Noisy, he left little doubt he was actually sick. "Ah," he called, "have any Kleenex?"

"No. For Christ's sake."

"That's okay." Sick or not, he was stalling, like a salesman with more faith in his pitch than his product.

"Hurry the hell up," I urged him back to the trail.

It was soon brighter. And less quiet. Through the trees were electric lights of some kind. "What is this?" I asked, getting nervous.

Suddenly, it was all familiar.

seventeen

WE WERE NEARING the expressway. In the early morning came the roar of eighteen-wheeled trucks. I followed Klijner to a clearing of sparse brown grass. On our right was an ice-covered pond drained from a large pipe under the road. The highway itself was on a rise.

"Where is she?" I spoke against the constant rattle and hum of traffic.

Klijner turned and faced me. He looked ordinary, maybe a little intimidated.

"Where is she?"

"I . . . here. Here somewhere."

"Where?"

"Here." He spread his arms. It was an unlikely place to bury someone, in full view of a major highway.

"Where is she? Show me the spot. The exact spot."

"I don't . . . I don't remember."

"Yes, you do."

"No."

"Don't fuck around, Roy. I don't want to think you dragged

me all this way for nothing. Show me where she is. If she's here."

"Don't shoot me."

"If there's something here, point to it. Just point."

"I don't know," he whined. "Believe me." He bent before a sudden gust of freezing wind, turning his back, putting his hand to his eyes.

"You think you can stall forever, but you can't. Hear?" Extending my arm, I pointed the gun and for a moment actually tagged his head. My finger curled over the trigger, though I could no longer feel the trigger or my finger. My eyes squinted involuntarily. The weapon refused to remain steady. I braced for the noise and recoil, turning away slightly, wondering if the thing would even fire in this cold.

"Don't . . ."

"Where is she? For the last fucking time."

"Over there."

"Where?"

He shuffled slowly to the edge of the forest, sniffling, shoulders stooped. "She's there." He pointed behind a large evergreen. "There."

I moved close to a small pile of leaves, dirt and rotting litter from the highway, paper cups frozen fast to the earth. "She's there?" I kicked a rusted oil can. "Come on."

"She is."

"Prove it."

He looked helplessly to the little mound.

"Dig," I said.

Klijner dropped to the ground, on his knees. He pushed and kicked away a top layer of leaves, litter and dirt. Time running out, his nose dripped on the frozen earth. He scraped at the ground again and again. Finally, he held out his hands, worked raw and bleeding. "I can't. It's frozen."

"Here." I dropped my knife on the ground. "Dig with this."

After a time, he had cleared away a large heap of dirt and

rock. Still no body, though he remained as grim as death, absorbed by the chore. And every moment I watched his hands working my knife into the soil. Giving him the knife was stupid.

Once he dug below the frost line, loose dirt flew, followed swiftly by an unforgettable odor. A cloud of unbreathable air billowed up from within the earth. I wanted to run. Klijner made soft, pitiable sounds in the back of his throat.

I stared at the growing excavation in horrified astonishment. She was there. A human being, beneath our feet. Someone we had known, laughed with, loved. Both of us.

"God . . ." Words grabbed in my mouth. And everything was dry and hot, as if the weather counted for nothing.

I saw a quilt. Even by indirect street light I saw the faded, dirty colors. Klijner was machinelike, clearing soil from it.

I took a step back. To come to this, finally. I didn't want to look.

He tugged the quilt away.

Her hair, thick and black, in bangs over her forehead. "Judy . . ."

Her face, only glimpsed. Was it white, eyes opened? Did I imagine that? Or did the light play tricks? I studied my feet, repelled by the thought of what I might find looking more closely at Judy.

"Oh . . ." I staggered away. Enough. "Cover her up. Cover her up."

Slowly, I dropped to the ground, sitting against a tree about twenty feet beyond. "Leave her alone. Cover her up."

He was already doing this. Very efficiently replacing the quilt. Scraping and pushing the dirt back on top of her.

"How could you do it? How could you do it?"

Judy had never betrayed me. But I found little satisfaction in that now. With all my heart I wished her alive.

Klijner continued to work. The terrible smell of human decay lingered, suffocating. Twenty feet away it infected everything, my clothes, the earth, the trees.

Poor Judy. I felt keenly that I'd failed her. And she died knowing this.

"How could you? How could you kill her? Just kill her?"

He was kneeling, fussing with the pile of leaves. Judy was reburied. The knife was in his hand. Suppose he came at me, wielding the knife. Suppose he did that. Let him. Let him try. I'll kill him. Shoot him. The bastard. I'd like to do that. Kill him.

"It was an accident," he mumbled. He stumbled toward me, flexing his knees. "What do we do now?" he asked softly.

I stood up to him, aiming the gun at his heart. I wanted it to go off.

"This is yours." He dropped the knife at my feet. I stooped to retrieve it. But I kept my eyes on him. He didn't move, seemingly resigned to whatever I might do. "Should . . . should we go back . . . the boy."

"Somebody should kill you. Somebody should kill you and dump you in a goddamn ditch. Somebody should kill you."

"Will you?"

"Move." I jerked the weapon. "Move. When I say move you move. Just give me an excuse. I'd be glad to do it."

He went up the trail. We left poor Judy. I wanted to get away. The stink was everywhere. "I'm sorry," he said.

"Even if it was true it wouldn't matter."

For him, the shock of seeing Judy was fading. Staying alive remained his primary concern.

"Somebody should kill you."

"Please."

"Please," I squealed, mocking him.

"You can't shoot me from behind like this."

"Turn around. I'll shoot you right between your fuckin eyes if I feel like it."

"You're going to shoot me?" He made an eerie, muffled sound. Stumbling, he fell to the ground, shaking, gasping.

"Get up, you asshole."

"I . . . I can't."

"Get up."

He shielded his face, as if he could repel bullets with his arm. "You can't shoot me. It wouldn't be right."

"It would be perfect."

"It was an accident, Bill."

"You should have an accident too." I couldn't see his face. That would make it easier. Pull the trigger. It just might work. Some hiker would find his body in the morning. Later, they would discover Judy's grave and guess that Roy had committed suicide out of remorse.

"Don't shoot," he muttered almost to himself.

"Get up."

On his feet, he was walking backward, mostly watching the gun, stumbling several times. "Don't kill me."

"You piece of shit."

"I know. I know. I don't sound very brave. But I'm afraid."

"You make me sick," I said.

"Wouldn't you be afraid in my place?"

"God damn me if I'm ever in your place."

"You don't understand," he complained. "It was an accident. I wouldn't lie about a thing like that."

We approached the yellow car. And if I killed Roy, what about the little boy? I couldn't just leave him. He'd freeze to death. The kid was going to be a problem.

Klijner caught himself on the hood and turned to me. "If you'd let me explain. You'd see how it could happen. You'd understand. You wouldn't want to kill me."

"Stop telling me what I'd want to do. I decide what I want to do." I moved carefully to the back of the car, aiming the gun at him every second. For his part, he never took his eyes from it. "Get in."

"You're not going to kill me?"

"Get in."

"It's the right thing." He opened the door. "I swear. It's the right thing." He slid onto the front seat, the child beside him in a deep sleep.

"What'll the kid think?" I climbed in back. "He grows up and finds out you killed his mother?"

"It's not like you say." Klijner was turned around in his seat. "It was an accident. I didn't kill her. I didn't."

"Here." I threw the keys to the front. "Get us out of here."

He searched the floor a full minute before retrieving them. I wondered if he had a weapon of some sort hidden under the seat. Good. Let him try something. I would shoot him after all. Point-blank. In the head. Again and again I thought of Judy. Dumped in a ditch at the side of the road. Covered with a pile of dirt and litter.

"I don't know if I can drive." He started the car. "I still don't feel so good."

"Drive the car."

"I will. I didn't say I wouldn't try. I'll have to . . . to back out of here. I'll have to look back."

I pressed against the passenger-side back door, diagonally across from Klijner. He put his arm on the back rest and looked out the rear window, steering with one hand. "I can hardly see."

"Does this help you to see better?" I showed him the gun.

We moved in fits and starts. Once, we stalled on a bank of earth and had to roll forward before resuming rearward progress. "I don't mind driving," he said. "You can't shoot me while I'm driving. We could all get killed that way. So, I don't mind driving."

"Shut up."

The car was quickly warm again, though the windows fogged badly. Occasionally, Klijner drove so poorly branches would scrape and crack against the windows, as if someone were trying to get in at us.

"I don't know why I'm this way," he said. "I never thought I'd be like this. But I don't want to be killed. You know? I'll beg to stay alive. It's not a high price . . ."

I decided not to answer anything he said. His hand was not far from the gun, propped on my knee. I studied his face, a shadowed object directly in my line of fire. A bullet would tear it apart.

Finally, we rolled onto the pavement of Hubbard Road.

"If you knew how it was," he turned from me, "if you knew, if I could explain. You'd know you did the right thing. When you didn't kill me, I mean."

As we drove up the road, everything was new. I was fascinated by trash thrown on the shoulder, puddles of ice in the swamp. And I had to remind myself, be alert. Back to the wall, this man was dangerous. He's a killer. But I couldn't erase the memory. The horrible smell. And the sight of her. Like an echo, fading a little each time, it played before me again and again and again.

"I could tell you how it happened. It isn't like you think. I'll explain."

We were swiftly on the main road. If we returned to Agnes Gallagher's house we would travel on the expressway and pass Judy's grave.

"I told the truth at the trial." His voice recovered some of its authority and timbre. "I just left some things out. I'm sorry I did that. But I didn't think anybody would get hurt. I thought you'd be found innocent. I was sure of that, you know."

I should kill him. He deserves it. Any other way, he'll get off. Coughlin had the right idea. Sometimes justice needs a push. I should kill him. At least it would shut him up.

"If you knew what she was like. To live with. Maybe you could understand then. She wasn't honest, for one thing. She had a lot of good qualities, I don't deny it. But she wasn't honest. She'd go off with someone. Man or woman. It didn't matter to her, by the way. And she'd convince herself it was an okay thing to do. Anything she did. She'd rationalize it."

And if I didn't kill Roy? What then? I was no better off than yesterday. I knew he was the murderer. But to prove it. I could take the police to Judy. But that hardly established my innocence. To the contrary.

"She could be faithful," Klijner complained. "But not all the time."

He was driving at a moderate speed. Once, a police car came from the opposite direction. Klijner, intent on making his explanation, didn't seem to notice. Amazingly, the grisly visit to Judy's grave had less effect on him than on me. My stomach was a sloshing bucket of rebellion, the coffee and banana threatening to come back. And I was drowsy for no reason.

"That day I wasn't even thinking about her," he said. "I took Michael here to my sister's and for some reason I had to go back home. I don't remember. Oh, yeah, now I remember, I'd forgotten something. A feature story Hennessy gave me to read. And I'd promised to read it. So I went back to my house. In my own car, big blue one I got. I parked it right across the street. I didn't park it in the driveway because I was just going to run in and out."

We were approaching the expressway. Klijner suddenly parked at the side of the road beneath a bank of mercury-vapor lamps. I could see his face clearly. It looked sickly, his complexion bathed by the bluish light. He was making a giant effort to convince. Establishing eye contact. Waving his hands expressively. He'd taken a risk even stopping the car. A little crazy, I might get mad, start shooting. But it was a risk worth taking. He was desperate to save his life.

"So," he said, "on that morning I parked the car across the street. And no one noticed it. None of the neighbors. You. You must've walked right past it. But you didn't notice it. It's a pretty ordinary-looking car. Not like this one here."

The child still slept. Klijner carefully modulated his voice. It was soft, rational. "When I got to the house, she had the car, you know, like you found it. Backed up to the porch. Suitcases inside. What the hell's going on? I wanted to know."

Now he faltered, swallowing, stepping back to that day. Approaching the moment when he killed her. "You think this whole thing was over affairs and like that," he said. "But it wasn't. You know what it was? It was an old argument. Four years old. Since before we got married. About who cared or didn't care. Who told the truth. Who lied."

The child babbled softly in his sleep. His father reached down and adjusted the blanket. "So we argued. And one thing led to another. She said things to me. Probably you don't want to hear those things. You only want half the story."

He looked over his shoulder at me.

"Anyway, at one point, I said something. I can't remember what. It was so unimportant and trivial. And she went crazy. Just crazy. Throwing things at me. And she ran off into the kitchen . . ."

Here it comes. It would be a lie. A smarmy, self-serving lie. And why even listen?

"She went in the kitchen, took a knife from the drawer. Butcher knife. First, she was going to . . . she threatened to hurt herself. I figured she was just putting on a show. So, I decided to get out of there."

He stopped for breath. "It's good to talk about all this," he said. "No one knows. No one. My sister? I told her I'd gone home that morning and found the house a bloody mess, the car gone, Judy gone. Well, everybody knew Judy and I, we did nothing but fight. So, I convinced my sister we had to lie. We had to say I was at the cottage with her all day. Or I'd be framed for whatever had happened to Judy. Agnes, she was scared. But I guess she believed me. She's my sister, she wanted to believe me. And eventually, with you arrested and all, she convinced herself I was innocent. Well, I am innocent. Really. But, I never actually told anyone the whole story. No one knows what really happened. Except me. And now you."

I was impatient to hear the story finished. But I gave no sign of interest.

"So . . . where was I? I walked out of the room. Out of the kitchen. And I was going to get in my car and go. But she came running after me, screaming. And she had cut her wrist. Just like that. She did these things all the time. Hurt herself. To get attention. Once, she got mad over something. We were driving somewhere. And she drove into a telephone pole. We were only going ten or fifteen miles an hour, on a side street. But, I mean, she did this deliberately, supposedly to hurt herself. Just turned right into it. Bam. Only I got the three stitches and she got off without a scratch. You can still see the scar. Right here if you've ever noticed."

Would he ever get to the point?

"When she tried this I guess she got a surprise. The knife was a lot sharper than she thought. God, there was blood everywhere. And she really went berserk then. Running into the kitchen, flailing all around. I knew if I didn't help her, I knew she might bleed to death. So I went in there. In the kitchen. Tried to calm her down. But she was hysterical. Wouldn't let me near. I kept saying, 'Calm down. I'll take you to the hospital. Calm down.' But she wouldn't let me near her. Kept backing away. Bleeding all over the place. I was scared. Telling her to calm down, but I wasn't calm either. And once, I got close, but she got tangled up with the kid's high chair. And she went down."

He looked at the boy. Klijner's lips were dry and tight.

"What happened?" I asked. "She fell. What happened next?"

"She fell. And she didn't get up."

"What?"

"She landed hard. All her weight. She landed against the corner of the refrigerator. Bang. The whole refrigerator got knocked out of place she hit it so hard. Her head went, like, at a crooked angle. Like, maybe she broke her neck?" He began stroking the child, whose deep, steady breathing accompanied the quiet clattering of the engine.

"She didn't move?" I asked.

"And I didn't know what to do."

"Did you call a doctor?"

"She wasn't moving." He was emphatic.

"Couldn't you call a doctor? If she was hurt. That's what I'd do. If somebody's hurt you call a doctor."

"She wasn't . . . she was gone. Gone."

"You just let her lie there?" I asked. "You just let her lie there and bleed to death?"

"She didn't bleed to death. She was already dead. There was nothing I could do."

"How do you know?" I asked. "How could you know for sure she was dead? You're no doctor."

"I took her pulse. I tried to find her pulse. I couldn't find one."

"How did she fall?"

"She tripped," he explained again. "Got her feet caught in the legs of the chair. And she went down."

"She tripped over a chair?"

"It was the way she went down. No chance to break her fall. And she went down, she went down hard."

"She tripped over a chair and died. I'm sure that happens a lot."

"It's true," he insisted. "She went down. With her arm out to me. Reaching. Like I should catch her. I'll never forget that. And she hit the fridge. Hard. Right on the corner. Hit it. With a noise. You wouldn't believe. Crack. What a horrible sound."

"So it was an accident?"

"Yeah. An accident."

"Then why didn't you call the police?" I demanded. "If it was an accident. Why not call an ambulance?"

"I should have done that."

"Call an ambulance. What any person would do. Any reasonable person with nothing to hide."

"I was afraid. There was blood everywhere. We'd been fighting. She was all packed to run away. And now she was dead on the floor. I was afraid to call the police. Afraid no one would believe me. I guess I was confused. I was confused and I panicked."

He was despicable. I shook my head. Lies just poured from him.

"I went into the front room," he continued. "I *was* going to call an ambulance. That was my first thought. I went to the phone. But I started thinking about what could happen to me. It didn't seem fair. I was going to go to work and I was worried because we were understaffed. That was my biggest problem an hour before. And now this. I kept going to the phone. I went to the phone three times. But I knew how it would sound. The way the police would look at me. So I was scared. You know? I got a quilt from the bedroom. Big, thick one. I wasn't thinking straight. Why did I want the quilt? I honestly don't remember. To make her more comfortable, maybe. I don't know. The things that go through your head . . . anyway, I took it to the kitchen."

He took a long, sad look at the boy. "She was lying there. Her head against the refrigerator at a crazy, unnatural angle. I tried to get a pulse again. I listened, listened for her heart. But she was dead. So I threw the quilt down. And I rolled her onto it. Once I'd done that I knew I could never go to the police. They'd ask, if it was an accident, why did you wrap her in the quilt? They'd never understand. I shouldn't have done that. So, now I had to hide the body. For some reason, that seemed the best thing to do. She was dead and I had to think of me and Michael. It wouldn't help her if they accused me of murder. Especially when I didn't murder anybody."

He sighed and began watching the highway. Cars passed constantly, coming from or going to the big city. Was there ever a time of day when cars did not speed along that road?

"When you came, Bill. When you came to the house and took the car away I was surprised it was you. It's true. I was in the house with her. And you took the car. I didn't know what to do. I wasn't thinking clearly in the first place. For a while, I thought about taking her in my car. But you came back. And you left this car in the driveway. So I took it."

"Your car wasn't parked across the street," I said. "I don't care what you say. I was going to meet your wife. Don't you think I was damn careful to look for your car?"

"Well, maybe you were. But you missed it. My car was there. But I took hers. I backed it up to the porch. I carried her out, wrapped in the quilt. I put her in the trunk. As carefully, as gently as I could. And I drove off to the reservation. I picked the roadside there cause the hikers stay away from the highway. Anyway, I was very, I don't know if this is the word, respectful. I buried her. Afterwards, I drove home, got my car and went right back to my sister's house. I forgot about the mess in the kitchen. I went to my sister's and started on a bottle. I tried to convince myself it was all a dream. You know, like it never really happened. I almost managed to do that. I was shocked when the police called me at the paper. I remember thinking, 'What a terrible thing. Who could have done it?' It's almost like couldn't remember, couldn't connect it."

"And when they arrested me? You still couldn't connect it?'

"I didn't want that," he said. "You arrested. I didn't."

I snickered.

"Really. I was sorry Judy had died. It was partly my fault. I didn't want anyone else to suffer. At first, I didn't think you'd be charged. But you were. Then, I didn't think you'd go to trial. But you did. If you were convicted. If you were convicted then I would have had to confess. Honestly, I was prepared to do that."

He studied the child again.

"Let me see," I said. "I want to get this straight. Judy's death. That was an accident. Then, when the police arrested the wrong man for her murder, namely me, and you said nothing, that was also an accident. Both accidents. Both lucky accidents for you."

"They were accidents."

"You must think I'm stupid, Klijner. Why should I believe you? Why should anyone? You've lied before. Under oath you lied, in court. Why should I believe you now? Your accidents happen strictly on purpose, if you want my opinion. I don't believe you. I don't even want to."

"Listen —"

"I've had enough of you, Klijner. I don't want to hear any more." I ordered him onto the expressway. Somewhere along the highway we passed Judy's grave. I was uncertain exactly where.

All talked out, Klijner drove in silence. It was past four o'clock and I wanted to sleep and forget. From nowhere a trailer overtook us at eighty miles an hour, roaring like a truck bound for hell. The storm in its wake rocked the compact car and threatened to suck us along after. Klijner fought for control of the wheel. "Damn truckers," he muttered. An unsettling incident, but at least it kept me awake.

When we reached the top of Seaside Lane, a thin, gray line marked the horizon of the dull, black Atlantic. I wondered if the police had returned, looking for Roy. "Wait a minute," I said.

"What?"

"Drive back to the expressway," I ordered.

"Why?"

"Don't ask why. Just do it." We drove on. "Yeah," I said. "We're going to your house. Drive us to your house."

He made no complaint, growing more sure of his safety. And, in fact, the longer I was with him the more remote became the prospect of killing him. At some point, I sank to his level even considering it. In fact, I lacked the stomach for murder, after all. I had respect for life. And this fact separated us.

More than anything now I wanted sleep.

We arrived at the Klijner house like a family returning from a long trip. Wrapped in the wool blanket, the boy was carried up the front steps. I thought of Judy, wrapped in a quilt, dragged out, dumped in the trunk.

Unlocking the door, Klijner went into the foyer and turned on the light. "I've got to put him to bed," he whispered. The house was temperate, dark and silent. He carried the boy upstairs. I followed at a distance, gun in hand. What was I doing here? What did I hope to accomplish? Was I to follow Klijner forever, pointing the foolish gun at him?

The boy whined softly as his father took off his suit. "You

sleep now. You sleep. Okay, little guy? Okay?" Michael's eyes opened for a second. He was still under the influence of the sleeping pill. I envied him.

I trailed Klijner downstairs. He yawned and so did I. It was peaceful here. My coat hung open. More lights came on. The house was neat, the furnishings Victorian. I could see Judy's hand in the decorating. She had a fondness for animals carved in wood. They were everywhere, including an elephant I had given her. All we'd seen that night. It was fading. I could no longer recall the smell. The details, that split second vision of her face no longer lovely, blurred. At one point, I actually tried to recall it and could not.

I caught a glimpse of the kitchen. The wallpaper in there was new, woodwork repainted, linoleum floor replaced by a rug. It might have been a different place.

Klijner waited in the living room. "What?"

"We still have a few things to settle."

"I know. I'm willing to do that. I'd like to talk. Get it settled."

"Good," I said.

"You don't need that gun."

"I'll keep it anyhow."

"Okay if you keep it," he said. "Just, I want you to know you don't need it. Tonight. I found out something. When I finally told the truth. You're the first person I told, really. And it felt good. Like I've been wearing a suit and tie for three months. And now I'm home. I can take if off and be myself. You can't imagine how good it feels."

We moved into the office. At his desk, Klijner switched on a lamp. Drawing the shade of the only window, I took a chair in the corner. It was a small den, but he was a full step from me. The gun still pointed at him. He could not forget it. I remembered, too late, that I was still intending to check the safety. Did it matter any longer?

"Well . . ." He yawned again. I yawned as though in sympathy. The whole arrangement suggested a bizarre job interview. His eyes were red, his face pale. I'm sure I looked worse.

"What do I do with you?" I asked. "I don't know what to do with you."

"I'll have to go to the police. That's all there is to it. I'll have to go to the police and tell them the whole story, exactly what I told you. And I'll just have to make them believe me."

"You'd love that. Go to the police. So you could charge me with kidnapping."

"I wouldn't."

"Klijner, you're full of shit. Now, if we could go up to the police and I could bring this." I tipped the gun. "But this's the only thing to get the truth out of you. Otherwise, you'll lie your ass off."

"I'm sorry you feel that way."

"So it all comes down to this, Klijner. What the hell do I do with you?"

"I wish you could trust me."

"I wish I pissed champagne."

"Suppose I wrote a letter?"

"Suppose I just blow your head off. It'll save on stationery."

"Please don't talk like that." He frowned. "When I say I'll write a letter I mean a confession. Explaining everything. On paper. In black and white. I couldn't take it back."

"You'll never pay for this. Goddamn lying weasel. You'll get off. No matter what. You'll find a way and you'll get off. And it's not right. It's just not right."

"I've paid. I've paid already. I've suffered."

"I don't believe it. I don't believe you feel anything for anyone. Except yourself."

And the child. Maybe he loved the little boy. But I didn't want to think about that.

"Let me try. Let me put something on paper. You see what you think." He opened a desk drawer and reached inside.

"Wait!" I sprang from my chair. "You fuckin wait!" I moved close. "What's in there?"

"Nothing." He slowly withdrew his hand, clutching a thin box. "Writing paper."

I sat down in embarrassment. Exhausted, I was overreacting.

Klijner began to write. How did he manage to stay wide awake? "Who should I address it to? The district attorney? Weisberg?"

"He's the assistant district attorney."

"Okay. I know that. Dear Mr. Weisberg. I can keep silent no longer on the matter . . . of, of my wife's death." He spoke as he wrote. "I write to totally exonerate Mr. Martell from any involvement in the tragedy. Is that strong enough?"

Damn his arrogance.

"My wife died accidentally. She is buried in the state reservation near the Monatiquot exit along the expressway. I have covered up my involvement out of fear. But conscience allows me to keep silent no longer. I act to end Mr. Martell's suffering and face the truth."

Like any professional, he reread the work, adjusting a word here and there. At a desk, he was the editor again, confident, condescending.

"It's pretty good," he decided. "Don't you think? Does what you want. Gets you off the hook. It's in black and white. In my hand. Here." He signed his name. "Will that do?" He held it up.

"Christ."

"What's wrong with it? If there's anything you want me to add? Tell me. I'll put it in."

"I'm thinking," I said, "I'm thinking this. Suppose I leave and you just tear that letter up. Or burn it."

"Here." He reached for an envelope. "Mail it yourself."

"Suppose I mail it. And it gets there. And you deny you sent it."

"It's in my handwriting. On my stationery. With my signature on it."

"Okay," I said. "Suppose it gets to Weisberg and you tell him you wrote it under duress? Suppose you tell him you wrote it with me sitting across the room pointing a gun at your head?"

"I swear. I wouldn't."

"Yeah. But that gets us back to the original problem, Klijner. I don't trust you for shit."

"Look —" He began scribbling. "P.S., I write this of my own free will. Is that better?"

"It doesn't prove anything."

"What do you want? Do I sign it in blood or something? I'm trying to prove to you I'm sincere. I want to tell the truth."

"Maybe you're sincere now," I said. "You're sincere tonight, with this pointed your way. Suppose tomorrow you change your mind?" I held the gun, but it was increasingly apparent that Klijner held the upper hand.

"I don't know what else to say." He leaned back in his chair. "There comes a point, no matter what, there comes a point where you have to trust me a little. Now, I give you this letter. You mail it. And even if I claim duress, it's still going to cast a lot of doubt. I can claim duress, but I can't prove it. No one saw us together. People will think I wrote this to relieve a guilty conscience. No matter what I claim in the morning. People will think that. But I'm not going to get cold feet. You mail this. And I'll stand by it." He reached for an envelope and began folding the letter.

"Wait a minute."

He looked up expectantly.

"I want to read that first. I want to make sure it says what you say it says."

The bastard almost smiled. "You won't be sorry." He unfolded the letter. "Here. Read it."

I stepped toward the desk, looking over his shoulder. As I did there was a sharp crack. My hand snapped. Bits of Roy's hair, skull and brains exploded, flying across the room. In a fine spray, blood covered the desk and the letter. It showered the light bulb, sizzling like overcooked gravy.

Roy's head dropped to the desk top. Blood gushed like a fountain from the top of his skull. On wheels, the chair squirted out from under him and rolled into the living room. He dropped heavily to the floor even as I stepped instinctively away. And still, blood poured from his wound. It fell, a Niagara from a puddle on the desk top. It gathered in a thick pond on the floor. It coated his face red.

I stared at the gun. "Roy?" But he wasn't answering.

eighteen

I HAD KILLED HIM. God. I had better get the hell out of here. Fingerprints? But I hadn't really touched anything. God. The man lay in a heap, on his side, hands on the floor near his belt. Never knew what hit him.

And the letter was on the desk. The confession. Speckled with blood. And he was shot in the head.

Suicide.

Of course. Make it look like suicide.

God, I wanted to get away. He deserved this. But it was horrible.

If it's suicide. If it's suicide. What? Think. Concentrate. What should I do? Jesus Christ. Clear my brain. Oh, God.

I looked down. The great puddle of red still growing. Nothing to stop it. I was afraid to move. Like a dream. It seeped to the toe of my sneaker. Now I was unable to move. It spread. As if Klijner reached out to brand me.

The awful pond threatened to completely surround my right sneaker. I moved my left foot away. But I couldn't move the other without tracking it everywhere. I had to think. A man doesn't commit suicide and leave bloody footprints all over the room.

Think. Don't just stand there and let it happen. Do something.

Pocketing the gun, I swiftly untied the sneaker, taking care to keep the laces dry. Carefully, I withdrew my foot.

Now what? I couldn't leave it there, my sneaker an empty white island on a lake of blood. Pinching it between finger and thumb, I lifted it from the floor, leaving a perfect print bordered in red. But the thick liquid soon began filling the void, first oozing into the tiny cracks between the floorboards.

I held the sneaker over the red pond. Blood dripped slowly off the rubber tread. I had to beware of worsening the situation by blundering into the mess at any other point.

And it was noiseless. Except for the clock, ticking. I stopped moving and listened, concentrating on the slightest sound, the settling of the house, the hum of the refrigerator. I was alone.

Then, I noticed Klijner. His tongue poked slightly between his lips and blood flowed from his nostrils in two neat streams. Great rushes of blood flowed down his forehead and cheek, while drenching his hair like red sweat. I didn t want to see this. But I held the sneaker close to the floor. It dripped slowly. And his face was just beyond.

Someone was behind me now. I could feel him standing there, staring, judging. Finally, I had to turn. No one was there. I was almost disappointed, hoping for a voice, someone to tell me this was not my fault.

Be careful. One drop of blood anywhere else in the house could destroy the illusion of suicide. I cupped my hand beneath the sneaker and carried it into the kitchen where Judy had died. I washed it clean in the sink, likewise the single drop of red on my palm. For now, I put the damp sneaker in my pocket.

Okay. What was the best way out?

"Jesus. Jesus." What had I done? Killed a man. "Jesus . . ." What choice did I have? I began breathing through my teeth, as though in pain. I never wanted this. What else could I have done?

I started toward the front door. But I stopped at the foyer.

The light was on here. Someone might see me leaving. If only one person did I would be charged with a second murder.

I returned to the kitchen, which was lit indirectly by the hall lamp. The back door had one chain lock and one snap lock. The snap lock would close automatically behind me.

I opened the door and storm door. The sky was deep purple at predawn. Cold swept in on me and I was grateful. It refreshed, helping me to think clearly.

I began to pull the door shut. The idea of running away from this house had enormous appeal. But . . . but what? Once I closed the door I would be locked out.

Fingerprints? Had I left fingerprints anywhere? Mentally, I retraced my steps, following Klijner up the stairs. I hadn't touched anything. I sat in his office, keeping my hands mostly on my lap. I had turned on the kitchen faucet with my elbow Even now, I used my coat to wipe clean the doorknob

Okay, no problem. I hadn't touched anything. Nor was I leaving anything behind. No dropped wallet or loose button. Not even the gun . . . the gun? The gun was in my pocket.

"Jeez!" How stupid could I be? I was walking out the door with the gun in my pocket. If Roy Klijner had committed suicide the weapon must be found by his side. I shuddered, considering how near to disaster I had come.

Now to go back. Back to that room. I would have to approach the body. All that bloody mess. Then, I must put the gun in his hand.

He lay exactly as before, on his left side, facing away from the desk, a curious landing. I saw him fall, head to the top and then to the floor. How he got in this particular position I could not remember. Already, the details of the killing were distant. There was the shot. Blood went everywhere. He fell. But it was all very hazy, as though it had happened to someone else. Not to me.

The pool of blood, incredibly, continued to grow, feeding glistening streams into the living room. I stayed well away from it.

A tiny red bubble appeared at the end of Roy's nostril. Then it fell and burst.

My God, he was alive. Alive.

I pointed the gun as though he were still dangerous. He was unlikely to even move, showed scarcely a sign of life. But he was alive.

"Jesus. Jesus."

What could I do? I looked to the pistol. Shoot him again. This time I could aim directly at his head. Make sure. Hands shaking, I raised the weapon, uncertain when it might go off again.

Wait. Don't be so fucking stupid.

No suicide ever shot himself in the head twice. Calm down. Don't panic. That's how you screw things up.

On hands and knees I studied the big man from a distance. "Roy?" I croaked. Except for that bubble of blood he seemed to be very dead. And still it poured in a steady, if diminished, stream across forehead and cheek.

While he might not be quite gone, he was bleeding to death, certainly. He would not survive to sunrise.

"Roy?"

I was talking to a dead man.

Now I decided to place the gun in his right hand. Cautiously, I circled him, hugging the wall and bookcase. I went to his feet. The blood was collected around his shoulder, oozing toward the living room.

Squatting, I used a Kleenex plucked from the desk to wipe the weapon of prints. Holding the barrel in the tissue, I slid it under Roy's right hand. His fingers, limply touching the floor, bent and sprang back over the butt. My stomach lurched. I bowed my head between my knees, tensing every muscle. No. If I vomited I'd never be able to clean the mess. And, in this house, there must be no trace of me.

Roy's entire body began briefly to move. "Gugg . . ." he quaked.

"*Ahh!*" I jumped back, banging into the bookcase. A large

photo album toppled flat to the floor. It seemed to explode as it landed, the noise reverberating, cutting through me.

Calm down. He is dead. Or dying. His body might shake. But his body is dead.

Nevertheless, as I backed away, I had the feeling he was aware of me. Surprised because I had shot him. And he had grown so positive I would not.

I crossed the living room rug, out of balance, one sneaker on and one sneaker off. The sky was beginning to lighten. Better get out before the milkman shows up.

There was something else. I stalled.

The boy.

I'd almost forgotten him, upstairs, asleep.

Klijner could lie undiscovered for days. And, in that time, anything could happen to an unsupervised toddler.

In the foyer, I watched the stairs. The house was still numbingly quiet. The pill should keep him out for a few hours yet. Someone was bound to come along. Klijner would be discovered, the little boy taken to a safe place.

Meanwhile, staying here, I was in real jeopardy.

But I delayed. This was Judy's child. Once, I'd actually promised to treat him as my own, to love and shelter him.

I imagined the boy on the top step, tottering, falling, screaming.

Leave now. Someone will come. Klijner's suicide will be in the afternoon paper.

But who would come? The sister was away.

The simplest thing would be to call the police. But even an anonymous call would give the lie to Klijner's suicide. If the call was recorded voice prints might identify me.

Would it be so terrible just to walk out? The kid's chances would be better than mine if I stayed.

Behind me the first dim morning light shot through the front window. A sick feeling in the pit of my stomach signaled time running out. I had to do something. Abandoning little Michael, I was no better than Klijner.

Suddenly, I turned on the television. The screen came alive with specks of black and white, dancing wildly. Broadcasting had not begun. As I adjusted the volume, the room filled with noise, almost unbearably loud and not unlike the cheering crowd at a sporting event. I swung the front door wide open.

Now, I hurried to the back.

Soon, programming would begin, blaring. With the door wide open this was bound to attract attention. And it would appear that Klijner had arranged it all for the sake of his son.

If it didn't work, then I could call the police myself, perhaps in the afternoon, pretending to be a neighbor, complaining over the noisy television.

In the back yard, I was cautious, pulling on my sneaker. It was beginning to grow lighter. I moved without haste to avoid attention. Somebody's car was roaring unattended in a nearby driveway, warming to the freezing weather.

I jumped a fence into a yard behind the Klijner house and walked to the street. It was several blocks before I saw another person. Head down, I kept moving.

I was proud of myself, concocting such a clever rescue for the boy. But would I live to regret it? The television. The open door. Would police read murder into these? Or had someone seen me leaving the house? Always something more to worry about.

Pam's car was on Seaside Lane. I had to retrieve it. "Need a favor," I called from a pay phone. "Can you do me a favor? One last thing. I hate to ask you. But there's no one else. So can you do this for me?"

"I don't know," Pam answered sleepily. "What is it?"

"Can you pick me up? Right now?"

"I guess so. In your car?"

"Yeah."

"What is it, Bill? Where's my car?"

"Don't ask me any questions. You're better off if you don't know." I stood in the phone booth, shivering. The knife was cold and as heavy as a rock in my pocket.

Waiting at a fast-food restaurant, I stared at breakfast, french fries, Cokes, a hamburg. Although I was hungry, a few bites was all I could manage.

So now what?

Get the car and go home. Act as though nothing has happened.

Act as though nothing has happened? Christ. Roy was dead. On the floor, gurgling. What if he wasn't dead? I imagined him crawling to the telephone, gasping, "Martell . . . Martell . . ." I saw him in his hospital bed, eyes unfocused, finger pointed at me.

Don't think about that. He's dead. He has to be dead.

When would they find him? Perhaps the police were there already, swarming over the house.

Suppose no one hears the television. Loud televisions, blaring radios, people ignore those things. Had I left the child to some disaster? Killing Klijner was no crime. It was self-defense and I might live with that or at least come to accept it. But the child.

Somebody will find him. Stop worrying.

Arriving in my car, Pam was apprehensive. "You look awful."

"Well," I said, "I haven't slept."

"What've you been doing? Where's my car?"

"Do you trust me, Pam?"

"What?"

"You said you believed me. That I'm innocent."

"What's happened, Bill?" She was rousing quickly now.

"I'll explain later. Right now we've got to get down to Horse Neck Beach. We've got to get your car."

"What's my car doing at Horse Neck Beach?"

"I'll explain. I told you. I'll explain." But when? And how?

Almost two hours had passed since I'd left Klijner's house. Little Michael would soon be awake, crying for his mother.

I insisted on driving, though mentally and physically exhausted. "I'll be okay, Pam. Just make sure I don't doze off."

"If you want," she said later, "you can come back to my place."

"That's nice. I appreciate that."

On the expressway, early morning traffic was building. Happily, it moved mostly in the opposite direction.

"I'm going to let you out on Seaside Lane," I said. "At the top of the street. And I'll drop you off. Your car is at the end of the street. I'm going to take off right away cause I can't afford to be seen here. Okay?"

She was increasingly uneasy. "What am I getting into?"

"Don't worry. You're just picking up your car. And beyond that . . . what you don't know can't hurt you."

Three hours had passed since I left Klijner. A television at high volume for three hours could not fail to attract someone. Further, the police must have been alerted by Klijner's abrupt disappearance from the cottage, especially concerned after his call to them last night.

But guessing that Judy's child was safe was not the same as knowing. Despite the risk, I stopped at a pay phone. I still knew the Klijner number by heart. It rang three times. A man answered, as I'd hoped. Nonetheless, I was terrified, as if it was Klijner.

"Hello," he said.

"Ah . . ."

"Hello?"

"Is Frank there?"

"Who is this?" The voice was deeper than Klijner's, though familiar.

"Oh. I'm sorry. I must have the wrong number." I hung up.

Judy's child was safe.

That morning, I washed at Pam's. Though it was uncomfortable to put on the same dirty clothes, it was refreshing to be clean. I lay on the couch, trying to sleep, trying to forget all I had seen and done in the last hours.

"I have to be home soon."

"You can stay," she said. "You can stay if you like." She sat beside me on the couch.

"You know," I said, "I could probably stay here all night."

"If you like."

"Suppose I did that? Stayed overnight."

"You mean tonight?" she asked.

"No. I mean last night."

"Last night? I don't get it."

"What if I tell the police I was here last night?"

"Why?" she asked.

"It's just an idea, Pam. I have to say I was somewhere."

"Why is it so important to say you were anywhere? Why should the police care? Or does it have something to do with what happened last night, Bill?"

She would know everything eventually. The smart thing was to tell her myself. Win her to my side. "Suppose I told you now. Suppose I said last night I saw Judy."

Her eyes widened.

"No. She's not alive or anything. I saw her in a ditch in the state reservation. Where Klijner dumped her. After he killed her. He confessed, Pam. Last night he confessed the whole thing."

"Confessed?"

"It wasn't any complicated insurance ripoff. The truth turns out to be simple, ugly and simple. As usual."

"He confessed to the police?" she asked.

"No. To me. And on paper."

"Then," she almost smiled, "you're in the clear."

"The thing of it is, Pam, is this. He confessed okay. And he took me to Judy's grave. But it wasn't what you'd call voluntary. I had to persuade him."

She was apprehensive, motionless. Now I'd started, she wasn't sure she wanted to hear it all. Nonetheless, I told her the whole story up until the gun went off. I wanted her to understand why it had happened that way.

"I threatened him, if you want to know. I told him, either he tells me where Judy is or . . . well, you know. So he told me. All the time, I was thinking about what you said about Judy hiding somewhere to collect insurance. But instead, she was all the time buried under a pile of trash. I still don't understand why. All I can tell you is he did it. Killed Judy. And buried her body."

"And he admits this?"

"He did."

"On paper?"

"And he specifically exonerates me."

"He'll stand by this?" she asked.

"No."

"How could he deny it. If it's on paper?"

"I don't think he'll deny it either."

"You're talking riddles."

"He's dead, Pam."

She flinched.

"I killed him."

"Mother of God."

"It was him or me. I had to do it. Can't you see that?"

"Don't —" She waved both hands. "This is — I don't want to know."

"Today you said you trusted me."

"I trusted you weren't a murderer. Now you tell me this."

"It was no murder. It had to be done. It was self-defense. What choice did I have? Please tell me that, Pam. What else could I have done? I didn't want to go to jail for the rest of my life for something I didn't do, killing Judy."

"The police will know you did this," she insisted.

"They won't. Because they'll think it's suicide. He's shot in the head at close range. With his sister's gun. He left a confession on the desk that'll pass for a suicide note, in his own handwriting. It'll be suicide. Only I know different. And now you."

She was staring at my hands. This would take a real selling job.

"He deserved it, Pam. Look at all the hell he's caused. You can't just kill someone, like he did, and that's the end of it. Killing someone. It's a whole chain reaction of misery and the person responsible shouldn't get off. And he didn't."

"Oh . . ." She began nervously folding and unfolding her hands.

"I know how you felt about Judy. But if you were with us last night. All he cared about was himself. The body, Judy, was right there. I was sick. I cried even. But it didn't bother him for nothing. All he cared about was himself, Pam. Saving his own skin. When I saw her, dumped in the woods like so much garbage . . . he wrote out the confession just to get me off his back. Today he would have denied the whole thing. I'd be right back in jail. This time for good. And, at the last, with the confession right there on the desk, it was him or me. And it just happened."

She looked away. Maybe I'd made a mistake bringing her into it.

"I've put you in a hell of a position, telling you this. I'm as sorry for that as for anything. I wish there had been another way. But I need your help, Pam. You're my only chance."

"For what? What do you want me to do?"

"All I want is for this to be over." I touched her shoulder. "We can have some peace. You and I. We can start our lives together. Like normal people."

"Yesterday you were going off without me."

"But I didn't. That's the whole point. I didn't go. I couldn't leave you." I added, with conviction, "I love you."

"I don't know what to do," she said.

"I understand if you're frightened by what I've done. I'm frightened too." I moved close. "Pam. I had no choice. Tell me I did right. Please. If you'll just tell me that, it won't matter what anyone else thinks. Just, you tell me I did right."

She was weeping as I took her in my arms.

For a few hours I slept. But the nap did not refresh me; rather, I was groggy and sluggish. Around noon, I headed home, across town, fighting the urge to drive past Klijner's house. I imagined the ambulance, attendants lifting the stretcher, steering it down the front stairs.

But I found no police at my apartment. Inside, it was precisely as I had left it. I waited by the phone. Why didn't they call? Why didn't they come for me? Finally, I fell asleep.

In the afternoon, they pounded on the door. I went, eyes barely focused.

Detective Reardon looked irritated. Matteo, behind him, watched the stairs. The young secretary from the apartment above was coming down. He followed her closely, looking up her coat and skirt.

"What do you guys want?"

"We want you to come with us," Reardon said.

"Why should I do that?"

"It's for your own good." His partner moved toward me.

"Am I arrested?"

"No," Reardon scoffed. "Of course not."

"Well, weren't you guys coming to arrest me the other night? At the wake?"

"I don't know where you get your information, Bill."

"If you weren't going to arrest me —" I was confused. "Why'd you chase me?"

"Never did," Reardon said.

"That was the undertaker," Matteo said. "Seems he got all upset because you jumped out his window. Most people use the door. But don't worry. We straightened him out. That's our pal, Bill Martell, we told him. He's just that way. Unpredictable."

"If I'm not arrested," I was half asleep still, "if I'm not arrested, why should I go anywhere with you guys? Why should I cooperate?"

"Go ahead," Matteo smiled. "Be an asshole. We could give a shit."

"Gotta come with us, Bill."

"Why?"

"Why not?" Reardon asked. "You afraid of something?"

"I talked to you guys before. It was a bad experience."

"We treated you right."

"My foot."

"Get your coat," Reardon said.

"Suppose I say no."

"We don't want to arrest anybody," he replied. "But we will get a warrant if we need to."

I was growing accustomed to the back seat of police cars.

"Away last night?" Matteo grinned.

"Staying with a friend."

"A friend?" Reardon turned from the wheel. "Does the friend have a name?"

"I'll ask her."

"Wouldn't be that little girl reporter?" Matteo smirked. "You mean her?"

"None of your business."

We drove through a familiar section, toward the Klijners' house. I saw it three blocks off. And despite myself, I couldn't look away. The yellow Pinto sat in the driveway. Police cars were everywhere. Reardon pulled to a halt behind one. "What are we doing here?" I asked.

"The assistant district attorney, Mr. Weisberg, wants to talk to you," Reardon said.

"Weisberg?"

"That's right."

"Why? Why here? Why don't we talk down the courthouse or someplace?"

"Mr. Weisberg wants to talk here. If that's all right with you."

"It's not. Not at all." I could feel my face getting hot with panic. It was difficult to know the least incriminating thing to do. How would an innocent man behave? "I don't want to go in there. That's Klijner's house. I don't want to see him."

"How can you be sure he's even in there?" Reardon asked.

"He lives here, for Christ's sake."

"Well, he was here earlier," Matteo said, "but I think he left."

They were trying to frighten me, pretending Klijner was still alive. But what if he was? I'd heard of people shot in the head who survived by some miracle, the bullet missing important parts of the brain.

"Let's go in," Reardon said.

"No. I don't want to go in there."

"You're afraid?" Matteo taunted.

"What are you afraid of?" Reardon asked.

"I want my lawyer first."

"You can call him from in there," Reardon said. "There's a telephone in there. You can call him. It's fine with us. You don't have to say a word until he comes. Here," he handed me a card, "that tells you. We can't make you do or say anything. Want me to read that for you?"

"I remember it."

"You're afraid to go in there," Matteo said. "For some reason you're afraid. What're you afraid of?"

How would it look? Driven to Klijner's door, but afraid to go inside. I took a deep breath. My stomach burned. All this tension was probably developing an ulcer.

"If I go in there, and he's in there, I'm leaving. Okay?"

"You can do whatever you want," Reardon said.

"He ain't in there," Matteo said.

The two detectives escorted me up the walk. Was I crazy to do this? I could only think of Roy. He was dead on the floor in there. And they wanted me to look at him. The police were gathered, waiting for my reaction.

What was the appropriate response? Surprise. But don't overdo it. I must appear genuine.

I measured my feelings on entering the house. Still under control, legs steady. In broad daylight, this place lacked much of its menace.

"This way." Reardon pointed me to the living room.

Here it comes. Be prepared. If the body is gone . . . if the body is gone, what? Puzzled. All the blood would be puzzling. Wouldn't it?

Uniformed police blocked my view of the office. I tried to be casual, but inside I was a twisted knot, heartbeat soaring. Just get through this. It will be over. Over.

"Come along." Reardon cleared a policeman aside. I saw the office and something unbelievable. The blood was gone. The photo album was returned to the shelf. And there was no body.

Klijner sat on the desk, smoking a cigarette, speaking with a policewoman.

I stopped, trembling. He was alive. As I staggered, Reardon caught me by the arm. How could he be alive? How?

"I'm sick." I went to the couch.

The man at the desk studied me with some satisfaction, lips in a near-smile. It was Weisberg. Somehow, I'd mistaken him for Klijner. It was nerves. The two men shared no obvious resemblance.

"I want to read you your rights." Reardon was sitting at my side. "Just a formality." He read loudly and clearly. Weisberg came near, hovering. "Do you understand that?"

"I told you, yes."

"And you've come here of your own free will without any coercion whatsoever?"

"Yeah," I said. "So I'm here. What do you want from me?"

"This is a release allowing us to ask you a few questions. You might want to read it before signing."

Carelessly, I signed.

"You don't look well," Weisberg said.

"Gas," I said. "My stomach. Gas."

"Can we get you something?"

"I don't know. What do you take for gas?"

"Detective Reardon, see if there's something in the medicine chest."

Beyond Weisberg were the office and a faint chalk outline of

Klijner's body marked on the floor alongside the desk front. In the living room, the edge of the red rug was dyed brown-red. So it hadn't been a dream. I had really shot him. He was almost certainly dead. And now I had aroused everyone's suspicions by nearly collapsing. Stupid.

"Do you know why you've been asked here?" Weisberg began.

"No. I assume it's about the case. I thought maybe you dropped the charges."

"Dropped the charges? Why would we drop the charges?"

"Because I'm innocent."

"Do you know what happened here?" Weisberg looked at the office.

"No."

"Why did you become faint when you walked in?"

"I didn't become faint," I insisted. "I just felt a little sick. The blood. The sight of blood makes me sick."

"Blood?" Weisberg asked. "Where do you see blood?"

"On the rug. The edge of the rug there is stained with blood."

The assistant district attorney walked to the edge of the rug. Strands of fabric had dried together in unsightly clumps.

"This is stained," Weisberg began.

"With blood."

"How do you know it's blood?"

"Sure looks like blood to me. Dried blood. Isn't it?"

"Do you know what happened here early this morning?" he asked.

"Sorry, no."

"Roy Klijner died here this morning," Weisberg announced. "He died of a bullet to the right side of the head, at close range, about an inch above the temple."

"Too bad," I said.

Someone handed me the stomach medicine, a spoon, and a glass of water. I prepared a teaspoonful, washing it down with the water. They placed the empty glass on the television.

"You don't seem very surprised," Weisberg said. "It's almost, I get the impression you knew what I was going to say here before I even said it. As if you knew Roy Klijner was dead."

"How could I know that?" I asked.

"Good question."

"But I'm not surprised. Not with all the blood there. And to me, it's no surprise Klijner committed suicide."

"Who said he committed suicide?"

"I . . . just a guess." It was a dumb mistake and Weisberg smiled. I looked with concern to a tape recorder spinning silently nearby. "What? Did someone shoot him then?"

"It's under investigation."

"You know, I think I need my lawyer."

"What's his name?" Weisberg asked.

"Fabiano."

"Oh, yeah. Detective Reardon, why don't you call Mr. Fabiano for Mr. Martell? Fabiano. You were better off with Coughlin."

"What's the number?" Reardon asked.

"I don't know," Weisberg said. "Do you know the number? He doesn't know it. Look it up."

Why hadn't they mentioned Klijner's confession? I didn't like this. Not at all. It would have been a simple matter for one of these men, finding the letter, to destroy it. What a vicious trick. And there was not a thing I could say without giving the game away.

"While we're waiting," Weisberg said, "there's one question. Will you answer it? One question?"

"You ask it. Then I'll let you know."

"My question is," Weisberg said, "Klijner died between two and six this morning, according to a preliminary report from the medical examiner. Now, can you account for your whereabouts during those hours?"

"Am I a suspect in this too?"

"Where were you between those hours? Two and six?"

"Asleep," I said. "In bed."

"Alone?"

"None of your business."

"You weren't at your apartment, Martell. We were looking for you. And you weren't there. Where were you?"

"Asleep."

"This Fabiano don't answer," Reardon muttered.

"Where? Where were you sleeping?"

"At a house. A friend's house."

"Miss Nealy's?" Weisberg asked.

"None of your business."

"Don't be stupid, Martell. Of course it's my business. The question is, will she give you an alibi?"

I stared back. Would she?

"What happened to the little kid?" I asked. "Judy's little boy."

"Slept through the whole thing," Weisberg grinned. "Upstairs in his crib."

"I guess he gets a hell of a start in life. Poor kid."

"A strange thing." Weisberg sat against the television console, folding his arms. "Last night Klijner was at his sister's house. With the boy. On Horse Neck Beach. And then, this morning, we found them both here. While the beach house, there's pretty definite signs of forced entry. Two. Two broken windows."

"Hmmm."

"And that's not all. The guy was covered with dirt. On his clothes. Under his fingernails. Abrasions on his hands. What do you make of that, Martell?"

I looked at the desk, cleared of papers.

"That all sound pretty strange to you?" the prosecutor asked.

"May I go now? I'm real tired."

"I can believe it. You sounded pretty mixed up on the phone this morning."

"On the phone?" I asked. "You been tappin the wrong phone, Weisberg. I didn't make any calls this morning. I was out."

"No. When you called here, I mean. This morning. I answered the phone myself. Sure. I recognized your voice."

"You're crazy," I said. "Why should I call here? You make about as much sense . . ." He was fishing. I would give him nothing.

The assistant district attorney followed me to the door. "Can you make it home on your own, Mr. Martell?"

"I'd prefer it, as a matter of fact. Policemen make me nauseous."

He held the door. "By the way, I forgot to ask you. About the letter. You dictated that letter. Didn't you?"

"He — I mean — what letter?"

Weisberg smirked, eyes sparkling with trickery.

"What letter?"

"Oh." He pretended embarrassment. "What am I saying? I'm sorry. I was thinking of something else."

nineteen

THE STORY RAN on the front page in the *Suburban-Citizen*.

Editor Dead in Shooting

Police are investigating the shooting death of the *Suburban-Citizen*'s assistant editor Roy Klijner in his home yesterday morning. Klijner's wife, Judith Anne, disappeared under suspicious circumstances three months ago. The trial of William Martell for her murder ended in a mistrial.

Martell was questioned and released in connection with Mr. Klijner's death. Police declined to rule Martell out as a suspect. . . .

The story was brief and incomplete. I read it three times. Each reading increased my panic. The piece implied that I was Klijner's killer. Okay. No surprise there. But, ominously, there was no mention of any suicide note.

"This isn't right," I mumbled.

The story horrified Pam. She dropped into a chair in my apartment, studying me. "If I tell them you were with me," she asked, "and they find out it's not true, am I implicated in the killing?"

"No. It's perjury. I mean, I won't lie to you. It's a serious charge. But it's not murder."

"This," she poked at the newspaper, "this doesn't mention any confession."

"There was a confession. Maybe they're going to study it before they announce it."

"I asked Burkhalter about a suicide note. He usually knows everything. He says there was no note. He's got lots of cop friends. And he says there was no note. No confession."

"There was, Pam. I swear."

"Then where is it?"

"For all I know they ripped it up and threw it away. I can't help what they do. I only know about me. I saw him write it. With my own eyes. There is a confession. I've told you the truth."

"I didn't expect this," she said. "I didn't expect to get involved in all this."

"I didn't either. Look, Pam, if I could have it any other way I would. In a minute." I put my hand on her, looked into her eyes. "I was in trouble and I needed help. And it seemed to me, it seemed to me there was no other way. No one else. No one else to turn to or trust. Except you. I knew I could trust you."

"I don't know . . ."

"Pam, I wouldn't let anything happen to you. So don't worry about that."

"How much will I have to do?" she pleaded. "How many lies? I'm not like that. I can't tell lies."

"The police are going to come to you with one question. Just one. And all you have to say is yes."

"One question? What question?" she asked.

"They'll want to know if I was at your place. Sleeping. The other night. When Roy was killed. All you have to say is yes. If they ask any more than that, we both stick as close to the truth as possible. I came to your apartment when I really came. Only I never left in your car. In fact, I never left at all. We went right to bed. To sleep. No conversation. No anything. Just sleep. In the morning we had breakfast at McDonald's. Can you remember that?"

"I need . . . I need to think."

"I want you to remember something," I began. "I could have run, back there. I'd be safe and far away if I did. But I stayed. I'm not exactly sure why I stayed. Except that you're part of it. When I looked at you, that day at the bank. I saw I had something to stay for, to fight for."

Her eyes were all questions.

"I stayed for you, Pam. At least I think I did. Maybe I stayed for nothing."

"No . . ." By degrees she softened. I worked on her for nearly an hour, flattering, begging, insisting that I loved her. Not everything I said was true, but I'd have been hard pressed myself to separate the fact from the fancy.

We made love in the bedroom. It seemed I had won. Yet, I stayed with her every second that day. She was nervous, preoccupied, and drinking rather too much. When the time came for work, I begged her to stay, dreading the hours she would be under the influences of others.

When she was gone, I called the office. "How are you?"

"Fine."

"You got your assignment for tonight?"

"Not yet," she said.

"Oh. I see. And, ah, has anyone, I mean, have people been talking to you?"

"Yes."

"That's good. Only, what, what about?"

"Work. About work," she said. "Nothing else."

"And the police haven't —"

"No. I haven't heard from the police, Bill. Will you please relax? You're going to make me a nervous wreck. If there's any problem, don't you think I'd call you?"

I called her twice after that.

I remained awake until she returned, around one o'clock in the morning. I looked carefully for some sign her attitude toward me had changed. In fact, she seemed less attentive. Of course, she was tired. Alarmed, I hustled to make her comfortable.

"You know," she said later, "I miss it when we're apart." She stayed the night at my apartment.

In the morning, I walked several blocks to a deserted street and dropped the shining steel knife down a sewer.

Shortly before noon on the following day I received a call from Lawrence Fabiano, my new attorney. I was instructed to meet him at the courthouse. "And bring along your girlfriend," he said.

"Pam? What for?"

"She's your alibi. Isn't she?"

We three gathered in the district attorney's consultation room. "What's this all about?" I asked.

"Weisberg," Fabiano whispered. "He wants to talk to us."

"Maybe I don't want to talk to him."

"I see your point. At the same time, it doesn't hurt to listen. He says he's got some new evidence on Judy Klijner's disappearance."

"Evidence? What?"

"I couldn't tell you. But he told me that his office is actively considering dropping the charges against you. And, if true, that should be appreciated as good news." The lawyer glowed as if he had accomplished this.

"He says he'll drop the charges?"

"He says he's considering it."

"Can we believe him?" I asked.

"Oh, he's honest enough. We want to be cautious in any case. Volunteer nothing. This man is not your friend."

But Fabiano knew nothing of Klijner's confession. Certainly, Weisberg had it, perhaps folded in his pocket. I refused to believe he was so evil as to suppress it permanently. No. He was analyzing it, reviewing and reassessing my testimony and behavior. Inevitably, he would conclude, as any fair man must, that Roy Klijner had killed Judy.

I sat at the end of a long table, studying the youthful prosecutor. Once, I thoroughly hated him. Now, I was full of anticipation. "I assume you want all this resolved," he said.

"That depends," I replied. "On how it's resolved."

"Well, resolved. I'm talking about getting to the truth."

"The truth. Sure. I'd like to get to the truth."

"Good. We appreciate your cooperation."

"Well," I said. "That's different. In this cooperating business only one thing counts. You guys think I'm guilty. So where's the advantage of my helping you do anything?"

"We don't necessarily think you're guilty anymore," Weisberg said.

"No?"

"I've had some new information. I'm reexamining our case, looking at this whole affair with an open mind."

"An open mind."

Weisberg hesitated solemnly. He stood and walked toward me. "We've found something. Just in the last twenty-four hours. A woman's body."

"Judy?"

"There's been no positive identification." He came almost to touch me. "That's where we'd like your help."

"You want me to identify the body?"

"Some items found with the body. Of course, it's up to you. Are you sincerely interested in resolving the matter or not?"

In a brief conference, Fabiano was scornful. "Cooperate with him? If I knew he was going to make that pitch I never would have talked to him even. Don't forget, he's trying to put you in jail."

"That's exactly the point," I said. "It's not really the law that puts me in jail. It's him. Weisberg. If I can convince him he's got the wrong guy my troubles are over. I mean, he's already considering it. And you yourself just said he's honest."

"He's a tricky bastard for my money. And my advice is to let him do his own identifications." Fabiano went on, lawyer-fashion, complaining at the prosecutor's "outrageous" conduct in dragging me to the Klijner house for the interrogation a few days before.

We drove in an official car toward the reservation. Weisberg and Fabiano sat in the front seat, Pam and I in the back.

"Where, exactly, are we going?" I asked.

"We're going for a little walk in the woods," Weisberg said. He and Fabiano chatted amiably, reviewing a long list of mutual friends. At one point, speaking louder than before, the prosecutor discussed a notorious case, a youth arrested for killing his father.

"This kid," he was saying, "a regular genius. Very bright. Plots it carefully. Wouldn't you know, he does something so stupid you'd think a three-year-old child would have more sense. Drops his cap at the scene. A thing like that. I've seen it a million times. They say there're guys who want to be caught. And you actually get to believe it. Some people are so unlucky it's got to be more than luck."

I took Pam's hand and squeezed. She nearly managed a smile. All the uniforms had set her on edge. Weisberg, peering from the rearview mirror, saw it too.

Down Hubbard Road we stopped at a cluster of police cars. Officers were everywhere in warm coats and boots. Reardon and Matteo leaned beside one car. "Everybody out," Weisberg said.

"Just remember," Fabiano took my arm, "anytime. We can leave."

"No. No, I want to cooperate. As long as these guys are going to be honest with us."

"It's your funeral."

We began our walk through the woods. It may have been the same trail Klijner and I had taken in the dark. Now it was daylight. I couldn't bear to see Judy in the daylight.

"What's this?" Fabiano joked. "Don't I get enough exercise chasing ambulances?"

All around, the woods were frozen by winter, without sound or color. Even the earth was hard and unyielding beneath our feet. I tried to remember it in summer, when Judy and I made love in her car, steaming the windows, growing slippery with sweat. One of nature's tricks, it seemed impossible this was the same place, that it would ever be warm and green again.

"Where are we going?" I asked.

"Just a short distance, be patient."

Pam lagged behind. Occasionally we passed police officers on the trail, remnants of a large search party. Weisberg would often confer with them.

"Is she there?" Pam asked. "Judy's body?"

"Keep your voice down," I said. "Forget you know where Judy is. Just forget."

"I can't take this anymore, Bill. I can't. I don't know why they wanted me to come."

I took her hand, cold as ice.

"I'm scared," she said.

"You don't have to come, dear."

"I don't want to see it. Her —"

"I understand. You go back. I'll tell them you're too cold."

"I'd rather go back."

"Don't get lost," I urged, as she moved quickly away.

"Where's she going?" Weisberg asked.

"Back to the car," I said. "She's cold. Besides, there's no reason for her to come. She doesn't know anything about this."

We walked up a hill and over an area of fallen trees and stumps. The trail narrowed.

"What's this all about?" I asked, stopping, hoping to sound

annoyed instead of afraid. "Why do we come all the way out here to identify these things?"

"Because out here is where we found them," Weisberg said. "We're still finding more."

My excuse for a lawyer was a few feet away, catching his breath, admiring a stream below the trail.

"We thought you could help by identifying certain items found with the body, clothing, jewelry."

"I see."

"You haven't changed your mind?" he asked.

"Well, could I be incriminating myself?"

"How could you be incriminating yourself?" the prosecutor asked. "You knew Mrs. Klijner intimately. That's not in doubt. You're only cooperating in the identification. And, at this point, cooperating with my office can only improve your position."

"I cooperated before and found myself on trial for murder."

"That was before," he said. "A lot has happened since then. Since your trial ended. Even in that short period of time a lot has happened." Weisberg was rocking and swaying, hands in his pocket, face an outrageous pink. "Let's go on ahead. I'm freezing my ass off, standing here." He gestured up the trail.

"I'm not going first," I said.

"No?"

"I don't know the way. I don't know where we're going."

"It's right on this trail."

"I'm not going first."

Weisberg led us.

"I love the woods," Fabiano said, taking great gulps of cold, fresh air. "I don't know why I don't do this more often." Yet his vigorous pace was slowing.

As we approached the expressway, the hum of traffic was constant, the air tainted by gasoline exhaust. In the clearing milled policemen of every type, including local, state and metropolitan police.

Weisberg paused on the pale, brown, flat grass and waited for me. I looked in his face, careful not to betray my knowledge of the grave.

"Where is this stuff?" I asked. If I was expected to look at the grave in daylight I wanted to get that done. It was to my left and slightly behind. I avoided looking in that direction.

"Have you ever been here before?" Weisberg raised his voice to compete with noise from the highway.

"No. Never. Except to drive past maybe."

"Never been hiking past this spot? Never in the vicinity?"

"I think I've answered that."

"Did you ever come here with Mrs. Klijner?"

"Is this a contest to see how many ways you can ask the same question?"

"So here's where you found her." Fabiano arrived.

"Over there," Weisberg pointed.

We looked at a shallow excavation at the edge of the forest, just behind a thick, wide evergreen. On the grass was spread the quilt, damp and eaten away at one corner. And it smelled. Not so much as before, but the odor was noxious and unmistakable.

"Phew," Fabiano said.

"Show a little respect," I muttered.

Weisberg led me to a plastic sheet spread beside a large tree, about twenty feet from the grave. On the sheet were arranged various items evidently found with the body. He displayed a plastic bag. Within was a necklace with a distinctive black stone. "Recognize this?"

"She wore it. Sometimes. She had it for the black thing there. She said it set off her hair. You know?" She must have worn it for me that day. Hoping to look her best.

"How about this?" Weisberg squatted and retrieved a silver bracelet, also in a plastic bag.

"I couldn't say. It looks like. It's probably hers. But I couldn't say for sure. I don't remember it specifically." Again, my stomach was burning with discomfort.

Weisberg bent again to his gruesome collection.

"Why did we have to come here for this?" I asked. "We could have done this at the police station."

"We came here to save time," the prosecutor said.

Leaning against a tree, I could see the grave. I felt acutely depressed. How could someone like Judy be dead? It was unfair. Incredible. The world didn't make sense.

Later, as Fabiano and I prepared to return to the car, the prosecutor approached us. "Hey, Charlie," my lawyer said, "can you bring a car around and pick us up on the expressway here?"

"I thought you loved walking in the woods, Larry?" Weisberg bent to tie his shoe.

"Oh, I do. But, you know, it's getting late. And I'm not used to all this walking."

"It won't kill you."

"You never know. Remember Coughlin."

"You dropped this, Martell." Weisberg stood. It was light brown, leather, a pine tree neatly stitched on the face. Not thinking, I reached toward it. Abruptly, I froze, hand outstretched, as awkward as an unfinished sentence.

"Isn't that yours?" Weisberg asked. Fabiano and a policeman looked on.

"Ah, no," I said. "What . . . where'd you get it?"

"From you. You just dropped it."

"What?" I smiled stupidly. "Not me."

"Yes. You. It just fell out of your jacket pocket." He looked to Fabiano. "He took his hand out of his pocket, like so, and this fell to the ground. Just, just two seconds ago." He turned the leather sheath over several times. "What is it? It's for a knife?"

"How would I know?"

This was a trap. Right from the beginning. I gave a fierce look to Fabiano. Some lawyer, to let me blunder into this. Obviously, Weisberg had found the sheath at the grave where I must have dropped it that night. Now he was trying to dupe me into claiming ownership.

Or had it, in fact, just fallen from my pocket? I couldn't be sure.

"This is yours, Martell," he pressed.

"No." I moved away.

"I don't understand. I saw this drop out of your pocket. Just now. Didn't you see that, sergeant?"

"You took your hand out of your pocket," the uniformed officer echoed, "and this come out. Dropped."

"I never saw it before."

"Well!" Weisberg affected a puzzled grin.

"How did it get in your pocket?" the sergeant asked.

"It was never in my pocket. I never saw it before."

"Why?" the prosecutor shook his head, as though questioning my sanity, "why should you deny it?" He presented the leather object between his hands. "It just fell out of your pocket. Just now. Why should you deny it?"

"This is a trick, Weisberg." I was furious with fear. "But it's not going to work." I wheeled, walking quickly up the trail.

The leather sheath was cheap, thin, pliable. It might have been folded in my pocket, unnoticed.

"This isn't yours?" Weisberg and his cop were at my heels.

"I told you once."

"This's almost brand new." He waved it in my face. "Very distinctive. I'll bet I can trace it to the store where you bought it."

"Only I didn't buy it."

"Where's the knife that goes with it?"

"I have no knife."

"Then I can keep this?" He slapped the leather, *crack*, against his hand.

"You can shove it up your ass for all I care."

"My," he regarded the object like a prize, "we have hit a sore point."

I turned on him. The three of us stopped in the middle of the cold, dead forest. "I know what you're trying to do, Weisberg."

"I'm not trying to do anything."

"You found that with Judy. Now, you want me to say it's mine so you can connect me to her murder."

"It fell out of your pocket, Martell. I only wanted to return it." He was so earnest, he could easily have been telling the truth. It wasn't likely, but possible. "What makes you think we found it here? You said you'd never been here before."

"You won't give up."

"What did you do with your knife?"

"I don't own a knife."

"I should tell you," he said, "someone's disturbed that girl's grave. Very recently. It occurs to me they used a knife to dig with."

"You know nothing. You can guess I killed Judy. You can guess I killed Klijner. But only I know if it's true. I'm the only witness to say if it's true. And I say it isn't."

"Not quite," Weisberg smiled. "There's one other person to say what's true and what isn't."

I shuddered in the cold.

"If she talks. Tomorrow. Or twenty-five years from tomorrow. I can wait. There's no statute of limitations on murder."

I hurried up the trail, frantic to know what Pam was doing, left alone among all those cops. Fabiano was far behind as I took long strides through the forest. Weisberg, however, stayed close.

On Hubbard Road some of the police cruisers were gone. Pam leaned against an unmarked car, chatting with Reardon and Matteo. She was almost smiling.

I burst beween them. "Come on, Pam."

The two detectives were amused. "Watch out," Matteo laughed, "daddy's here."

We walked a few yards down the road. "What are you doing talking to those guys, Pam?"

"What?"

"What did you tell them? What'd they ask?"

"I . . . I don't know. It was just small talk."

"Did they ask about the other night? When Roy was killed?"

"I just told you," she replied. "It was small talk."

"Okay, if you say so. But I've got to be sure."

"Do you think I'm lying?"

"No, Pam. But I have to protect myself, you know. These guys are full of tricks. So I have to know. Did they mention Roy? Anything like that?"

She stared toward the bog, saying suddenly, "I love you, Bill. And I've done things I never would have done except that I love you. And, you know, if we're in this together it's okay. But I don't want to be used. Because it just wouldn't be fair. It wouldn't."

' "I love you too, Pam."

"Do you?"

"Of course."

"Maybe you do," she said. "Then again, maybe you haven't decided. But, at least you could trust me."

"I trust you."

"You know, you can love someone and not trust them. And I can tell you from bitter experience, Bill, it's better to be lonely than to live like that."

She didn't smile, looking distant, her face cheerless, cold. And she certainly hadn't answered my question about the police.

"You're right," I spoke quickly as we moved back toward the car where Weisberg watched us intently. "Don't pay any attention to the things I say now. You can see I'm all screwed up by all this pressure. All this mess. But I know. I've got to see beyond it. Someday all these problems will be in the past. And we'll want to go on with our lives together."

She didn't answer, hurrying out of the cold to the assistant district attorney's car.

We climbed into the back seat. "Let's warm this thing up." Weisberg fired the engine. Fabiano was still shuffling through the forest. We could see him far down the trail, moving slowly, holding his side.

"About the other night," the prosecutor said. "When Roy Klijner was killed. I wanted to ask you, Miss Nealy. Is it true Bill here spent the night with you?"

I looked out the window, flushed.

"Excuse me?" she said.

I couldn't bear to look in her face. I didn't want to see her expression if she betrayed me. Why should she risk so much to lie for me?

"Was Mr. Martell with you," Weisberg said, "on the morning that Roy Klijner was killed?"

"With me?" she replied. "Yes. Like I told Detective Reardon. We were together. All night."

"You're sure he didn't leave at some time during the early hours of the morning?"

"We were in the same bed, Mr. Weisberg. If he had left, I think I would have noticed."

"While you were asleep?"

"I didn't sleep. Not very much that night."

"You know, Miss Nealy, it's a serious crime to lie about a thing like that. Even though you're not under oath. You're obstructing justice."

"I'm not lying," she retorted indignantly, her hand finding mine. "You've no right to say that. I'm not lying."

The prosecutor appeared neither happy nor surprised.

Fabiano climbed in, collapsing on the seat. "Oh, my God. I haven't walked so far since I was a teenager. My God." He was snorting and gasping for air. "Well. Have I missed anything?"

Weisberg drove up the hill. I left Hubbard Road for the last time.

/ 338

Twenty

In the afternoon, Weisberg announced that Judy's body had been found. Her death was tentatively attributed to a sharp blow to the head. He released Roy's confession, a photocopy that reproduced the spots of blood in black.

The press conference was low-key, in contrast to my arrest. There were no television cameras, though Fabiano had made calls to every station. In fact, only three reporters, including Burkhalter, attended.

"Does this mean Mr. Martell is no longer a suspect in either of these deaths?" someone asked.

"We have dropped the charges," Weisberg said. "The case remains open."

"I'm so glad for you," Burkhalter insisted in the hallway. "I want you to know I never believed it. Some people in the newsroom thought you were guilty. But I never lost faith."

"What will you do now?" asked another reporter.

"Will you and Pam get married?" Burkhalter was always keen for a good story angle.

"Well," she smiled, "who knows?"

"How about it, Bill?" someone asked. "Planning to buy a ring?"

"Well . . . I don't know." I put my arm around her. Pam smiled up at me. "She's the boss."